SHATTERED EXILE

THE CHRONICLES OF FREYLAR

- VOLUME 3 -

by

Liam W H Young

First edition printing, 2018

ISBN 978-1-78926-193-6

Copyright © Liam William Hamilton Young 2018.

All characters appearing in this work are fictitious. Any resemblance to real persons, living or dead, is purely coincidental.

All rights reserved. No part of this book may be reproduced in any manner without written permission except in the case of brief quotations included in critical articles and reviews. For further information, please contact the author.

Cover Illustration Copyright © Liam William Hamilton Young 2018, moral rights reserved by Hardy Fowler.

A catalogue copy of this book is available from the British Library.

Printed and bound by Createspace.

www.thechroniclesoffreylar.com

ACKNOWLEDGEMENTS

Foremost, I would like to thank Hardy Fowler once again for the excellent cover art illustration for this book. Hardy is an absolute pleasure to work with, and really understands my vision for the world of Freylar.

Again, I would like to thank Matthew Webster for his enormous contribution to this book, and the series as a whole. Matt continues to be an amazing sounding board for this ongoing project, and I am extremely fortunate to have him along for the ride with his invaluable editing services.

Always, my thanks go to Kevin Forster for his experienced counsel regarding the correct use of medieval weaponry.

Lastly, thank you to Tibor Mórocz for proofreading this book. His keen perception continues to challenge me, giving me the impetus I need to complete my storytelling.

I dedicate this book to all those who have been touched by cancer. During the writing of this book, numerous family members, friends, work colleagues and aquaintances of both my wife and I have suffered this seemingly indiscriminate disease. Many are still with us today, though sadly others have lost their fight and will never read these words. Advances in medical science have allowed us to better understand and combat this life-changing adversary, nonetheless, its unwanted presence leaves a mark on all those caught in its wake.

TABLE OF CONTENTS

ONE Alone

TWO Darkness

THREE Calling

FOUR Affirmation

FIVE Impression

SIX Expulsion

SEVEN Emotion

EIGHT Promise

NINE Confrontation

TEN Concealment

ELEVEN Trials

TWELVE Interference

THIRTEEN Portent

FOURTEEN Reverence

FIFTEEN Separation

SIXTEEN Secrets

SEVENTEEN Reprisal

EIGHTEEN War

NINETEEN Hurt

TWENTY Pursuit

TWENTY ONE Duplicity

TWENTY TWO Release

DRAMATIS PERSONAE

ONE
Alone

She had no one. The domain and all of its inhabitants had forsaken her. Exiled to the unforgiving waste of the borderlands, abandoned by her kin, left to fade into nothingness; this was to be her fate – she had personally seen to it. There was no one to blame but herself. Her actions alone had led to her current lot. The allure of scrying both the past and the future had taken hold of her – indeed, she zealously sought its intoxicating caress. Knowledge was power, and the desire for power had consumed her entirely. Ethical considerations had played no part in her quest to know everything. The Freylarkai were wary of her – they feared what she knew. Subterfuge, murder, love, adultery; these acts became as transparent as glass. No Freylarkin could hide their past actions or future intent from her second sight – including Queen Mirielle. Yet her insatiable thirst for the relentless pursuit of knowledge had ultimately led to her ruin. Her actions had not gone unnoticed. In pushing her ability to its extreme, she had inadvertently painted a target on her back, one that was not easily removed.

Wearily, she rolled her head onto its side, allowing her left cheek to press against the cold dirty floor upon which she lay. She stared vacantly at the bronze metal mechanical claw attached to the stump of her left wrist. She subconsciously engaged her second sight, travelling back to that ill-fated cycle just moments prior to the loss of her organic hand. The past imagery now assaulting her mind was absent of any dialogue, though she recalled well the events leading up to her disfigurement, and subsequent exile, at Scrier's Post.

'Darlia, your actions can no longer go unpunished. You have repeatedly defied Freylarian law and the will of the ruling council. This cannot be allowed to continue!'

'What gives you the right, Mirielle, to curtail the development of the Freylarkai when you yourself flaunt your own ability?!'

'The ability of a shaper does not extinguish free will.'

'And yet you exiled Krashnar for his works!'

'They were monstrous constructs.'

'As were your own failures, Mirielle, need I remind you of that fact?'

'Enough! I am your queen, and you have defied Freylarian law for the last time, Darlia. As of this point, you are banished from Freylar. You will never again step foot in this domain. The Blades have standing orders to enforce this ruling by any means available to them, including release.'

'You cannot do this – you have no right! Kirika, surely you do not support this? Stop this unjust madness!'

'I cannot. The ruling council has already voted on the matter.' her sister had replied meekly from the front row of the gathered ensemble.

'Mirielle, if you do this, word of your unwarranted action will spread throughout Freylar, inciting others who seek to explore their abilities.'

'That will not come to pass. Let what is about to happen here be a reminder to all those who seek to follow your forbidden path, Darlia. Marcus...take her hand!'

'No! You cannot do this Mirielle! The ruling council's judgement on this matter is biased. Marcus is your willing lapdog and Aleska has always followed her own agenda.' she remembered pleading desperately.

She recalled the ominous moment when Marcus purposefully drew his bastard sword from the scabbard at his waist. The Blade Lord strode coldly towards her with an unflinching expression etched across his normally charming face. Despite her dogged stance on the matter, she had failed miserably to convince her kin of their impending atrocity. She tried to end her scrying by disengaging her second sight, desperate not to relive the painful memory, yet her feeble starved physique and dominant subconscious dictated otherwise. She watched again in mute horror as Marcus mercilessly brought the edge of his blade down across her left wrist. Her body immediately went into spasm as her mind replayed the agonising moment when the shock of losing her left hand wracked her body. In her mind's eye blood spurted from her severed wrist, splattering her disconnected left hand, which fell lifelessly upon the hard bedrock of the courtyard. Her once beautiful slender hand lay as an orphaned bloody mess. The sound of her own screams filled her ears once again, cried out against the backdrop of the stunned observers – including her own sister, who looked on dejectedly in silent horror. She recalled dropping to her knees and instinctively clutching her ruined stump as more blood gushed from the clinical wound. Marcus had already turned his back on her and was walking slowly towards her dazed audience. The Blade Lord flicked his blade abruptly, casting aside the blood that clung to its razor sharp edge. Mirielle also turned her back, prompting her entourage to follow suit, with the exception of Kirika, whose conflicting loyalties caused her to falter momentarily. Her eyes filled with tears, due to the increasingly unbearable pain, and she howled again in agony whilst her body fully acknowledged its traumatic loss. She looked towards Kirika at the fore of the dispersing crowd. Kirika too wept uncontrollably, though she struggled to make out her sister through watery eyes and strands of purple hair clinging to her face.

'Help me Kirika!'

'Darlia...'

Mirielle overheard her pitiful plea and strode purposefully towards her sister. She grabbed Kirika by the left arm and promptly escorted her younger sibling away.

'Kirika, your sister has brought this upon herself. Let us put this ugly business behind us and move forward.'

'Sister, please, I beg your help!'

She cursed herself for being so conceited, for failing to scry the future for both herself and Mirielle sufficiently, having grown comfortable with her false sense of security.

Having sated its amusement, her second sight suddenly disengaged, releasing its hold over her. The future became the present once more, abandoning her to lie alone upon the filthy floor of the Meldbeast's pen. Her body began to relax again, and slowly her numbing depression returned with the promise of its comfortable embrace. She turned her head back towards the chamber's opening above, beyond which Krashnar had permitted his hideous mutated pet its first taste of freedom. The insidious shaper's monstrous creation had at last been freed from its dingy prison, carrying upon its carapace back her since-departed lover. Driven by the need for vengeance and fuelled by Krashnar's hollow promises of revenge, Lileah had finally left her side, carried away by the abhorrent Meldbeast along with its twisted creator. She had lost everything; she could no longer return home, had lost the respect of her kin, her sister had been coerced from her side and now her last support structure had been kicked out from underneath her – Lileah had left. Her world was in ruin, and both her physical and mental states were rapidly following suit. For an entire cycle she had lain upon the cold hard dirty floor of the Meldbeast's pen, her only company being misery, depression and regret. Despite her insatiable desire to further her knowledge, the cost of realising her potential had been too great. The steep price of her unlawful transgressions had not only cost her own soul but had also demanded the souls of others. Many Blade Aspirants had been released during their recent failed invasion of Freylar, at Scrier's Post, and more souls would travel to the Everlife in the wake of Lileah's renewed path of bloody vengeance. Though Lileah now bore scars of her own, following their last encounter with The Blades, nonetheless, the impetuous telepath's disfigurement only fuelled her desire for revenge. The overwhelming need to balance the score sheet guided Lileah steadily towards her inevitable doom. Lileah's renewed invasion – carefully steered by Krashnar's own machinations – promised nothing but further pain and misery for all. She tried to scry the outcome of Lileah's ill-fated plan on several occasions while lying on the floor of the chamber, but the strands of fate were too numerous to examine, given the scale of the telepath's intent and ultimate lack of presence. Even so, none of her scrying had shown a glimpse of a positive outcome. The result of any war was always the same: everyone suffered. She did not need to scry Lileah's future to know that the Freylarkai would be devastated by further conflict, so soon after the massacre at Scrier's Post, even in the event of an unlikely victory. Families would be devastated by the loss of those released in battle, and trauma would become an unwanted bedfellow for the survivors of the inevitable horrors to come. Despite the hypocrisy of her now altered perception, having lost everything – not just her hand – she could not permit the future to play out as was likely written. In spite of her deep-seated personal loathing towards Mirielle, the Freylarkai were still her kin, and the fate of her people could not be tied inexorably to the actions of a single individual. Though she could never fully align herself with Mirielle's rule – the loss of her hand ensured as much – she now conceded the point that there did indeed need to be a tighter rein on scrying, something she had come to learn through her own experiences. Perhaps the ruling council was right to take her hand, she mused. Maybe Freylar *needed* her to be that example, to deter others from following the same path to ruin she had regrettably taken. However, public exile was another matter entirely. Her actions had not warranted such severe punishment; banishing one from their home, denying them of their loved ones, friends and family was unforgivable. Mirielle's efforts to push her away had failed catastrophically. The raw hurt she felt following her exile would never allow her to fade into obscurity. The torrent of distasteful emotions, along with her physical pain, festered during her time in the borderlands, slowly turning to hatred. Mirielle's ill-conceived judgment had been the catalyst for her changed disposition, which in turn had led her along a dark path of destruction back to Freylar. Although Lileah willingly joined her campaign of bloody vengeance, ultimately she was responsible for those released at Scrier's Post. And now Lileah was out there, threatening to repeat what was now a part of Freylar's history.

Thoughts continued to churn in her mind as she remained in her numb state. Her physical health had declined; her lips had begun to crack and she was dehydrated.

She awoke on the second morning of her self-imposed penance to the gentle patter of rain upon her face. The welcome moisture initially stung her dry lips, and the occasional stray droplet caused her tired eyes to flutter. After a short time spent staring up at the wintery sky, the rain intensified, presenting her with a dilemma: remain and get soaked, or...

'Do something!' she whispered to herself. 'You must not allow her to repeat your mistakes.'

Her clothes began to feel damp, and the rain falling through the opening in the cavern became heavier.

'Get up!'

Impulsively she raised her head slightly off the ground and allowed it to fall, landing with a dull thud. The sudden impact momentarily roused her from her cloddish state, though on its own it was not enough to rid her of her despair. Lifting her head once more, again she allowed it to drop to the filthy floor – this time with an audible thump.

'Get up, now!'

Still her body refused to obey her mind's instruction. Again and again she struck the hard floor with the back of her head, ultimately causing it to feel sore. Slowly her limbs began to stir, until eventually her body grew weary of its self-flagellation and finally permitted her to sit slowly upright. Her muscles ached painfully and her joints were stiff, thus it took some time before she was able to push herself off the grubby floor. She stood for a moment, unsteady on her feet, after which she began to walk gingerly around in an attempt to shake off the last of the fog still clinging to her mind. She eased her body back into motion, by slowly pacing around the chamber's circumference several times.

Setting her body to purpose once more, she followed the dark exit tunnel back to Krashnar's dingy workshop. She had grown accustomed to the gloom shrouding the Meldbeast's pen, thus the tunnel appeared lighter now than when she had first stepped foot into its foreboding darkness. As expected, the workshop remained empty, exactly as the insidious shaper had left it. She supposed it unlikely that Krashnar had any plans to return to his hide. So assured were they of their success that neither had given any thought to securing his subterranean abode prior to their abrupt departure. Seeing the grizzly workshop again up close stirred painful memories. She took no solace in the role she had played in restoring Lileah back to health. Lileah's altered form – now one of fused metal and flesh – was both disturbing and wondrous to behold. Although Krashnar had been the one to ultimately save Lileah from certain release, it was she who had prevented the restored telepath from becoming an androgynous construct wrought from the twisted shaper's lacklustre imagination. Krashnar's works were at best functional – though more often abhorrent – in their appearance, therefore she had made the conscious decision to prevent the same stigma from afflicting her former lover. During Lileah's restoration, she had painstakingly directed Krashnar's work, ensuring that her lover retained at least part of her femininity despite the shaper robbing her of the rest. The result of their combined efforts was horrifyingly beautiful; Lileah's entire torso was now fused with a bronze metal alloy. The work was extensive – necessarily so – to prevent the spread of infection from Lileah's grievous wound, caused by the Blade Paladin Nathanar, which had been the final hammer-blow in their defeat. Yet despite their successful efforts to save Lileah from release, the impetuous

Freylarkin had lost much of her manoeuvrability and could no longer bear children.

Quickly putting the shaper's awful place of work behind her, she rounded up the barely edible goods remaining in Krashnar's food stores. She then tended to the poor state of her attire and fixed her matted hair. After setting right some of her visual erosion, she began the unenviable process of restoring her physical health. Keeping down some of the overripe fruit she had gathered proved to be a struggle, but she managed, as she needed her strength if she was to stand any chance of returning to Freylar.

'Rayna wake up!' she said, shaking Rayna firmly by the shoulders, attempting to rouse the light bringer from her unnatural slumber. 'Nathaniel, how long has she been this way?'

'I do not know exactly. When I returned home from the arena last cycle, I noticed signs of her return. I went to check on her and found her here, in her room, sleeping. I thought little of it at first, assuming the journey back to Freylar was responsible for her fatigue, but when she failed to wake this morning I became duly concerned. I have checked her condition and – physically at least – her body is fine, with the exception of a few bumps and bruises which I have since seen to. I simply cannot explain it Kirika. Aside from journeying south to speak with the Knights Thranis or tracking down Anika – wherever she may be – I have no one else to turn to. I am loath to put you in this difficult position Kirika, but regardless, will you help?'

'I understand Nathaniel – yes of course I will help.'

'I would not ask this of you if not absolutely necessary, but I need to understand what caused this.'

'Nathaniel, what use is my ability if I cannot use it to save a fellow Blade sister? Let me worry about the ramifications of my personal scrying, should word of my actions reach unwanted ears.'

'Those ears will not hear it from me, this I swear!' Nathaniel declared.

'You need not swear an oath to me Nathaniel. I would like to think that the trust between us transcends such public declarations of loyalty.'

She leaned over Rayna's motionless body and gazed deeply into the light bringer's unflinching open eyes. Typically, Rayna's eyes were brown-orange in colour – subject to the light's influence – but now they appeared darker, as though stained with watery dark ink. Although he had failed to notice the portent upon initial inspection that morning, The Teacher had soon discovered Rayna's unnerving wide-eyed stare, along with her seemingly paralytic state. Gazing into the vacant visage of her immobile Blade sister, she engaged her second sight, moving backwards through time to shortly before the ill-fated moment when Rayna first succumbed to her current condition. She watched intently as Rayna returned to Nathaniel's tree, and subsequently climbed the stairs to her room. She smiled whilst observing the curious light bringer study her own body in the bedroom's dresser mirror – it pleased her immensely to see Rayna properly acquainting herself with her feminine physique. Eventually Rayna called an end to her self-analysis and climbed into her bed, ready for an early night. She skipped forwards in time whilst Rayna slept, that is until someone new entered the room. Initially she found it difficult to identify the interloper, who expertly clung to the shadows creeping across the room. When at last she caught a clear glimpse of the intruder's face, she gasped in disbelief, unable to fathom the truth of what she saw.

'What is it, what do you see?' asked Nathaniel anxiously.

'You!'

'What?!'

'You...you were here!'

'Kirika, what are you talking about? I do not understand.' replied Nathaniel, who was clearly bewildered by her preliminary analysis.

More of the ominous images flowed through her mind's eye: she saw Nathaniel's inexplicably aggressive behaviour towards Rayna, as he forcibly pinned her down onto the bed, before finally the identity of Rayna's attacker revealed itself.

'Krashnar!'

'What?! Kirika, are you telling me that wretched shaper did this – to Rayna?!'

She watched intently as the exiled shaper's ugly visage slowly revealed itself, whilst Nathaniel's own slipped from sight. All was clear to her now. Krashnar had infiltrated the vale using Nathaniel's likeness. The devious shaper had passed right through the forest, completely undetected by its inhabitants, and had forced his way into their home. Yet it was the images to come that truly disturbed her. She watched in horror as Rayna desperately tried to fend off her attacker. Despite his decrepit looking countenance, Krashnar seemingly possessed unnatural strength, which allowed him to hold Rayna down. Then came the ill-fated moment when the vile shaper coughed up some kind of black fluid, which dribbled from his mouth onto Rayna's face. The horrid looking substance moved of its own volition, desperately seeking a means of violating Rayna's body – which it eventually did, up through the hapless light bringer's nostrils. She cringed as Rayna's body went into spasm, whilst the parasite infiltrating her body gained a measure of control over her; although unable to manipulate Rayna's motor functions, the wretched thing instead found a way to paralyse its new host. The heinous violation seemed to entertain Krashnar – the repugnant shaper appeared joyous as he keenly observed the abhorrent act. Seeing the shaper's obvious amusement caused her unease. She wanted nothing more than to disengage her second sight, yet there was more to come. Having claimed his prize, Krashnar – in what was presumably some kind of twisted celebratory act – lowered his head towards Rayna's own. He flicked out his long tongue and slowly drew it across the side of her face, visibly savouring the moment of perverse pleasure. Krashnar then pulled back from the bed and lingered for a moment in the shadow, offering Rayna a leering wide smile.

'Night-night puppet. Sweet dreams.'

She read the foul words on his lips, after which the shaper quickly took his leave, leaving behind the comatose light bringer.

She ceased her scrying, having learnt all that she needed to know, before making her way unsteadily towards the bedroom window. Seeing her obvious unease, Nathaniel pushed the window open, allowing the fresh air to steady the contents of her stomach.

'Kirika, has Krashnar returned to the vale? Did he do this to Rayna?'

'Yes!' she replied, exhaling deeply.

Her body was shaking – she could feel it – and for the first time, in a long time, she felt truly afraid. Krashnar had indeed returned to the vale, having clearly chosen to defy the terms of his exile.

'He is here, in the vale – Nathaniel, he could be anywhere...or anyone!'

'Try and calm yourself Kirika.' replied Nathaniel, who laid his reassuring hands upon her trembling shoulders. 'Think clearly and tell me exactly what he did to Rayna.'

'I am uncertain. He violated her – put some kind of evil parasite inside her, which I believe is responsible for her paralysis.' she replied.

'Then we have to get it out, else she will surely not survive.'

'How? You have already tried yourself to revive her, and few renewalists are capable of surpassing your ability to restore our kind, Nathaniel.'

'Then we must find another way! I cannot lose my daughter for a second time,'

'What do you mean by that Nathaniel?' she asked, completely taken aback by his heated response.

The Teacher chose not to respond at first, instead he bowed his head in shame – clearly, The Teacher regretted his leading choice of words.

She decided to press upon the matter, in an attempt to learn the truth of Nathaniel's slip. 'Alarielle travelled to the Everlife shortly after Rayna released the Narlakin imprisoning her soul – are you implying that did not happen?'

'Kirika...I wanted to tell you, but I made a promise.'

'What promise?'

'Rayna needed time to come to terms with the...arrangement.'

'Nathaniel, what arrangement? You speak in riddles – none of this makes any sense?'

'When Rayna released that Narlakin, my daughter's soul was freed from its dark imprisonment. Alarielle saw her own body and tried to reclaim it. In part she succeeded, though upon discovering the presence of Rayna's own soul, Alarielle chose to accept a subservient role. She is now a passenger in her own body, no longer in control of its actions, yet her consciousness remains fully aware.'

She gasped at Nathaniel's impromptu confession. Previously she had been unable to put her finger on it, but now, finally, some of Rayna's recent odd behaviour at last made sense – the light bringer's body housed two souls.

'Who else knows of this?'

'Just Lothnar – he loved my daughter and blamed himself for her release. Rayna felt that he should know. She planned to inform you too Kirika, but then you disclosed Darlia's identity, Aleska retired and Marcus had her seconded to the Knights Thranis, all of which took place in rapid succession. The timing was all wrong – Rayna never intended for you to learn of Alarielle's return like this. She thinks of you as her sister.'

'I know...and I understand. Although hearing your words comes as a shock, we can discuss them at length later – right now we have more pressing concerns. If you cannot restore her body, perhaps we can find a way of communicating with Rayna...or Alarielle? Then, perhaps, we might learn more about the parasite – such as where it is. Maybe then we can cut it out.'

'Agreed. I will go and find Lothnar. He will surely help us.'

'No, I should be the one to find him.' she replied, sternly.

'Why is that Kirika?'

'Because of the other matter you and I have discussed. It is in our interests to maintain the public's perception that there remains bad blood between yourself and Lothnar. If you are both seen wandering around together, questions will be asked. We cannot tip our hand and divulge our knowledge of Queen Mirielle's privately reneged stance on Freylarian law concerning scrying.'

Nathaniel sighed wearily before replying, 'You are right of course. At least one of us is politically sensitive to such matters. Go then, find Lothnar and bring him back here as soon as possible. Check with Ragnar first – he will likely know Lothnar's current whereabouts.'

'I shall. And Nathaniel...we *will* save them!'

TWO
Darkness

'*Callum! Get your shit together now and listen to me damn it!*' said Trix sternly over the analogue communications device attached to his ear.

'Shut the hell up!' he replied tersely.

'*Look, I know you're pissed...*'

'Pissed?! There's a man dying on the floor in front of me Trix – a man I killed, because of you!'

'*You can accuse me of all that later. Right now, we need to act fast, before the Peacekeepers are apprised of the situation. Look, if you won't do it for me, do it for yourself!*'

He chose not to respond to Trix's hollow words. Instead, he continued to watch the expanding pool of dark red liquid beneath the fallen gentleman's head. The fatal wound – incurred when Mr L. Cameron's head struck the hard bedroom floor – was a result of *his* actions. He had been the one to push the elderly gentleman to the floor during their struggle. Yet if it were not for Trix's wretched siren forcing his hand, the situation could have been avoided entirely. Instead, he had inadvertently murdered the senior citizen. The thought of the atrocity – by his own hands no less – made him sick. He retched abruptly over the deceased gentleman's feet and began to breathe rapidly. Panic clawed at him; he was on the edge of losing control.

'*Callum, you must cut out his bio-key! We need to reconfigure it immediately to transmit a healthy signal.*'

'You speak as though I don't have a choice. I'm not carrying out your macabre proposal Trix.'

'*If you don't do this now, his life, and all our work, will be for nothing. Please Callum, cut it out!*'

Trix continued to bleat in his ear, like unwanted background noise. He felt lightheaded and the room began to move – or so it seemed. Sensing he was on the cusp of fainting, he stumbled towards the room's window and slid it open, hoping the fresh air would clear his head. After a few minutes the world ceased spinning and he quickly regained his balance. He turned his attention back to the prone body of Mr L. Cameron. The blood seeping from the man's head injury had slowed considerably now. Spotlights studding the ceiling reflected brightly in the motionless pool of dark red liquid, which surrounded the gentleman's head like some kind of demonic halo. Though he knew very little of medical science, by now Mr L. Cameron was surely dead. He lingered aimlessly, absently regarding the deceased, whilst Trix continued to twitter uncaringly in his ear; the detached software engineer clearly held little regard for the lives of those inhabiting the metropolis – including his own, perhaps. Yet regardless of the heinous crime orchestrated by Trix – realised by his own naïve hands – there remained the inescapable truth: that he would soon be detected. Unless he sought to disappear, along with the rest of his kin, he would need to act fast.

Casting aside his morals – albeit temporarily – he moved towards Mr L. Cameron's right arm and dropped to his knees. Grabbing his knife from the side of his belt, he pressed the blade's point deep into his victim's skin and drew the knife down the length of the deceased's forearm. Blood immediately saturated the man's arm, running towards its limp hand before dripping onto the floor. Dropping the knife, he dug his fingers into the fresh wound, and began feeling around under the surface of the gentleman's skin. It did not take him long before he felt the familiar rough surface of the owner's bio-key. Pinching the small piece of tech between his thumb and forefinger, he teased the bio-key free from its host.

'OK, I have the fucking thing – are you happy?! Trix, are you listening?'

'Yes, yes... I thought for a minute there that you were going to bail on the plan.'

'Your plan – this is on you!'

'Fine, whatever...is there an access panel in the room?'

'Yes.'

'Good. Use the bio-key to gain access and I will guide you through the rest.'

Holding the bio-key stolen from his victim – still slick with gore – in front of the holographic display at the foot of the elderly deceased's bed caused the access panel to spring to life. Immediately he was on the Infonet – it had been sometime since he had last accessed the vast network of data.

'OK, I'm in – where am I going?'

'First, I need you to access level twelve.'

'You're kidding right? I've only ever accessed level three.' he replied, taken aback by Trix's request.

'Callum, there are twenty-eight levels on the Infonet – that I know of. You have not been previously aware of their existence, simply because you have never been given access to them.'

Immediately he navigated his way to the Infonet's main lobby. From there he could clearly see barrier twelve, along with many more. It was the first time he had acknowledged more than three data access levels on the Infonet – his virtual world just got significantly larger.

'Trix, there are thirty-four barriers here!'

'Son of a bitch! I knew his clearance was high, but still... Regardless, access level twelve.'

'Why not level thirty-four?'

'We don't have time for your questions – access level twelve, now!' replied Trix, tersely.

He sneered at the hacker's words; Trix's personality – or lack thereof – grated on him. All he wanted now was to complete the objective, so that each of them could go their own separate way. Despite being a fellow Shadow class member, his opinion of Trix had soured dramatically in light of Mr L. Cameron's death – he had little appetite left to stomach the socially awkward hacker. As he passed unchallenged through the barrier to level twelve, the holographic access panel grew and expanded around him, like an ethereal bubble, giving him a better view of his virtual surroundings.

'Are you there yet?'

'Yes!' he replied, irritably.

'Good. Access sector seventy-two.'

He rapidly navigated his way across level twelve, paying little attention to the torrent of data streams flowing around him. Sector seventy-two was easy enough to locate, however, a fresh barrier blocked its access.

'There's a barrier here – it looks complex.'

'Of course it is – I built it.'

'How do I gain access?'

'Repeat after me. Zero, seven, echo, nine, delta...'

'Right, zero, seven...'

After what seemed like an eternity of repeating numbers and characters, the barrier opened, allowing him access to sector seventy-two. He reiterated thirty-two characters in total before breaching the barrier – he counted diligently on his fingers and thumbs whilst repeating Trix's sequence. Though he was able to memorise information reasonably well, the access code was simply too long for him to remember, and Trix knew it.

'What is this place?'

'*Think of it as one of your subterranean bolt-holes in the Wild, but instead buried within the Infonet.*'

Though he comprehended little of what he was seeing, nevertheless he understood enough to confirm that Trix's virtual space was akin to his real space – untidy. Complex data streams and objects were haphazardly strewn across the sector, with no apparent effort spent ordering or sorting them; this was not a bolt-hole, he mused – this was a playground.

'More like a sandbox.' he said, sardonically.

'*Check the stream-meta. Look for one with a timestamp approximately a month ago – it will be titled "Project Phoenix".*' commanded Trix, who ignored his retort.

'What is "Project Phoenix"?'

'*Enough of the questions Callum. Do you want to bring Mr L. Cameron back from the dead, or not?*'

The pain in her torso was nearly too much to bear. With each bounding stride of the Meldbeast's powerful legs, her body screamed defiantly, reminding her that it could no longer cope with such stresses and strains. She could feel herself slipping and sliding around on the beast's thick chitin carapace, which covered the entire length of the top half of its body and part of its tail. Without the aid of the flesh straps, securing her legs to its flanks, Krashnar's abomination would have long since discarded her from its armoured back.

'Argh...' she cried again in pain, as the Meldbeast landed heavily on yet another adverse camber.

The awkward angle caused her body to twist, pulling at the flesh-metal of her torso, causing fresh tears to spill from her eyes. The pain was agonising, yet they needed to press on regardless, given that time was against them. Their journey across the hard, dusty relief of the Narlakai borderlands had been punishing; she had felt each leap and every painful landing made by her frenetic mount, as it expertly navigated the cracked landscape with unerring agility. Nonetheless, her ghastly mode of transport had carried her across the borderlands at breakneck speed, as though Krashnar had specifically designed the monstrosity for such a task. Despite their rapid pace, she had routinely reigned in the beast with her mind, forcing it to rest – the Meldbeast seemingly cared little about its own wellbeing – lest it burn itself out before they could complete their task. Since the beast had been caged in a filthy pen since its grisly inception, Krashnar's abhorrent creation was now enjoying its first taste of freedom. In spite of her strong telepathic link with the chaotic creature, its desire to roam and explore was insatiable, making it difficult to keep the unnatural creation under her control. Though she managed to dictate the beast's heading, she could do little to ease its rapid pace.

For two cycles they had combed the borderlands in search of the withdrawing Narlakai herd, which had ultimately taken a back seat during her and Darlia's short-lived invasion of Freylar. Occasionally they would pass small isolated groups of soul stealers, aimlessly drifting across the near-barren landscape, yet they had failed – thus far at least – to locate the mass of Narlakai she had previously gathered to her side. They had limited their hunt to the night, given the nocturnal disposition of the Narlakai and their natural aversion to light. Searching at night was far from ideal, though fortunately she had – in addition to her own above-average night vision – three more sets of nocturnal eyes at her disposal, courtesy of her many-headed mount. Each of the three dire wolf heads attached to the Meldbeast's body keenly scanned the rugged landscape, whilst the hybrid construct continued its relentless advance across the harsh terrain. Each dawn, she fought with the beast's mind, coercing the Meldbeast to go to ground, ultimately forcing it to sleep. However, since she was unable to remove the creature's flesh straps without forcibly tearing them, she had little choice but to both eat and sleep in her saddle. Had she successfully managed to pull herself free from the skin wrapped across her legs, she would have never again been able to mount the beast – unassisted at least – let alone remain on top of it.

The Meldbeast continued to bound across the unforgiving landscape at speed, causing her short raven-black hair to flap in the cold night breeze. Although she no longer felt the cold as keenly as she once had, nonetheless she could still feel the encroaching winter biting at the exposed flesh of her arms and legs. In hindsight, she should have prepared better for her journey, though her sudden introduction to Krashnar's monstrous pet had distracted her from such trivial concerns. She looked up towards the black sky to gain her bearings; the sky was devoid of any cloud cover, allowing the Night's Lights to shine brightly, guiding her way. Given their current lack of success, it was possible that the herd had fallen back much faster, and in a more orderly fashion, than she had expected. Following her revised train of thought, she chose to alter the Meldbeast's course by directing it deeper into the borderlands rather then combing the breadth of the frontier. After a while, the terrain started to change; the ground fractured even further, and what little cover there was became increasingly sparse. The once-familiar sight of the arid borderlands was morphing into something more sinister and unwelcoming. As the Meldbeast drove deeper into the inhospitable land, she no longer recognized the strange new environment rapidly consuming them. The air began to feel dry, and huge chasms started to split the landscape, restricting their movements. It was then that the obvious suddenly dawned on her: they were no longer in the Narlakai borderlands – they were in Narlak.

The moment she set foot into the arena, she felt its occupants tracking her hurried steps with understandable intrigue. It was rare that she visited the arena, typically only doing so when in urgent need of Nathaniel's counsel – and yet The Teacher was notably absent. Unsurprisingly, Lothnar was also nowhere to be seen – a quick scan of the arena confirmed his lack of presence. However, at the far end of the arena, the Captain of The Blades sparred vigorously against several Blade Masters, each of whom struggled to turn the light bringer's monstrous axe. Ragnar rarely used a shield – although skilled in its use – preferring instead the powerful swing of a double-handed axe. He used the weight and reach of his weapon to devastating effect, drubbing the shields of his opponents and controlling the crowd with wide arcs. She noticed that one of the Captain's opponents had lost the use of their shield, courtesy of Ragnar who had buried the bite of a backup hand axe into it; the armour was now too heavy and cumbersome for its former wielder to bear. Ragnar's fighting style was nothing short of aggressive. The Captain of The Blades loathed hanging back, and instead loved to engage his opponents using raw strength to overpower them. Despite their technical skill, Ragnar's sparring partners struggled to deal with his brutish assault.

'Kirika!' boomed the Captain, who had clearly seen her enter the arena despite the melee around him. 'Come fight with us!'

Typically, she ignored such passive-aggressive comments, especially when spoken by the Captain of The Blades, but it was high time that she challenged such childish jibes in front of her peers. Irritated by his words, she reminded herself of her secret pact – to be more assertive – and decided then to tackle his goading remark head on. Realising that her own voice would not carry the distance, she strode towards Ragnar, trying her best to feign confidence.

'Do you require assistance Ragnar?' she said, after closing the gap between them.

Ragnar offered her a quick sneer as he continued to battle his opponents.

'Some of us no longer recall *your* fighting style – perhaps you can refresh our failing memories?' mocked Ragnar, before swinging his double-handed axe in a wide arc, forcing his attackers back once more.

'They say that memory abandons us all, with age. Shall I scry your past and recall the missing details for you?'

Her mocking retort clearly irked the Captain. She realised then that it was sometimes necessary to lower one's tone in order to effectively manage those who sought to belittle others.

'What do you want, Kirika?'

'Simply to confirm if you will be attending the opening duel of the Trials, two cycles from now.'

'Of course I will!' replied Ragnar, who thrust the top of his axe into an encroaching shield, driving back its wielder once more and creating the separation he needed to swing his enormous weapon once again.

'And Lothnar? Might you know if he too will be present?'

'How should I know?' replied Ragnar, tersely. 'Can you not see that I am busy? Go ask him yourself!'

'If I knew his location, I would.'

'Search east of the bridge. You will likely find him throwing those knives of his into a fresh tree, close to the riverbank.'

It was unusual for Ragnar to be so cooperative; either her feigned confidence afforded her a modicum of respect, or – as was more likely the case – the gruff light bringer simply wanted her gone. Either way she had the information she required, and promptly left the arena, leaving the Captain behind to continue beating down his fellow Blades.

Despite the eventual arrival of winter, the air temperature was kinder back down in the vale; she had forgotten how exposed the Tri-Spires actually were, due to their elevated vantage point along the southern ridge. The heart of Freylar was well protected against the elements, blessed as it was by the natural shelter afforded by the mountains flanking the vale.

She soon arrived at the aging timber bridge spanning the breadth of the river, after her quick descent from the arena. The river ran the length of the vale, providing fresh water to both the local forest dwellers and those who lived in the Tri-Spires. The venerable bridge had become a nexus between the forest dwellers and those Freylarkai choosing to make their home within Mirielle's artificially constructed granite spires. Despite favouring her comfortable lifestyle high up in the Tri-Spires, she envied the honest land, along with its way of life, and the genuine warmth of the community amidst the charming forest dwellings; life within the Tri-Spires had a more formal – or stale, according to Nathaniel – feel to it. The bridge acted as a natural hub for lively gossip and commerce. The landmark served as a place of communion between those living either side of the river, and thus the atmosphere was typically inviting. Yet something sinister had clearly befallen the site, casting a grim shadow across the gathered Freylarkai.

'Kirika!' cried the voice of a young female, who spotted her approach. 'You need to see this – it is truly awful!'

Following the direction of the noise – making her way politely past the crowd of worried faces – she approached the front of the anxious congregation gathered on the south side of the bridge. She gasped as she saw the released body of a male Freylarkin, recently pulled from the river. The unnaturally pale corpse lay naked on the southern riverbank, adjacent to the bridge, and had been stripped of its clothing. Disturbingly, the Freylarkin's legs were mutilated, well beyond any practical use – both were fused together, which would have made it impossible for the victim to walk, let alone swim. The male Freylarkin was young – she estimated him to be about her age – and had good-looking features, albeit now spoiled by the early stages of decomposition. She felt instantly saddened seeing the youth in such a miserable state – so much potential, laid low by the heinous actions of another.

'My word...when did this happen?' she asked, addressing no one in particular.

'We do not know. The body was found only a short while ago, wrapped around one of the bridge piers. A few of us helped to pull him from the river, but he is well beyond the capability of a renewalist.' replied one of the male forest dwellers.

'This is horrible!' she replied, appalled by the manner of the victim's release. 'His face looks familiar to me, though I cannot place it – do we know who he is?'

'It is Riknar.'

'What...you mean Keshar's elder brother?'

'Yes – he was well known throughout the local community.' continued the Freylarkin. 'We were about to send word to Keshar.'

'That will not be possible; she is currently beyond the vale, carrying out an errand for me, no less. However, I will have word sent to her as soon as possible.'

'Kirika,' asked the voice of another, 'Can you help us determine who was responsible for this crime? We need to protect ourselves from this monster, plus Keshar deserves to know who released her brother.'

'Of course.' she replied.

She knelt down beside Riknar's body and touched his right hand with her own. Although she no longer needed to touch the subject of her scrying, nonetheless, physical contact with her target facilitated the process, allowing her to see more clearly. Engaging her second sight, she allowed the grisly images of the events leading up to Riknar's release to flood her mind. She saw the released Fraylarkin's attacker first-hand, along with the heinous shaping wrought upon Riknar's legs, before he was unceremoniously dumped into the river, left to the mercy of its gentle current.

'Krashnar, what are you up to?' she whispered quietly to herself.

The same dread she had felt earlier that cycle, when scrying Rayna's past, now clawed at her again. Not content with just the one victim, now there were two – how many more Freylarkai would fall foul of his evil before the cycle's end, she wondered apprehensively. In any event, she could not allow her judgement to become impaired by fear; she needed to act clearly and decisively, now more than ever. Despite the expectant faces around her, she paused for a moment to consider her options; she could ill afford to incite panic amongst the Freylarkai by disclosing Krashnar's presence within the vale, yet at the same time they needed to take precautionary measures, in order to protect themselves against the hidden threat at large.

'Kirika, tell us, what do you see? Who would commit such an awful crime?'

Digging deep, she found the necessary resolve needed to command her audience; she rose to her feet and stood tall in the middle of the anxious sea of faces rapidly amassing around her.

'Gather your loved ones now and stay in your dwellings until further notice.' she said, with new-found authority. 'As of now, a curfew is in effect, throughout the vale, until we can resolve this matter. Go now, inform the others, and then stay in your homes.'

'You heard the Fate Weaver!' cried a voice from the growing crowd. 'Alert the others, and then get to your homes.'

The crowd immediately began to disperse as those around her moved quickly in response to her command. It was an odd feeling, seeing so many Freylarkai carry out her orders. She felt reassured knowing that the curfew would restrict Krashnar's movements – the insidious shaper would find it difficult moving around the vale unseen, with her kin having gone to ground.

THREE
Calling

He sat alone, quietly, resting against the trunk of an old fallen tree, listening keenly to the occasional sounds of wildlife foraging through the bare woodland. He enjoyed relaxing whilst listening to the ambient sounds of the forest, unerringly identifying each one – the practice kept his skills sharp. Sometimes he would play the same game during those nights when he had trouble sleeping, whilst scouting the Narlakai borderlands alone. Often, on clear nights, he had difficulty sleeping; the soft glow of the Night's Lights frequently distracted him, making it difficult to switch off. He recalled fondly the last time he was in the heart of the vale; Ragnar had tried his hardest to sneak up on him. The Captain's eager attempt was ultimately futile, nonetheless he appreciated Ragnar's effort, which had brought a smile to his face – he enjoyed the Captain's gruff companionship, and the fruitless repeated attempts to outsmart him. He wondered – in light of his recent string of failures – whether the Captain would now fare any better. Knowing that Kirika's sister had used him like a puppet to bait The Blades, and that her telepathic accomplice had twice surpassed his own ability, laying him low in the process, had rocked his confidence. It had been summer when Ragnar last tried to spook him, with the vale in full colour. Now autumn had eroded most of that colour, and the encroaching winter promised to wash away the rest with its cold icy rain, dark skies and howling wind. One could always find shelter, even in the borderlands, and so he tolerated the rain, but the wind habitually riled him – there was no escaping its touch.

Krisis lay next to him, content to while away the remainder of the morning. Occasionally the dire wolf's ears would twitch – seemingly of their own accord – as they too detected the ambient sounds of the woodland. He enjoyed having his fleet-footed companion at his side, and the eager dire wolf was keen to serve its pack leader. In the short time they had spent together in the borderlands, Krisis had proven his worth repeatedly. Perhaps it was time to introduce Krisis to his scouts, to induct the loyal dire wolf formally into their ranks, he mused. His thoughts on the matter were cut short, however, by the sound of someone close by, stalking through the woodland. Krisis' ears twitched repeatedly; the black-furred dire wolf promptly stood up and began to snarl, directing his muzzle towards the west. He too had heard the faint sounds, and had quickly risen to his feet, ready to face the potential threat headed towards them. The sound intensified, though only slightly, before the shape of a female Freylarkin emerged through the trees. Treading quietly through the forest was Kirika – instantly recognisable by her long purple waterfall-braided hair and pale skin. The young scrier carefully picked her way through the woodland, making very little sound.

'I am impressed that you made it this far, before we detected you that is.' he said loudly, clearly startling the Blade Valkyrie.

Kirika turned towards the sound of his voice, adjusting her heading accordingly. After a brief moment scanning the forest, she singled him out against the backdrop of the woodland, followed shortly by Krisis; his worn attire and the dire wolf's black fur camouflaged well with their surroundings.

'Lothnar, is that you?'

'Who else are you expecting to find out here, Kirika?'

'If that is truly you, Lothnar, explain to me now the recent events that have brought you and Nathaniel together.' replied Kirika, tersely.

Kirika's cryptic response was unexpected, so too was her posture – the Blade Valkyrie had adopted a defensive stance. Krisis also sensed that something was wrong; the loyal dire wolf stood firmly by his side and continued to snarl aggressively at the scrier.

'Kirika, what is going on?'

'Answer the question!' demanded Kirika.

'Fine...Aleska's work, at Scrier's Post – does that answer your question?'

Kirika exhaled deeply and began to look at ease; she seemed to visibly relax after hearing his response.

'Lothnar, I am glad to have found *you*. I require your assistance.' said Kirika intently, only now daring to approach them. 'There is trouble in the vale, and both Alarielle and Rayna need your help.'

'What is it Kirika? Tell me, what has happened?!'

'Krashnar is back in the vale! He has already released a local fisherman by the name of Riknar, and has since infected Rayna with some sort of parasite.'

'What?! Is she OK?'

'I do not know – she seems to be experiencing a kind of paralysis. Nathaniel is with her, back at his tree.'

'What about Alarielle?'

'I cannot say. We are unable to communicate with either of them in their current state, though perhaps, with your ability, you can.'

'Take us to them now, Kirika, and I will do what I can.'

'Thank you, but alas, I cannot join you both. I must warn Marcus of the threat. Krashnar is stealing identities, in order to infiltrate the vale.'

'You should have realised that Krisis here cannot be fooled so easily – neither can I.'

'Of course. I was not thinking clearly. This situation has everyone on edge, myself included.'

'Regardless, you have responsibilities, I understand. You need to report this to Marcus.'

'Do either of you know the way to Nathaniel's tree?'

'Vaguely, but the forest dwellers will aid us.'

'That is unlikely.' replied Kirika. 'I have ordered a curfew – the Freylarkai are going to ground.'

'Makes sense.' he replied. 'No matter, I will have Krisis here follow your scent to Nathaniel's tree. We shall accompany you back to the bridge, Kirika, after which we shall leave you to find Marcus, and apprise him of the situation.'

'Very well.' replied Kirika, with a look of concern.

'Whatever this is, Kirika, we will find a way to beat it.'

'I sincerely hope that you are right, Lothnar, and that you are able to expel whatever evil has infected The Guardian.'

His dry lips stung as they cracked in the wake of his ever-widening smile. He could still taste the tang of the light bringer's sweat on his tongue, which he slowly slid across his bottom lip. The Guardian belonged to him now, and with Freylar's mysterious benefactor removed from the board, Lileah's chances of success were greatly improved.

'Ha, *The Guardian* – how disappointing.' he said, musing aloud.

Lileah, too, had become his unwitting puppet; it was a simple enough task to compel the impetuous Freylarkin to join him, thereby advancing his own agenda. The abnormally powerful telepath would provide a useful distraction whilst he sought to realise his own ambition. Although Lileah had made for an amusing pastime, ultimately the gaunt raven-black-haired Freylarkin meant nothing to him. Once she had served her purpose, Lileah would no longer be of any significance. Despite admittedly being in awe of her supremely impressive telepathic ability, in truth, he had little time for the disrespectful youth. He paid lip service to the Freylarkin, purely to ensure her cooperation. Her former lover, Darlia, however, was an entirely different proposition altogether. He liked the purple-haired scrier – more so than perhaps he cared to admit – and despite Darlia's crushed resolve, he enjoyed having her around. There were times – many in fact – when he had considered forcibly violating her flesh, purely to sate his own dark desires. Perhaps, once his plan had come to fruition, he would return to his hide and ravage Darlia's sumptuous body – assuming, of course, that she had not since abandoned his subterranean abode. Though given her severed ties with Freylar, and in light of Lileah's decision to leave her, it was unlikely that Darlia would leave the relative safety of his hide.

Without any warning, the ambient noise outside the store – in which he was currently holed up – notably increased, bringing with it an end to his otherwise pleasant mood. All pleasurable thoughts of violating Darlia's body came to an abrupt end, along with his – relatively – pleasant disposition. Keen to learn the reason for the irksome commotion responsible for disrupting his thoughts, he quickly shuffled towards the closed door at the front of the store. Pressing his one good ear against the narrow gap between the door and its frame, he listened attentively to the sounds of Freylarkai shouting outside in the alley.

'Go home, all of you!' cried a voice from outside the store. 'A curfew is now in effect. Stay inside and await further news.'

It was too soon, surely, for Lileah's renewed invasion of Freylar. The hot-headed telepath was in the borderlands, busying herself with the task of consolidating the retreating Narlakai herd, before ultimately driving them once more towards Freylar. It was foolish to think that Lileah could have rounded up the Narlakai so quickly – he convinced himself – so why then would the Freylarkai impose a curfew now, he wondered. Eager to learn more about the impromptu curfew, he continued to linger by the door, listening with keen interest to the growing number of panicked cries outside.

'What is going on?' cried several of the voices, all lacking harmony.

'They found Riknar's released body, down by the old bridge.' proclaimed another. 'Kirika has imposed a curfew whilst The Blades investigate the crime.'

'Riknar...' he repeated quietly to himself.

The name was hauntingly familiar, though try as he might, he simply could not place it. His leering smile began to wither, as the vital clue continued to vex him. Eventually the voices began to fade; presumably, the Freylarkai were going to ground, and the messenger had since moved on. Deciding, finally, to give up on his failing memory, he turned towards the store's proprietors – mother and daughter – and began to walk slowly towards them. Their wide eyes were filled with terror, and both were shaking uncontrollably. He imagined being able to smell their fear, though given that his poor sense of smell was worse than his memory, such thoughts were entirely fanciful. Nonetheless, he could clearly see their dread, which was enough – for him at least – though the lodger inside of him craved more. Since agreeing to become the parasite's host, the thing inhabiting his body had become increasingly difficult to appease. His early exploits had been sufficient to sate its twisted desires, but as time marched on, it required increasingly heinous acts. Or perhaps the cravings were in fact his own – he could no longer tell. Regardless, his dark companion had fulfilled its end of their bargain. Since allowing the parasite to infiltrate his body, he felt growing power inside of him, despite his dishevelled appearance – of which he was keenly aware. The parasite had altered his body, turning it into that of a predator; in addition to his abnormal strength, he could now *see* the fear in his prey – an unexpected side effect of the joining process, which...he enjoyed.

If they could have screamed, they would have, but their sealed mouths prevented such attention seeking behaviour. In addition to fusing their lips together, he had melded their clasped hands behind their backs. He had also given consideration to fusing their legs, thereby completely thwarting any attempts to escape, however, he enjoyed watching his victims resist. Seeing them now, thrashing frantically at the ground with their legs, trying desperately to push themselves away from him, filled him with joy. The struggle was always better than the final, inevitable, act of release.

'Ah, yes...the fisherman. Now I recall.' he said aloud, to no one in particular.

During his infiltration of the vale, he had initially stolen the identity of a local fisherman. Casting his mind back to that moment, he recalled now one of the natives calling him by that very name – Riknar – when first he crossed the old bridge leading to the heart of the vale. When carelessly dumping the hapless fisherman's body into the river, he had clearly paid no attention to the direction of its current. Subconsciously he had assumed the river flowed towards the setting sun, but in reality that was clearly not the case. The drowned body of the Freylarkin must have been dragged downstream by the current, towards the old bridge, thus drawing the attention of the forest dwellers.

'You fool!' he said, chiding himself.

The unwanted attention would surely slow him down. With a curfew in place, there were bound to be fewer Freylarkai wandering the alleys, making his task more arduous. He would find it difficult, in future, stealing fresh identities and blending in with the crowd. Originally, he had planned to assume the hapless mother's identity – the thought of posing as a female amused him. However, this setback now altered his plans. He could sense his dark companion's growing frustration, realising now that its host would be forced to lie low and demonstrate patience. Having come this close he could ill afford to take any rash actions; timing was critical, and he would not allow his plan to be undone, especially not due to the simple boredom of the thing he harboured. Despite the shorter cycles, thanks to the arrival of winter, there was still plenty of time before dusk; in the meantime, he would need something to occupy his mind – at least until sundown – and to appease the hungering darkness inside him. He stopped his slow advance just short of the hapless females, bound and gagged before him. Their backs were pressed firmly against the rear wall of the store. Both were petrified and whimpered incessantly, like newborn Freylarkai. No doubt they clung to the futile hope that The Blades – or perhaps even their pathetic, beloved Guardian – would step forward to save them. He knew better; there was to be no salvation for the cowering pair now. He licked his lips again, almost tasting their fear. The anticipation was euphoric, and he could feel new strength coursing through his body as the growing darkness inside him caused his body to judder with excitement.

'So, which of you would like to go first?' he said, widening his black pupil-less eyes. 'Oh, how forgetful of me. Neither of you can speak! Perhaps I should help you with that...or maybe instead, I should be the one to decide?'

'Kirika, tell us, what is so pressing that it could not wait until our next scheduled council meeting?' asked Mirielle, tersely.

Previously, Freylar's queen had been far less direct with her questions, though since the events at Scrier's Post, there had been a notable change in Mirielle's behaviour; her inviting demeanour had eroded in part, revealing glimpses of something sour that lay beneath. Marcus remained largely stone-faced by Mirielle's side, though she could sense The Blade Lord's unease at the blunt manner in which the queen commenced their impromptu meeting.

'I apologise for calling this unscheduled meeting, but I believe that the matter in question cannot wait.'

'What have you to report, Kirika?' asked Marcus in his habitual welcoming manner.

'Krashnar has returned to the vale.'

'What?! Why would that vile shaper return to Freylar?' asked Mirielle, who was clearly shocked by her announcement.

'A good question, one to which I do not know the answer – at least not yet.'

'Kirika, what evidence do you have of his return?' asked Marcus calmly.

Prior to calling their meeting, she had thought in depth about whether or not to disclose Rayna's current condition. She had ultimately concluded that doing so would only serve to draw unwanted attention; by now, Lothnar would surely be at Rayna's side, and she could not convincingly explain the Paladin's reason for being there, knowing – courtesy of her second sight – that Marcus would choose to check in on The Guardian's progress. Past friction between Nathaniel and Lothnar was well documented – why then would Nathaniel accept Lothnar's aid, when numerous other telepaths throughout the domain could lend their assistance? Until she had a better understanding of Mirielle's reasons for reneging on Freylarian law, she decided it was best to withhold the information and play her cards close to her chest. Whether Rayna chose to acknowledge the fact or not, The Guardian had become a local hero – in particular amongst the forest dwellers – and had quickly earned the respect of her peers. Due to Rayna's native home amongst the Sky-Walkers, The Guardian's revered status had become an incredibly powerful tool; she could not therefore afford for the light bringer's legacy to be undone by reports of her demise at the hands of an outcast shaper. Rayna was undoubtedly loyal to both her and Nathaniel. If things turned sour when finally she confronted Mirielle about Aleska's activities at Scrier's Post, she would likely need The

Guardian's support, and along with it the support of the people. Unwittingly, Rayna was now a rising power in matters of state, and she intended to keep it that way – indirect access to the support of the people was no small thing, and an advantage she would continue to nurture.

'Riknar's body was found mutilated down by the old bridge. It had been dumped in the river, and subsequently washed up downstream. When scrying the body, I learned of Krashnar's presence; he used Riknar's likeness to infiltrate the vale. I became aware of the situation earlier this cycle, and immediately instated a curfew.'

'Kirika, you have overstepped your authority in this matter. You were not authorised to investigate the crime, plus issuing a curfew will only create widespread panic amongst the people.' proclaimed Mirielle sternly. 'You should have consulted us first, before making such a rash decision.'

Holding on firmly to her new-found conviction, she dug deep, finding the courage to defend her decision. 'With respect, Queen Mirielle, I did what I felt was right and in the best interests of the Freylarkai. Panic had already started spreading amongst those present; Riknar was renowned for his skill as a fisherman and was well liked amongst the forest dwellers – this crime has shaken them badly. Krashnar is *here* – in Freylar! He could be anywhere, passing as anyone. He has already released one of our kin, and could well seek to release more in the pursuit of his objective – whatever that is. Whilst I have deliberately refrained from divulging any details, surely we have an obligation to act to protect them?'

'Regardless of your justification, Kirika, the decision was not yours to make alone.' replied Mirielle, who had a cold look on her face.

Mirielle's words incited her anger, not helped by Marcus' seeming lack of support, yet she was forced to bite her tongue – figuratively speaking. The Blade Lord appeared divided on the matter, which was not entirely surprising; Marcus was loyal to a fault, and with Mirielle's increasingly questionable judgement, that single character flaw necessitated that she tread carefully around him. For a brief moment, she considered raising the issue of Aleska, but that was her anger threatening to get the better of her judgement. The timing was poor, in light of the latest threat to Freylar, and given Marcus' current reaction, she needed to speak with him privately on the matter first.

'Please accept my apologies. May I ask where we now stand on the Trials, in light of this situation?'

'Am I correct in assuming that all the preparations are complete?' asked Mirielle.

'Yes, however, would it not be prudent to cancel the proceedings, in light of Krashnar's current unknown whereabouts?'

'No – I will not have that wretched Freylarkin interfere with our traditions. In two cycles, the Trials will proceed as planned. Assuming that she returns from her assignment in good time, Rayna *will* meet Lothnar's challenge for the opening duel in the arena.' said Mirielle resolutely. 'I trust Marcus to apprehend Krashnar – if indeed the vile shaper still lurks within the vale.

Mirielle was no longer thinking clearly, of that she was certain. The release of so many Blade Aspirants at Scrier's Post had obviously affected Mirielle's judgement, placing their queen under a great deal of stress, more so perhaps than she had initially presumed. She glanced once more towards The Blade Lord for support, yet there was none. Caught between a rock and a hard place, Marcus chose to say nothing on the subject. The Blade Lord continued to stand motionless, though she could see now the conflict in his eyes. Despite her new-found confidence, she had clearly lost this round to Mirielle. She recalled the promise she had made to herself, back in the study hall, prior to Rayna's departure for the Knights Thranis at their Ardent Gate stronghold. So far, she had delivered on that promise – twice in fact – during the current cycle. She would not allow Mirielle's latest questionable decision to stunt her personal development. However, for the time being at least, she recognised the need to toe the party line. In any event, she now had more pressing concerns to deal with – Rayna's welfare and ability to participate in the Trials being chief among them. If Lothnar failed to rouse Rayna from her paralysis, she would require an alternate means of expelling the evil inhabiting the light bringer's body.

It was starting to get late, and moving around after dusk – with Krashnar potentially on the prowl – was unwise. Come the morning, she would return to Nathaniel's tree and check in on Lothnar's progress, but for now she needed to rest. Realising that she would have no option but to yield to the queen's decision regarding the continuation of the trials, and seeking to bring an end to the debate, she nodded respectfully to Mirielle.

'As you wish, my queen.' she said politely.

'Good. Is there anything else you wish to discuss, now that we are all assembled?'

'No, not at this time.' she replied, offering Mirielle another polite, well-practised, smile.

'Very well then, if there is nothing more, we shall meet again after the Trials. If, in the meantime, there is word from

Marcus regarding the exiled shaper, we shall meet again to discuss any further action.'

She nodded courteously towards Mirielle then turned slowly to take her leave. As she approached the door, Marcus finally chose to speak.

'Kirika...we *will* catch him.' said The Blade Lord sternly.

She paused for a moment to consider her response carefully. Apprehending Krashnar was all well and good, but allowing the Freylarkai to go about their business, pretending that no threat existed – when clearly one did – was irresponsible in her mind. If nothing else, lifting the curfew would allow Krashnar to move more freely again. It occurred to her then that Mirielle had in fact only implied that the curfew be cancelled – she had not been asked directly to terminate it, nor would she rush to do so.

'I have no doubt, Marcus, but at what cost?'

FOUR
Affirmation

'Relax! Kirika sent me.'

Nathaniel narrowed his eyes, as though the act of doing so would allow him to see more clearly – which it would not. The Teacher shifted his critical gaze towards Krisis, and then back to him. Satisfied, finally, that they were indeed who they claimed to be, Nathaniel nodded in acceptance towards him, before inviting them in.

'Please, come in. I apologise for my lack of hospitality, but I needed to be certain that it was you.'

'I understand – Kirika informed me that Krashnar is back in the vale.' he replied, as both he and Krisis entered Nathaniel's tree.

'I trust that no one saw you come here?'

'Nathaniel, Riknar has been released – by Krashnar no less. They found the fisherman's body down by the old bridge. Kirika has since instated a curfew; no one will have seen me come here.'

'I see. The situation is escalating.'

'How is she? Has her condition worsened?'

'Physically, there is nothing wrong with her – hence there is little I can do to help. Her body is not actually damaged in any way, but the *thing* is still in there, controlling her mind in some ghastly manner.'

'You refer to the parasite Kirika saw?'

'Yes. We have not been able to identify its origin. But it appears to have a hold over Rayna's mind. She seems to be experiencing some kind of paralysis, or maybe the beginnings of a fugue state.'

'That bastard!'

'Please, keep your emotions in check Lothnar – we can deal with Krashnar later. You need to clear your mind and focus. Perhaps *you* can help Rayna to expel it from her mind?'

'Take me to her.'

At once, Nathaniel led them both up a narrow set of spiralling stairs towards the top of the tree. Lying in her room upon her bed – seemingly asleep – was Rayna. The light bringer lay unnaturally still. He had expected to see Rayna's chest rising and falling regularly, in the manner typically expected of one deep in slumber. Instead, there was little or no movement; Rayna was either breathing extremely shallowly, or not at all. Krisis approached cautiously, with his slanted yellow eyes fixed on the motionless light bringer. The dire wolf sniffed at the air around Rayna's motionless body, then began to snarl incessantly.

'Krisis senses the evil within her.' said Nathaniel warily.

'Yes, there is very little which passes him unnoticed.' he replied. 'Though I have to ask, Nathaniel, is she still with us?'

'Yes, I am certain of it, despite being unable to communicate with Rayna. However, both Kirika and I hope that, with your ability, you will succeed where we have clearly failed.' said Nathaniel expectantly.

He could see the quiet desperation in Nathaniel's eyes. Although Rayna was not technically his daughter, The Teacher clearly cared a great deal about her wellbeing – the two had an inescapably close relationship. Although Rayna now inhabited his consenting daughter's body, Alarielle's soul also resided within it – if only as a silent observer. Yet despite the strange state of affairs, Nathaniel had accepted the arrangement for what it was. When Alarielle's soul was ripped from its moorings, the sad tale had almost destroyed The Teacher. However, Callum's unexpected rebirth as Rayna – in his fallen daughter's body no less – gave Nathaniel renewed purpose. Rayna had become Nathaniel's surrogate daughter, and when she released Alarielle's Narlakin captor – recovering his daughter's soul in the process – that relationship had been cemented. Nathaniel now stood upon a precipice, ready for a jump towards uncertainty; if he failed to connect with The Guardian's mind, Nathaniel stood to lose not only Rayna, but Alarielle too. He tried to clear his mind, ready for what needed to be done, though his recent failures continued to prey on his mind, causing him to doubt his own ability. Nevertheless, he needed to try; as a former member of his scouts, he owed Alarielle that much. Turning his attention back to Rayna's prone body, he opened a conduit to his mind, inviting in whatever dark cacophony preyed on the light bringer's soul. He dearly hoped that he would not fail Alarielle – not for a second time.

Project Phoenix: further proof that Trix had indeed orchestrated the killing of Mr L. Cameron. Murdering the retired software developer was clearly not a recent agenda item – Trix had been planning the event for some time. In all likelihood, the software engineer first conceived the distasteful plan prior to the inception of the government's policy to forcibly relocate their kin – the Shadow class – who referred to the unethical programme as the Rout. The abhorrent policy, specifically targeted towards his class, was designed to move the growing number of Shadow class members elsewhere. The official manifesto claimed that the Exodus – the government's title for the initial proposal –

would enrich the lives of the Shadow class, by providing them with the opportunity to start over. In reality, rounding up the Shadow class was a heinous operation. Squads of Peacekeepers had been deployed throughout the metropolis, sanctioned to use cruel weapons in order to subdue members of the Shadow class, before loading them into unmarked transports – a process reported by the media as "escorting". The final destination of the windowless mobile prisons was never made public – to his knowledge at least – though it was generally believed that it was beyond the perimeter wall of the metropolis. Government officials had claimed that anonymity was entirely appropriate, and indeed necessary to facilitate the Shadow class' forced emigration.

The Project Phoenix data stream contained numerous data objects, all designed to carry out specific functions. Although the object code ultimately meant nothing to him, the associated meta-data was at least readable by the layperson. Most of the objects had nonsensical names that meant nothing to him, though there were others, which he could in fact interpret – one in particular stood out: 'siren-one-seven-one'. The cursed object briefly riled him; the code was presumably the routine programmed into his analogue communications device, responsible for attracting the attention of the bloody corpse lying by his feet. Trying desperately to contain his anger, he closed his eyes and regulated his breathing, attempting to calm his rapidly beating heart.

'*This shouldn't be taking you so long.*' bleated Trix annoyingly in his ear.

'If you weren't so fucking messy, it wouldn't!'

Trix did not respond to his terse reply – presumably, even the socially awkward hacker knew when to shut up. At any rate, his eyes were opened once more, and so he resumed his search for the required data object.

'Found it: "one-seven-one-remote-console" – this is the object, correct?'

'*Yes, execute it.*'

'How is this going to connect you to my access panel?'

'*It won't – at least not directly – but I can connect to it, and it will then interface with your access panel.*'

'Connect with what – there is no networked tech in my hide.'

'*I will use the data-strap.*'

'But you severed that thing's data-link!'

'*I did, just not permanently.*'

'I misjudged you Trix. You deceive and withhold information; nothing is straightforward with you.' he said, scornfully.

'*Irrelevant. Execute the code Callum.*'

It was pointless debating ethics with Trix. The self-proclaimed software engineer had tunnel vision and would do almost anything to achieve his own goals. He realised now that he had judged Trix poorly, and in doing so had inexorably tied his fate to that of the untrustworthy hacker. Swallowing his pride, he ran the code as instructed. Several lines of code flashed across the holographic access panel, yet aside from the brief display of meaningless text, nothing – visually at least – appeared to happen.

'I've run the code, what happens now?'

There was no response from Trix. Perhaps, having completed his task, Trix no longer required his unique skills, he mused. Doubt started to cloud his mind, and he began to wonder if indeed he had done the right thing by giving his accomplice an invitation to the access panel.

'Trix!'

'Be patient! I'm trying to establish a connection.'

'Fine. I'll just stand here next to the dead elderly gentleman, shall I?'

'No, you can dispose of the body. Just leave his bio-key connected to the Infonet. I will do the rest.'

'What?!' he replied, completely bewildered by Trix's lack of empathy.

'The body needs to be disposed of else the hab will reek once it starts decomposing.'

'Are you serious?' he said, still shocked by Trix's words.

'Why wouldn't I be?'

Trix's response horrified him, but there was no point in arguing the toss over their opposing perspectives on the issue. In point of fact, Trix was likely correct. The body *would* eventually decompose, and the stench would potentially draw others to the crime scene. Still, disposing of a body within the metropolis was completely unrealistic. He supposed it unlikely that Trix had given the matter any real thought, since his immoral accomplice had clearly intended for him to resolve the issue himself. Since he could not exactly light a fire within the hab, he supposed that his best course of action would be to contain the smell. Finding the means to isolate the stench of a decomposing cadaver, however, would be difficult. He pinched his arm to remind himself that he was not in fact going mad, and that the scenario playing out before him was actually happening. Everything seemed surreal to him now, like a dream – or rather, a nightmare. He felt cloddish and detached from the world, more like a spectator than an actual willing participant in the dangerous game they were playing. Trix was in control now, and he had unwittingly allowed himself to be manipulated by his wicked accomplice. Although the reward, dangling before them, was becoming ever more tangible, the cost of realising their goal had increased dramatically. In a single day his moral fibre had been dealt a massive hammer-blow. He was now a murderer, and only one step away from becoming a "cleaner" too. He knew with all certainty that his actions would become a stain on his psyche. Whether they succeeded or not, there would be no erasing the day from his memories.

'Fine, I'll sort it out.'

'You are not Rayna! Who are you?'
'Am I not speaking with Rayna?'
'She is unavailable right now.'
'Then who are-- Alarielle?!'
'Yes, I am she.'

Hearing the words shocked him. Although Rayna had informed him and Nathaniel of the presence of Alarielle's soul shortly after the events at Scrier's Post, part of him, it now seemed, had doubted the light bringer's claim, if only on a subconscious level. Now, Rayna's unlikely claim had been validated, first-hand, by himself no less. The inescapable fact that Alarielle's soul still clung to Freylar made his head spin. Since losing her soul to her former Narlakin captor, he had chided himself repeatedly for her loss. Despite bringing Alarielle's body back that cycle, after their ill-fated mission to the Narlakai borderlands, neither he, nor his scouts, had been able to save her soul. The loss had affected them badly. Though he had never openly admitted his affections towards her, losing Alarielle had been hard – not least on Nathaniel, who had been devastated by the loss of his daughter. Fortunately, Kirika had managed to pull Nathaniel back from his overwhelming despair.

'Alarielle! It is me, Lothnar!'

'Lothnar! How is this possible?'

'Through my ability, although...I was expecting to connect with Rayna, however, your soul must be dominant right now.'

'No, I am merely an observer. I cannot, for instance, operate our shared body. Only Rayna can do that.'

'Nonetheless, it is good to hear your voice – or rather your thoughts – once again.'

'It is good to converse with you too Lothnar.'

'I have missed you. We all have.'

He wanted to say more, but the notion was a purely selfish one, and besides, the timing was poor. Nathaniel and Kirika were depending on him. He was determined not to let them down, and in doing so further add to the stain of his recent poor achievements.

'But...where is Rayna?' he asked, eager to learn of the light bringer's fate.

'The black liquid inside us clouds Rayna's mind. It is influencing her thoughts and has locked her within a dark prison of her own making; it is forcing her to relive her darkest memories.'

'If the parasite is responsible for her catatonic state, how then can we disrupt its hold over her?'

'I have been trying to contact her, but the black liquid is thwarting my attempts to do so. Perhaps, if we work together, we will have the necessary fortitude to cast it out?'

The thought of working alongside one another – if only with their minds – filled him with renewed vigour. Perhaps the joint undertaking would also see his fortunes improve, he mused.

'Yes, I believe you are right, though where do we start? I do not sense her presence.'

'Right now, her mind is looking inward – it seeks to avoid external contact. However, I have been searching for it since the black liquid violated her, and have discovered its whereabouts. Let me guide you.'

'Natalya, are you going to take the bet or not?'

Their impromptu meeting with The Blade Lord had been intense, and the cycle long, with their meeting concluding late in the evening. All she sought now was a moment's peace, the contents of her cup, and the warmth of the hearth to stave off the encroaching winter's cold caress. She had the latter two, but the Captain of The Blades robbed her of the third. The red-haired giant sat upon a narrow bench opposite her, next to Nathanar. It amused her to see the unlikely duo sat adjacent to one another; one was an axe-wielding brute, who thrived on battle, whilst the other was – aside from Marcus of course – a poster boy for the Order. To her left, sat Thandor. The highly skilled duellist sat casually, and appeared entirely uninterested in Ragnar's attempts to goad her into accepting the wager. Perhaps it was time to pull Thandor off the fence she thought mischievously.

'Tell you what, *Captain*. I will take the bet, provided Thandor also agrees to your wager.'

Upon hearing her words, Thandor finally displayed signs of life; the veteran Paladin raised his eyebrows and cast a languid gaze towards her.

'Excellent, so you are both in then!' pressed Ragnar, enthusiastically.

'Steady Captain, I do not believe Thandor has officially accepted your terms.' said Nathanar, looking to broker the wager.

'Come, Thandor. Is a mighty Paladin such as you scared of a friendly wager?'

Thandor said nothing. She watched with interest as her bench companion continued to maintain his nonchalant posture. Most assumed that Thandor simply cared not for the mundane trivialities of the domain in which they lived. However, she had fought alongside the skilled Paladin many times, and knew him will enough to know better. Thandor gave nothing away, but behind his seemingly disinterested exterior lurked a sharp cunning, waiting for the opportune moment to strike. Thandor's choice of weapon lent itself well to his masked disposition. The rapier was a potent weapon when wielded by one skilled in patience and precision – as well as possessing a little luck. Although the unconventional choice of weapon robbed the Paladin of half-swording and its associated attacking options, such as the murder stroke, nonetheless, Thandor preferred the extended reach and tip agility offered by his rapier. The Blades rarely fought heavily armoured opponents, therefore Thandor's decision was not without its logic. However, despite his compelling reasoning, she still favoured the vastly extended range of her bow.

'Your terms do not appeal to me, Ragnar.' replied Thandor, who then took a slow sip from his cup.

'Ha, more like you are scared that the light bringer will lose to Lothnar.'

Again, Thandor chose not to immediately respond. The Paladin was well practiced in managing Ragnar's quips, and met each one with a measured – if not irksome – response.

'I am not interested in wagering services. I will, however, agree to your terms *provided* you are willing to wager a favour.'

Upon hearing Thandor's words, Ragnar's body stiffened noticeably, as the Captain of The Blades tried to fathom the wily Paladin's play. Intrigued, Nathanar leant forwards to meet the cunning Paladin's stare.

'Well played, Natalya, using another to put the Captain on the defensive.' said Nathanar, with a curious smile.

Ragnar snorted derisively, clearly unimpressed with the turn of events.

'What is your game, Thandor?' said Ragnar gruffly.

Thandor took another sip from his cup, prolonging the tension, then turned his gaze at last towards Ragnar.

'If Rayna loses, both Natalya and I will work for you personally, for ten cycles each, performing the required administrative functions necessary to run our Order. However, if Rayna wins, you will owe each of us a favour.'

'What favour?'

'Who can say? That is the blind nature of a favour.'

Ragnar grunted in annoyance, before throwing his cup – along with its contents – into the hearth. The flames flared energetically as they reacted violently to the liquid's unwanted presence. Engaging her ability, she plucked the discarded cup from the flames with her mind, and set it down neatly between them upon the stone floor. Ragnar sneered, as even his attempt to vent his frustration had been thwarted.

'Calm down. The cup does not deserve your ire.' She said, further infuriating Ragnar.

'Captain, will you accept the revised terms of the wager?' asked Nathanar politely, who was clearly trying to diffuse the situation by quickly drawing their attention back to the heart of the matter.

'Fine, it matters not. Rayna shows promise, but she will not be able to match Lothnar's skills.' said Ragnar, pointedly.

'Then we have ourselves a wager.' she said, hoping that with the matter settled, she would finally get the moment of peace that she craved.

Ragnar stood up, towering above them, and grunted once more before taking his leave. The Captain of The Blades offered each of them a curt nod, then strode out of the chamber, leaving the three of them to enjoy the late-night warmth of the hearth.

Following the Captain's departure, she sat quietly, for a moment at least, enjoying the welcome peace that was finally hers. Content with the company of her brothers, she languidly watched the flames dancing silently in the hearth, rapt by their mesmerising allure. Lost in the moment, her thoughts began to wander. She found herself pondering the unlikely possibility of an upset victory at the Trials. Ragnar was right; The Guardian certainly did show promise, though sparring against novices in the arena, and using her ability to destroy the Narlakai, would not be enough to secure a victory against Lothnar. Perhaps she had been too hasty in accepting the Captain's wager, she mused. Yet despite her tardy concerns, she clung to the knowledge that Thandor too had tied his fate to that of Rayna's own. Thandor was not known for taking chances, meaning that the veteran Paladin was no doubt confident that The Guardian would in fact succeed. As such, she felt reassured, despite logic and reason suggesting otherwise.

'I do not like it.' said Nathanar, ushering in an end to their brief moment of silence.

'Like what?' she asked irritably, annoyed by the sudden interruption.

'The Trials.' replied Nathanar, who now seemed buried in thought.

'What is there not to like about the Trials?' asked Thandor, who only now began to take an active interest in their conversation.

'Perhaps he no longer believes that he can win.' she said aloud, with an amused smile.

'It is not that.'

'Well then, perhaps you could be less vague? Neither I, nor Thandor, are telepathic, you understand?'

'Please accept my apologies. It was remiss of me to utter my musings aloud.'

'Oh, come on Nathanar, you cannot leave us both hanging.'

'Spit it out.' said Thandor, before taking another sip from his cup.

'I...just feel that it is irresponsible – going ahead with the Trials that is. If there is an immediate internal threat to Freylar, surely we should reschedule the games?'

'Careful brother. Imagine the Captain's displeasure if you denied him his habitual games.' replied Thandor, with a wry grin.

She laughed. The thought of Nathanar informing the Captain that there would be no games for the current pass amused her. Knowing Ragnar, the Captain would ring Nathanar's head like a bell, using the butt of his axe, at such a blasphemous notion.

'Nathanar, let me ask you a question.' continued Thandor, who leaned forwards, finally giving up his casual posture. 'Do you trust Marcus?'

'What? Is that a trick question?' replied Nathanar defensively.

'No trick...do you trust him?'

'Of course I do. However, the decision to go ahead with the Trials feels wrong. Surely we should *all* be focusing our efforts on locating such a dangerous exile?'

'Agreed, but let me ask you this: do you think that *he* made that decision?'

Nathanar exhaled deeply through his nose and turned his gaze from Thandor to her. The Blades' newest Paladin looked uncomfortable, and clearly had no desire to answer Thandor's leading question. She offered Nathanar a warm smile, attempting to put him at ease once more.

'Nathanar, you may speak candidly, you are amongst friends here. I suspect that your thoughts – at least in part – coincide with our own.' she said calmly.

'Natalya, with respect, we convened here immediately after meeting with The Blade Lord.' replied Nathanar, factually. 'Neither of you has had the opportunity to discuss this matter in private.'

'Verbally no, but we have known each other long enough to be able to read one another's body language. I do not believe that this decision sits well with Thandor either – am I right?' she said, glancing towards the famed duellist.

Thandor smiled before replying, 'Indeed, you know me well, Natalya. This decision is worrying, on two accounts.'

'Would you care to elaborate?' asked Nathanar, turning his attention back to Thandor.

'Of course, provided, however, that you first answer my question.'

There was a momentary pause in their conversation as Nathanar took the measure of Thandor. On a personal level, neither knew the other particularly well. However, she sensed that both Freylarkai respected one another, for both their skill with a blade, and their ability to reason both logically and calmly.

'I suspect that the decision split the council.' said Nathanar, bringing about an end to the temporary lull in their conversation.

'That is also my belief. Kirika would not have sanctioned the decision, given that she was the one who instigated the curfew, which brings us to the heart of the matter.

'Meaning that the decision is likely the result of the queen's will alone?' Nathanar interjected.

'Yes! But more worryingly, this would imply that Mirielle overruled the others – assuming Marcus did not in fact abstain.'

There was another pause in their conversation, as they each digested Thandor's sobering perspective on the matter. There was no denying that Mirielle's rule had been a boon for Freylar, however, over the passes their aloof queen had become increasingly fickle and capricious. Mirielle's recent controversial decision was far from an isolated case; since the Narlakai invasion, their queen had displayed increasingly questionable judgement. The previously strong backbone of leadership underpinning Freylarkin society was beginning to buckle. Subtle cracks, once easily attributed to stress, were now widening, giving cause for concern. She sighed heavily, as she ran her fingers through her shoulder length blonde hair. She tried to find fault with Thandor's deduction, yet there was none – they could not deny the inescapable logic behind his reasoning.

'Natalya, what is your view on the matter?' asked Nathanar, regarding her now with a grim expression.

'Although I am loath to admit such thoughts – especially aloud – nonetheless, I agree with Thandor's assessment entirely.' she replied, casting her gaze towards the hearth. 'The Narlakai invasion has rattled Mirielle, though I suspect that her greatest enemy now is self-doubt. Consider the facts: two exiles – one of whom is possibly still present – have infiltrated our domain, and both have released our kin. It was by Mirielle's will alone that the Freylarkai, to whom I referred, were exiled.'

'An interesting point.' said Thandor, musing over her words.

'In any event, this recent poor decision, along with others which you have not been privy to, on account of your recently promoted rank, leave me questioning our queen's clarity of mind.'

'What are you implying, Natalya – a coup?!' asked Nathanar abruptly.

'No. A few bad decisions are hardly the basis for leadership reform alone. A successful coup – as you put it – requires more than mere evidence of one's error in judgement. Damning critical analysis must go hand-in-hand with an alternative solution.'

'Such as...?'

'A principle, or rather an ideal – something which the Freylarkai can rally behind of their own free will.' she said, musing aloud.

'Interesting.' said Thandor, who clearly agreed with her thinking.

A dark mood descended upon their previously light-hearted gathering, as they each paused for further reflection, allowing the hearth's greedy mesmerising flames to consume their gloomy thoughts. Her nagging doubts about Mirielle's continued ability to rule effectively preyed on her mind, as she further considered Thandor's deduction in addition to her own.

'Let us suppose, for a moment that is, that such evidence was presented. Where then would one find such an icon?' asked Nathanar boldly.

'I find it ironic that you should be the one to air such thoughts aloud, being the *role model* that you are – or at least I thought you were – for our Order. However, I believe that I may have an answer to your question.' replied Thandor. 'Look to the opening duel of the Trials in two cycles. I believe there, you will find the answer you seek.'

FIVE
Impression

It felt good to get out of hab one-seven-one, away from the crime scene of his own making. With the inevitable break of dawn drawing ever closer, the reassuring darkness outside began to recede, as daylight crept over the obscured horizon. The stars above were barely visible now, reaffirming the inevitable: that time was against him. He knew exactly what needed to be done, and he needed to do it fast. Using the NGDF's ghost data – designed to monitor the global movement of weapons – in conjunction with Trix's own predictive heuristics, they were able to locate a nearby Peacekeeper patrol. According to Trix, the patrol was a two-person team operating only a few structures away, not far from the residential habs. Although the laggy ghost data was not entirely accurate, it was all they had. Prior to leaving D-zero-zero-three, he had hurriedly memorised the route to the patrol, in addition to its predicted trajectory. Having unwittingly played his part in Trix's macabre plan to execute project Phoenix, the deceased Mr L. Cameron's hacked bio-key vitals now reported to be stable. Coupled with Trix's spoofed remote access to the Infonet, the unethical hacker now seemed largely disinterested in his movements. Trix was now consumed with the need to gain access to the source code used to develop the bio-key tracking software, subsequently abused by the government and its Peacekeeper enforcers. Trix's intricately conceived plan relied on gaining access to the Infonet by leveraging their victim's high-level clearance, who in another life had worked as a private contractor for the government, developing the software used to locate the members of the Shadow class.

With so little time now remaining before dawn, he had no choice but to forgo stealth in favour of speed. His heart thumped in his chest as he ran down the wide streets of the metropolis at breakneck speed. He tried hard not to think about the prospect of being detected as he sprinted past the metropolis' pristine white and glass buildings. Upon reaching his destination, he crouched at a street junction, peering gingerly around the corner of a tall white building. To his surprise, the patrol he sought was nowhere in sight. In his haste, he had seemingly gained more ground on his target than originally anticipated. Breaking cover, he turned right at the junction and ran down the adjacent street until he approached the first of several parked vehicles. Keeping low, he moved to the rear of the first vehicle, offering it a cursory glance to ensure that it was in fact empty. Pressing on once more, he passed the second and third vehicles, inspecting both for occupants as he moved swiftly alongside them. Before he could approach the fourth, he suddenly froze at the sound of faint whistling. Turning to inspect the noise, he noticed a narrow alley between two of the seemingly endless columned buildings flanking the street. He approached quietly with caution, following the noise, which grew louder with each closing step.

Peering into the gloom, his keen eyes spotted a single Peacekeeper, whistling jovially whilst pissing against the left wall of the alley. The lone law enforcement officer had his back towards him, and was seemingly unaware of his presence. Pressing his back against the opposite wall, he moved swiftly along the alley towards the unsuspecting officer. Unlike the rest of the inner core, very little of the metropolis' ubiquitous light penetrated the dark passage. However, despite the welcoming embrace of the shadows, his heart pounded ferociously in his chest, reminding him of the ever-present danger of being caught. As he neared his target, he unexpectedly began to panic as the realisation of the task at hand suddenly dawned on him. Although he had been in plenty of scuffles in his time spent bouncing between children's homes, as well as during his life on the streets, he was a brawler, and certainly not a professionally trained combatant. Playing out the scenario in his mind, he quickly realised that he did not possess the knowledge, or skill, necessary to disable the Peacekeeper quietly. Since he could not account for the location of the Peacekeeper's absent partner, logic dictated that it was unwise to cause any kind of commotion. Perhaps there was another way of acquiring the item he needed, he mused, wondering if in fact retreat was now the better option. Either way, his options were about to change, as the sound of splattering urine ceased abruptly.

'*Rayna, can you hear me?*'

'Shit!' he cursed aloud, turning towards the entrance to the alley.

There was no one there. He expected to see the other Peacekeeper standing at the end of the alley, boxing him in, and yet there was nothing – aside from the silent gloom. He turned his attention back to the first Peacekeeper. The armoured law enforcement officer had not moved, and appeared to be paralyzed, as though frozen in time.

'*Rayna! Concentrate on my voice.*'

'Who's there?'

'*Rayna, it is me, Alarielle.*'

'What is this?' he said, turning his head left and right in confusion. 'Who is Rayna?!'

'*That is your name. Your mind is clouded – you are not thinking clearly.*'

'Show yourself!'

'*I cannot, for I am also you.*'

'This makes no sense!'

'*Let me help you. You need to let go of this endless torment consuming your mind.*'

'If you truly want to help, show me how to disable the Peacekeeper quietly, and without killing them? Perhaps then I shall listen to what you have to say.'

'*Very well. Slide your left arm around the front of their neck.*'

'Ah, you intend for me to induce syncope?'

'*I do not know what that is – you will be executing a rear naked choke. In any case, please do as I ask.*'

Not wanting to keep his mysterious benefactor waiting, he did as instructed. He slid his arm around the thick neck of the motionless Peacekeeper, applying pressure against the officer's throat.

'*Not yet. First, grab your upper right arm. Next, place your right hand behind their head.*'

Again, he did as requested, following the voice's instructions to the letter.

'*Good. Now apply pressure by bringing your left elbow inward.*'

Time suddenly resumed once more, and he could feel the startled officer clawing desperately at his left arm, trying in vain to break his chokehold. He did exactly as the voice had instructed, pulling his left elbow inward, thus performing a blood choke on his victim. Much to his astonishment, the technique was effortless, as though he had rehearsed it many times before – though in practice, it was the first time he had ever attempted such a move. Throughout the hold, he felt a curious sensation, a sense of familiarity, as though invisible hands were guiding his actions. The voice – which called itself Alarielle – had somehow left an impression in his mind, seeded deep enough that his benefactor's words had evolved into something akin to natural instinct. The Peacekeeper thrashed their arms wildly, and started kicking their legs defiantly as he lowered his opponent quietly to the ground. The move was effective; in little over ten seconds, the Peacekeeper was slumped before him, rendered unconscious.

He rolled the Peacekeeper's prone body over and hurriedly attempted to unfasten a pack strapped to their back. The rear pack refused to let go, prompting him to tug at it aggressively until finally his prize came free. The body of the Peacekeeper heaved suddenly, and the downed officer began to cough hoarsely as they started to come round. He threw the pack across his shoulder and immediately got up and ran back along the alley towards the parked vehicles. Breaking into a sprint, he tore down the starkly lit street until he arrived back at the junction, where he turned left, retracing his route back to D-zero-zero-three.

When eventually he made it back to hab one-seven-one, he collapsed into a high-backed chair in the main living space. His muscles were tense, and he struggled to calm the continued thumping in his chest. On reflection, tearing around the metropolis had been irresponsible, if not downright stupid. He was certainly no adrenaline junkie, although part of him had enjoyed the rush of sailing so close to the wind. Breathing deeply, he relaxed into the surprisingly comfortable chair, contemplating his uncharacteristically rash course of action. Perhaps, subconsciously, he had *wanted* to be caught, he wondered, as light from the morning sun crept into the room. Regardless of the circumstances, he had taken a life. Surely, then, he deserved to be caught and punished accordingly.

'*That was not your fault.*'

Particles of dust floating in the air, illuminated by the caress of the morning sun, suddenly became fixed in place, and the flicker of light at the far end of the room's adjoining corridor – emanating from the bedroom's holographic access panel – abruptly ceased. He felt the same odd sensation when first he had heard Alarielle's voice, as though time had suddenly stopped, and the world around him ceased marching forwards.

'What is this? What are you doing?'

'*We are communicating.*'

'This isn't simply communication, you are doing something to me. I don't understand how, but you are changing me – I can *feel* it!'

'*Does it matter?*'

'It matters to me. I did not consent to this!'

'*So, you want this regret? This debilitating guilt which is feeding on your mind?*'

'That guilt is mine, and I alone deserve it. You have no right to take it away from me.'

'*That is not the Rayna I know talking. That is the darkness influencing your subconscious thoughts, locking you away inside this place of eternal torment.*'

'My name is Callum!'

'*It was, yes, but you were released from that shackle.*'

'Get out!' he said angrily. 'You have no right violating my mind like this!'

'*You have a duty to The Blades, to Freylar, and to me.*'

'Whatever it is you are doing, stop it now!'

'I am sharing my experiences with you; only then will you understand.'

'I killed an unarmed man – an elderly gentleman at that – in cold blood. There is no absolving the fact'

'You did not do so willingly; you were coerced. During my time with the Order, prior to our merging, there were many times when I released the soul of another. In battle, such action is inevitable, but it is not the action itself that defines us – it is the reason for the action.'

'There is no justification for murder!'

'These emotions you are feeling are new to you. The darkness inside of you feeds on them, sating its ravenous appetite, and in doing so traps you in this place for its own amusement. I am now sharing with you my own experiences of release, and in doing so you will learn to accept its necessity in times of strife and conflict.'

'No wait, I do not ask for...'

She loitered awkwardly by the door to Nathaniel's tree, wondering how long to wait before knocking again. The surrounding forest was unusually quiet. Despite Mirielle objecting to her impromptu curfew, she had done little to inform the Freylarkai of their queen's differing point of view. In addition, with Riknar's release now common knowledge, few wanted to venture far from their homes, despite their queen's reassurances that Marcus would deal with the potential threat. She was about to knock once more, when the door to Nathaniel's tree opened abruptly.

'I apologise for keeping you waiting Kirika, please, do come in.'

It was clear to her that Nathaniel's tardy appearance was a result of a hurried attempt to make himself look more presentable, which had, sadly, failed. His dishevelled appearance implied that he had endured a rough night, with very little sleep as a result – if any at all.

'You look tired Nathaniel.' she said, stepping over the threshold into the downstairs living space.

'I feel tired.'

'Has Rayna's condition changed at all?'

'No. Lothnar is with her. He has been at her side all night, as have I.'

'What does Lothnar say?'

'Nothing – that is exactly what has me worried! His mind has been connected to Rayna's throughout the night, yet Lothnar has said nothing. It is as if he too has succumbed to Rayna's catatonia.'

Before she could respond to Nathaniel's concerns, there was a loud thump against the ceiling, followed by the muffled sounds of cursing. They glanced at one another for a brief moment, then quickly ran upstairs to Rayna's room. Lying on the floor, flat on his back, was Lothnar. The downed Paladin banged his right fist against the wooden floor, clearly angry and frustrated.

'What has happened? Please, tell me!' asked Nathaniel, concerned by the sudden turn of events.

'I have lost my connection!' replied Lothnar, who accepted Nathaniel's hand to assist him in regaining his feet.

'You must try again – I cannot lose them Lothnar!' implored Nathaniel, desperate for the master telepath to redouble his efforts.

'It is up to Alarielle now.'

'What do you mean?' she asked, puzzled by Lothnar's choice of words.

'Together, we were able to establish contact with Rayna's mind. The parasite is feeding off of her darkest emotions, forcing her subconscious to relive troubled memories so that it can savour them.'

'Then how do we stop it?' demanded Nathaniel, whose face was awash with concern.

'*We* do not. Only your daughter can do that now. I believe that Alarielle remains in contact with Rayna's mind, and is able to manipulate it on a subconscious level. If your daughter is successful, *she* will be the one to wake Rayna from her nightmare stupor.'

'I see.' replied Nathaniel, thoughtfully. 'For a while, I thought that perhaps I had lost you all.'

'Nathaniel, what do you mean?'

'Lothnar, look outside – dawn approaches. You have been *in there* most of the night.'

'That is not possible!'

'The sun disagrees with you. See for yourself.'

Lothnar strode towards the room's only window, allowing the weak morning light to spill across his tired visage. He paused for a moment, appearing to consider everything that had recently transpired. Lothnar then turned towards them with a preoccupied stare.

'This is fascinating.'

'What is?' she asked, eager to understand the Paladin's cause for confusion.

'Events seem to be passing at a slower pace in Rayna's mind, presumably due to the parasite's influence. But regardless of Rayna's curious mental state, Alarielle has found a way to communicate with her at a more rapid pace, within her subconscious.'

'So this *thing* is slowing down Rayna's subconscious thought processes, whilst Alarielle is actively speeding them back up?'

'I do not understand.' replied Nathaniel, who seemed to be growing agitated. 'Does this aid Rayna's recovery in any way?'

'I am uncertain.' replied Lothnar, frankly, 'A mental duel is being waged inside Rayna's head. Her mind has become the battlefield upon which your daughter and the parasite currently fight one another.'

'There must be something more we can do? I refuse to sit by and wait for my daughter and that thing to tear Rayna's mind apart whilst battling for supremacy.'

'Nathaniel, there is nothing more we can do for Rayna right now. Lothnar has set Alarielle's mind to purpose, and has since been cast out. Neither you nor I have the ability to further aid Rayna at this stage.'

'Kirika, can you not at least scry the outcome, to end this torment of mine?'

'Nathaniel, Rayna's future is unclear. Your daughter's body has become a vessel for multiple souls, albeit with a single commander – currently under siege – at its helm. Rayna's future actions are highly uncertain. Scriers, myself included, can only glimpse fragments of her destiny. I cannot end your renewed emotional torture.'

Nathaniel sighed heavily as he considered her words. The pain etched on his face was clear to see. She wished dearly that she could do more to help the tortured Freylarkin, who had become a father figure to her over the many passes since her induction into The Blades.

'I realise how personal this is to you Nathaniel, but do not regress back to that broken Freylarkin I found slumped upon the floor in The Cave of Wellbeing in the wake of your daughter's initial release. You know your daughter far better than I, but I know this much: Alarielle is an extremely capable Freylarkin. Trust in her.'

A single tear rolled down her cheek as the morning sun broke cover over the eastern horizon, its weak wintery light revealing the presence of her former home. Filled with conflicting emotions, she stared down towards the heart of the vale – home to the forest dwelling Freylarkai – whilst fighting back the tears welling along the bottom of her eyes. She no longer recalled how many passes had come and gone during her time spent scratching out a living in the inhospitable borderlands. Surviving in the Narlakai borderlands was a constant battle, and thoughts of home had quickly abandoned her when practical issues, such as the need to eat and drink, occupied her waking thoughts. Yet despite the hardships of her exile, and the challenges it posed, thoughts of her sister were never far away. She missed seeing Kirika, more than she had ever thought possible, and now, the prospect of reconnecting with her sister distracted her. She lingered at the top of the Eternal Falls, watching silently as the shadows slowly retreated across the vale. As the morning mist slowly began to clear, her gaze drifted idly towards the Tri-Spires – the heart of Mirielle's rule, and now her sister's home. Unable to contain her disgust, she offered the unnatural structure a venomous sneer, whilst rubbing the fusion of flesh and metal that joined her ornate bronze claw to the stump of her left wrist. Whilst focusing intently on Mirielle's marvellous construction, dark thoughts began to take shape in her mind: she imagined her claw clutched tightly around the neck of Freylar's queen, ready and eager to serve its own brand of retribution in response to her unjust exile. The hatred inside her burned with desire; with a single squeeze of her claw, Freylar would be ushered into a new era of leadership, one that would likely reverse her current sentence. Fanciful thoughts, she mused, before breaking suddenly from her reverie as the sound of the falls drew her back to the cold reality of her miserable existence.

After finally taking the decision to abandon Krashnar's abhorrent abode deep in the borderlands, the way ahead had – for a time at least – seemed clearer to her, but now, reality started to cloud her judgement. Realistically, the chance of reaching Kirika unnoticed, way up in the Tri-Spires, even with her ability to scry, was slim. Therefore, she had decided to throw her lot in with her sister's closest confidant, Nathaniel, who lived a modest life in the heart of the vale, amongst the forest dwellers. The Teacher had a chequered history, and it was her hope that Nathaniel would at least hear her out, potentially brokering a discreet meeting with her sister. However, now that the vale was within physical sight, doubt started to gnaw at her. Unable – thus far at least – to muster the courage necessary to act upon her new-found conviction, she loitered by the edge of the falls, attempting to scry the likely outcome of her intent. Once more, the way forward was unclear to her, in much the same vein as when she had attempted to scry the conclusion of hers and Lileah's failed invasion of Freylar. Could it be that she was destined to cross paths with The Guardian for a second time, she considered, pensively. For who else had the ability to confound her second sight? As she battled with her growing insecurities, the sun slowly rose higher in the sky, eventually signalling the arrival of noon. Her stomach growled, reminding her of the need to eat, though a cursory glance at

Krashnar's spoiled wares quickly silenced any further bodily grumbles. Turning her attention back to the vale, she noticed something curious at the edge of her view: her keen vision sighted movement within the majestic pool below, which formed the base of the Eternal Falls. Focusing her attention on the disturbance, she saw a fully clothed Freylarkin swimming slowly towards the edge of the pool. The unidentified male reached the far edge of the pool, dragging his sodden body from the crystal-clear water. After unsheathing a long, peculiarly shaped blade from his back, laying it neatly on the ground, the Freylarkin carefully started to remove his clothing. She watched with interest as the Freylarkin wrung the cold water from his soaking wet clothes and emptied his boots. Curious to learn more about the interloper – in particular the means of his sudden unorthodox arrival – she climbed down to the base of the falls and formally announced her presence, knowing full well that the Freylarkin would likely see her descend from the falls' summit. After reaching the base of the falls, she regained her composure and walked calmly towards the Freylarkin, who had since re-dressed himself from the waist down. Judging by the well-defined musculature of the Freylarkin's arms and torso, in addition to the large curious weapon that lay by his feet, she supposed that the Freylarkin was a warrior of sorts – though he was clearly not a member of The Blades.

'Afternoon to you.' she said, approaching to within five paces. 'Do you require assistance?'

'Warmest greetings to you, and thank you for the kind offer, however, I believe that I am OK.'

The warrior seemed unperturbed by her presence, and paid very little attention to her left hand. He seemed to have no intention of reaching for his weapon, but continued to wring the last of the water from his shirt.

'May I ask how it is that you suddenly arrived here?' she asked, politely.

'I am afraid that I cannot say, however, I am looking for a Freylarkin called Rayna, whom some might refer to as The Guardian. Apparently, she lives in these parts, along with another by the name of Nathaniel – often called The Teacher. Perhaps you could help me find them?'

Her thoughts frantically jostled for position inside her head upon hearing the mysterious Freylarkin's new information. This unexpected news complicated matters. She knew very little about the entity now inhabiting Alarielle's body. Her only knowledge of The Guardian came from their brief encounter during the conflict at Scrier's Post, along with second-hand scraps of information tossed to her by Krashnar. It was impossible to know how The Guardian would react to her arrival, and whether the chance of a second encounter would have any bearing on her already challenging discussions with Nathaniel. This increased risk threatened to jeopardize everything. She paused for a brief moment whilst considering the facts available to her. Logic demanded that she make a hasty retreat, back to the borderlands, yet there remained nothing for her there. Besides, she had come too far to turn back now, and the presence of another would help to deflect attention away from her own – likely unwanted – presence in Freylar.

'Yes of course. Follow me.'

SIX
Expulsion

The Narlakai herd had moved much quicker than she had expected. Despite the distance covered since its withdrawal after the battle for Scrier's Post, the herd had remained relatively intact, although its shape had curiously changed. The herd was now stretched out into a long meandering column, reminding her of a funeral march. Its silent retreat was methodical; each dimly sentient Narlakin diligently followed the next, as they collectively drifted further into Narlak. It was impossible to discern their numbers with any accuracy, due to the volume of Narlakai and their close proximity to one another, their flailing tendrils blurring the gaps between them. Regardless, her gifted mind could sense their collective presence, which was formidable; the mass of Narlakai trailing across the cracked landscape before her would ultimately be sufficient for her needs. She cared not for the herd's miserable existence. The Narlakai were nothing more than a tool to her; marionettes, waiting for their strings to be pulled.

Opening her mind fully, she established hundreds of weak conduits to the Narlakai, hoping to assert her control over as many of the soul stealers as her mind would allow. Immediately the column began to falter, with gaps appearing as some of the Narlakai broke formation and began hesitantly drifting towards her position. Some of the nightmare horrors appeared to be confused, loitering, whilst others continued their blind march towards the heart of Narlak. Her initial attempt to alter the herd's trajectory had seemingly failed, causing them to flounder instead. However, she would not be beaten. Redoubling her efforts, she channelled renewed mental energy along each conduit, in an attempt to impose her will on her tentative subjects.

'You will follow me!'

More of the Narlakai broke formation and started to drift eerily towards her. Her Meldbeast mount reared its three dire wolf heads, each of which sniffed at the cold air, as the black writhing sea of Narlakai on the horizon gradually altered its heading. The strain on her mind was immense, unlike anything she had previously experienced. When she had initially gathered the herd – at Darlia's behest – the task had been relatively straightforward, albeit slow. Gathering the Narlakai together piecemeal was a simple test of her ability, especially after discovering that one only needed to control a small percentage of the slow-witted horrors in order to guide the rest, due to their herd mentality. Trying to command the driven mass to alter its previous course, without fracturing it, however, was another matter entirely. Although the bulk of the herd was now heading silently towards her, she could sense parts of the horde breaking off, bent on pursuing their prior directive. Quickly realising that her ability alone would not be sufficient to bind the confused mass to her will, she turned her attention once more to Krashnar's abhorrent pet, ready to impart fresh orders to her eager mount.

'Round them up! Drive them south!'

Using its boundless stamina, the Meldbeast leapt forwards, eager to shepherd its newly-assigned nightmare flock. Once more, the beast's jarring movements pulled at her flesh-metal torso, causing her to wince as agonizing pain shot through her upper body. More tears spilled from her eyes as her fervent mount raced towards the herd's right flank. The Meldbeast's powerful limbs propelled the creature across the landscape at impossible speed, which – by now at least – she should have been well accustomed to. Yet, despite her experience riding the creature, she continued to bounce around painfully on top of its chitin carapace, barely held in place by the flesh-straps securing her legs to the flanks of the chimera. The Narlakai withdrew from the beast's colossal presence as the frenetic chimera approached the herd's right flank, thus consolidating its mass. Those soul stealers that had previously begun to break away along the right flank of the herd, quickly re-joined the main mass, clearly not wanting to be singled out by Krashnar's monstrous creation, presumably on account of its size. With the right flank's fledgling separatist groups rapidly falling back into lockstep, she commanded the Meldbeast along the rear of the formation, ensuring that no more of the Narlakai splintered off from the herd. Whilst the Meldbeast tore down the rear of the formation, the dark clouds above signalled their displeasure, dumping heavy rain across the inhospitable landscape. The impromptu rainfall quickly washed away the bodily fluids and dried excrement staining the rear of the Meldbeast's carapace. Despite the agonizing pain wracking her tortured body, seeing the shaper's uncouth prophecy come to fruition prompted her to laugh aloud, unexpectedly. Oblivious to her twisted amusement, her impressive mount continued to power down the rear of the Narlakai's formation, reinforcing the herds' renewed purpose. Soon, the Narlakai would be back under her control – where they belonged – and those who had shunned her existence would once again feel her wrath.

'Nathaniel, I am sorry, but I really must be getting back to the Tri-Spires. My presence will be needed to coordinate the final preparations for the Trials.' she said, before finishing her drink.

'I understand.' replied Nathaniel, who paced restlessly whilst she and Lothnar sat opposite one another.'

'You *will* contact me if you need anything?'

'Yes...of course.' replied Nathaniel distantly.

She turned her attention to Lothnar. The bored Paladin lazily slouched in the rocking chair opposite, staring vacantly at the grubby window adjacent to them. Krisis lay on the floor, across Lothnar's feet. The black-furred dire wolf appeared entirely uninterested in their discussions.

'Lothnar, please, will you stay with him?'

The master telepath offered her a sidelong glance, displaying his obvious displeasure at her request.

'Please, Lothnar.' she implored softly. 'He should not be alone right now.'

'Fine – I guess I shall have to read some of these dusty books.' he replied, shifting his eyes towards the piles of literature surrounding them.

'Thank y--' she began to reply, when suddenly a thump sounded above them.

She immediately rose from her chair, though Nathaniel was already ahead of her and running frantically up the stairs. Lothnar, however, reacted slowly, due to Krisis immobilising him – the animal's ears simply twitched in acknowledgement of the sound.

'Come on boy – shift yourself.' said Lothnar, who was eager to join Nathaniel and check on Rayna's condition.

Eventually Krisis took the hint; the large dire wolf slowly rose and moved to find a better spot, behind one of the dusty book piles.

'Come quickly!' cried Nathaniel, his muffled voice loaded with urgency.

Together they ran up the curved wooden stairs, in single file, leaving Krisis to enjoy his renewed slumber. Upon entering Rayna's room, they found the light bringer on the floor, pushed up on her hands and feet. Rayna appeared to be struggling to breathe and was retching violently, as though trying to expel something large that was stuck in her throat. As Rayna's head rocked back and forth, she saw black liquid streaming from the light bringer's eyes, in addition to trace amounts seeping from her nostrils. Nathaniel was crouched by her side, attentively, holding Rayna's left arm, trying to steady her. Once more Rayna retched, causing the vile liquid seeping from her eyes to run down her cheeks, before dripping onto the floor. Again, and again, the light bringer retched, until finally a substantial mass of black liquid projected from her mouth onto the wooden floor with a wet splatter. Rayna's ashen face immediately regained some of its natural ochre colour and she began to breathe more easily. She gasped in horror as the expelled liquid began to slither away from where it fell, reconstituting itself as it connected with the multitude of other dark pools heaved upon the floor. The vile liquid quickly consolidated its form in the centre of the room, and in doing so grew in size to form a large black puddle. However, before it could claim a fresh victim, Rayna staggered to her feet and began to harness pure white light in her closed left hand. The brilliant white light quickly grew in intensity, spilling between the gaps in Rayna's clenched fist, bleaching the room with its genesis.

'Look away!' she cried, as Rayna unsteadily directed her left arm towards the evil fluid.

She turned and closed her eyes as brilliant white light flooded the room, threatening to blind its occupants irrevocably. Despite closing her eyes, shutting them tightly, Rayna's light permeated the skin of her eyelids and stung her retinas. For a brief moment she felt disorientated and unstable on her legs, however, the phenomenon quickly passed, allowing her to open her eyes, gingerly, once more. The dark puddle no longer existed. Instead, in its place, were flecks of grey ash, strewn across a carpet of fine white powder.

'Rayna!' cried Nathaniel, grasping his surrogate daughter by her shoulders, trying to steady her.

'What did you do to it?' asked Lothnar, as Rayna sought to compose herself.

'Lothnar, please, give her a moment.' she said pensively. 'She is probably quite disorientated.'

'It's OK, Kirika.' replied Rayna, straightening her back. 'Whatever that thing was, it's gone now – it hates the light.'

'How did you manage to expel it?' asked Lothnar curiously.

'It was feeding on the darkness of my past, causing me to become trapped there. Alarielle helped me to see things differently.

'I am so glad to have you both back.' said Nathaniel, who was now visibly more at ease.

'As am I, sister.' she said, stepping round the fallen ash to offer Rayna a welcoming embrace.

'I'm glad to be back. But where's Krashnar?'

'We do not know. He released a local fisherman – Riknar – and could conceivably still be lurking in the vale.'

'Kirika, he must be stopped!' replied Rayna, regaining some of her characteristic determination.

'I agree, however, Mirielle is more concerned with maintaining the status quo. She has entrusted Marcus to deal with the threat. In the meantime, she expects you to compete against Lothnar in the opening duel of the Trials.'

'Kirika, I do not understand why Mirielle would be so irresponsible. Krashnar poses a real threat to the Freylarkai. We should secure the civilians and hunt him down, without delay.' replied Rayna fervently.

'Again, I agree with you, however, I cannot go against the Queen's decision on this matter.'

'But you are on the ruling council – surely there is something you can do?'

'Sadly, there is not. I have already tried. Marcus is loyal to Mirielle; therefore he will not readily challenge her edicts. I have thus been overruled. In addition, Mirielle does not endorse a curfew which I instated, following the news of Riknar's release.'

'Kirika, we have to stop him. Marcus is going to need our help.'

'Then you oppose the will of our queen?' asked Lothnar with a curiously raised eyebrow.

'I oppose *any* decision which puts the lives of innocents at risk.'

'Then there is more you should kn--' Lothnar began to reply, before being abruptly cut off by a loud knocking on the door of Nathaniel's tree.'

'Nathaniel, are you expecting company?' she asked, concerned by their unexpected company.

'No, I am not.' replied Nathaniel pensively. 'Stay here – all of you.'

Nathaniel left the bedroom and promptly made his way down the curved wooden stairs. An uncomfortable moment of silence passed between them whilst they stared awkwardly at one another, unsure as to who would attempt to seek an audience with Nathaniel at such time. Those who knew The Teacher well – including the local forest dwellers – were keenly aware that Nathaniel habitually returned late from the arena. Who, then, would know that he would be home, shortly after noon? They stood silently, hoping to glean the occasional word of dialogue between Nathaniel and whoever it was that sought an audience with him – yet they heard nothing. Time passed, and she could sense both Rayna and Lothnar growing restless. She was about to raise her hand to ask for their continued patience, when suddenly they heard the sound of footsteps ascending the stairs. Shortly afterwards, Nathaniel re-entered the room, looking the worse for wear, more so than when she had first laid eyes on him that morning.

'Nathaniel, what troubles you?' she whispered quietly, concerned by his ominous appearance.

'I think that you should all come down and see for yourselves – though I urge you all to exercise restraint.'

She offered Rayna and Lothnar a curious glance, before swiftly following Nathaniel back down the stairs into the main living space. There were two Freylarkai standing in the centre of the room. The first was a male of respectable height, with short raven-black hair, shaved at the sides, and piercing blue eyes. He carried a long blade across his back, and stood a full pace forward of his companion. The other – a female – wore a brown robe, fitted around the waist, adorned with fine metal chains and with an elaborate metal collar affixed to it. The slender Freylarkin had long dark purple hair, tied back in a loose ponytail, and deep violet eyes similar to her own. She took a step forwards to the right of the male, seeking to better observe her female counterpart. It was then that her lips parted in disbelief, as she suddenly realised who in fact stood before her. Slowly, the female Freylarkin opposite slid her left hand out from behind her back, revealing an ornate prosthetic bronze mechanical claw. Her heart skipped a beat, and tears immediately began forming along the bottom of her eyes. She tried to move closer, but her limbs stiffened, and her movements became awkward whilst her mind struggled to process that which her body already knew to be true. In that single moment, her world was – once again – turned upside down.

'Darlia! You have come back!'

She smiled to herself whilst she watched her new protégé diligently practicing the meditation techniques she had recently imparted. After aiding Nathaniel to track her own movements to Scrier's Post, Keshar had inadvertently become the first of her students. Despite their short time together, the young scrier was already exhibiting signs of great potential, nurtured by her experienced tutelage and under the protection afforded to them by Scrier's Post. The formerly abandoned site – originally erected as a sanctuary for scriers – now stood rejuvenated, courtesy of Krasus' masterful ability. Under her direction, and with the blessing of their queen, Scrier's Post was now restored to glory – though with a modern twist. The original gothic feel of the sanctuary and its surrounding courtyard had been eroded by Krasus' ability to bend the laws of nature. Now the site had a much sleeker feel, with stylish curves and sharp lines littered throughout its new design. The site's previously rough organic surfaces were now smooth, like glass, giving the place of meditation an almost crystalline quality. Her new direction for Scrier's Post had seen its former dark and sombre existence raised into the light, in accordance with her vision. The site was now the fulcrum of Mirielle's renewed stance on scrying, and together they would work to avoid repeating the tragedies responsible for the sanctuary's tarnished repute. Scrier's Post would no longer be mired in the unfortunate events that stained its past; the site had renewed purpose, and would once again serve as a sanctuary for Freylar's scriers. Under her watchful eye, Scrier's Post would allow them to bring the art of scrying into the light. No longer would the ability be seen as taboo. Whilst there would still be the ongoing necessity for certain restraints – lines never to be crossed – her students would be indoctrinated in the use of their ability. No longer would scriers operate in the shadow, under tight regulation; instead, her kin would embrace their ability, whilst being both mindful and well informed of the dangers wrought through over-indulgence.

'Aleska, my time here is coming to an end. I trust that you are satisfied with my work?'

'Indeed I am. You have done an excellent job. I know of only *one* capable of surpassing your masterful ability.' she replied, with a warm smile. 'I shall inform *her* that you have exceeded my expectations.'

'There is no need to inform our queen.'

Once again, she detected the familiar hint of arrogance in the shaper's voice. Krasus was a master shaper – a fact he was keenly aware of – who often failed to keep his hubris in check. Despite greatly appreciating his help to restore Scrier's Post, she preferred to work with those who exhibited a more modest work ethic. The overconfident artisan began talking in detail about the alterations he had fastidiously wrought upon the site, though she found his delivery unnecessarily verbose and conceited. Krasus' lips continued to move, yet she paid the talented shaper little further attention as her mind began to wander. She wondered if perhaps seeing the site now would ease Nathaniel's stance over their renewed direction on scrying. There was no doubt in her mind, that the site's new facade would go some way to distancing the sanctuary from its grubby past, thus allowing them to usher in a new era of acceptance for Freylar's scriers.

'So, you see, it was necessary to spend the additional time ensuring that--'

'Your efforts are appreciated.' she replied abruptly, seeking an end to Krasus' pompous verbal tirade. 'If you wish, you may return to the Tri-Spires tomorrow morning. In the meantime, can you please finish the memorial in the courtyard, which we discussed?'

'It will only take me a moment to complete.' replied Krasus, seemingly unfazed by her interjection.

'Good. After it is done, your work here is finished.'

Krasus nodded cordially, then turned and strode out of the sanctuary into the courtyard. Throughout their conversation, Keshar had remained intently focused on her meditation. She smiled again as she resumed her observation of the young Freylarkin, watching with interest whilst ensuring that the young scrier did not attempt to overstep the boundaries of her new-found freedom. Although Keshar was her only student – for the time being at least – she remained confident that others would follow her teachings, once word of the sanctuary's restoration became public knowledge. Having decided to remain positive, she convinced herself that Mirielle would find a way to overcome the lingering stigma attached to Scrier's Post. She hoped dearly that the reimaging of Scrier's Post would aid the queen by facilitating their shared ambition, which, ultimately, was in the interests of the Freylarkai. But despite her confidence, there remained the ever-present possibility that Mirielle would summon her back to the Tri-Spires, to assist with future recruitment. To that end, she required that Keshar be ready. Moreover, she *needed* the young scrier's unwavering loyalty; if Mirielle indeed chose to recall her, she would need a Freylarkin whom she could trust to manage the sanctuary in her absence.

'Keshar, you may stop now.' she said, as she approached her eager apprentice. 'It is now time for you to move on, for I have another lesson for you to learn.'

'Come in.' he said, using his mind effortlessly to open the door to his private quarters.

Two of the Tri-Spires' guards entered the room and promptly stood to attention. As was habitually the case with the house guards, the Freylarkai standing opposite him appeared rigid, like statues. He took their measure whilst smiling cordially, hoping to put them at ease. But instead, the well drilled guards stiffened their backs, appearing tenser now than when they had first entered his chamber. He sighed in response, bemused as to why they persistently greeted him in such a way, despite his continued efforts to soften his demeanour in their presence. Typically, he had little difficulty winning over his audiences, but there was something sterile about the house guards, which granted them immunity to his charm offensives.

'At ease.'

Despite ordering the guards to relax, very little changed in their stoic demeanour. Both continued to stand at attention, as though physically restrained by some unseen force. Bemused by the guards' strict adherence to protocol, he laughed quietly to himself, wondering if there was ever a time when Ragnar practiced the same level of restraint. Unfazed by his personal amusement – at their own expense no less – the guards remained perfectly still, presumably waiting for his formal request for their report. How stale the chain of command was, he mused. Regrettably, there were few who questioned his authority. Although this state of affairs ultimately made the task of commanding The Blades easier, he missed the mental stimulation of justifying his own thought processes. As a direct consequence, he spent a great deal of time buried in his own thoughts, debating issues silently to himself. Secretly, he had hoped for the prompt return of Rayna from her secondment to the Ardent Gate, where he had instructed her to spend time with the Knights Thranis, seeking to earn their trust. However, as fate would have it, Rayna remained absent from the vale. Though her lack of presence was a good sign – suggesting that the knights had not dismissed The Guardian out of hand – her absence did nothing to placate his own needs. Whilst his fellow Paladins and Valkyries were often a good source of debate, their own views were typically self-serving, frequently driven by personal agenda. Occasionally both Ragnar and Nathaniel made for good sounding boards, however, Ragnar lacked imagination and Nathaniel had become increasingly distracted since Rayna's arrival in Freylar. Deciding not to leave the guards hanging any longer, he gave them the formality they sought and stood before them, ready to receive their report.

'What news do you have to report?'

'My lord, I regret to inform you that there has been no further sighting of the exile. We believe he has since fled the vale.'

'What evidence forms the basis of your assumption?' he asked, toying with the unfortunate guard who chose to speak.

'We have checked everywhere, my lord.' replied the other guard, who now warranted his attention.

'An impossible task, I am sure. Besides, why would Krashnar travel to the vale, simply to release a local fisherman? Mark my words – he is *still* here.'

The guards stiffened once more, no doubt finding his response uncomfortable.

'What are your orders, my lord?'

'Continue your search. And remember...he could *be* anyone.'

'Yes my lord.' the guards replied in unison.

'Is there anything further to report?'

'My lord, there are reports that The Guardian has been sighted in the vale.'

'When was this confirmed?' he said, failing to mask his surprise.

'Two cycles ago. One of the forest dwellers reported seeing her return from the north.'

'The north – are you certain?'

'My lord, it is possible the Freylarkin was confused. The report, however, is accurate.'

'Understood. Then, if there is nothing else, you are both dismissed.' he said, followed by a quick wave of his right hand.

The emotionless duo promptly left the chamber, closing the door firmly behind them. He wandered over to the room's single large window, casting his gaze towards the distant forest on the other side of the river that ran the length of the vale. If the report was accurate, and Rayna was indeed back from the southern lands, why then would she delay in reporting to him regarding her mission, he mused. In addition, the report mentioned nothing of Anika – had the pair become separated, he wondered. For a fleeting moment, he thought about contacting Rayna by paying her a personal visit at Nathaniel's tree, though he quickly reminded himself of the Trials, and The Guardian's imminent duel with Lothnar. The smart move was to await Rayna's report – undoubtedly, she would approach him when she was ready. Besides, with Krashnar's whereabouts still unaccounted for, gallivanting around the vale in search of Rayna was unwise. The Blades had already been tasked with chasing one shadow; he could ill afford to start potentially chasing another.

SEVEN
Emotion

'You have come back!'

Having spent countless cycles wondering if she would lay eyes on her sister again, seeing and hearing Kirika now was almost too much to bear. During their time apart, she had battled tirelessly with herself, trying to remain strong by suppressing her feelings and keeping them in check. Now, those defences – which she had worked so hard to erect – were being rapidly torn down. She watched, trembling, while her sister's eyes filled with tears, mirroring her own. She tried to speak, but her mind failed miserably to recall the words necessary to convey the torrent of emotions now assaulting her psyche. Blinking hard, in a futile attempt to clear her vision, she felt streams of tears rolling down her cheeks, collecting under her chin, before dropping to the floor. Her breathing was shallow and her body now trembled uncontrollably. She tried to approach her estranged sister, but her muscles tensed against her will, thwarting her attempts.

'Stay back!' cried a stern voice from a male Freylarkin at the bottom of the stairs. 'Take another step closer, Darlia, and I *will* release you where you stand!'

Directing her watery vision towards the threatening voice, she blinked heavily once more. Her vision cleared – albeit temporarily – allowing her to quickly recognise her male aggressor. It was Lothnar. Beside the Paladin scout was a red-haired female, who stood barely clothed, and looking somewhat the worse for wear. Sifting rapidly through the chaotic thoughts and emotions assaulting her mind, she quickly realised that the female Freylarkin opposite was in fact the enigma Krashnar had warned her about. Standing before her – in the same room no less – was the Freylarkin responsible for her failed invasion of Freylar.

'The Guardian!' she whispered under her breath.

'Darlia, what is going on?' asked Vorian, turning towards her. 'How is it that you know one another?'

'*She* is responsible for the release of our kin!' proclaimed Lothnar vehemently. 'Explain to us now, stranger, why it is that *she* is an apparent associate of yours?'

'Lothnar relax – his name is Vorian; he is a Knight of the Knights Thranis.' replied The Guardian, whose gaze now shifted towards her mechanical claw.

'You *know* him?' asked Lothnar, clearly taken aback by The Guardian's knowledge of her companion.

'Yes – he is well regarded amongst the Knights Thranis and is entirely trustworthy.' continued The Guardian. 'It's good to see you again Vor, though I'd not expected it to be so soon. Please forgive us – your arrival is...unexpected, so too the presence of your companion.'

'It is good to see you too, Honorary Knight Rayna. My companion and I have only recently met.' replied Vorian. 'Darlia offered to be my guide, and I accepted her kind aid.'

'Your guide to what, may I ask?' enquired her sister, softly, who had since wiped some of the tears from her eyes.

'To finding The Guardian.' replied Vorian, who then turned his attention back to Rayna. 'It is urgent that I speak with you privately, Rayna.'

'Speak your mind, Vorian – you have no enemies here.' replied Rayna casually.

'That one is an enemy, to the entire domain no less!' proclaimed Lothnar, directing his left index finger directly

94

towards her. 'Queen Mirielle had you exiled from Freylar, *witch*, so why is it then, that you are here?!'

A prolonged moment of awkward silence followed, as each of them regarded her with mixed emotions. Lothnar glared at her with utter contempt, whilst Nathaniel and Vorian showed measured restraint. Her sister remained noticeably shaken, but most curious of all was The Guardian, who seemed genuinely intrigued by her sudden unforeseen arrival. Swallowing hard, attempting to clear her throat, she cut straight to the heart of the matter, attempting to salvage a modicum of credibility, despite deserving none.

'I am responsible for the heinous events which transpired at Scrier's Post – I do not deny it – but I am not the one who drove the Narlakai towards the sanctuary. Her name is Lileah, and right now she is raising her forces again, with the intention of releasing you all!'

'Ha! How can we believe a word of what you say?' replied Lothnar sharply. 'You instigated an invasion of Freylar, responsible for the release of our kin, were subsequently defeated, and now you expect us to believe the words which spill from your venomous tongue!'

'We should at least investigate her claim, Lothnar' replied The Guardian, calmly.

'She is a threat, Rayna, all the while she remains in the vale.' argued Lothnar. 'We have a responsibility to protect the Freylarkai.'

'Agreed, but we should not dismiss this information out of hand.'

'And if she *is* indeed telling the truth, what then?' Nathaniel suddenly interjected.

'And what if she is not?' retorted Lothnar, maintaining an unwavering stance on the matter. 'Nathaniel, we cannot trust her!'

'Quiet!' cried Kirika, bringing a quick end to the heated, short-lived, debate. 'Sister, the punishment bestowed upon you was too severe; your actions did not warrant a life of exile. Nonetheless, you broke Freylarian law. Moreover, you were subsequently responsible for the release of our kin! Surely you expected such a reaction to your claim?'

'I believe that she speaks the truth.' said Vorian flatly.

'Rayna says that you are trustworthy – and I believe her – but how, Vorian, can you blindly accept Darlia's claim of a renewed invasion?' demanded Lothnar.

'Rayna, if we may speak in private, I believe that I can validate Darlia's claim.'

'Then speak now, Knight, to us all!' demanded Lothnar, whose anger now threatened to get the better of him.

'Vorian, I appreciate the need to safeguard certain information pertaining to the Knights Thranis, but as you can see, emotions are somewhat frayed right now. Please, if you can indeed validate this claim, find a way to do so publicly.' said Rayna, who was clearly looking for a way to diffuse the tension between them.

'Very well.' replied Vorian, with a look of resignation. 'The means by which you returned to the vale has been compromised. We believe that it has been infiltrated by another.'

'You mean by someone outside the Order?'

'Correct – the source of the activity came from the Narlakai borderlands.'

'And its destination?'

'The vale.'

'Krashnar!' Kirika interjected. 'He recently showed up in the vale, alone, released Riknar, and subsequently tried to release Rayna too. Queen Mirielle has tasked Marcus with bringing him to justice.'

'Krashnar was with Lileah. They were both seated upon the back of some hideous mutant pet beast of his, shaped by his own ability no less.' she said, surprised by her sister's account.

'Then they have since parted ways.' replied Kirika matter-of-factly. 'Perhaps a difference of opinion has led them down separate paths?'

'No. Krashnar was manipulating Lileah, he would not have abandoned her after going to such lengths to coerce her into cooperating. Lileah is impetuous, and difficult to control. This must be some kind of ruse.'

'*You* are the one trying to deceive us, Darlia!' Lothnar interjected. 'Your presence here is ruse enough.'

'Kirika, you *must* believe me, sister.' she implored. 'Lileah *is* going to attack the vale. There will be no subtlety in her approach; she will round up as many Narlakai as her mind will permit, and heard them straight towards the vale. Please, you must stop her, else she will release thousands, whether she succeeds or fails in her attempt.'

'*Why* must I believe you? Darlia, you attacked us before!'

'That was different. I would be lying if I said that I did not want to release that bitch, Mirielle, along with that obedient lapdog of hers who is responsible for *this*,' she said, raising her bronze metal claw, 'But foremost, I wanted to overthrow her rule, not to release our kin. The flanking Narlakai herd was directed specifically for that reason. My strategy involved drawing out The Blades and infiltrating the

Tri-Spires – I would have been able to calm Lileah's impetuous desires *after* ousting Mirielle. However, I did not foresee The Guardian's ability to disrupt my second sight, which ultimately led to the events that transpired at Scrier's Post. What happened there was a tragedy – one for which I am ultimately to blame. Believe me, sister, when I say *that* atrocity weighs heavy on my soul. I *know* that I cannot be absolved of my past crimes, nor can I fully atone for them, but please...let me at least try.'

There was another long, awkward moment of silence, as everyone present regarded her sternly, trying to ascertain the truth of her words. She expected Lothnar to blast her, again, with another of his cutting retorts, but instead the Paladin stood silently, gazing intently at her. Concerned that she had failed to convince her audience of her sincerity, she was about to continue, when suddenly The Guardian spoke confidently.

'Darlia, I believe you.'

'And I have no desire to see another of my students fall in battle.' followed Nathaniel, curiously lending his support.

She watched nervously as her sister offered Lothnar a sidelong glance, attempting to discern whether in fact the master telepath was conveying his thoughts to Kirika telepathically. After a brief moment, Lothnar took a deep breath, before exhaling loudly. The Paladin turned to her and approached ominously.

'If you truly have nothing to hide, Darlia, allow me to search your mind. If indeed your claim is valid, I will know of it.'

She stared at the Paladin intently, considering whether or not to reason with him further. Lothnar was evidently not the type to readily accept the word of another – he needed to see for himself – suggesting, therefore, that further reasoning would achieve very little. She desperately needed the incredulous Paladin on side, and if that meant willingly exposing her innermost thoughts, so be it.

'Very well – I have nothing to hide.'

Without any warning, she felt the weight of Lothnar's mind pressing upon her own, seeking to uncover the truth behind her presence. There was no subtlety to Lothnar's mental approach; the Paladin wanted answers, hard and fast, and had little interest in her own mental welfare as he sought to justify his doubts. At first, the pain was uncomfortable, and she felt pressure building inside her head. The invisible force assaulting her mind then suddenly shifted up a gear, causing her to wince in pain.

'Lothnar, careful, you are hurting her.' said Kirika sternly.

'Almost there.' replied the Paladin firmly, who clearly had no real interest in her discomfort.

She cried out in distress, although her protest was not due to any direct physical pain. Lothnar had discovered her feelings for Lileah, and was now reopening the barely cauterised wound, subjecting her once more to the hurt and despair caused by their miserable parting of ways. Again, she cried out as Lothnar continued to dig deeper, violating her mind, dredging up hurtful emotions which she would sooner lay to rest. She dropped to her knees and began to weep, whilst the unrelenting Paladin ruthlessly pressed on, hollowing her out, leaving no stone unturned.

'Lothnar! That is enough.' said Kirika, whose eyes began to water once more upon witnessing her suffering.

Despite her sister's proclamation, Lothnar continued to burrow deeper into her mind, in his quest to disprove her words. She began to sob, uncontrollably, whilst Lothnar replayed the raw emotions of her past, forcing her to suffer their torment again. Desperate to prove her claim, she clung on to her strained psyche, determined not to give in – yet maybe that was the point of Lothnar's interrogation, some part of her mused. Perhaps he wanted her to break, so that he could pick over the remnants of her shattered mind, satisfying the wrath he harboured for both her and Lileah in the process.

'Enough!' cried Kirika, glaring angrily at the master telepath.

Once again, Lothnar ignored her sister, prompting Kirika to grab his left arm angrily.

'I said enough!'

'Quiet! I cannot hear myself think.' he said, agitatedly, casting his malevolent black pupil-less eyes towards the thing writhing in the dark corner opposite.

The shaping of his newest creation had provided a welcome distraction throughout the night, and in turn had sated the hungering darkness inside of him – temporarily at least. However, the fledgling creature's genesis had since done little to ease his mood, due to its constant muffled moans. His futile attempts at passing the cycle asleep, upon the hard stone floor of the store, had largely failed, leading to his growing irritation. Perhaps he should have found a quieter way to violate its flesh, he mused, as he tried to block out the incessant moaning of the gibbering construct – formerly the mother and daughter proprietors of his current accommodation. Their previous whimpering had been like sweet gentle music in comparison, unlike the monotonous drone that now emanated from the creature's sealed lips. Perhaps his newest creation was simply hungry, he thought –

it had been a good cycle since last they had fed. Desperate to put an end to the whining torment, he pushed himself off the cold stone floor and began to rifle haphazardly through the store's abundant wares. The establishment predominantly supplied tools, for both agriculture and hunting game, though his keen eyes quickly located a small section towards the rear of the structure that held a limited selection of fresh fruit. Using his good hand – still retaining all of its digits – he greedily snatched a handful of fruit, before gorging himself on the ripe produce. It had been some time since last he had eaten; recent events had distracted him, causing him to neglect his own wellbeing, including his noisy stomach. After eating his fill, he grabbed more of the deliciously sweet produce and casually tossed it onto the floor, close to the store's former proprietors. Quick to react, the creature pulled at its leash, desperate to close on the source of nourishment carelessly discarded just beyond its reach. He groaned with annoyance as he watched the pathetic aberration miserably attempting to edge closer to the discarded produce. The creature clumsily used all of its eight limbs to push itself towards the abandoned fruit, however, a thick rope of flesh, which he had used to tether his creation to an adjacent wall, thwarted its attempts. He sighed loudly, before kicking some of the ripe fruit towards the creature in an unexpected moment of compassion. The aberration turned its heads towards the produce and attempted to ingest the fruit, but with both of its mouths sealed shut, it became increasingly distressed by the fleeting promise of nourishment.

'Pathetic!'

Despite being the architect of the creature's miserable existence, he had no remorse for its wretched being.

Experience told him that melding key bodily components ultimately lead to failure, thus he had taken a different approach with his latest work. Rather than swapping limbs and significantly reworking the flesh, he had instead decided to adopt a more simplistic approach, choosing to graft the mother's torso onto the back of the daughter's own. Together they crawled awkwardly across the floor, with arachnid-like movements. Both retained their original limbs and head, however, the front of the mother's torso was now fused to the back of her own daughter, forcing the pair to work in unison. Their heads were bowed low, due to their own weight, which in turn caused their long hair to drag across the floor, further obscuring their vision. For a brief moment he considered tying back their hair, yet it amused him to watch their continued struggle. However, despite his personal amusement, he could not permit the creature's release; he still had a use for the aberration, so he approached the wretched construct, which recoiled in his presence, and proceeded to separate its lips.

'There – now you can eat. Now be quiet! Do not make me regret this decision.'

He turned his back on the deformed mother and daughter and once again lay down upon the hard stone floor. With his creation no longer whining, he could think clearly about the path ahead. During his time spent holed up in the store, he had overheard a number of conversations in the street outside, despite the meddlesome scrier's impromptu curfew. Conflicting advice had filtered down from the Tri-Spires, as guards patrolling the streets openly reaffirmed public safety, informing the Freylarkai of the queen's decision to proceed with the Trials. Some of the civilian Freylarkai appeared to welcome the news, though most had said nothing, suggesting a lack of faith in their queen's conviction. The general hesitance in accepting Mirielle's proxy sermons meant that the streets would remain largely empty – for the time being at least – thus providing him little in the way of cover to mask his movements. Nevertheless, Mirielle's hubris meant that ultimately the Freylarkai would push ahead – albeit reluctantly – with their pompous Trials, thus populating the streets of Freylar again. A leering wide smile formed across his pitted face, as the fact crystallised in his mind; news of the Trials was most welcome indeed, and would provide an opportunity to advance his agenda once more. Yet despite the fortunate turn of events, he remained frustrated, forced as he was to exercise restraint. Breaking cover now would only lead to his detection; he needed to remain patient. Eventually, come the cycle of the Trials, he would slip unnoticed through the busy streets of Freylar, ever closer to his imminent goal. The thought caused his mouth to salivate incessantly, which in turn saw black liquid collect at the corner of his lips, before dripping to the floor. His pupil-less eyes widened as he licked his cracked lips. In just over one more cycle, his patience *would* be rewarded. He laughed quietly to himself, amused by the path fate had chosen for him, courtesy of Mirielle's own poor judgement. His amusement was short-lived, however, as the renewed sound of whimpering quickly began to grate on him once more. The thing opposite had finished its meal and was now starting to irritate him again. He groaned audibly and rolled over, facing away from the fledgling construct.

'For the last time, be quiet! Any more noise, from either of you, and it will be the last noise either of you hears.'

Lothnar's mental interrogation of her sister ceased abruptly, ending his hold over Darlia's mind. Hurriedly, she moved to help her sister, who struggled to rise to her feet. Lothnar's methods were blunt and intrusive, the result of which had left Darlia reeling. She held onto her elder sibling tightly, who rocked back and forth on the balls of her feet, clearly struggling to compose herself. Darlia's eyes were full of tears, and she could feel her sister trebling in her arms.

'You love her, this Lileah?' said Lothnar impassively.

Darlia looked up, and stared teary-eyed at her former interrogator.

'More than your ransacking of my mind will ever allow you to know.' replied Darlia, who continued to cling to her closely.

'You realise, of course, that this will not end well for you both?'

'Lothnar, my actions hasten such outcome. Lileah's success or failure is now irrelevant to our future together, which has already ended. All I wish now is for the chance to atone, and to spare the unnecessary release of our kin.'

'Including that of your lover?'

'If I am able, though I fear Lileah may have already sealed her own fate.'

'And as a scrier, you *accept* this?'

'Lileah cannot be swayed from her cause, one which we once shared, but is now solely hers. Her impetuous need for revenge against those who have wronged her, or those whom she cares for, has now consumed her entirely – she *must* be stopped.'

'Very well.' replied Lothnar, at last softening his voice. 'Your mind confirms your sincerity, in addition I recognise the courage required for you to come here. I will therefore consider your counsel.'

'Thank you.' she said, relieved that Lothnar would at least hear her sister out.

Darlia wiped the tears from her eyes and nodded respectfully to Lothnar. The tension in the room immediately eased, like thunder clearing the humid summertime air. Sensing a degree of acceptance amongst those gathered, Nathaniel offered Vorian and her sister the rocking chairs at the far end of the room. Both readily accepted his kind offer, and promptly seated themselves, though Darlia still required her aid. As they began to relax into the large wooden reading chairs, their host hurriedly gathered a couple of wooden stools for her and Rayna, after which Nathaniel perched himself upon one of the dusty piles of books nearby. Lothnar chose to stand, leaning against one of the walls with his arms firmly crossed. Ever the opportunist, Krisis seized the chance to lie across his master's feet once more, sharing the Paladin's body warmth with his own.

'Please forgive the lack of space – we do not typically receive so many visitors.' said Nathaniel, who tried to get comfortable on his makeshift perch.

'There is no need. It is you who must forgive our unannounced arrival.' said Vorian respectfully.

There was another awkward moment of silence. She could see the mounting expectation on everyone's face, as each of them waited respectfully for the other to commence their proceedings. Stealing a leaf from Rayna's book, she chose to begin the discussions by cutting straight to the heart of the matter.

'I am afraid that a proper reunion between us will have to wait, sister. Tell us, *when* will Lileah most likely attack the vale?' she asked.

'I cannot say for certain, though it is likely that we still have a little time. By now, Lileah will have likely gathered up the retreating Narlakai herd. Despite their natural aversion to the light, there are numerous subterranean caverns that run beneath the surface of the borderlands. Lileah will exploit these passages to mitigate the Narlakai's ponderous movements, by keeping them moving whilst it is still daylight.'

'I have seen those caverns – you used them yourself.' said Lothnar, further validating her sister's account.

'Correct. Although they do not run the length of the borderlands, they will significantly advance Lileah's schedule. We cannot delay our response, in my opinion, longer than a cycle.'

'Nor can we permit the Narlakai to enter the vale.' said Rayna sternly.

'Then we must assemble The Blades immediately, if we are to meet this new threat.' said Lothnar grimly.

'Agreed, however, Mirielle will not consent to such action based on my sister's claims alone, despite your confirmation Lothnar. Darlia is an exile and would be treated as such.' she said flatly.

'And if we speak to her together, what then?' asked Lothnar.

'She would likely feel pressured – maybe even threatened – by such a display of unity, and therefore react unfavourably towards each of us. The Queen has displayed increasingly capricious behaviour as of late.' she explained.

'We could speak to Marcus first, win his fav--' said Nathaniel, before she rudely cut him short.

'That would be a mistake!' she said, commanding the gathered ensemble's absolute attention. 'My apologies Nathaniel, I did not mean to interrupt. However, what you are proposing would be seen – by Mirielle at least – as a betrayal of her trust. We need to find a way of forcing the Queen's hand, thus denying her the decision.'

'And how do you propose that we achieve such an end?' asked Lothnar, suddenly pushing himself away from the wall, disturbing the contented dire wolf, before moving closer.

'If we could win over the Freylarkai, and sow the seeds of our desire amongst them, they would ultimately force the issue for us.' she said, musing aloud.

'Careful, sister, for you talk of insurrection. Besides, such an act – even *if* successful – would surely take too long. We do not have the time necessary to politic our way out of this one.'

'Actually, Darlia, that is not strictly true.' said Rayna, unexpectedly.

'This should be interesting.' said Vorian, who until now had remained largely silent. 'What it is that you propose, Rayna?'

'Vor, I am glad that you ask.' replied The Guardian, offering the Knight a playful wink. 'My proposal is simple, though it is not entirely without risk.'

'Rayna, every moment spent dallying sees Lileah approach one step closer to the vale – we are already at risk.' she said, eager to learn of the light bringer's thoughts.

'Very well, Kirika, then ask yourself this question: are you finally ready to step out from Aleska's shadow?'

EIGHT
Promise

He woke suddenly, startling himself. The weak light of a new dawn encroached into the living space of hab unit one-seven-one, rendering it in full colour for the first time since his initial infiltration. The large space was as he had imagined; minimalistic, polished and above all, expensive. Even the high-backed chair – in which he was now slumped – looked costly, with its silver frame and black suede upholstery. The room itself was well kept, with no visible marks or signs of dust; the space appeared barely lived in, causing him to wonder if Mr L. Cameron contracted in outside help to assist with its upkeep. He made a mental note to apprise Trix; after coming so far, the last thing either of them needed was the added complication of an unsuspecting cleaning contractor exposing their dirty secret.

Working his way around the metropolis, whilst skilfully avoiding detection, had taken its toll on his body; he felt weary, and his limbs ached. Loath to move from the comfortable chair, he turned his head towards the large metal avant-garde table, stationed in the centre of the room. Upon its highly polished surface was the pack that he had wrestled from the blood chocked Peacekeeper earlier that morning. He stared vacantly at the black container, wondering if the trouble incurred whilst obtaining it, had in fact been worthwhile. Willing his tired body into motion, he approached the ostentatious table. He opened the pack inattentively, turning it upside-down to empty it and scattering its contents across the table's polished metal surface. He scanned the items for anything of note – medkit, light, restraints, ammunition – and there it was, the reason for his recent troubles: a single large ominous black sack. He grabbed the body bag and walked back down the corridor to the master bedroom. The holographic access panel was still active, suggesting that Trix was still in the system, poking around for his prize. Ignoring the tech, he cast his gaze towards the floor and the body of the hab's lifeless owner. The pool of dark red liquid on the floor had ceased expanding, and the cadaver itself had already changed colour with the conclusion of pallor mortis. It would not be long before rigor followed, so he needed to act quickly, before the grim task ahead of him became that much harder. He knelt down beside the pallid body, and carefully unrolled the sack ready to receive its occupant. Seeing the body bag laid out before him brought back painful memories of his kin disappearing into the black void of other such sacks, never to be seen again – within the metropolis at least. Ironically, the situation was now reversed, yet the thought of stuffing any human, dead or alive, into one of the ominous bags sickened him.

'*Callum, are you there?*' Trix suddenly blurted out, through the antiquated communications device still attached to his ear.

'Yes, what is it.'

'*I checked the logs. You've been busy, so it seems. Why did you leave the building?*'

'You asked me to get rid of the body.'

'*I did, but not to leave the building.*'

'Then, next time, I suggest that you be more specific.' he said, knowing in fact that there would never be a *next time*.

'*Why did you leave?*'

'I needed something.'

'Are you deliberately being evasive?' replied Trix tersely.

'Like you?'

'You're acting childish.'

'You used me!'

'Irrelevant – we've talked about this. What we are doing benefits both of us.'

'You forced me to murder him!' he said angrily, unable to mask his emotions.

'Do I have to remind you that he made the Rout possible? He facilitated the forced relocation of the Shadow Class – our kind Callum! Besides, we needed his access – he would not have given it to us willingly.'

'We didn't give him the choice.'

'What choice did he give us, when they rounded up the Shadow Class like animals, before shipping them off?'

'That doesn't make it right.'

'Callum, the world isn't right – deal with it.'

He chose not to reply, which caused a temporary lull in their conversation. Despite the mediocre reception of their communications, plagued by random white noise, he could still hear the morally grey software engineer's heavy breathing through his earpiece; Trix had an answer for everything, except for silence, it seemed.

'What was the thing you needed?' asked Trix suddenly, intentionally breaking their awkward silence.

'I required one of their black sacks.'

'You stole a body bag from the Peacekeepers?!'

'Yes.'

'Are you insane?'

'That's not it.'

'Then what is?'

'I'm not convinced that I give a shit anymore – I feel numb.'

'Obviously I underestimated the effect this would have on you, but for both our sakes, you need to get a handle on the situation. We're in too deep now – we need to see this through. You and I can part ways after, if that's what you want.'

'What I want is to not have to bag up the dead elderly gentleman in front of me.'

'Then you're in luck.' replied Trix confidently.

'What?'

'Technically, Mr L. Cameron is not dead. I have re-engineered his bio-key to relay healthy vitals. In a sense, he's alive – so far as the authorities are concerned at least. Plus, I do not consider someone responsible for tracking down our kin to be a gentleman, as you put it.'

'Screw you Trix!'

'You're welcome.' replied Trix sarcastically. *'I have left some instructions on how to provision Project Phoenix; you may find the data objects useful. I have copied them – along with the instructions – to Mr L. Cameron's own...how did you put it...sandbox? You will find some other interesting data objects in there too. I suggest you spend the day familiarising yourself with them – that is, after you're done with the old man's body.'*

'Saying goodbye already?'

'I made you a promise; these tools will help you gain access to the Infonet. In addition, I have located the tracking software. Typical programmer – as I predicted, he copied the source code to his private sandbox. Once I have reverse engineered it, we will be free to come and go as we please, using our new identities.'

'You're suggesting that I should acquire more bio-keys?'

'*If you want to live in the metropolis, you'll come around to the idea.*'

'You're sick!'

'*Irrelevant. Anyway, come nightfall you will need to get back to the Wild. But in the meantime, don't you have a body to be getting rid of?*'

She felt different now; her soul no longer ached with the burden of her past. Having previously sensed the change – immediately after expelling the darkness inside her – it was only now that she began to understand the consequences of the impressions gained from sharing Alarielle's history and perspective. Aside from waking unassisted from her latest nightmare – for the first time since her arrival in Freylar – she felt properly rested. Alarielle's own experiences had somehow desensitised her to death, killing and other such dark acts. The result of this left her feeling at ease, as though her mind had since reconciled the grim events of her past. Lying quietly in her bed, enjoying the feeling of acceptance, she stared curiously at Kirika, who lay sleeping beside her. Due to the lack of space in Nathaniel's tree, she had offered both Kirika and Darlia her bed for the night. Kirika had gladly accepted the offer. Darlia, on the other hand, respectfully declined, choosing instead to make do with one of Nathaniel's rocking chairs. Vorian agreed to keep the exiled scrier company for the night, leaving Lothnar, who favoured the hard wooden floor of Nathaniel's room, alongside Krisis. As she continued to watch Kirika silently, sleeping peacefully beside her, conflicting thoughts occupied her mind. Kirika was an attractive Freylarkin – there was no denying the fact – yet her body was different now. In the past, her physical and emotional reaction to the close proximity of a beautiful woman had been predictable. However, since her arrival in Freylar, everything had changed. Now she felt lost and confused, no longer certain of her personal desires. Her mind turned to thoughts of the Ardent Gate, and her time spent with Heldran, whiling away the cold nights within the heart of the knights' stronghold. She had greatly enjoyed the Knight Lord's company, and missed their late evening soirées. Having seemingly reconciled one set of emotions, she now faced the challenges of dealing with others.

'If you wish, I can help you with that.'

Alarielle's impromptu offer caught her off guard, sending her mind spinning. She quickly slid out of the bed, careful not to wake Kirika, and proceeded to get dressed. After sitting down at her dresser, she stared vacantly into its mirror, whilst fixing her hair, distracted by Alarielle's intriguing proposition.

'I'm not ready to take that step – not yet at least.' she finally whispered in response.

'The cycle will come when you fully accept who you are, and when it does, remember that you need only ask.'

She nodded towards the dresser mirror and set down her hairbrush, before proceeding quietly downstairs.

Unsurprisingly, Nathaniel was already awake; he was speaking earnestly with both Vorian and Darlia. Lothnar was nowhere to be seen, suggesting that the Paladin either remained asleep upstairs or – more likely – had already left.

'You slept unusually well.' said Nathaniel.

'I certainly did. Perhaps expelling the invading darkness inside of me also exorcised some of my own.'

Nathaniel gave her a curious look – she could tell immediately that her attempt at misdirection had failed to convince him. Regardless, now was not the time to attempt to articulate Alarielle's new-found ability to leave lasting impressions on her mind. It had been several cycles since her return to the vale; she was duty-bound to report to The Blade Lord to be debriefed about her time spent with the Knights Thranis, and – more importantly – she had a promise to keep.

'Perhaps indeed,' said Nathaniel, flashing one of his wry grins, 'And most fortunate, given your imminent duel with Lothnar. Will you be spending the cycle training in the arena?'

'No, I need to report to Marcus, plus there is the matter of The Vengeful Tears to resolve.' she replied. 'Besides, if I am not ready by now, one more cycle spent training will be of little consequence.'

'Actually, I was going to suggest that you refrain from training this cycle; better to allow Lothnar to discover the fruits of your efforts *during* the Trials – not before.'

'They should have nicknamed *you* "Fox" instead.' she said, with a grin of her own.

Darlia looked confused by her choice of words; it seemed that Kirika's sister was not yet aware of her former life. Vorian, however, appeared entirely unfazed – such was his habitual demeanour.

'Perhaps you can explain my past to our guests during my absence?'

'By the time I am done with all that, you will be home for dinner no doubt.'

She laughed at his dry response – a positive sign that Nathaniel was in good spirits, despite the recent turmoil and the uncertainty of events to come.

'No doubt. Please give my regards to Kirika, and I will see the rest of you later this cycle, after I have dealt with some loose ends.' she said, nodding politely to Vorian and Darlia, before grabbing some food for her journey to the Tri-Spires.

It was mid-morning by the time she reached the foot of the southern slope, on the opposite side of the river, leading towards the arena at the base of the Tri-Spires. She decided to visit the arena first, presuming that The Vengeful Tears would be busy training alongside the other Blade Novices. Walking casually through the west gate, she was greeted by her fellow Blades, many of whom offered her a respectful nod as she made her way towards the centre of the arena. The Vengeful Tears were seemingly absent, although she quickly spied The Blade Lord, who sat high up in the tiered stone seating, overlooking the arena floor. Ragnar was also present – the Captain of The Blades was busy presiding over several enthusiastic Blade Adepts, sparring tirelessly before him, over by the east gate. Despite the close attention he paid the Adepts, Ragnar noticed her impromptu arrival and offered her a respectful nod of his own. She returned the gesture, before ascending the stone steps towards Marcus, near the back of the arena.

'I was beginning to wonder if you were deliberately avoiding me?'

'What do you mean?' she replied, before sitting down next to The Blade Lord.

'You were sighted *north* of the vale, a few cycles ago, yet only now do you return to the Order – is it something I said?' explained Marcus, followed by a warm smile.

'I needed some time alone to clear my head – the cycles have been rather eventful since my arrival.'

The Blade Lord regarded her silently, with an expectant look about him. She suspected that Marcus sought more detail, and that he had assumed that she would elaborate further – which she did not.

'Did you give my regards to Heldran?' enquired Marcus, finally accepting her brief explanation.

'I did, though he seemed largely unimpressed.'

'Ha, as expected. You had no luck then?'

'On the contrary, I won his favour.' she said, grinning mischievously.

'And...?' prompted Marcus, whom she could tell was eager to learn of her time spent with the knights.

'Anika has decided to remain at the Ardent Gate, as a Knight of the Order. In addition, the Knights Thranis have agreed to train The Vengeful Tears, and – should they accept, and subsequently prove themselves able – they too will be welcomed into the Order and trained to become Knights themselves. Anika has agreed to facilitate any transitions.'

'Excellent – you have achieved that which I could not. My faith in you, Rayna, was well placed I see.'

'Perhaps you should reserve judgement – there is more that I need to tell you.'

'Go on...' said Marcus, who seemed unfazed by her sobering remark.

'The Knights Thranis will not fight for our Order, but, they *will* fight for *me*.

The Blade Lord straightened his back and narrowed his eyes, whilst he digested the information she had imparted. Given his sudden change in body language, she considered the possibility that her proclamation had incurred Marcus' ire. However, such thoughts were quickly dispelled, when

Marcus' initial stony expression slowly changed to that of a wry grin.

'Rayna, your news is not entirely surprising. I have never personally known the Knights Thranis to lend their support readily. That they will fight alongside you – if requested – is achievement enough. You have accomplished the first steps in rebuilding a new trust between our orders. I applaud your efforts.'

'Thank you, Marcus. It was never my intent to offend, or indeed to undermine your command.'

'I have no doubt. Besides, a Freylarkin in my position quickly learns to develop a thick skin – Ragnar taught me that lesson well.'

Marcus' quip put her at ease; they savoured the moment of shared amusement, all the while watching the subject of his comment below, who vigorously bellowed commands to a group of Adepts within earshot.

'So...are you ready?'

'To face Lothnar, you mean?'

'Yes. I gather there has been much talk about your impending duel in the arena.' said Marcus, changing the subject.

'I must admit, the reality hasn't sunk in yet.'

'It needs to. Next cycle, these seats will be filled with Freylarkai, all eager to witness The Guardian duel one of Freylar's finest at the Trials.'

'Perhaps I should have shown more restraint during the war council, shortly after my arrival.' she said, followed by an audible sigh.

'Maybe, though perhaps you should see this as an opportunity.'

'To advance my standing within The Blades, you mean?'

'Exactly.' replied Marcus, who leant forwards to better hear the Captain's brazen barking below. 'Your unconventional arrival in Freylar, coupled with word of your actions at Scrier's Post, continues to win favour with the forest dwellers. Yet you still have doubters, in particular amongst the upper echelons of The Blades, and those civilian Freylarkai who live within the Tri-Spires.'

'I am curious – is Ragnar aware that you are grooming me?'

'Ha, you know the Captain shares your boldness, Rayna, though he lacks your perception – the combination is refreshing.'

'Do you think that you will answer my question?' she pressed, offering The Blade Lord a casual wink.

'Oh, I think he knows – in fact, I believe he is counting on it. However, you cannot expect to command The Blades without their unwavering loyalty. Rallying the Aspirants and Novices is one thing, and you have done well to earn the respect of several high-ranking members of the Order, in addition to wining favour with the Knights Thranis. However, the remaining members of our Order will not follow you until you have proven your mettle in that arena.'

'No pressure then.'

'Not unless *you* create it.' replied Marcus, who turned to face her. 'When you enter that arena, ensure that you do so with clarity of mind – that will be your greatest weapon. Few can match Lothnar's skill, and of those, most have much more experience than you. If you mean to best him through skill alone, you will fail. You will need to find another way.'

'Others have imparted similar advice.'

'And well they should. Your unique reputation now balances precariously upon a fulcrum. You can choose to either serve as a rank and file member of the Order, or alternatively, you can use the momentum you have gained to become something more.'

They sat in silence for a moment, whilst she considered her options from Marcus' perspective. The Blade Lord's use of the words "rank and file" was curious. Reading between the lines, she could disappear into comfortable obscurity within the Order, or instead capitalise on her increasing popularity, and push herself, in the hope of elevating her rank. As a former member of the Shadow class, however, she had very little career ambition. Yet now an opportunity presented itself, which – in theory at least – would allow her to make a difference. Given that losing to Lothnar would ultimately decide her fate, the crux of the matter, therefore, was the extent to which she was prepared to go to in order to succeed. Thinking back to her duel with Knight Lord Heldran – albeit, one that was cut short – she recalled the thrill of the encounter, along with her desire to succeed. Heldran had applauded her creativity in her attempts to best him, yet he had also urged her to dispense with etiquette. *"Combat is not an art form"* – she recalled the Knight Lord's words well. Since that time, she had learned first-hand the merits of Heldran's counsel, and had adapted her fighting style accordingly. Her long years spent surviving in the metropolis, in addition to her intense combat training in Freylar, had developed her battlefield cunning. She knew how to fight dirty, and she had become good at it.

'Make sure that you have a front row seat.' she said, once again grinning mischievously.

'Good. I look forward to it.'

She stood up and stretched her neck muscles. Below, Ragnar continued to drill the Order's Adepts, who tried their best to meet the boisterous Captain's lofty expectations. She sighed as Ragnar caught her eye, subsequently directing his left arm towards her.

'Well, that was a mistake.' said Marcus, in an amused tone.

She turned her head and offered The Blade Lord a dreary sidelong glance, prompting him to laugh aloud.

'Rayna! Get down here and show this lot how it is done!' bellowed the Captain of The Blades.

'Marcus, I have to go now – I made a promise to the Knights Thranis, one which I intend to keep.'

'Understood. Please give The Vengeful Tears my blessing should they decide to accept Heldran's offer.' Marcus replied. 'Oh, and please do not keep *him* waiting – he is even harder to work with when riled.'

'Indeed I shall not. And don't worry about Ragnar – this won't take long.'

Her attempts to reach her personal quarters were thwarted repeatedly, following her return to the Tri-Spires. Upon entering the base of the organic citadel, she was immediately set upon by numerous aides, all clamouring for her attention. Each was understandably anxious about the final preparations for the Trials. Although she appreciated their concerns, and their need to discuss certain matters with her, nonetheless, her mind remained distracted by the impromptu arrival of her sister, and the likely ramifications of Darlia's return. She had tried numerous times that morning – whilst lying in bed – to scry the outcome of their planned course of action, however, Rayna's involvement had hindered her second sight, as Darlia had predicted. The Guardian's latent ability to disrupt scrying was curious. Just as a stream would part around a rock, fate – so it seemed – appeared to flow around The Guardian. Anyone, or anything, in contact with Rayna exhibited the same phenomenon – albeit for only a brief time – as though granted temporary immunity to the fates as a direct result of The Guardian's presence. A sense of foreboding lingered in the pit of her stomach, given her inability to foresee the outcome of their intent. She hoped dearly that when the moment finally came, any anxieties which she had would be dispelled, and play no part in hindering her role in their carefully orchestrated ruse. Rayna's involvement, however, ensured that there would be no guarantees that their efforts would bear fruit. Regardless, they had unanimously agreed that support from The Guardian would strengthen their position.

'Kirika, we have received word from the Cave of Wellbeing: eight renewalists will be present at the Trials, three of whom will be masters.' explained Kayla, one of her closest aides.

'Good. Nathaniel will also be present.' she said, hurriedly, struggling to manage the growing number of Freylarkai around her.

'Kirika, the number of delegates attending has been confirmed.' said another.

'Thank you. Please ensure ten percent contingency when finalising the catering arrangements.'

'The Blade Lord has confirmed the queen's security detail – and additionally, telekinetics will be present.'

'Understood.'

It was some time before she finally made it to her private quarters, having appeased her aides. Their eager support made it possible for her to manage the increasing number of duties assigned to her, although at times their presence was overwhelming. She had no desire to become suffocated by her assigned entourage, yet despite her wishes, Mirielle had insisted that she use the resources provided to her. With the last of her aides finally dismissed, she collapsed into a comfortable chair in her quarters. She stared vacantly at the door to her chamber, half expecting another aide to come scuttling through. As she relaxed into the chair, her mind began to wander once more, with thoughts straying towards the potential ramifications of their agreed course of action. She tried to reassure herself that their decision had been solely in the best interests of Freylar, yet the steps they were about to take would be frowned upon by those with more politically attuned minds. The path ahead would be a difficult one, fraught with uncertainty – a concept with which she was largely unfamiliar. She closed her eyes, and was about to drift off, when a loud knock abruptly sounded at her door, startling her.

'Come in.'

Kayla appeared once more, who she mistakenly thought had been appeased.

'What is it Kayla?'

'I am sorry to disturb you, yet again, Kirika, however, the Queen has asked that you report to her at your earliest convenience; she wishes to discuss the final arrangements for the Trials with you.'

She said nothing at first, and instead stared blankly at her aide. It was clear that Mirielle's trust in her was far from absolute, not helped by their differing opinions over the recent curfew, and how best to manage Krashnar's likely continued presence within the vale.

'Please inform the Queen that I will meet with her shortly.'

Kayla nodded in acknowledgement, before taking her leave, closing the door behind her. She sighed heavily. No doubt Mirielle had noticed her recent absence from the Tri-Spires, and would use the opportunity to dig deeper into the reason for her lack of presence on the run up to the Trials. She had no qualms about being selective with the information she would present – if indeed an explanation was asked of her – however, the almost certain need for early subterfuge unsettled her. Steeling her nerves, she prepared herself for the challenges to come.

NINE
Confrontation

It was late afternoon when she finally tracked down The Vengeful Tears. The tight-knit group of disillusioned Blade Novices were gathered in a clearing, east of the old bridge, despite their assigned duties. It had taken her some time to locate the absent band of fanatical warriors, whom she had finally tracked down by piecing together information gleaned from local civilian Freylarkai, in particular the workers spread across the southern riverbank.

'You're a difficult bunch to locate – I expected to find you all in the arena.' she said, clearly catching them unawares.

'Guardian.' said a male from the group, who was notably taller than his peers. 'Your presence honours us.'

She quickly recognised the Freylarkin as Dumar, a prominent voice within the group.

'I gather you are all hunting Krashnar.' she said, cutting to the heart of The Vengeful Tears' current whereabouts.

'That is correct.'

'Yet you were ordered to continue your training in the arena.'

'With respect, Guardian, we should be hunting down the exile, not practicing the same tired moves beneath the unflinching gaze of wary eyes.'

She paused for a moment to consider Dumar's point of view. Since the massacre at Scrier's Post, The Vengeful Tears had earned their name as a result of their changed dispositions, wrought by the horrors they had faced. She too had suffered alongside the former Blade Aspirants, but the darkness she already harboured had allowed her to weather the harrowing encounter with the Narlakai, thus she had endured the mental ordeal relatively unscathed. Regrettably, for the remainder of the surviving Aspirants, the traumatic event had caused lasting repercussions. Despite her notable exception, each member of The Vengeful Tears had returned to the vale changed by their experience – for the worse.

'I do not disagree; however, your actions only serve to incite the ire of your fellow Blades.'

'We serve the founding principle of the Order – to protect the Freylarkai – and cannot do so from within the arena.'

'I understand. You serve the Order, not its members.' she replied, much to Dumar's obvious surprise.

'Yes – you *do* understand.'

'I understand plenty, and I know that this is not the right place for The Vengeful Tears.' she said, commanding his attention.

Dumar was clearly taken aback by her unexpected proclamation. The vocal Blade shifted uncomfortably, before narrowing his eyes as he held her stare.

'Consider this – *all* of you.' she said, deliberately raising her voice, so that every Freylarkin present could clearly hear her words. 'Anika has chosen to remain with the Knights Thranis, at the Ardent Gate. She is now a Knight of the Order and has sworn fealty to the Knights Thranis. Her actions have helped to create an opportunity – one that is open to you all: the Knights Thranis have further extended their hospitality, and are prepared to welcome each of you into their Order, so that you may test your mettle by training to become Knights yourselves. *If* you choose to accept their invitation, and prove yourselves worthy – as Anika did – you will be expected to swear fealty to the Knights Thranis.'

Intense discussions quickly broke out amongst The Vengeful Tears upon hearing her words, as they hotly debated the surprise opportunity presented to them. Based on the group's body language, and the snippets of enthusiastic conversation that she managed to glean, she sensed rising excitement amongst those gathered before her, at the prospect of a fresh start.

'Guardian, with deepest respect,' cried a voice suddenly, from the rear of the group, 'We have already sworn our allegiance to The Blade Lord.'

'Should you decide to take the knights up on their offer, I have been authorised to inform you all, that each of you will have The Blade Lord's blessing.'

'Ha, then we are no longer wanted!' replied Dumar sardonically.

'Correct, and I would not insult you by suggesting otherwise.' she replied, hoping that her candid gambit would pay off.

Dumar looked shocked by her words, along with the remainder of the gathered Blades. She paused for a moment, affording Dumar and the others time to compose themselves.

'What would *you* do?' asked Dumar sombrely, after a moment of quiet introspection.

'Since the massacre at Scrier's Post, all of you have changed. The horrors you witnessed came too soon in your military careers, the memories of which will not fade anytime soon, should you continue to serve The Blades. The release of your brothers and sisters will haunt you tirelessly, unless you make peace with it, or...accept the knights' invitation.'

'What are they like, the Knights Thranis?' asked a voice from the gathered crowd.

'They're like family. They do not function in a highly disciplined fashion, as per our Order, nor do they have any real concept of rank or hierarchy. However, they will demand your complete devotion to their cause; as Knights, you would bunk in the same quarters, prepare each other's meals, repair the Order's armour, and it is expected that you will fight with all your heart – against impossible odds. The Knights Thranis are not compartmentalised like The Blades. Each Knight is respected equally, and each is expected to put the wellbeing of their comrades above that of their own. You will only have each other out there, on Freylar's southern fringe. If you decide to go, there will be no returning to The Blades. However, if you crave adventure, a fresh start, and above all else, real purpose, then I strongly advise that you accept their invitation.'

There was another lull in their group discussion, whilst The Vengeful Tears considered the opportunity she had presented to them. She had been bold in her delivery, though by doing so, she had hoped to convince the troubled Blades of the sincerity of the knights' offer. The changed disposition of The Vengeful Tears no longer aligned itself to Marcus' disciplined regime. Going forwards, they required a more simple and honest environment within which they could thrive. The Vengeful Tears' zealous nature would be a good fit for the headstrong Knights of Heldran's southern defenders.

'As you know, next cycle I will face Lothnar in the arena. Therefore, I will be taking my leave imminently, so that I may begin my final preparations for the encounter. Whilst I do not deliberately seek to rush your decision – for I understand its importance – nonetheless, there is currently a representative from the Knights Thranis in the vale, whom

I shall report to shortly. His name is Vorian, and – should you wish it – I will arrange for you to meet with him. You have until I leave this clearing to decide your destiny.'

'Thank you!' Dumar replied quickly in response.

'What for?'

'For being honest with us – it is appreciated.'

'Dumar, if you decide to join the Knights Thranis, know that they will guard their secrets from you – at least until you prove your worth – however, they will not deceive you.'

Dumar took a deep breath, then nodded respectfully, before turning his back on her to discuss the matter further with his kin. She tilted her head back gently, and gazed languidly towards the cold sky above, hopelessly seeking to glimpse the sphere of light responsible for bringing her to Freylar. She wondered what the enigmatic entity thought of the world, which it seemingly contained, and indeed, whether it even cared. Its brief conversation with her had been blunt and sterile, devoid of any emotion; perhaps it held the Freylarkai in the same lacklustre regard, she mused.

'Guardian,' said Dumar suddenly, disrupting her reverie, 'We have decided. Please kindly introduce us to this Vorian.'

'Come in.'

She entered Mirielle's personal chamber and quietly made her way towards the queen, who sat alone, beside a wooden table. Mirielle was staring vacantly at several ornate stone fragments, presumably the remains of what must have been a complex structure, now shattered and strewn across the bench. As with any Freylarkin gifted with an ability, she assumed that Mirielle was not exempt from failure. She wondered, therefore, if the broken structure before her was proof of such, or instead the result of venting one's frustrations. Wary of the latter, she approached cautiously, trying to assess the queen's mood, prior to announcing her presence formally.

'My queen.'

'Ah, Kirika – please sit down.' replied Mirielle, in a distracted tone.

'I gather that you wish to speak with me?'

'That is correct.'

There was a curious delay before the queen began their impromptu meeting; Mirielle appeared to remain distracted by the fragments littering her desk. That, or her silence formed part of some clever tactical ploy, which would soon reveal itself. Regardless, Mirielle eventually reengaged with the world around her, and subsequently wasted no time in addressing business.

'Your updates regarding arrangements for the Trials have been infrequent. I thought it best, therefore, that we catch up on the matter, in person.'

'Please forgive my lack of information – I sought only to shield you from the administrative minutiae which habitually plagues the organising of such events.'

'Your concern for my welfare is appreciated, however, I would prefer to be well informed going forwards.'

'As you wish.' she said, followed with a well-practiced cordial smile. 'Hopefully you will be pleased to hear that everything is in hand for the Trials, and that The Guardian will indeed be facing Lothnar in the opening duel.'

'Good. I want everything to proceed smoothly, and to ensure that the delegates enjoy the festivities. I do not want them distracted by this business with the rogue exile.'

'I understand.' she replied, careful not to commit herself to Mirielle's vision.

Once again, the queen seemingly disengaged from the world, deciding – temporarily at least – to bury herself in private contemplation. She could not discern whether there was something genuinely bothering the queen, or instead, if Mirielle was simply playing her, hoping that she would fill the silence by volunteering information freely. If indeed Mirielle sought the latter, she had no intention of contributing – a lesson she had learnt well, having been burnt by past experiences.

'I noticed that you have been absent from the Tri-Spires recently – anything there I should be made aware of?'

There it was – the inevitable heart of their discussion, she mused. Although not unexpected, she was somewhat disappointed by Mirielle's obvious delivery. Historically, the queen had conducted her affairs employing a more subtle, if not cunning, approach. Since Aleska's official retirement, however, Mirielle's politicking had adopted an increasingly blunt trend, suggesting that she was underutilising The Blade Lord's strategic acumen.

'I met with Rayna, following her return from the Ardent Gate – I am still assisting The Guardian with her transition.'

'Yet you did not think to inform Marcus of her return?'

'It was not my place to do so. I decided it best, therefore, not to interfere with Blade operations. My only concern was Rayna, given that her welfare is one of my direct responsibilities.'

'I see.' replied Mirielle, narrowing her pupil-less eyes.

It was impossible for her to understand what Mirielle saw, courtesy of her altered vision. Although she was aware of Mirielle's ability to see the sphere of light in the sky – responsible for The Guardian's arrival in Freylar – she cursed herself for having failed to ask Rayna what their queen saw when studying the Freylarkai; other than Mirielle, Rayna was the only Freylarkin she knew who had directly experienced the unusual means of sight.

'As a courtesy, perhaps next time you could inform Marcus – assuming a similar situation arises in future.'

'As you wish.' she said, smiling politely once more. 'Is there anything else that you wish to discuss?' she asked, seeking a swift end to her informal interrogation.

'Not for the time being. I will leave you to finish your final preparations.'

She nodded politely to Mirielle, before calmly taking her leave; she took care not to appear eager to depart the queen's company. After leaving Mirielle's chamber, the tension in her body quickly eased. Although happy to put the brief uncomfortable meeting behind her, she was mindful that – come the Trials – the awkward encounter would be the least of her concerns.

Following his socially inept companion's advice, he spent the remainder of the day familiarising himself with the data objects Trix had made available to him. The task was taking much longer than he had anticipated; his mind repeatedly distracted him, relentlessly replaying the grim events of Mr L. Cameron's recent bodily disposal. He had been loath to manhandle the cadaver for a second time, especially given the effort required to scrub his hands clean after cutting out the elderly gentleman's bio-key, at Trix's grizzly behest. Yet, irrespective of his personal disgust regarding the matter, the abhorrent and unenviable task needed to be undertaken, and between Trix and himself, he was the only viable candidate for the job. He tried to focus on a sophisticated search algorithm Trix had developed, but his mind kept replaying the ghastly moments prior to the last time he had seen the elderly gentleman's face. His reaction to the corpse's skin had sickened him the most, unprepared as he was for its harrowing death chill – further validation of the heinous crime he had committed. Indeed, the act of simply touching the body had been more disturbing than stuffing it inside of the Peacekeeper's commandeered black sack. He would never forget the moment when he sealed the last of Mr L. Cameron's body inside of its unorthodox black tomb. The holographic access panel before him flickered vigorously once more, seeking his attention, yet he remained unable to focus on the present. Visual memories were not the sole cause of his distraction; touch sensations and sounds also assaulted his mind, like the noise of the victim's body bag scraping along the polished floor, as he dragged it towards its final resting place. There were very few suitable hiding places within the minimalistic hab, in which to adequately conceal the body. Though far from ideal, he had settled upon a low storage cupboard at the other end of the hab, in what appeared to be a guest bedroom. The cupboard was a good fit and would help to contain any cadaverine managing to escape the Peacekeeper's tightly sealed sack. Despite the storage area's positive credentials, its location meant – rather unfortunately – that he had to drag the body bag some distance, therefore prolonging the awful sound of the sack scraping along the floor. Ultimately, he managed to drag the corpse to the guest room without incident, however, the operation's horrid soundtrack stuck with him, including the sounds of heavy muffled thumping which had ensued whilst manhandling the sealed cadaver into its faux coffin. After completing the wicked assignment, he had lain upon the guest bed for a time, contemplating his actions. He recalled closing his eyes, trying to make peace with himself, hoping, somehow, to absolve his sins. Yet there was no absolution – his life going forwards was destined to be one of penance. As he stared vacantly at the holographic access panel, he could feel his mind collapsing in on itself, due to the overwhelming mental burden, desperately trying to bury the memories of the appalling crime he had committed.

'*Callum, are you there?*'

'I haven't left the hab again – assuming that's what you're wondering.' he replied, unenthusiastically.

'*I didn't mean it like that.*'

'Was that...an attempt at remorse?'

'*Look, I know you're still pissed with me, but...none of that matters now.*'

'Of course it matters!'

'*No...it really doesn't. I've found something, and--*'

Despite the poor quality of their communications, he detected a change in the tone of Trix's voice; the habitual sound of the software developer's monotone vocals now exhibited a dread-like tone.

'What have you found?'

'*Meet me on level thirty-two, sector eighty-four.*'

'What is it?'

'*Just come – you need to see this for yourself.*'

Using Mr L. Cameron's security credentials, he accessed the Infonet's main lobby once more, this time ascending to barrier thirty-two. The holographic access panel grew once more, expanding around him, as he breached another of the Infonet's lofty barriers unchallenged. His virtual surroundings stretched out before him, affording him a better view of the digital landscape, moreover the sea of data streams alongside which he now swam – figuratively speaking. He navigated his way to sector eighty-four, his interest piqued by the foreboding tone of Trix's request. The sector itself was vast, appearing to be some kind of digital archive – a virtual graveyard for discarded information, which humanity was not yet prepared to delete indefinitely. Instead, the historic data had been neatly recorded, catalogued and filed amongst the virtual shelves of the seemingly endless sector.

'What is this – some kind of massive data library?'

'*That's exactly what it is.*

'So what am I looking for, specifically?'

'*Peacekeeper engagements.*'

'I thought the priority was to reverse engineer the bio-key tracking software?' he replied, with a hint of agitation.

'*It was – I mean, it is. I was waiting for some code to decompile, and found this place.*'

'Let me get this straight. You have a go at me for wandering, yet you are guilty of the same crime!'

'*Your risk of exposure was significantly higher than my own.*'

'Irrelevant.'

There was a brief moment of silence whilst Trix considered the ironic use of his own words, now used against him. Typically, he was loath to engage in petty bickering, but recent events had chipped away incessantly at the outer layer of his very being, exposing beneath a torrent of raw emotions, no longer held in check.

'*Look for the data stream titled "Exodus".*' said Trix, ultimately deciding it best to ignore his retort.

Rifling through the alphabetically catalogued data streams, he identified the one marked Exodus and proceeded to analyse the data. There were countless data feeds, including mass transcriptions, relevant legislation and video feeds. The amount of data contained within the stream was overwhelming.

'Check the video – the government has been recording feeds from Peacekeeper operations.'

'What! You mean *all* Peacekeeper activities?'

'So it would seem, given the quantity of data present. I'm sending you a time index.'

A fresh data object appeared before him, containing the time index Trix proclaimed to be of particular importance. Using the information, he quickly navigated his way to the designated time index, and immediately began playback of the specified video feed.

A barren wasteland stretched out before him, towards the horizon with its ruddy sky. Littering the blasted landscape were the remains of numerous structures, now little more than unrecognisable ruins, poking out of the scorched cracked earth. The ground was visibly hard, scoured clean of vegetation, and appeared utterly devoid of life. The empty scene unfolding before him suggested that he was observing the surface of a dead planet, home perhaps to a once great civilization. Suddenly the desolate view panned down and to the right, it was then that he realised he was witnessing events through the eyes of another. His unknown host had turned their attention towards the instruments in their current mode of transport. Based on the configuration of the cockpit, he appeared to be on board an armoured Peacekeeper transport. The view panned upwards, confirming his suspicion; a column of windowless boxy carriages, escorted by lightly armoured transports flanking the main procession, extended before him. Light from the distant sun glinted off the carriages, which cut a direct path towards an ominous dark line stretched out horizontally across the landscape, just short of the horizon. He sped up the video feed's playback by sixty percent, watching with interest as the dark line morphed into a shadow as it drew ever closer. What was once a line continued to grow in depth, until finally revealing its true nature; they were heading towards a large crack in the landscape, which had widened considerably, essentially forming a ravine. He reduced the playback speed to ten percent of its original pace, watching intently as the carriages lined up neatly alongside the drop, ensuring ample space between them, whilst the escorts spread out to form a protective perimeter. Scores of Peacekeepers promptly exited from both the carriage cockpits and armoured transports, with the latter contingent quickly taking up defensive positions against an invisible assailant. Those exiting the carriages hurriedly stationed themselves around the back of their vehicles, targeting the rear doors eagerly with their weapons. The thick metal barriers flung open abruptly, in unison, disgorging additional Peacekeepers, each armed with a shock rifle or other such heinous weapon – which he keenly recognised. Satisfied that there was no immediate threat to their operation, the Peacekeepers closest to the carriages shouldered their weapons and began unloading the contents of the carriages. Groups of Peacekeepers, working in pairs, pulled numerous black sacks from the mobile containers. They manhandled the sacks, tossing them onto the hard floor alongside one another, close to the edge of the ravine, to form a ragged black line. Two of the Peacekeepers, stationed at either end of the developing line, pulled curious devices from their packs and began scanning each of the sacks in turn. Occasionally they would direct their hand towards a given sack, prompting those closest to fire stun rounds into the identified targets. After the process was complete, there seemed to be a momentary lull in their operation. Although the video feed included audio, this amounted to little more than ambient background noise. He assumed, therefore, that the Peacekeepers received their orders via a neural interface, or perhaps courtesy of some other means not captured within the feed – that, or the communications data had been redacted. Either way, he could not discern the reason for the curious delay, until suddenly, the obvious dawned on him.

'I can't watch this!' he said, pausing the feed abruptly.

'*Callum, you have to!*'

'No good can come of this.'

'*Damn it Callum, this is our history! You must bear witness to this, as I did – this crime cannot pass unremembered!*'

'This is last rites stuff – you cannot make we watch it!'

'*Actually...I can.*'

Without any intervention on his part, the video feed resumed suddenly. The Peacekeepers approached the line, and immediately began pushing the black sacks over the edge of the precipice with their heavy booted feet. One by one, the sacks fell into oblivion, swallowed whole by the unforgiving ravine, consumed by its gluttonous appetite. Unable to tear his sight from the images unfolding before him, he felt nauseous, and his stomach churned violently whilst the atrocity played out before him.

'Turn it off!' he said, overcoming his momentary paralysis. 'Turn the fucking thing off!'

He turned his back to the access panel and ran towards the bedroom window, desperate to fill his lungs with fresh air in a futile attempt to quell his unease. Unable to keep the contents of his stomach in check, he retched over the sill before backing up awkwardly, partially hunched over. Lifting his head, he stared vacantly at the vomit splattered across the wall beneath the window. Distracted by the heinous images, now fresh in his mind, he was only dimly aware of the meagre former contents of his stomach, which now trickled slowly towards the floor. As his mind began to process the images he had just seen, his initial shock and disbelief rapidly dissipated, giving way to something far darker.

'Why?!'

'Because we're nothing more than vermin to them; society's cancer, best cut out and destroyed.'

'But these are people, Austin – how can we do this to ourselves?!'

'Callum, you already know the answer to that question. It's the nature of humanity: class, wealth, influence, religion, race – time and again, we find ways to differentiate ourselves.'

He stood upright and closed his eyes, seeking to regain some of his composure. He tried to suppress the rising anger and hatred inside of him, but the raw dark emotions refused to be quelled. He could hear himself breathing more heavily with each passing breath, as violent thoughts assaulted in his mind.

'This changes everything! How can we live amongst these people, knowing the atrocities they have committed against our kin?'

There was no immediate answer from Trix, just the software engineer's familiar laboured breathing – due to Trix's obvious lack of personal fitness. Trix was not built to gallivant around the metropolis, thus even the smallest increase in the hacker's heart rate was easily discerned.

'Again, you already know the answer to that question – we cannot!'

TEN
Concealment

It took them some time to make their way to the west gate, due to the number of Freylarkai loitering in the alleys surrounding the arena. Any lingering thoughts of a curfew had rapidly dissolved in the wake of the increasing hype and excitement leading up to the Trials. Together they politely pushed their way through the growing throng, single file, deftly navigating the path of least resistance towards their goal. Eventually they broke free of the crowd and half stumbled into the arena – afforded access courtesy of their rank – where proceedings were clearly more civilised. Despite the maelstrom of jovial chaos that surrounded the venue, the final preparations taking place within the arena were being carefully conducted in a calm and controlled manner. Although public spectators were now slowly trickling into the arena, it would be some time before the venue reached capacity. Freylar's queen was already present; Mirielle was seated front and centre upon the tiered stone seating which spanned the southern edge of the arena. The Blade Lord sat to the right of Mirielle, with an empty space to her left – presumably reserved for Kirika. Ragnar sat next to Marcus; the broad Freylarkin occupied almost two spaces. Adjacent to to the Captain was Lothnar, followed by a number of empty spaces – presumably reserved for them, The Teacher and a host of Blade Masters and Mistresses still yet to arrive. Stretching left across the front row were numerous administrative aides – presumably attached to Kirika, whose absence was curious. She had expected an honorary space to be reserved for Aleska, however, the current seating arrangements along the front row implied otherwise. Perhaps Aleska's recent aloofness had prompted the venerable scrier's omission from the front row, or maybe Aleska simply did not intend to attend the festivities, she mused.

'May I escort you to your seats?' enquired an eager young Freylarkin, overseeing the event's seating arrangements.

'Thank you for the kind offer, however, I believe we already know our places.' replied Thandor, who offered the young female a polite smile.

'She is a bit young for you, do you not think?' she said, attempting to tease Thandor as they made their way to sit beside Lothnar.

'If you were less coy, I would not need to broaden my horizon.' he replied, followed with a devilish smile.

She enjoyed Thandor's company immensely – there was something about his semi-aloof enigmatic presence which drew her in; he was like a complex puzzle, which she absolutely needed to solve. Yet regardless of their obvious mutual attraction, their habitual flirting and teasing had thus far failed to evolve into something more. Her relationship with Thandor was a curious one; she often wondered if the thrill of the chase appealed more to them, as opposed to the actual claiming of their prize. Putting aside her habitual musings regarding her relationship with Thandor, she focused her attention once more on the present and took her place in the front row next to Lothnar. Lying at the nomadic Paladin's feet was the black dire wolf Krisis, who she had noticed accompanying Aleska, and more recently Lothnar, since his recent return to the vale. The powerful animal sat on his hindquarters, keenly observing the Freylarkai busying themselves on the floor of the arena before them. Lothnar offered her a respectful nod as she made herself comfortable beside the duo.

'Mind if I stroke your new companion?'

'Be my guest – Krisis enjoys the affection.'

The dire wolf eased into her left hand as she enthusiastically rubbed the thick black fur at the scruff of his neck. Krisis made numerous pleasurable deep rumbling noises, signalling his desire for her to continue massaging his neck.

'I am curious. Should you not be preparing for your imminent duel with The Guardian?'

'I have already completed my preparations. Besides, I wanted to ensure that Krisis and I had a good seat for the remainder of the festivities.'

'You seem rather relaxed, despite being asked to participate in the opening duel.' she replied, surprised by the Paladin's blasé attitude towards his imminent encounter with The Guardian.

'I am not concerned.' the Paladin replied, unconvincingly.

Lothnar's short response betrayed his unease; she could sense a hint of doubt in the Paladin's voice, however, she decided it wise not to potentially agitate him by needlessly pursuing the matter further.

'I see.' she replied, redoubling her efforts to sate Krisis' appetite for continued affection. 'I look forward to the duel – it should be an interesting encounter.'

Lothnar said no more on the matter, thus bringing a swift end to their brief conversation. The Paladin stared blankly at the arena floor, seemingly distracted by thoughts unknown to her. She turned to Thandor, who had clearly overheard their conversation; she could tell by the narrowing of his eyes that her exchange of words had piqued the duellist's interest. Something was obviously bothering Lothnar, and now Thandor's keen mind was working tirelessly to discover the cause. With Lothnar in earshot, she knew that Thandor would remain tight-lipped on the matter, and so she turned her attention back to Krisis, who by now had become an eager member of her personal entourage, easily won over by her ongoing affections. As she continued to massage the dire wolf's neck, she thought back to their conversation with Nathanar – specifically Thandor's own words. *"Look to the opening duel of the Trials"* – his words were still at the forefront in her mind, perpetually renting space. Assuming The Guardian could indeed score an upset victory against Lothnar, would Rayna subsequently ascend to become the very ideal she herself had coined, she mused. Rayna's controversial arrival had already sent ripples throughout Freylar, like a stone cast into still water, and now Alarielle's successor stood upon the cusp of more profound events to come. Victory over Lothnar would see The Guardian's popularity soar to even greater heights. What would happen then, she mused, if Rayna became more revered than Mirielle, or more importantly...Marcus.

He was done hiding in the shadows. The growing number of Freylarkai flocking to the alleys surrounding the arena, in the run up to the Trials later that morning, meant that he could once again resume his infiltration of the Tri-Spires. Mirielle's hubris, especially in proceeding with the Trials, had brought about a swift end to the curfew, thus permitting him freedom of movement once more. The hungering darkness deep inside him fuelled his desires, urging him onwards, having had its fill of the gibbering construct cowering in the gloomy corner of the store. Before taking his leave, he severed the flesh leash shackling his newest creation to one of the store's interior walls, and left the establishment's main entrance ajar. No longer bound to its cell, the creature now possessed the freedom to roam outside – indeed, he was counting on the inevitability. With the timing of Lileah's renewed invasion unknown to him, he required an alternate means of distraction to tease the remaining house guards from the Tri-Spires, thus ensuring his successful infiltration. Although it was unlikely that the mother and daughter monstrosity would venture far anytime soon, in his prolonged absence the abhorrent creature would no doubt seek to escape its confinement in search of aid. Policing the Trials, along with its attending citizens, and dealing with the inevitable panic his arachnoid construct would ultimately bring, would see Freylar's domestic security stretched thin. In all likelihood The Blades too would be preoccupied, revelling in the festivities, therefore making his task of infiltrating the Tri-Spires that much easier.

Prior to leaving the store, he dressed himself in the mutilated mother's discarded attire, which he had torn from the Freylarkin's body before working on the pair. Naturally, he had thought about posing as the daughter, but even his mastery of manipulating the flesh had its limits; the size difference between the young female and his own frame was unlikely to go unnoticed. Given his inability to reduce his own mass significantly – even on a temporary basis – he had resigned himself to playing the role of the mother. Regardless of his preference, the fresh experience was exhilarating. Despite having previously stolen numerous identities, never once had he adopted the appearance of a female. His gender-defying masquerade was uncomfortable at first; specifically, the role demanded a conscious effort on his part to stand up straight, which irked him no end. Nonetheless, he quickly adjusted to his altered form, working his new physique hard as he moved unnoticed through the growing throng of Freylarkai crowding outwards from the arena. Although mimicking the voices of others remained beyond the reach of his ability, those Freylarkai who ultimately recognised his faux visage were quickly dismissed with a friendly wave of his right hand – which still retained all of its digits. He pushed his way past the enthusiastic revellers, all of whom appeared eager to watch the Trials. His successful pretence of posing as a female amused him immensely, in ways he had never previously imagined. The darkness lurking inside his body also approved of his brazen disguise, savouring his own experience in equal measure. How ironic, he mused, that one of Mirielle's exiles now walked alongside her own people. Together they mocked the Freylarkai in secret, passing through the gathered host without a second glance. He laughed quietly, in unison with his dark companion, taking pleasure from the ease with which he had deceived his unsuspecting kin.

'Soon...' he said, quietly under his breath, in his habitual raspy tone, 'Your skin will dance to my touch.'

He quickened his pace, in line with his rising excitement, conscious now that he was incessantly licking his lips. His short-lived discipline was now faltering badly in the wake of his growing anticipation. Having exercised patience and restraint for so long, now his body – more than ever – craved the object of his desires. Soon Freylar's queen would be within his grasp. Lucid thoughts of how he would violate Mirielle's marble-like skin swarmed in his mind, making him feel giddy amidst the press of the overbearing crowd. The promise of euphoria was now close to intolerable; the prospect flooded his mind, making it difficult for him to concentrate. He could feel the muscles in his face twitching with glee, making it difficult to maintain his current visage. Realising now the precarious nature of his situation, he increased his pace, carelessly pushing past those in his path, attempting to break free of the dense crowd. Several Freylarkai cast their gaze in his direction, bemused by his strength, which obviously exceeded that of a normal female. He paid them no attention and continued to fight his way past the gathered Freylarkai. After finally breaking free of their undisciplined ranks, he started to regain his composure as his dislike of densely packed crowds abated. The muscles in his face ceased twitching and the mounting elation, which had threatened to overwhelm him, quickly receded. Once he was satisfied that he had regained control of his facade, he glanced over his shoulder, offering the mob a quick sneer, before pressing on towards the Tri-Spires.

She watched with interest as Rayna prepared herself for the opening duel of the Trials; the enigmatic light bringer diligently performed the breathing techniques commonly practiced by The Blades, which, almost certainly, had been imparted to her by The Teacher. She supposed that Rayna sought to compose herself, in readiness for Lothnar's challenge, yet, given The Guardian's resolve at Scrier's Post, the pre-combat ritual seemed largely redundant. She shifted her gaze towards her sister, who observed Rayna's choice of breathing exercises; Kirika had a curious look on her face, full of conflict and mixed emotions. After The Guardian's arrival in Freylar, her sister was tasked with overseeing The Guardian's personal development, and in doing so had apparently grown attached to the light bringer. It was understandable then, that Kirika would exhibit a certain amount of pride, watching favourably as her protégé prepared for what promised to be a fascinating duel. Yet on the other hand, Kirika was about to commit an act which would potentially see her sister lose her seat on the ruling council, or worse, become exiled – as she herself had been. Having only just reconnected with her sister, she was heartbroken to learn that her arrival now placed Kirika in an impossible situation. Now, more than ever, she needed to scry the future – for her sister's sake – yet Rayna's involvement continued to confound her ability. Due to her unpredictability, and the colliding destinies that she represented, The Guardian was anathema to all scriers, regardless of their level of mastery. It was impossible to foresee the strands of fate interwoven with The Guardian's own, and right now, their destinies were inexorably linked. If Rayna won her duel with Lothnar, and subsequently lent them support, their gambit, and in all likelihood Kirika's future, would be secured. However, failure would weaken their position; she remained unconvinced that Vorian's testimony alone would be sufficient to ensure that her voice was heard. They needed the Freylarkai on side, and the key to earning their favour was popularity.

'Are you nervous?' asked Vorian, who had remained diligently by her side since her return to Freylar.

'It is hard not to be.' she whispered, whilst tugging at the hood of her robe with her good hand, ensuring that her identity remained hidden.

Smuggling her into the buildings adjoining the arena had been relatively straightforward, given her sister's level of influence. Nonetheless, she remained conscious of her mechanical claw, and the need to ensure its continued concealment – for the time being at least. If a single Freylarkin caught sight of her ornate prosthetic, their carefully orchestrated plan would quickly unravel. Thus, she ensured that Krashnar's work remained out of sight, buried beneath the folds in her robe. She was now a stranger to Freylar, yet despite this fact there could be no room for complacency, given the risk each of them shouldered. Kirika was about to lay everything on the line to ensure that her voice was heard and judged by the people – the very least she could do was to reciprocate her sister's level of commitment.

After completing her exercises, The Guardian casually wandered over. Rayna leaned with her back against the wall, adjacent to herself and Vorian, whilst Kirika busied herself with another of her aides, who seemingly appeared from nowhere. The Guardian said nothing at first, appearing content simply to stand in their presence whilst she waited to be called to the arena. She expected the silence between them to be cold and awkward, yet there was something about Rayna that put those around her at ease, herself included.

'Don't you just hate waiting?' said Rayna, suddenly.

The direct nature of the light bringer's question caught her by surprise.

'I have actually become rather good at it. But, in answer to your question, yes – waiting can be tiresome.'

'Does it hurt?' continued Rayna, who cast her gaze towards the mechanical claw concealed beneath her robe.

'It was agony at first, and, still to this cycle, it causes me pain, although, I have learned to accept the discomfort – a small price to pay, for a working hand.'

'Must be pretty *handy* in a fight?' said Rayna, who beamed at her with an amused look.

'Yes.' she replied, with an honest smile – it was the first time anyone had openly made light of her disability. 'I suppose so, although, I have never tried to strike an opponent with it, or use it to *disarm* them.'

Rayna laughed, despite Vorian's obvious lack of perception apropos of their brief exchange of quips.

'Nothing is taboo for you, is it?' she said, her curiosity piqued by Rayna's free disposition.

'Well...it got us talking, and that's a start.'

'By that I take it that you wish to know me, and yet you should abhor me, given the events at Scrier's Post.'

'I have done things myself, which I am most certainly not proud of. It would be awful if we were unable to leave behind the dark places that haunt us. Moreover, what would be the point in continuing if they weighed us down indefinitely? Someone close to me recently taught me that it is possible to accept our past for what it is, and make peace with it. I have to believe that we can come back from our mistakes, and rediscover ourselves, so that we can move forwards.'

She had not expected such musings to spill from The Guardian's lips. Taken aback by the unexpected thought provoking words, she struggled to find her own. She felt strangely drawn to Rayna, wanting to learn more about the enigmatic light bringer's presence in Freylar, specifically whether there was a higher purpose to her curious arrival.

'I am no longer certain that I can move forwards.' she said, struggling to envisage a personal application for Rayna's counsel.

'Rubbish – you're doing it right now. No one forced you to come back to Freylar. You could have remained in exile and allowed the comforting numbness of depression to have its way with you. But instead, you are here, risking your soul in an attempt to save countless others. You have already taken the first steps upon your road to redemption.'

Rayna's frank assessment emboldened her spirit, threatening with it the dangerous promise of hope.

'I may fail.'

'No, you won't – and neither will I.'

'How can you be so certain – you are no scrier; you have no means of foretelling that which is to come.'

'I have faith.'

'You have faith – in what, may I ask? I gather such notions are moot, since your arrival.' she said, generally interested in Rayna's perception on the matter.

'I have faith in us.'

'Are you not confusing your faith with determination and ambition?' she replied, seeking further clarity on Rayna's viewpoint.

'Perhaps…maybe – does it really matter?'

'I suppose not. Regardless, I am not convinced that I share your level of *faith*.'

'You have the determination, of that I am convinced, else we would not be having this conversation. And after I defeat Lothnar in that arena, I hope that you will come to share my faith.'

She was about to respond to The Guardian's analysis, when a young female called to them from the passage leading to the arena.

'Guardian, Lothnar has entered the arena.'

Rayna pushed herself away from the wall and turned to offer her a playful wink.

'I guess it's time I finally did this.' said Rayna, who then looked to Kirika with a sidelong grin, before casually making her way towards the thunderous applause which echoed along the passage.

'I would wish you good luck,' she said, as Rayna calmly set of down the passage, 'Though I can see now that you clearly make your own.'

The sound of the roaring crowd was almost deafening, as he deftly vaulted over the dwarf wall that ran the perimeter of the arena floor. Following Mirielle's brief public speech – announcing the start of the Trials – he wasted little time ushering in its opening duel. Despite having managed to distance himself from the hype and excitement leading up to his duel with Rayna – largely due to his absence from the vale – nonetheless, the relentless ambient chatter concerning his imminent encounter, which he had overheard whilst waiting for the tiered stone seating of the arena to fill up, had succeeded in agitating him. Shortly after Natalya had accompanied him to the front row, he had quickly grown to regret his decision to bide his time amongst the crowd. Despite his anti-social demeanour, the showmanship of his unconventional means of taking to the arena floor was well received; the crowd cheered his entrance enthusiastically. Though typically not one for such cocky public displays, he presumed that Rayna would be waiting within earshot, therefore his deliberate ploy to incite the audience, thus strengthening his position, was no bad thing – the art of duelling was as much about strategy as it was displays of physical skill. He turned around to face the tiered stone seating and offered the sea of assembled faces a quick nod of his head. The crowd roared again, with thunderous applause, as they noisily approved of his subtle acknowledgement of their lively support. Numerous Freylarkai rose to their feet, continuing to clap and cheer fervently. Playing once more to the crowd, he acknowledged their support one final time, with another fleeting nod that sent his audience into a complete furore. Though not as well liked as Marcus or Nathaniel, nonetheless, his rank of Blade Paladin meant something to the people; he required no introduction – the crowd both respected and knew him as a champion of Freylar, a privilege rightly deserving of Paladin and Valkyrie alike. The Captain of The Blades was also on his feet; Ragnar clapped hard with his club-like hands, alongside Krisis, who barked energetically in front of Natalya. Savouring the moment, he inhaled deeply through his nose, before breathing out slowly through his mouth, attempting to slow his eager heart. Watching the raucous crowd react wholeheartedly to his presence shored up his weathered confidence; thoughts of Lileah quickly melted away, along with the creeping self-doubts over the mastery of his own ability.

After what seemed like an eternity of cheering and clapping, the lively crowd began to settle back down, as the eager spectators found their seats once more. After reseating themselves, the atmosphere in the arena quickly abated. As was expected of him, he took up his position, off centre, towards the east gate, where he silently waited for his opponent to emerge. Given The Guardian's forthright disposition, he – as well as the audience – had expected Rayna to emerge promptly, but instead, they were left unexpectedly hanging, like overripe fruit refusing to drop from a tree. From the corner of his left eye, he noticed heads turning, as the audience looked to one another in obvious confusion. Palpable tension began to build quickly in the arena; it manifested in the air, until almost tangible. He began to feel a little awkward and self-conscious, and his mouth became dry. Officially, their duel had not yet started, but already he had underestimated his opponent, who was no doubt playing for time, deliberately, in a bid to rob him of his early momentum. The familiar self-doubt, which had previously stalked him, quickly returned; it lingered over him, like an ominous black cloud with the promise of rain.

'Damn you.' he whispered slowly to himself.

Whilst there was no doubt in his mind that Rayna would ultimately make her appearance, it was clear to him now that – before deciding to do so – The Guardian would first make him sweat. Typically he was unaffected by such obvious ploys, but the fact that he had not predicted the cheap move concerned him. It was clear to him now that Rayna had no intention of fighting fairly, which – given his superior fighting skill – was an understandable logical move. He wondered whether Rayna herself had coined the strategy, or if another member of The Guardian's growing entourage had played a part in executing the cheap trick.

'Clever girl,' he whispered, again to himself, 'Although, you have also made a mistake – you played your hand too early!'

ELEVEN
Trials

'I think you have kept them waiting long enough.' said Kirika over her shoulder.

'You're probably right.'

'And remember what we talked about.'

'I haven't forgotten.'

'Well then – enjoy the fight.'

'I will...'

The crowd were on their feet the moment she stepped foot into the arena. The sound of cheers emanating from the audience was deafening, causing her to feel a little lightheaded. Though she had anticipated welcoming cries of support, nothing had prepared her for the uplifting roar that now assaulted her. She casually approached the centre of the arena, then turned towards the sea of faces shouting the word "Guardian", repeatedly, in unison. She raised her left hand in a balled fist, acknowledging their support, which in turn prompted renewed applause from her enthusiastic supporters. Despite having spent so many cycles training in the arena, only now did she began to fully appreciate its generous size; seeing the mass of cheering Freylarkai neatly sat adjacent to one another emphasised the enormity of the crescent shaped amphitheatre. Amongst the many faces, she recognised numerous forest dwellers who chanted her name fervently, in addition to others she had seen habitually loitering by the old bridge. Rather unsurprisingly, there was also a large contingent of Blades present, who were no doubt eager to watch the combat prowess of their peers. Sitting calmly in the centre of the front row, adjacent to Marcus, was Freylar's queen; Mirielle stared eerily towards her with her white pupil-less eyes. By contrast, The Blade Lord wore his ever-present welcoming smile; Marcus' genial manner helped to calm her nerves, which threatened to get the better of her, despite her seemingly calm exterior. Nathaniel was also in the front row, adjacent to Thandor – both seasoned Blades sat with their arms folded and nodded reassuringly to her as she caught their eye. Seeing so many familiar faces, all of whom had come together to witness Lothnar's challenge play out, caused the reality of her current situation to hit home. She felt unexpectedly overwhelmed, as she now fully realised the reality of the task ahead of her. She tried to convince herself that her imminent duel with Lothnar was just another fight – no different to her duel with Knight Lord Heldran. In a relatively short space of time, since her arrival in Freylar, she had faced the Narlakai horrors, survived charges from the brutal Ravnarkai, and even expelled the darkness manifesting inside her inherited body. Yet there was something different about her previous challenges. Despite accepting the role of the underdog once more, there was something different this time; previously there had been no real expectation on her part to succeed, but now the Freylarkai had become accustomed to her bucking the trend. Now, plain to see, etched upon the many faces in the audience, was the expectation that she *would* succeed, despite her opponent's obvious superior combat prowess. Now, feeling the pressure of her changed circumstances, she breathed slowly and deeply, in an attempt to still the butterflies raging in her stomach. Keenly aware that the pressure of the current situation was getting to her, she smiled and winked playfully to the crowd, maintaining the illusion that she was still very much in control of her nerves. After doing her part to appease the audience, she took her position opposite Lothnar; the nomadic Paladin gave nothing away, courtesy of his stoic disposition. She briefly considered shaking her opponent's hand, but the opportunity passed as The Blade Lord suddenly rose from his seat, commanding the eager crowd to silence without a single gesture or word.

'I welcome you all to the opening duel of the Trials. Lothnar, Rayna, you will face one another in this opening contest of skill.' said Marcus, in his habitual warm but commanding tone. 'I trust that you are both familiar with the rules of this engagement, however, for the benefit of the audience, I will reaffirm the expectations as follows. Your duel will be a contest of skill – not ability. You are not authorised to use your abilities during the duel. Whilst this will be a full contact engagement, you will refrain from executing moves which court release – contravening this directive is punishable by Freylarian law. I trust that I am clear on this point?'

Both she and Lothnar nodded respectfully towards The Blade Lord in acknowledgement.

'Good. Furthermore, I grant you both the aid of a renewalist, twice, during your duel, requested immediately by raising an open palm. During this time, the duel is suspended. Lastly, the duel will end once blood has been drawn three times from your opponent, thus declaring the victor of the engagement. With that said, you are both free to select your weapons of choice – I wish you both the best.'

After finishing his speech, Marcus retook his seat and pressed the tips of his fingers together, against his chin, as he regarded them both with interest. Two of Kirika's aides appeared behind them, ushering forth a large mobile wooden rack, adorned with an array of weapons, including large double-handed axes, bows, daggers, shields and morning stars. The Blades' mainstay weapon of choice was also present – the falchion. They both turned and made their way towards the cache of weapons, eager to make their selection. She yearned for Shadow Caster and The Ardent Blade, though sadly neither was present. Likewise, the custom dirks that she had previously seen Lothnar deftly toying with were absent. Freylarian law dictated that only stock weapons be permitted for use when training or duelling in the arena. Lothnar wasted little time in selecting a number of throwing knives, which he slid into a sheath strapped to the underside of his left arm. In addition, he chose two dirks and attached them to his belt. Satisfied with his selection, the Paladin took his position towards the east gate, without so much as even glancing in her direction. Turning her attention towards the weapons, she selected a pair of falchions, before making her way to her designated position towards the west gate. Although heavier than her Dawnstone twins, nonetheless, she was well adjusted to the weight of the blades in hand. Having selected their weapons and taken their designated places, they both stared intently at one another. Though tempted to turn her gaze towards The Blade Lord for further instructions, Nathaniel's sermons burned in her mind, ensuring that she did not lose sight of her opponent. She studied the distance between them; it was clear that Lothnar had the tactical advantage. She needed to close the gap, and that meant entering his area of threat, whilst the Paladin remained beyond her reach. With no throwing weapons of her own, and no means by which to defend herself on approach, she would be utterly reliant on her speed and agility. No doubt Lothnar had also considered the scenario playing out in her mind, thus she needed a means to distract her opponent. However, before she could consider her options further, a loud deep wind instrument sounded from the direction of the crowd, followed by a short command from The Blade Lord which would forever remain etched in her mind.

'Engage!'

Their journey south via the subterranean caverns was unbearably slow, yet they served their purpose, allowing her to continue to drive the Narlakai herd towards Freylar, specifically the vale, despite the harmful rays of the weak autumnal sun. During their march south, her abhorrent mount had been instrumental in shepherding the Narlakai, which in turn had eased the mental strain upon her. However, shortly prior to entering the caverns, the three-headed construct had begun to show signs of fatigue; the Meldbeast had bowed its three heads low whilst breathing hard, struggling to draw in enough air to sustain it. Concerned about the creature's stamina, and its readiness for the inevitable battle to come, she had afforded the creature a brief interlude during which to hunt, prior to commanding it underground, along with the writhing gaseous black mass stretched out before them. During its brief respite, her kindred mount had little trouble tracking the scent of one of the borderlands' many dire wolves, known to roam the sparse landscape. After temporarily abandoning the herd in favour of a well-deserved meal, she had revelled in the beast's excitement as it tracked its prey to a thick isolated copse, east of Black Thorn. The chimera had demonstrated little trouble locating its prey, which it promptly cornered and savagely tore apart to sate the hunger in its belly. Though partly composed from dire wolves itself, the Meldbeast had shown no qualms devouring one of its kin. She recalled the ugly sounds of the Meldbeast's feasting from atop her mount, her legs still fixed in place, courtesy of its flesh straps, whilst the creature noisily devoured its well-earned meal; the grim sounds of sinews tearing and bones crunching had been notably amplified against the borderlands' quiet ambiance. She remembered watching the numerous sets of yellow eyes lurking in the copse that had studied them intently, whilst the Meldbeast devoured their unfortunate kin. A small part of her had felt remorse for the lupine onlookers silently mourning the loss of their companion, however, this fleeting emotion paled in comparison to the feeling of supremacy facilitated by the power of her mind and the physical strength of her obedient mount. After finishing its meal, she decided to follow suit, having not eaten in cycles. After taking no pleasure in gulping down some of the spoiled wares from Krashnar's hide, she had commanded the Meldbeast back to tend to its flock. The abandoned writhing mass of Narlakai had barely moved, making the task of funnelling them underground relatively straightforward. Initially their subterranean progress had been steady, but as the winding passages gradually narrowed, their dogged march became increasingly constricted. Their overall pace through the caverns was far slower than she had liked, having hoped that her previous experience managing the herd in such confines would have served her well. However, the stark reality was that the caverns had too many choke points, which – coupled with the Narlakai's inherently slow movement – meant their throughput was inevitably limited. However, the experience was not entirely without reward; their restricted path forced her mount to identify other means of running the length of the advancing column, thus keeping it in check without the constant need for her ability. With its path regularly blocked, the Meldbeast experimented – tentatively at first – by running up and down the side of the caverns over short distances. The beast soon discovered, however, that its cruel father had furnished it with the tools necessary to climb the interior rock face; the Meldbeast's iron-like claws pummelled the cavern walls, splintering them with ease, thereby allowing the chimera to find grip at seemingly impossible angles. Without the aid of Krashnar's flesh straps, the creature's gravity-defying feats would have seen her quickly thrown from her mount. Instead, her only concern was the agonising pain racking her body with each new feat from Krashnar's enthusiastic monstrous pet. She thought about reigning in the Meldbeast's daredevil acrobatics, purely to ease the agony shooting through her metal-infused flesh, but the pain she now experienced was a part of her, and something that she needed to become accustomed to – according to Darlia. As the increasing torment assaulted her unnatural body, she began to think of Darlia, specifically the manner in which she had abandoned her lover. She wished dearly that the conflicted scrier had come around to seeing things as she now did, but – for the time being at least – the motivation for their respective actions was no longer aligned. Darlia's soul was broken, and harboured a pointless need to repent, where as her own – by contrast – had hardened, galvanized with vengeance and hate. All of the injustices that both she and Darlia had suffered could be traced back to Mirielle's arrogant reign. Her desire to see that reign reduced to ash, and deliver retribution for Freylar's ongoing prejudice, fuelled her ongoing vendetta. More pain speared through her body, disrupting her private thoughts; her mount executed yet another audacious move, as it grew increasingly confident in its abilities. The supremely agile creature flew over the top of the writhing gaseous black stream funnelling through the narrow space, as it leapt towards the opposite wall of the cavern. Rock splintered again as her maniacal mount crashed into the hard surface of the opposing wall, punishing it dearly. Her stomach lurched due to the thunderous impact, causing her to retch yet again, although she did so with a curious smile, knowing that the pain she felt would be visited a hundredfold upon her haughty kin. The baleful thought prompted the release of cruel laughter from her, as she savoured the notion. Giving herself over entirely to the comforting embrace of revenge, she used the power of her mind to incentivise the Meldbeast once again, giving it another of her mental kicks. The abhorrent creature moaned in discomfort, after which it redoubled its efforts, now more determined than ever to appease *her* – its mistress.

'Engage!'

Tightening her grip on her falchions, she immediately sprinted headlong towards Lothnar, arcing towards his left flank with the intention of wrong-footing the Paladin. From the corner of her right eye, she could see the crowd on their feet, cheering and screaming at her impetuous assault. It was clear from Lothnar's reaction that the Paladin had not anticipated the extent of her alacrity, although the astonishing speed with which he drew from the sheath attached to the underside of his left arm, mitigated her own reckless abandon. Instinctively she dived into a shoulder roll, moments prior to Lothnar's first throw. Despite failing to witness the projectile's trajectory, a collective gasp from the crowd, and the absence of any pain, implied that her acrobatics had borne fruit. After exiting the hastily executed roll, she used her forward momentum to quickly regain her feet, thus allowing her to resume her assault – or at least, that was the theory. With impossible speed, Lothnar drew another of the stock throwing knives from the sheath strapped to his arm. Little more than ten paces now separated them, which – combined with Lothnar's unprecedented skill – meant there was very little she could do to avert the Paladin's second throw. Instinctively she tried to block the fresh projectile's path with her falchions, however, countering the pace with which the knife found its mark proved to be beyond her skill, prompting another gasp from the audience. Her left leg quickly buckled and gave way, sending her crashing to the floor of the dusty arena. Despite her familiarity with the arena's hard surface, having endured countless undignified lessons first-hand from The Teacher, she was unprepared for the painful sensations caused by the knife's sudden impact. Immediately after the blade punctured her limb, she felt a strange tingling sensation, followed by the rapid onset of heat rising in her left leg, and finally, lots of pain – excruciating pain! She cried out in agony, raising her hand with fingers splayed; swallowing her pride, she signalled her request for the aid of a renewalist.

'Hold!' cried Marcus immediately, announcing a temporary reprieve from their duel.

One of the renewalists stationed on the arena floor, over by the east gate, immediately ran towards her. The young healer passed Lothnar, who turned and offered a confident smirk to the crowd. The diligent renewalist ignored the Paladin's obvious gloating and rushed to her side, eager to repair the damage to her leg.

'Please, keep still whilst I remove the blade.' said the renewalist, clearly out of breath after his short sprint. 'This will hurt!'

'It already bloody hurts!'

The renewalist grinned at her retort and pulled the throwing knife from her leg in one fluid motion. Thick blood gushed from the wound, lapping around the side of her left leg, before dropping to the floor, staining the arena's dusty surface. Stemming the flow of blood, the renewalist placed his hands over the wound and immediately began to knit the cut flesh together using his ability. Amidst the pain, she cast her mind back to the times when Nathaniel had tended her wounds, recalling specifically how the recovery process had been a much slicker and calming experience. The sensation now felt different to Nathaniel's previous ministrations, as though laboured or perhaps carried out with a blunt instrument.

'May I ask what level you are?' she said, whilst wincing in pain.

'Regrettably, Guardian, I am still an Adept. We only permit Adepts, Masters or Mistresses of our ability to administer those who fall during the Trials. Where possible, those of my rank are expected to provide aid so that we can practice our skills under pressure.' the renewalist replied self-consciously. 'Would you like me to request a Master or Mistress instead?'

'I meant no offence.' she said, trying hard to block out the throbbing pain. 'A Freylarkin of your ability would be deeply respected amongst the Knights Thranis – perhaps you should enlist.'

The renewalist smiled politely, accepting her unconventional praise.

'I know little about knights, but I do know that you will be back on your feet shortly. Also, there will be no scarring once the wound is fully healed.' the renewalist replied, whilst diligently finishing his work. 'However, I do sincerely hope that you have a strategy which does not involve getting stabbed again.'

'What's your name?' she said, catching her benefactor off guard.

'Galadrick.'

'That's a mouthful – may I call you Gal?'

Galadrick briefly looked up from his work and nodded to her with a welcoming smile.

'In answer to your question, Gal – absolutely not!'

Galadrick glanced at her once more, this time with a look of confusion.

'Do you mean to say that you have no strategy, or that you do indeed plan to get stabbed once again?'

'Both. Lothnar won't expect me to take another hit like this; he'll assume that I will favour a more defensive stance. As for a plan, surely if I have no plan, he cannot therefore counter it?'

Galadrick stared at her with a puzzled look, clearly bewildered by her unconventional analysis. The confused renewalist was obviously lost for words, and offered no comment regarding her alternative approach.

'See what I mean?' she continued, offering the bemused renewalist a playful grin.

'I am not sure that I follow you, Guardian.'

'And that's the point.'

'Well then, I hope for your sake that he sees it that way – or rather, that he does not see it.' replied Galadrick, finishing up his handiwork. 'You should be able to stand again now.'

'Thanks Gal, I appreciate it.'

'You are most welcome, Guardian.' replied Galadrick earnestly. 'Please ensure that you await Marcus' command to engage, before commencing your impromptu offence.'

'I will.'

'Oh, and there is one more thing.'

'What's that?'

'Kick his arse!'

'Cora, we have to leave.' she said to her daughter, in an unconvincing voice.

There was no response from Cora, just the continued sound of whimpering, muffled beneath the thick hair hanging down across her daughter's face. She tried to lift her head to displace some of her hair, pulling it away from her daughter's own, but the added weight of Cora's body made the task extremely difficult.

'Please, my love, we have to get help.'

Still there was no response. Though she could not see her daughter's face, Cora was clearly distraught and in pain. She wished dearly that she could embrace her own daughter, offering her the reassurance that a child so desperately needed when coping with trauma. However, their vile tormentor had cruelly taken that basic right away from them. She vowed to release the heinous shaper if ever their paths once again crossed. Though for now, such ugly thoughts were fanciful – they desperately needed help, and in order to seek that help she first required her daughter's own.

'Cora, please! You must help me.' she pressed, raising her voice, so that her daughter might hear beneath the combined matted mass of hair. 'I cannot do this alone – I am not strong enough! I need you Cora.'

'Mother, I am scared!'

'My love, I know that you are. I am too. However, we need to work together. We must get away from here before that vile monster returns.'

'But what if he catches us?' replied Cora hysterically.

'Cora, calm down.'

'Mother, if he catches us, it will be far worse!'

'You cannot think like that, and we cannot survive like this. We must get help. Please, Cora, you have to be strong, for both of us.'

Her daughter began to sob once again; Cora was clearly struggling to come to terms with their abhorrent reality.

'Please, Cora!' she implored sincerely.

Relenting momentarily, she gave her daughter time to register her words. Eventually Cora ceased her sobbing; she was about to try to coerce the cooperation of her daughter once more, when unexpectedly she felt upwards pressure. Her daughter suddenly propelled them forwards; despite the vicious pain that wracked her torso, she began to move her own arms and legs, doing her best to guide Cora towards the gap in the door opposite. Working in unison, they crawled awkwardly towards the store's main entrance, which had been carelessly left ajar – an oversight on their tormentor's part, she mused, anxiously. Reaching out with her right arm, she grabbed the side of the door and pulled it open. Cora cried out in pain; the act of wrestling the door open tugged at their fused skin, stretching it mercilessly – her daughter clearly suffered as she did, and it was the distress caused by that thought that brought tears to her eyes, rather than their actual physical pain.

'Good girl, be brave.'

Together they crossed the threshold of the store clumsily, into the alley outside. The weak light penetrating the clouds above stung her eyes, as she craned her neck back to better survey their surroundings. In light of their recent ghastly ordeal, she had completely lost track of the cycles.

'Cora, wait here for a moment.'

Shaking her head to clear her matted hair away from her ears, she listened carefully to the ambient sounds of Freylar, hoping to locate one of their kin for assistance. In the distance, she could hear the roar of the crowd in the arena, suggesting that the Trials were already underway. She cursed their poor timing; with so many of the Freylarkai engrossed in the Trials, their task would be even more arduous. Refusing to let despair consume her, she continued to listen carefully, desperate for a thread of hope to cling to. In the background, she fancied hearing the incessant bickering of several Freylarkai. Although she could not discern the nature of their discontent, it mattered not, for she had found their hope.

'Cora, turn to the right.'

'Mother, what is it?'

'Our salvation – I hope.'

Her daughter whimpered again in pain as they adjusted their heading. After the painful manoeuvre, they began crawling towards the direction of the sound she had previously identified. Their progress was slow due to their laboured movement, but desperation drove them onwards. Eventually, they reached the junction at the end of the alley. They were both exhausted; her arms and calves ached incessantly, due to their imposed configuration. She imagined that her daughter suffered similarly – in all likelihood, Cora's knees were bloodied and bruised due to scraping across the hard ground.

'Rest here for a moment.'

The sound she had previously heard was much louder now; she could hear the distinct voices of three Freylarkai, each of whom seemed to be bickering about the Trials, specifically their inability to secure access to the venue in order to witness the spectacle. In light of their own hardships, she cared little for the group's insignificant troubles. Moreover, their pathetic words angered her, given the heinous mutilation both she and her daughter had been forcibly subjected to.

'We need one last push – now, Cora.'

Riding the agonising pain, they moved once again in horrific unison, around the corner of a building into direct line of sight of the squabbling Freylarkai. She craned her neck back once again and stared imploringly at their horrified onlookers, each of whom appeared frozen in terror.

'Help us!'

TWELVE
Interference

The crowd roared as she rose to her feet, following Galadrick's ministration. Her left leg still felt sore from the knife's impact, but the wound itself was no more, and her leg felt strong – she stamped her left foot on the ground a few times, just to be certain.

'How does it feel?'

'A little sore, but otherwise it feels good.'

'The pain will pass. Sometimes it takes a little while for the mind to catch up with such rapid changes to the body.'

'Thanks Gal, I appreciate your efforts.' she replied, after which the Adept renewalist offered her a smile, before promptly returning to his position over by the east gate.

She cracked her neck in a circle and shook her arms to loosen any tension in her muscles, before nodding to Marcus, who remained standing at the front and centre of the tiered stone seating. Although most of the crowd were on their feet, shouting and cheering, Mirielle remained calmly seated, staring at her with vacant eyes. When she had first met Mirielle, she had experienced a cool, but inviting, demeanour. Now Freylar's queen seemed changed; whilst she could not quite put her finger on it, Mirielle appeared now to be more imposing than when first they had met.

'First blood to Lothnar!' cried Marcus, confirming that the challenge she faced was now greater than before.

The crowd roared again, following Marcus' official confirmation of the score. The Blade Lord allowed the audience to have their raucous moment, before turning his attention back to them, ready to recommence their duel.

'Engage!'

She immediately sprinted headlong towards Lothnar at breakneck speed; the Paladin instinctively snatched at the sheath attached to the underside of his left arm, reaching for another of his throwing knives. As she had accurately predicted, when receiving treatment from Galadrick, Lothnar's scrappy movement was purely reactionary – a far cry from the slick motion she had previously witnessed. Caught off guard by her – perhaps reckless – audacity, the Paladin had been placed under pressure; maybe in his haste, Lothnar would struggle to read her movements. Before her mind could devise her next move, however, time – it seemed – abruptly stopped, crashing to a complete halt. She recalled experiencing the strange phenomenon before, when Alarielle had somehow meddled with her mind, leaving behind a lasting impression that had ultimately altered her perception. Previously Alarielle's interference had taken place during the retelling of one of her suppressed memories, perpetuated by the parasitic evil that had violated her body. However, her duel with Lothnar was not a dream; in a similar vein, Alarielle – it now seemed – had found a way to disrupt her reality.

'What are you doing?!'

'*I am helping you.*'

'Alarielle, this is my fight.'

'*No, it is our fight. My future is linked inexorably to your own. This duel is no longer about a simple challenge between you and Lothnar. There is far more than pride at stake here. Your priority is to strengthen your popularity amongst the Freylarkai, and to perpetuate your demi-god status, thereby allowing you to lend credence to Darlia's words.*'

'Why do you care about her future? By inciting the Narlakai, she was – in a sense – responsible for your own demise.'

'The irony is not lost on me, but Freylar's fate still matters to me. Freylar is home to my father – and us, for that matter.'

'I can defeat Lothnar myself.'

'I admire your confidence Rayna, but determination and creative thinking alone will only take you so far. Perhaps that is enough, but, given the stakes, I would rather see your chances of success increased. I ask, therefore, that you consent to my aid; my current state of being affords me little bearing on the world – please, do not deny me purpose.'

'You do not require my consent Alarielle, but...I appreciate your point of view, and besides, this body we share is not mine alone, indeed you are its rightful owner.'

'Never think like that, sister. This body is yours now, though I still have a vested interested in it.'

'Nonetheless, you have my consent.'

'Thank you. Then let us get to work.'

Time suddenly resumed, albeit not unexpectedly – she was prepared. For a second time now, Alarielle had left a lasting impression on her psyche, empowering her to access knowledge previously unknown to her. She adjusted her legs to perform a powerful slide towards Lothnar, channelling the furious momentum of her charge in a way she had not previously considered. The unorthodox move kicked up a plume of gravel and dust from the arena floor, providing her the opportunity she needed. Caught off guard by the move, Lothnar recoiled and attempted to shield his eyes with his left arm. The Paladin tried to track her movements, but the cloud of dust hindered his visibility, affording her a window of opportunity. Scrambling back to her feet, she swung her right falchion towards the Paladin's torso, whilst turning anticlockwise to follow up the sweeping blow with a slash from her left blade, which she angled downwards. Her first attack clanked against one of Lothnar's hastily drawn dirks, though fortuitously, the second caught the side of his right thigh, flush. The crowd gasped as a thin trail of blood fell to the arena floor. Lothnar grunted audibly in pain, before staggering backwards. His hasty withdrawal, coupled with the residual momentum from her assault, meant that several paces now separated them. The cloud of dust was also rapidly dispersing, and along with it, Lothnar's need to shield his eyes; the Paladin quickly reached for his second dirk, signalling that Alarielle's opportunity had been spent. Wasting little time, she renewed her assault against Lothnar, deciding instinctively to maintain the pressure on her opponent. Lothnar's awkward body language suggested that she had successfully pushed the Blade Paladin out of his comfort zone. Nonetheless, there was no escaping the fact that his skill with a blade far exceeded her own. Despite her unfavourable snap assessment, she charged headlong towards the Paladin yet again, as though she was back in the southern lands, fighting alongside the Knights Thranis against the Ravnarkai menace. Lothnar held both dirks in a knife forward stance, relying on his superior reflexes as his primary means of defence. His right thigh continued to bleed, but the Paladin's professional pride denied him the luxury of any medical aid; Lothnar was a proud Freylarkin, a trait that she would do well to exploit. In a bid to further increase pressure on the Paladin, she leapt forwards and drew back her right arm, whilst using the falchion in her left hand to shield her torso as best she could. Lothnar's eyes widened, but the Paladin's extraordinary reflexes countered her audacious move, leaving her vulnerable to his riposte. Lothnar deftly rotated clockwise, narrowly avoiding her strike, before abandoning his right dirk, contrary to The Teacher's sermons. The blade thumped heavily on the arena floor, freeing up his right hand, which he used to grab her outstretched arm. The Paladin then drove the dirk in his left hand into her arm, immediately sending her body into shock. The sensation was not unlike her previous stabbing, although the attack felt significantly more impactful. Her resolve would have undoubtedly been broken in that single moment, if not for Alarielle's intervention once again. The former Blade Adept had been stabbed many times as an active member of the Order, thus Alarielle's experiences were instantaneously passed down to herself. Alarielle's newest impression mitigated the mental effects of Lothnar's blow, preventing her mind from paralysing her body. Therefore, still able to function, she rapidly bent her left knee, kicking the heel of her boot hard into the Paladin's genitals.

'Bitch!' said Lothnar audibly, as he instinctively doubled over from her dishonourable blow.

She followed up her brawler's move with a slash from the falchion in her good hand. Lothnar performed a deft backwards shoulder roll, attempting to evade her attack, but the tip of her blade caught the Paladin's right shoulder leaving its bloody mark. Noise from the crowd thundered once more across the arena, as their enthusiastic audience rose to their feet in unison, clapping, screaming and cheering fervently. Both were left reeling from their brief violent exchange. Lothnar was clearly suffering from her low blow – less so from his actual wounds – and she could no longer fight effectively with his dirk still buried in her right arm, the throbbing pain of which was now beginning to manifest notably. As much as she wanted to press her assault, the blade protruding from her arm dictated otherwise. Reluctantly she raised the open palm of her left hand, signalling for further aid, although she now knew specifically who to turn to.

'Galadrick!'

The screams and cries from their onlookers broke her heart, filling her soul with despair. Cora's resolve was also broken by the group's tactless response, and she began to sob once more.

'Help us!' she implored again, with growing frustration in light of her daughter's distress.

Despite soliciting their aid, the Freylarkai continued to act irrationally, with their continued screaming and shouting.

'Stay back!' cried one of the females, promptly followed by 'Be gone, demon!' from another.

Their uncaring words fuelled her daughter's upset, causing Cora to moan and weep incessantly.

'Please, you cannot leave us like this. Help us!' she continued, her frustration now rapidly turning to anger.

The group remained at a safe distance from them, whilst others ran out into the alley, from neighbouring buildings, swelling their nervous ranks. She realised then how upsetting – horrid even – their mutilated bodies must seem. Nonetheless, the disappointing reaction of their kin threatened to poison her increasing anger, turning it into something far darker.

'Please, you must help us!' she screamed hysterically, allowing her raw emotions to get the better of her.

Her raised voice only escalated the situation, prompting further harsh responses from their scared audience. Others were now beginning to enter the alley, and she could hear the sounds of Freylarkai gathering behind them.

'My daughter and I need your help – you cannot leave us like this!' she cried.

A voice of reason suddenly cut through the callus remarks from their raucous audience, making itself known. She recognised the familiar tone of the single benevolent voice, which belonged to one of the neighbouring store proprietors. The renowned dressmaker typically plied her trade within the Tri-Spires, which was ultimately good business. However, with space at a premium within Mirielle's artificial construct, Larissa also operated a small warehouse locally, which she used to hold stock, in addition to vibrant coloured fabrics and other raw materials.

'Larissa, help us, please!' she wailed emphatically.

The celebrated dressmaker – also known for speaking her mind – pushed her way through the frightened crowd, before promptly running towards them with outstretched arms. Larissa dropped to her knees in front of them and gently reached for Cora's head, trying to console her daughter, before pushing back her own matted hair, so that she could better understand their plight.

'Hanarah, who did this to you?'

'Call for the house guards.' cried a voice from the growing agitated crowd.

'Quiet!' Larissa shouted in return. 'Can you not see that they are in distress?'

'That thing is a monster – someone call the guards, now!'

Larissa's face was loaded with anger. She did not know what was worse – the horror visited upon them by their sadistic creator, or the overwhelmingly unsympathetic reaction of their kin. A sense of dread began to claw at her mind, more so than when their evil tormentor first laid his vile hands upon their skin.

'I must alert the Queen – surely she can undo this.'

'No, Larissa, please stay with us!' she implored.

'I must – you need help.'

'Do not leave us.' Cora whispered meekly, at last finding the courage to speak.

'But I do not have the ability to undo this--'

'Right now we need your protection – that is more important.' she said vehemently.

'Protection from who?'

'Them – the Freylarkai!'

Her heart began to pound in her chest as the tip of Rayna's blade caught Lothnar's shoulder, tracing a thin line of blood across the arena floor. She leapt to her feet and immediately began clapping earnestly. Unsurprisingly, Thandor remained seated, with his arms neatly folded; the aloof Paladin maintained his habitual cool demeanour. However, the remainder of the audience – or at least the vast majority – followed her lead; the Freylarkai were on their feet, screaming and shouting words of encouragement. Even Marcus rose to applaud both combatants, for what was proving to be an extremely decisive duel. Typically, engagements in the arena commenced with a feeling out process, as opponents tested each other's defences, but the duel between Lothnar and Rayna had – thus far at least – defied convention. Even Krisis was enjoying the spectacle;

the adolescent dire wolf barked enthusiastically, and was no doubt keen to see his master prevail. She glanced to her right and spied The Teacher standing tall, with a deep-seated grin stretched across his face. To her left, Ragnar was also on his feet, although the Captain looked conflicted; it was common knowledge that he shared a close friendship with Lothnar, yet it was also rumoured that Ragnar had been sighted aiding Rayna with her training. Regardless, the contest of skill was fascinating to watch, and entirely unpredictable.

'What do you think?' she said loudly, turning to Thandor.

'Interesting...'

'That is it – that is the sum total of your analysis?' she said, attempting to coax Thandor into divulging further insight.

'OK, I will bite – on this occasion.' replied Thandor, who now also chose to stand up.

'So come on then – who do you think will win, given the current state of play?' she enquired enthusiastically.

'It could go either way at this point. Rayna is inexperienced – this we know – but I do not believe that her aggressive stance is in any way rash. By accelerating their encounter, she has placed Lothnar under pressure with her deceptive reckless abandon, and is gambling on the final cut. It is an interesting ploy, but necessary, given Lothnar's superior level of skill. Of course, this risky strategy has only been possible due to her unconventional style. Although now she will need a different approach – self-sacrifice will no longer serve her, in their race to the deciding cut; she needs to draw blood *before* Lothnar.'

'I see – so you think she has been manipulating Lothnar?'

'Indeed. Lothnar will be agitated now; the fact that he chose *two* dirks suggests to me that he did not expect to receive any cuts. Until now, he has relied entirely on his speed and reflexes, yet Rayna employed creative thinking to circumvent both. Now, Lothnar has self-doubt to contend with, in addition to his opponent.'

'So you favour The Guardian's chances then?' she asked, trying to pin Thandor down on the matter.

'I think that is enough for one day – after all, I have a reputation to uphold.' replied Thandor, offering her a wry grin.

Having exhausted her source of information, she turned her attention back to the arena floor. Rayna was receiving aid from the same renewalist who had last tended to her. Lothnar, on the other hand, had requested no such aid, and was instead tying a length of fabric around the cut on his leg, thereby reducing further blood loss. There was an audible cry of pain from The Guardian, as her benefactor removed the dirk still lodged in her arm. After removing the weapon, the renewalist passed the blade to Rayna, who then, curiously, attached it to her belt.

'Why take the weapon?'

'Perhaps for no other reason than to keep us guessing, and Lothnar for that matter; after all, that is her style – she is unpredictable.'

'I sense that you admire her.' she said, with a wide goading smile.

'Rayna's behaviour is not unlike your own.'

'Since when?'

'When was the last time that you conformed to the stuffy doctrine of The Blades, eh?'

'I may be somewhat carefree on occasion, but unpredictable – that is a stretch.'

Thandor said no more on the matter; the aloof Paladin was, in all likelihood, teasing her. Instead, he sat back down and turned his attention towards the arena once more. The renewalist was still diligently tending to Rayna's arm, which had clearly sustained a decent amount of damage from the latest stabbing. Lothnar, however, had finished patching up his leg, and was now retrieving the dirk that he had abandoned earlier during the duel. The nomadic Paladin walked slowly back to his original position from prior to the interlude, whilst flicking the blade between his fingers with unparalleled skill. Upon returning to his position, Lothnar adopted his knife forward stance once more, however, this time he held his left arm vertically in front of him – no doubt with the intention of grappling her arms, in order to wrestle her weapons from her. Lothnar focused intently on The Guardian, who was still receiving aid for her injury; she could tell by Lothnar's business-like attitude that he was agitated and keen to end their encounter.

'He looks pissed off.' she said, as she sat back down and promptly began stroking Krisis once more.

The black-furred adolescent placed his head in her lap and narrowed his eyes, as she ran her slender fingers across the top of his head – clearly, the dire wolf was a willing slave to her affections.

'Indeed. But that pride and emotion of his is a double-edged sword; though it will undoubtedly fuel his desire to win, it could just as easily damn him, *if* it impairs his concentration.'

'She is going to win.'

'Really? You think…or you hope?'

'Both. It is obvious now that she is playing for time – Lothnar knows it, and that will only agitate him further.'

'Playing for time will not secure Rayna victory.' replied Thandor, matter-of-factly.

'It is more than that.'

'Oh…'

'Although he is rarely present in the vale, nonetheless, Lothnar represents The Blades, moreover, what we both know and are comfortable with. Rayna, however, is new and exciting; she represents something fresh and different – dare I say: change.'

'Interesting. So you think the Freylarkai – perhaps even Lothnar himself – consciously, or maybe even subconsciously, desire change?'

'Exactly. That change is coming Thandor – I can feel it in my soul.'

'I think, perhaps, that you have let him stew long enough now, Guardian. Besides, I do not know how much longer I can maintain this pretence – the wound is fully healed.'

'Thanks Gal, I'm sure that will be enough. Oh, and call me Rayna – my friends call me Rayna.' she replied.

At the edge of her peripheral vision, she could sense Lothnar's steely gaze, as the Paladin maintained his unflinching stance, ready to engage. If her hunch was right, Lothnar's current emotional state was almost certainly tempestuous – evidenced by his stony demeanour. It was time now to heed the Knight Lord's council and act upon the advice given to her by Heldran, during her secondment to the Knights Thranis.

'Very well – Rayna.' replied Galadrick with a warm smile, before taking his leave to join the others renewalists, gathered by the east gate.

She rose to her feet, prompting another loud cheer from the crowd, and flexed her right arm, trying to relax its newly healed muscles. Turning her head towards Marcus, she nodded courteously, signalling her desire to continue with the duel, after which she focused her gaze on her opponent once more.

'Are you ready?' she whispered to herself.

'*Of course – you forget that I know him Rayna, well enough to believe that this ruse of yours might actually work.*'

She tightened her grip on her falchions, narrowed her eyes and stared intently at Lothnar, waiting for the inevitable signal from The Blade Lord.

'Engage!'

The crowd screamed and shouted once more, as she charged, yet again, headlong towards Lothnar. Once more, the Paladin made no attempt to close the distance between them, content to let her expend energy by doing so. Before entering the reach of his weapon, she misplaced her footing, causing her to trip and crash into the dusty floor of the arena. Her grip loosened on her blades immediately upon impact, allowing them to slide across the floor, well beyond her reach. Her vision temporarily blacked out, due to the hard impact, though promptly returned when a firm grasp on her right shoulder violently rolled her over, forcing her to stare into the face of her opponent. Lothnar held his right arm above her, ready to rain down his dirk and drive it through her left shoulder.

'Lothnar – it is me!' she said, perfectly mimicking Alarielle's tone of voice and facial mannerisms.

Confused, Lothnar hesitated, staring at her in silent horror, as though having just witnessed a ghost. The sudden unorthodox distraction afforded her the opportunity she sought; using Lothnar's own teachings – imparted through Alarielle – she deftly drew the dirk, still attached to her belt, with her right hand. With enhanced speed, courtesy of her benefactor's repeated intervention, she thrust the blade upwards, towards the bemused Paladin's left shoulder. Lothnar reacted instinctively, attempting to deflect the weapon's trajectory with his free arm; he narrowly blocked the dirk, forcing her to miss its intended target, but the Paladin's lack of focus meant that she caught his forearm with the deflected strike. Visibly enraged, Lothnar rained down the dirk in his right hand. His facial expressions betrayed his intent, affording her the opportunity to block his own attack. She raised her free arm, but its awkward placement prevented her from successfully deflecting his attack. Instead, the Paladin's dirk impaled her left palm, stopped only by his hand, firmly clasped around the weapon's grip.

'Damn it!' he thundered furiously, aware that his forearm was in fact bleeding.

Angrily, Lothnar yanked the dirk violently from her hand, sending blood through the air. She cried out in pain, her body now registering the severity of the wound. Grinding her teeth, she tried to suppress the agony she felt, yet she was unable to hold back the tears gathering along her lower eyelids. The crowd were on their feet yet again, but the familiar shouts and cheers abruptly gave way to gasps, and other sounds of disbelief. Irrespective of the considerable number of the spectators who had clearly supported her during the duel, it was apparent now that, despite their enthusiasm, very few had actually expected her to win the engagement. Shocked by the unexpected outcome, the volume in the arena dropped rapidly as the stunned audience began to wrap their minds around what they had just witnessed.

'Damn it!' said Lothnar aloud once more. 'You have *no* honour!' he shouted, ensuring that the entire audience clearly heard his words.

Cradling her bloody left hand, she rolled onto her side, using her right hand to push herself upright. Rising to her feet, she slowly turned to face the infuriated Paladin, ready to defend her actions.

'Enough! Since my arrival in Freylar, I have tolerated your disparaging remarks, but there shall be no more – this is the end of the matter!' she said, in a commanding tone. 'Whilst you may not approve of my methods, regardless, you were beaten – deal with it. I was never going to surpass your skill with the blade, even with Nathaniel's teachings. You rank amongst the best of us Lothnar. It will be a great many passes before I come close to your level of combat prowess. For me to have faced you in a contest of physical skill alone, in this arena, would have been folly.'

'So your incessant training was what – some kind of ruse?'

'Partially; I required a degree of skill to make our duel look convincing. However, someone told me *"There is no respect in combat. Release your opponent and do it quickly, any way you can, lest they do the same to you."* – I believe in those words. The Narlakai have no concept of honour, neither do the Ravnarkai; affording either such, invites release. We cannot indulge in such fanciful nobility if we are to defeat Freylar's enemies, nor could I offer you the same if I was to stand any chance at defeating you, Lothnar.'

'You fought dirty!'

'I fought and won.' she replied, pointedly. 'If you asked it of me, I would gladly fight *alongside* you, not against you – I would have your back until the end, defending our people by *any* means necessary. Lothnar, I respect you.'

Following her words, she offered the Paladin an olive branch in the form of her good hand, whilst still cradling her left, which continued to drip blood onto the dusty floor. She fixed her gaze intently on Lothnar, staring earnestly at him. Now was not the time for her typically playful demeanour; Lothnar was a proud Freylarkin, and further embarrassing the Paladin would only widen the gulf between them.

'Please Lothnar, let me fight alongside you.'

THIRTEEN
Portent

Together, they lingered by the end of the passage, which led into the arena. They were careful to remain out of sight throughout the duel, yet they managed to snatch the occasional glimpse of the fight that routinely brought the crowd to its feet. Regardless of the outcome, the encounter would be analysed and discussed for passes to come - she regretted not being able to take her place alongside Mirielle for the occasion. However, her sister desperately required her support, and she would not abandon her for a second time. Although she had successfully calmed her nerves once already, they promptly returned when a collective gasp from the audience suggested that their time grew short. Knowing the likely repercussions that their actions would incite only increased her anxiety.

'Are you ready?' she asked, turning to her sister.

'I am nervous.'

'We both are, but we must stand resolute when we do this.'

The noise from the arena died suddenly; they both listened keenly to the ensuing discussion between the combatants, desperately hoping that Rayna's promised outcome had indeed come to fruition. There was an ominous lull in the heated dialogue, during which The Guardian extended her hand, offering Lothnar the chance to forge a new relationship between them. She could sense the audience holding their breath as the proud Paladin considered the chance to make amends. After what seemed like an eternity, Lothnar grabbed Rayna's hand, shaking it once, firmly. Thunderous applause filled the arena, the likes of which she had never previously witnessed. Her heart thumped loudly in her chest against the backdrop of the crowds' fervent clapping, which echoed down the passage behind them. Sensing their time had come, Vorian promptly appeared from the gloom of the passage; the Knight's unfazed appearance and piercing blue eyes set the tone for what they were about to do – she hoped dearly that she would emulate his demeanour when facing Mirielle and the citizens of Freylar.

'It is time.' said Vorian matter-of-factly. 'You must be the one to lead us out, Kirika. Both Darlia and I will flank you.'

'Agreed.' she said, turning to face the arena, and her destiny.

The time for musing and worry was over. Steeling her nerves, she stepped out of the gloom and into the arena, marching directly towards its centre, paying little notice to its combatants. Playing their part well, both Lothnar and Rayna offered her – and her entourage – a cold hard stare; all had agreed that the unannounced interruption needed to appear authentic, not staged. Once more, the applause from the crowd died abruptly, replaced instead with murmurs and whisperings as the audience tried to understand the meaning of the unexpected disruption. Continuing with their resolute march, they made their way to the centre of the arena, where they stopped to address Freylar's queen and The Blade Lord. It was clear that few – if any – of the Freylarkai actually recognised her sister; Darlia continued to conceal her identity well beneath her generous robe. However, despite the subterfuge, The Blade Lord, Nathaniel and a handful of others rose to their feet, fixing their gaze intently on her sister.

'What is the meaning of this, Kirika?' asked Marcus, calmly.

'Please forgive the interruption, though I have news which cannot be delayed – under any circumstance.' she replied, working hard to suppress any signs of nervousness in her voice.

'You have *our* attention.' replied Marcus, narrowing his eyes.

'Freylar is being invaded – *now!*'

The audience gasped at her words; no doubt the previous invasion was still fresh in their minds.

'What?!' snapped Mirielle, who promptly rose to her feet. 'There is no invasion.'

'With respect, Freylar's scouts were garrisoned in the wake of the massacre at Scrier's Post – *we* have been blind to this renewed threat.'

'Kirika, what proof do you bring of this claim?' asked Marcus firmly.

The Blade Lord looked to Vorian, before turning his attention to her sister, where his gaze lingered uncomfortably.

'This is Vorian, from the Knights Thranis – I believe The Guardian has already met him.' she said, turning to Rayna for validation.

'Yes, we have met – it is good to see you again Vor.' replied Rayna, taking a step towards them.

'The telepath responsible for inciting the Narlakai is herding them once more towards Freylar. This information has been confirmed by the Knights Thranis, and was brought to my attention by my *sister*.'

Following Kirika's cue, she pulled back her hood and revealed her mechanical claw, previously hidden beneath the folds in her robe. Mirielle regarded her in mute horror, whilst silent panic began to spread throughout the civilian Freylarkai. Even The Blade Lord appeared taken aback by her presence, evidenced by his lack of words. Ultimately, Captain Ragnar spoke first, in his typical blunt manner.

'You have the *audacity* to bring that witch here?! Are you mad?' asked Ragnar angrily, directing his rage towards her sister.

Kirika was about to retort, before she interrupted by raising her prosthetic hand, with its menacing claws fully outstretched.

'You need not defend me, sister.' she said calmly, 'I did not come here of my own volition, expecting to be welcomed.'

'Why are you here?' asked Lothnar tersely, advancing several paces to stand alongside The Guardian. 'You realise that the punishment for an exile's return is release?'

She glanced towards Lothnar, who offered her a disapproving sneer. Although he was simply playing the role assigned to him – and playing it well – she wondered if the Paladin's condescending facial expression was in fact sincere.

'I am aware, though the fact that I court release is not important.' she replied, now turning her attention back to Queen Mirielle and The Blade Lord. 'I have not come here to seek forgiveness. I am – in part at least – responsible for the crimes that transpired at Scrier's Post, but I am not the one who drove the Narlakai towards the sanctuary. Her name is Lileah. She has rebuilt her forces, and marches on Freylar with her black host. Lileah has one goal: to release you all!'

Her blunt words stunned the panicking audience, bringing with it a surreal sense of temporary clam.

'*If* what you say is true, why would you help us?' asked Marcus, sternly.

'*You* did this to me, Marcus.' she said, raising her mechanical claw once more, prompting further gasps from the audience. 'For many passes I wanted nothing more than to rip out your throat, with this *thing* that has now replaced my hand, which you severed in your obedient service to *her*.'

'Take her away!' commanded Mirielle sternly, directing her gaze towards one of the house guards stationed inside the arena.

'Delay that!' replied Kirika, inciting an even louder gasp from the audience. 'Darlia speaks the truth – this time you *will* hear my sister out!'

'Guards, get her out of here!' cried Mirielle irritably.

'Time and experience have altered my perspective; I have made peace with my physical punishment – I no longer *hate* you Marcus, for blindly carrying out the will of our queen. I accept my physical deformity, and the deterrent it represents, however, the punishment of exile was too great, and one that no Freylarkin should be made to endure; the forced separation from loved ones, and our kin, is unjust – the sentence did not fit the crime. Nevertheless, despite the injustice I suffered, I have no desire to see my kin, and indeed my sister, released – especially due to the events set in motion by our queen.'

'Take her now!' cried Mirielle angrily.

'Ralnor, please stand down.' her sister commanded, turning to face the advancing guard. 'You know me – the young unconfident female who grew up in the forest, who now spends her every waking moment serving the people.

You know that I would do anything to protect our kin, even if it means suffering our queen's ire. Please, heed my sister's warning – she speaks the truth, despite her past transgressions.'

The guard hesitated upon hearing her sister's words. She too knew Ralnor, from her misspent youth, and saw the mutual recognition in the Freylarkin's conflicted eyes.

'I lost my Aspirants due to your feud with our queen,' Nathaniel interjected, 'I have no desire to witness the release of any more of our kin. If what you say is true, let *him* validate your claim.' continued The Teacher, pointing his right hand towards Lothnar.

'Will you consent?' The Blade Lord promptly followed.

'Very well – if you need further proof of my claim, so be it. However, I ask that my privacy be respected.'

'Something to hide?!' sneered the Captain of The Blades disdainfully.

Ignoring the Captain's disparaging quip, Marcus nodded towards Lothnar, giving the Paladin the required authorisation to violate her mind – for a second time. She readied herself, as best she could, knowing first-hand the extent of the mental anguish to come, as Lothnar fixed his steely gaze on her. Again, she felt his mind touch her own, although the experience was very different to the rough encounter she had previously endured.

'I have little interest in raking through your mind for a second time – it would be cruel and unfair. That said, you need to put on a good show, therefore, I will share some personal insights with you. If the Freylarkai see sense in your words, and subsequently march out to meet your lover in battle, know that I will personally seek an audience with Lileah. I will offer her no mercy, only a slow and agonising

release. In that moment, she will experience the full extent of the pain she has visited upon our kin – I will make certain of it. This I promise you!'

After delivering his private message, the Paladin promptly disengaged his connection to her mind. His vehement delivery left her feeling numb and empty. The callous words burned in her mind, leaving room for little else. She wiped the tears from her eyes, which threatened to roll down her cheeks, and nodded slowly in acceptance. She knew that Lileah had humiliated the proud scout, but now it was apparent that she had robbed him of something more than simple pride. Curiosity demanded that she use her second sight to discern the exact cause of Lothnar's hurt, yet frivolous use of her ability had been the catalyst for her current lot. The Paladin's cold promise sent a chill up her spine, causing her to tremble visibly; from a dramatic perspective, Lothnar had achieved his goal – she hoped dearly that he would not realise the other.

'She speaks the truth.' Lothnar said aloud, ensuring that everyone present heard his words.

'Take her away!' Mirielle repeated once more.

'No. We need to meet this threat head on, on the field of battle, and my sister must join us – she is the only one who can possibly get through to Lileah, and potentially avert further conflict.' replied Kirika.

'How?!' Mirielle snapped in return.

'Lileah and I were lovers. Though I cannot condone her current course of action, nonetheless, I still have feelings for her – I expect the reverse to also be true. I may be able to talk her down.'

'You expect me to believe your deceitful words?'

'I have not lied, nor do I do so now.'

'Marcus, we *need* her.' said Kirika firmly.

'Agreed.' said Rayna, whose words prompted the full attention of the audience. 'At the very least, Darlia will serve as a useful distraction when we march out to meet the enemy – and you all know how I favour a good distraction.'

'You want to march out – meet the Narlakai head on?'

'Marcus, we *cannot* fight them in the vale.' replied Rayna.

The Guardian's words resonated with the audience, prompting verbal affirmation from a number of the concerned spectators.

'You do not need to remind me; indeed, we are left with little choice in the matter, so it would seem.' replied Marcus, who shifted his critical gaze towards her sister. 'Knight Vorian, what counsel do you offer, given your timely presence?'

'I second The Guardian's favoured course of action.' replied Vorian efficiently, wasting no time on unnecessary dialogue.

There was a long pause, during which The Blade Lord carefully studied those standing before him. She could *feel* his stare, as though it were something tangible, whilst he regarded them with a critical eye. It was clear – to her at least – that Marcus saw through their carefully orchestrated façade, however, the overwhelming evidence, and Rayna's sway over the crowd, left him little room to manoeuvre.

'My queen, the evidence supports the exile's claim – I advise that we act accordingly, and with haste.'

'I will not be forced to send the Freylarkai to war!' replied Mirielle, tersely.

'War is already upon us! We must defend ourselves, and meet this threat head on.' said Kirika firmly, stoking further support from the crowd.

The public support of her sister, Vorian and The Guardian, in addition to Lothnar's validation, ensured that her claim was irrefutable. They had successfully forced the hand of Freylar's queen; Mirielle had no choice but to accept her course of action. Kirika had made the right decision to follow through with Rayna's bold strategy. If they had been brought solely to the ruling council's attention behind closed doors, her words would have been dismissed outright – or worse, disseminated in line with Mirielle's own agenda. Instead, the truth was now freely available in the public domain, laid bare for all and sundry. Mirielle's face was awash with anger, as Freylar's queen recognised the weak position she held in the matter. Watching Mirielle's choler rise was bittersweet; despite having successfully warned her kin of Lileah's intent, she had also damned her lover in the process. Though her own future was unclear – due to The Guardian's involvement – Lileah's own followed a path to certain ruin; failure would see Lileah released by Lothnar's hand, but success promised a hollow existence, devoid of love and full of hatred. Her ability was a curse; she could revisit the past with unerring clarity, yet she could do nothing to alter those events that had already come to pass.

'The defence of Freylar is your responsibility Marcus, therefore, I will be guided by *your* counsel, and not that of an exile.' replied Mirielle, offering her sister a hard stare.

'As you wish, my queen. Captain,' commanded Marcus, turning to Ragnar, 'Ready The Blades for battle!'

'Kirika, a word alone, please.' said Marcus.

The Blade Lord quickly guided her towards an isolated spot at the edge of the arena, which was rapidly filling up with Blades, all preparing for war.

'Who else was involved in this little *stunt* of yours?'

'You know that I cannot answer that question Marcus.' she said, determined – at the very least – not to patronise The Blade Lord.

'*If* we survive this, you realise that there will be repercussions?'

'Of course – and I shall meet them head on.'

'Whilst I am glad that you have finally found your voice, this was clearly not the right forum for the occasion.'

'I disagree. The Queen would have dismissed my sister's claim out of hand, if not for the external pressures this forum ultimately provided.'

'You used your relationship with Rayna to capture the mood of the people, and thus their support; did you manipulate her into helping you with this dangerous strategy of yours?'

'Do not underestimate her Marcus.'

'Well then, perhaps I have underestimated you both – know that it will not happen again.'

They both paused for a moment, staring into each other's eyes, attempting to discern whether their mutual trust had been broken. Although her actions had not stained Marcus' own reputation, nonetheless, she had allowed her professional courtesy to lapse, by failing to forewarn The Blade Lord of her intent.

'You are loyal to the queen, but she is not the leader she once was, Marcus – you must know this.'

'This is neither the time nor the place to discuss the matter.'

'Very well, then what about my sister – do I have your word that she will be unharmed?'

'You have it, but know this: she is *your* responsibility now Kirika, at least until all this is over. Should we somehow manage to repel her lover's invasion, Darlia's fate will be decided by the ruling council – is that clear?'

'Understood.'

'Good. Now do us both a favour and remove her from Mirielle's sight.'

'You know I respect you Marcus. It had to be this way, due to the urgency.'

Marcus did not respond, instead The Blade Lord offered her a subtle nod, before turning his attention back to The Blades, who were still hurriedly assembling in the arena. She watched for a moment, in awe, as the Freylarkin responsible for the domain's defence commanded The Blades effortlessly, setting them to purpose. Typically, during such moments, Freylar's soldiers rallied behind the Captain, whilst awaiting direction from The Blade Lord himself. It was interesting viewing, therefore, watching many of The Blades present flock towards The Guardian, seeking motivational sermons from their newest icon, elevated by the unexpected win over Lothnar. Curious to see how the situation before her would unfold, she moved to join her sister for a better view, who stood lost in the middle of the arena, amidst the growing tempest of gathering Blades.

'What is to be my fate?' asked Darlia, as she arrived at her sister's side.

'Amnesty – for the time being at least. But after this battle is fought, we shall have another on our hands.'

'You believe that we can win this war then?'

'I believe in you…and in *her.*' she replied, tipping her head towards Rayna, and the growing number of Blades standing between them.

Before she could finish her train of thought, Kayla swiftly joined them, along with the rest of her aides, each clamouring for her attention.

'Kirika, what do you need us to do?' asked Kayla, who had a concerned look about her. 'The Queen has left the arena, and we need guidance.'

She cast her gaze towards the front row of tiered stone seating, and the notable absence of their queen.

'Where did Mirielle go?' she asked, whilst scanning the increasing number of empty seats.

'We do not know.' replied Kayla.

'I see.'

'Do you want us to begin evacuating the vale, as before?'

'No, not this time.' she said, much to Kayla's obvious surprise. 'Lileah will crash upon us like a hammer – there will be no clever trickery this time. We must do everything we can to reinforce the war effort. Coordinate with the smithies to have them bring every available arrow, brazier and torch to the front line. In addition, please gather as much tinder and any wadding you can procure from the seamstresses. Fire will not destroy the Narlakai, but the light from the flames will slow their advance.'

'Understood.'

'Also, ensure that The Blades are well stocked – they need to keep their strength up, and we do not know how long they will be in the field before engaging the enemy.'

'As you wish.' replied Kayla enthusiastically.

With renewed purpose, her closest aide turned to the others and began assigning duties. She loathed being followed around by her entourage, however, she found it immensely useful being able to delegate tasks.

'I see you have done well for yourself during my absence.' said Darlia, who keenly observed Kayla instructing the other aides.

'They make my position viable, nothing more. I have no interest in the perceived level of influence or the attention they bring.'

'There are many who would crave such authority, even if only an illusionary thing.'

'Indeed – but I am not one of them. I just want to serve the people Darlia, to the best of my ability, and help guide them along a safe path. Mirielle is confused – her judgement is impaired.'

'I too wanted to guide the Freylarkai, although I mistakingly thought that I could do so using my ability alone. I did not believe the excessive use of scrying would lead to my downfall – I see now that it is a dangerous obsession, attempting to understand every facet of what is to come – on that point, at least, Mirielle and I are in agreement.'

'I believe that her views have since changed, Darlia. Mirielle seeks to control our kind through the illusion of freedom, but freedom must be real – false hope only leads to discontent.'

'You are referring to the more recent events at Scrier's Post, I assume?'

'Yes, although I also question her judgement on other recent issues, including dismissing the curfew.' she said, thoughtfully.

'It is likely that Krashnar still lingers in the vale. Allowing the people to believe otherwise, without confirmation, is pure folly. This public spectacle should have been postponed until he is apprehended, or his lack of presence is confirmed.'

'Darlia, I agree with you, but the decision was not mine.'

'You are a member of the ruling council.'

'What ruling council? Marcus is loyal to Mirielle and will not challenge her, ergo my voice carries little sway in our council meetings. Occasionally I am able to influence Marcus on matters, and in turn, massage Mirielle's thought processes. However, that relationship is now damaged; his trust in me has waned due to my actions this cycle.'

'Kirika, the fate of our domain should not rest upon a single Freylarkin – that was the guiding principle upon which the ruling council was founded.'

'Agreed, but that principle has long since been abandoned. Aleska still bends Mirielle's ear, and Marcus is loyal to a fault – I cannot change this state of affairs by myself. The council is broken: three members is insufficient.'

'A moment ago, you said that you believe in me, and I appreciate your faith. You should know that the reverse is also true: I believe in *you*, Kirika, and that is why I risked returning to the vale. Furthermore, you are no longer alone in your campaign.' noted Darlia, directing her gaze towards Rayna, now barely visible beyond the throng of Blades before them. 'You have the support of Rayna – along with those who fervently follow her – in addition to your aides, who clearly value your leadership. Nathaniel will also back you, and – for what it is worth – you have me.'

'Thank you. Your support means a great deal to me, especially given how I wronged you.'

'You opposed the decision to exile me.'

'Still, I could not present a case compelling enough to overturn the decision.'

'Mirielle sought to make an example of me; I became a deterrent, another means of control, to ensure that her subjects would not surpass her own prowess. There were others before me – other exiles – Krashnar being one, each of whom Mirielle perceived as a threat to her rule. No amount of compelling reasoning would have dissuaded her, Kirika.'

Darlia's absolution was almost too much to bear – she deserved no such pardon. Though she had indeed opposed her sister's punishment, nonetheless, she was a part of the committee responsible for Darlia's sentencing. For passes she had flagellated herself emotionally, due to her guilt by association. Yet despite the injustice Darlia had suffered, her sister now took a pragmatic approach when analysing the miserable events. She smiled at Darlia through watery eyes; the act prompted her sister to follow suit, though before either could succumb to the onset of tears, Rayna finally spoke, deciding at last to address the host of expectant Blades gathered in attendance.

FOURTEEN
Reverence

'Thandor, are you coming?'

'You go ahead – I want to catch up with Lothnar, before we march on the Narlakai.'

'Very well, I will see you later.'

Abandoning the aloof Paladin to pursue his own agenda, she vaulted over the low wall separating the seating area from the arena floor, and made her way towards the growing number of Blades gathering before The Guardian. Standing tall amidst the throng was Nathanar, who until now had been strangely absent from the arena.

'Nathanar, hey!' she cried, seeking to gain the attention of The Blades' newest Paladin.

Nathanar turned to face her with his piercing blue eyes, softened only by his welcoming smile.

'Where were you – did you see the duel?' she said, eager to canvas his thoughts.

'Apologies for my absence, Natalya, I was busy preparing for my own trials. Though I did manage to glimpse the duel from the east passage.'

Before he could speak further, the ambient chatter suddenly abated, as The Guardian motioned to speak. They both stared intently at Rayna, eager to understand how their enigmatic Blade sister intended to motivate her eager followers.

'Ironic – the last time you all stood before me, I had to blind you all to get your attention. Now each of you stands here, freely, of your own volition, yet I have not sought as much. I see you looking at me, perhaps expecting some kind of clever ploy or strategy to thwart the enemy, but the truth is, I do not have one – at least, not yet!' said Rayna, followed by a playful wink, which incited laughter from the crowd. 'I believe that last time I mentioned something about getting out of bed – that's still true. We sent these horrors back to the abyss once already, with little more than a detachment of freshly trained recruits. This time the Narlakai will face our combined might; together, we will drive them back into the void, else they will feel the wrath of our imbued weapons. This is not an expression of wish, or an empty proclamation – this is fact! When we march on Bleak Moor, we do so with the following in mind: either Darlia finds a way to end this peacefully…or we end the Narlakai!'

Rayna clenched her left hand – still requiring the attention of a renewalist – allowing blood to drip from the ball of her fist onto the floor, signalling her bloody oath.

'Who amongst you will join me, and send these horrors back to the abyss?'

'I will join you!' cried Nathanar unexpectedly.

Nathanar typically spoke with a soft voice, but now The Blades' newest Paladin made his presence felt.

Nathanar drew a dirk attached to his belt, then cut his left palm. He clenched his hand into a tight fist then re-opened the palm, before raising it high above his head, allowing blood from the minor self-inflicted wound to trickle down the length of his arm. Inspired by Rayna's words, and emboldened by Nathanar's unforeseen actions, she requested the dirk from the Paladin and followed suit.

'I too will join you!' she cried passionately, swept up in the moment.

Following her proclamation, several Blades standing to her right unsheathed similar blades of their own, and promptly repeated the action, swearing the same blood oath as she had done. All around them, more Blades swore the same oath, before raising their bloody hands in affirmation. Before long, the entire congregation had followed in Nathanar's stead.

'See what you have gone and done – some role model you turned out to be.' she whispered quietly to Nathanar, whilst grinning from ear to ear.

The Paladin offered her a sidelong smile, before turning his attention back to Rayna, who stood defiantly at the head of the congregation. Unsurprisingly, the display of fealty had not gone unnoticed. The Blade Lord, accompanied by the Captain of The Blades, quickly wandered over to sate their curiosity. Marcus' face bore a curious expression, as he cast his analytical eyes over the impromptu gathering, before finally she felt The Blade Lord's gaze fixed intently on her. She considered lowering her hand, but that was not her style – Marcus knew as much.

'I expect this sort of behaviour from you, Natalya,' said Marcus, widening his eyes, 'but *you*…Nathanar, you surprise me.'

'What a bloody mess.' said Ragnar gruffly, who bore a discreet grin of approval.

'Quite – I had hoped to engage the Narlakai with our renewalists at full strength.' said Marcus sternly. 'At any rate, get yourselves cleaned up – once you are done here. Oh, and Rayna, you can lead *this* new-found flock of yours; when the time comes, your detachment will be at the forefront of the offensive, alongside the Captain, who will lead the charge.'

Ragnar flashed his teeth with a wide smile; his talents were wasted behind a bench, managing The Blades' mundane daily affairs. It was common knowledge that the

Captain craved the field of battle, and the glory of victory. Now, with the Narlakai bearing down on them, Ragnar would once again be in a position to answer his true calling. Having made their presence felt, both Marcus and Ragnar returned to the heart of the arena and continued to coordinate preparations for the battle to come. When the Narlakai invaded Scrier's Post, there had been a sense of dread and anxiety amongst The Blades. By contrast, the atmosphere now had a more fervent feel. Despite their losses during the recent invasion, The Blades were now eager to engage the enemy, no doubt keen to deliver a measure of vengeance.

'Oooh…that is going to leave a blemish on your otherwise perfect record.' she said, teasing Nathanar.

'Behave yourself.'

She smiled in the face of Nathanar's retort – it was good to see the tall Freylarkin's disposition finally ease. For passes, Nathanar had been a stickler for Blade doctrine – never one to go against the grain. Yet since his command at Scrier's Post, something had changed in the Freylarkin. Although a far cry from her own carefree disposition, nonetheless, the Paladin was developing signs of a rebellious nature, much to her admiration. She turned her attention back to Rayna, and thought back on the events that had transpired since The Guardian's impromptu arrival in Freylar. Despite not being responsible for the recent turbulent affairs, which now plagued their domain, nonetheless, Rayna's presence was somewhat of a catalyst. The Guardian's unorthodox approach – to just about everything – had caused the Freylarkai to review, perhaps even question, their own actions and way of life, prompting some to step outside of their comfort zones. Rayna had introduced a sense of non-conformaty to the Freylarkai, by demonstrating that, with enough determination, virtually anything was possible. Before Rayna's arrival, the eager flames of such mischievous heralds had been snuffed out – Darlia being a case in point. However, The Guardian's demi-god status had allowed Rayna to avoid such end. The icon they had discussed, that night by the fire, was now manifesting before them, drawing towards it those who welcomed change. She could feel The Guardian's presence pulling her closer, yet she did not intend to fight it – she wondered if Nathanar felt the same.

'You heard The Blade Lord – it looks like we will be the ones sending the Narlakai home!' said Rayna, with a mischievous grin.

Loud cheers and applause broke out amongst the gathered Blades, and those who had lowered their bloody hands quickly raised them once more. It was naïve to think that they would each return from their confrontation with the Narlakai, or even win the impending battle. However, with The Guardian now leading them, *if* they failed to return, it would not be through lack of effort.

'What is going on? Where are you running to?' she shouted tersely, as a group of house guards ran straight past her, without so much as acknowledging her presence.

Her body was tense – like a coiled spring – and the muscles in her neck were stiff. Since Darlia's return, during the Trials, she had been on edge, more so than normal. She had not expected to see the disgraced scrier again, not since Darlia's public exile and the physical punishment bestowed by Marcus. However, Darlia's return was not the sole reason for her anger – Kirika's actions alone were reason enough for her dark mood. She desperately needed to relax and unwind, although she could not hope to do so with the eyes of the people constantly watching her, analysing her actions, wondering how she would react to the sisters' public display of defiance. It galled her knowing that Kirika had circumvented her authority so brazenly in public. She needed to return to the Tri-Spires and collect her thoughts, yet her attempt to do so now appeared to be in jeopardy, due to the growing panic manifesting in the alleys surrounding the arena.

'Apologies my queen.' replied one of the guards, who promptly doubled back following her summons. 'There has been an incident; some kind of abomination has been sighted in the streets.'

'Show me.'

'With respect, my queen, you should not--'

'Show me now!' she snapped, uninterested in the guard's concern for her personal safety.

The guard looked startled by her reaction, and was clearly confused as to how to respond. No doubt Marcus had impressed upon them the importance of her safety, but she refused to be caged by his security protocols any longer.

'If you are concerned about The Blade Lord, do not be – my authority trumps his own, as I am sure you well appreciate.'

'Yes, my queen – please, follow me.'

The guard slowed his pace to that of a brisk walk, due to her cumbersome attire. As Freylar's queen, she was duty-bound to look the part during public events. However, her long thick dress, which she had chosen specifically for the Trials, was far from conducive to running along the streets surrounding the arena. She cursed the trappings of finery hindering her pace, desiring nothing more than to be free of their regal yoke. After turning down a number of alleys, the ambient noise level increased dramatically, so too the number of Freylarkai loitering in the streets, a good number of whom were shouting and panicking.

'Calm down!' she cried, trying hard to make her voice heard above the raucous onlookers.

Several members of the crowd moved aside as the guards forced their way along the street towards the source of the disturbance. The gathered Freylarkai parted before them, allowing her to catch a glimpse of the abomination that had riled the bystanders. Crawling awkwardly on the floor, in tandem, were two naked Freylarkai – both female – fused together at the torso, one in front of the other. Adjacent to the unnatural pairing was the renowned dressmaker, Larissa, who she quickly recognised, having previously procured her services. Larissa was crouched alongside the arachnoid creature, trying her best to comfort the victims, despite the scared and angry mob surrounding them. After her initial shock, she took a deep breath and pushed her way towards the centre of the chaos, whilst the guards did their best to suppress the growing crowd.

'How did this happen?'

'The exile, Krashnar – he did this!' replied Larissa, angrily.

'Where is he now?' she asked, concerned now that he would soon strike again.

'We do not know; he saw fit to work his ghastly touch on Cora and Hanarah, only to then abandon them. That Freylarkin is a monster!'

The names were familiar – she had heard them before – but she failed to place them. She wondered if perhaps the unfortunate pair were related. Regardless, it was clear that they desperately required aid.

'Please, my queen, will you help them?'

'I am not sure that I can.' she said reticently, taken aback by Larissa's plea.

'But you are a powerful shaper – you alone built the Tri-Spires.'

'Yes, but…this requires manipulating the flesh – that is not my area of expertise.'

'But you have done it before; the gift of your eyes is testament to your ability.' Larissa pressed, trying earnestly to make her case.

'You do not understand. My eyes are not a gift – they are a curse! Besides, working the flesh permanently requires a sacrifice. If there is inadequate resource, more will be required – they would require a donor.'

'Forgive me, but I do not understand. Surely enough material is already present; he joined them together – I believe nothing was taken.'

'Even if that is indeed the case, Krashnar is a master of this abhorrent craft. I do not possess the skill or experience to work with such intolerances. I cannot separate them neatly, ergo, without additional resources I could inadvertently release them both.'

'Please, you must try!' implored Larissa, overstepping her boundary.

'Larissa, *I will* not take that risk.'

'Yet every cycle your decisions court risk, for all of us – *you* were the one who exiled Krashnar from our domain. Now he has returned, and we are the ones paying for that decision.'

'There is no "We" – this is one incident. Who can say what goes on in that shaper's deranged mind; likely the result of his self-experimentation.'

'With respect, my queen, you are wrong in this matter – it *is* we who are enduring his sadistic revenge, or have you forgotten Riknar? When she learns of her brother's fate, Keshar will not forget so easily!'

'Do not preach to me, Larissa,' she replied sternly, 'I do not require a lesson in history.'

'You owe it to them to at least try – they cannot exist like this.'

The presence of the guards only incited the crowd further, causing them to taunt and jeer whilst jostling to find positions to better observe the events unfolding.

'Please, help my daughter!' Hanarah meekly interjected, as the crowd condemned them once more. 'Whether I survive the separation is irrelevant – just ensure that my daughter is well.'

'You cannot ask this of me.'

'Cora is my daughter, and I have every right to ask this of you. The council saw fit to lift Kirika's curfew, falsely proclaiming our safety. Furthermore, it was you who exiled Krashnar, giving rise to this very situation.'

'I acted in the best interests of the people!' she replied vehemently.

The jeers from the crowd grew louder, making it difficult for her to think, let alone carry out the ugly request. She longed for Aleska's counsel once more – the venerable scrier was a skilled politician, and saw paths which she could not. Still, with her closest ally busy, beyond the reach of the vale tending to other important affairs, she was alone, again. Doing nothing would only incite her people further, but carrying out Larissa's request was risky, with a high chance of failure. Once again, the burden of leadership weighed heavily upon her. Regardless of her decision, the outcome would inevitably be the same; she felt her soul erode with each impossible decision. Tipping back her head, she looked to the sky and silently cursed the thing that lingered there. Were such events preordained, she mused; perhaps this was how the entity fed, slowly digesting the souls it ensnared by introducing them to pain, anguish and despair.

'I beg you – please, save my daughter!' said Hanarah, effectively making the decision for her.

'Very well…'

'No! Mother, you cannot!'

'Cora, this is not *your* choice. One cycle you will have children of your own – then you will understand.'

'Mother, no!' Cora protested, before weeping inconsolably.

'Larissa, help me get them inside, I need to concentrate – I cannot attempt this here.'

How delicious, he thought to himself, amusedly. The Freylarkai were so easily distracted. He wondered if perhaps there was even a need to impersonate anyone else, given how easy it had been to draw out the house guards.

'So much for Marcus' security protocols.' he muttered hoarsely, before spitting at the ground in open disgust.

Realising the error of his actions, he briefly glanced around – there was no one present. Fortunately, his ill-conceived behaviour had gone unnoticed. After quietly chiding himself, he commenced his infiltration of Mirielle's egotistical structure, safe in the knowledge that his stolen identity continued to serve him well. Ultimately, news of the store proprietors would spread to the Tri-Spires, thus mitigating his disguise. However, this inevitability was of little concern to him. By the time news of his latest work eventually reached to the Tri-Spires, the opportunity – provided by his newest creation – would have been spent. The Freylarkai were naturally inquisitive, a racial trait which fit neatly in with his plans. Unable to contain his excitement, he laughed cruelly again to himself, before disappearing into the organic-looking warren at the base of the Tri-Spires. Although still getting used to his newly adopted female form, he made good progress as he hastily made his way through the structure, along countless winding polished granite tunnels. Eventually, after a number of wrong turns, he found the small antechamber adjoining the Waystone chamber itself, which provided access to the spires. Surprisingly, the antechamber was also unguarded; Mirielle's absence from the structure, in addition to his creative distraction, had stretched security unworkably thin. However, his run of luck quickly ended after passing through into the Waystone chamber beyond, where a lone guard promptly approached him.

'Please state your business.'

Without even bothering to acknowledge the guard, he thrust his right hand towards the Freylarkin's face. Grasping the unsuspecting guard's cheeks with his grubby fingers, he pushed the Freylarkin's lips together vertically, which he then fused, making a complete mess of the hapless guard's face.

'My business is none of yours.' he rasped, before flashing a wicked grin.

Having silenced his prey, he used his unnatural strength to knock the guard backwards off his feet, towards the Waystone promising him access to his prize. The defeated guard flew briefly through the air, before crashing violently against the Waystone's pedestal in a crumpled heap. He could feel the darkness inside him, growing in strength; the parasite continued to feed off his macabre rapture, strengthening him in the process, in accordance with their mutually beneficial relationship. He laughed at the ruined mess lying before him; the unsuspecting guard was battered and bruised, possibly even released – either way, he cared not. The pathetic fleeting obstruction, which had sought to derail his ambition, was no longer a concern. He casually strolled towards the crumpled guard and touched the broken Freylarkin with the remaining digits of his left hand.

'Unfortunately, you cannot take a nap here.' he said aloud, regardless of his deaf audience.

With his free hand, he touched the Waystone leading to Mirielle's chamber. He grinned excitedly as his surroundings elongated and disappeared from sight.

'If we depart now, we should reach Bleak Moor during the night.'

'Ragnar, if we do that, we could find ourselves fighting both fatigue *and* the Narlakai.'

'I agree with the Captain.' Rayna interjected. 'If we delay, we could end up fighting this war in the vale.'

'I thank you for your counsel, Rayna, but your detachment needs you. Please see to their final preparations.'

Rayna smiled cordially, before returning to her newly assigned detachment. Although he had not deliberately intended to dismiss Rayna so flippantly, nonetheless, he needed space to think, and managing one impetuous light bringer was difficult enough.

'Kirika, how are your preparations coming along?'

'We have managed to secure ample wadding and torches – the rest we can do en route.'

He paused for a moment, hoping that some other solution would present itself, though none did. He was loath to rush into battle, but the circumstances demanded it. They could ill afford conflict in the vale, especially with Kirika foregoing an evacuation – which he agreed with. They had precious few light bringers during their last engagement with the Narlakai and, with the release of Kryshar, their ranks now numbered one fewer. In a war against the soul stealers, he needed every available trained light bringer, but there were simply not enough. Given the time constraints, he would have to make do with his lot, and use his resources creatively.

'Ragnar, signal The Blades to march out, as soon as preparations are complete. Kirika, you will march behind us – along with your sister – whilst completing your preparations.'

Both Kirika and Ragnar nodded in acceptance, before quickly scattering to complete their assigned duties.

He had hoped to gain a quiet word with Mirielle, prior to their departure, to both assess their queen's state of mind and clear the air. Darlia's portent, and the manner of its delivery, was akin to a stone cast into still water; the ripples of her actions were being felt across the domain, as the Freylarkai scrambled – once again – to meet this latest threat. In her soul, he knew that Mirielle valued the scrier's warning, but the way in which the information was received no doubt stung her pride. Of all the Freylarkai fate could have chosen to deliver such a message, it had to be one whom their queen had publicly denounced – as a threat to their domain no less. The irony was not lost on him. Indeed, there would be further political battles ahead, if they somehow weathered Lileah's renewed invasion.

'Have you seen the Queen?' he asked abruptly, as one of Kirika's aides passed within earshot.

'I am sorry my lord, but I have not – no one has. She left shortly after the interruption.'

'Thank you.'

He considered searching for Mirielle, but the timing was poor, and The Blades needed him more. Besides, the house guards had standing orders to escort her at all times, and she was not the vulnerable porcelain-faced Freylarkin some believed her to be – a Freylarkin capable of building the Tri-Spires, unaided, would certainly give an attacker cause for concern. Satisfied that the present circumstances were of sufficient import to keep him from their queen's side, he surveyed the arena once more, confirming that each Freylarkin present had purpose. Whilst casting his keen gaze around, he curiously spied Rayna conversing ardently with the Knight, Vorian, who still lingered in the arena. Amidst the initial chaos, he had all but forgotten about the lone knight. Now, as he watched them both talking enthusiastically, he began to wonder if there was more to the Knight's impromptu arrival. He was keenly aware of Rayna's new relationship with the Knights Thranis, having personally encouraged its development. However, he remained uncertain as to the extent of her newly forged ties to the estranged Order, and the robustness of the newly established trust between them. Rayna had provided a solid account of her secondment to the Order, however, it would be the details that told the full story – and she had yet to disseminate these. He had hoped to use Rayna's special relationship with the Knights to enlist their aid, but recent unforeseen events had expedited matters. Calling upon their assistance now, so soon after rebuilding the bridge between their Orders, would undoubtedly harm the fledgling relationship. Besides, time was short and Lileah's nightmarish host would soon be upon them – even with the aid of Sky-Skitters it would take too long to communicate with the Knights to be of use. Once again, The Blades would stand alone against the invading Narlakai horde, although on this occasion it would not be due to a lack of willingness, but caused instead by the pressing circumstances at hand. Still, his plan had not been entirely without fruit; Rayna's time spent with the Knights Thranis clearly had a positive influence on her ability to command and, given the present situation, he desperately needed those capable of command. Whilst the Paladins and Valkyries provided much-needed inspiration on the field of battle, and were themselves tremendously skilled fighters, few had the ability to lead – effectively at least. Although they could rally The Blades and bolster the ranks where needed, each rarely saw beyond the reach of their own ambitions. It would be an injustice to accuse them of being selfish, though it would be a fair assessment to liken them to a disfunctional family. Whilst The Blades needed their heroes, more importantly, they needed someone who could unite them. Since his ascension to the role of Blade Lord he had done well to heal the damage caused by his predecessor, but even he had struggled to get the Order pulling in the same direction. Rayna's exploits potentially offered him the opportunity to achieve something greater. In order to crystallise his ambitions, however, he needed to keep Rayna separated from the domain's politicking. Aside from her increasing demi-god status, it was The Guardian's raw purity, and determination to succeed, that endeared her to the Freylarkai. Regrettably, Mirielle's own disposition had hardened during recent events. Although he had achieved a measure of success in breaking down the barriers caused by her aloofness, nonetheless, her connection to the Freylarkai was noticeably weakening. Mirielle wielded the authority necessary to lead the people, but her charisma was lacking. If he could somehow align the pair and guide their combined direction, their influence would galvanise the Freylarkai and strengthen the domain. Perhaps this Lileah's rash invasion would provide him the opportunity to achieve such, he mused. Then again, if the vengeful Freylarkin succeeded, there would be little left remaining worthy of uniting.

FIFTEEN
Separation

'Natalya!'

She glanced over her shoulder to see a fleet-footed Freylarkin jogging towards her – it was Thandor. She smiled at seeing the Paladin work up a light sweat, before turning her attention back to the front of the column. Eventually the Paladin caught up with her and promptly fell into lockstep with the rest of her detachment.

'If I had known that you were not going to break step, I would not have bothered calling after you.'

'I like having you run around after me.' she said, with a wide smile.

'So I have noticed.'

'I thought you were assigned to Marcus' detachment?'

'That is correct. But we have had little chance to talk since we left the arena, and – truth be told – I needed the workout.'

'You do not fool me Thandor; you just want to know why I enlisted with The Guardian.'

'Not just you – Nathanar as well!'

'It was you who suggested that we might find our *icon* in the arena.' said Nathanar, who had clearly been eavesdropping on their conversation.

'That I did, although I had not expected you both to throw your lot in with Rayna so readily.'

'Well...I was bored; the Trials were over prematurely, Darlia had done her thing, and I needed further entertaining.' she said facetiously.

There was a brief pause in their conversation, before Thandor replied, 'I realise now that I have made a mistake – Marcus' company is in fact more stimulating.'

She smiled at Thandor once more – she enjoyed stringing the Paladin along whenever the opportunity presented itself, and appreciated his witty retorts, which habitually amused her.

'Nathanar, do you want to tell him, or shall I?'

'You mean to tell him to run back to Marcus?'

Thandor rolled his eyes at Nathanar's remark – it was rare that she vexed him to such extent.

'Her carefree attitude is rubbing off on you – that is in no way a good thing.'

They each smiled as they enjoyed the fleeting moment of friendly banter; in less than a cycle, there would be no smiling, not once The Blades stood across the Bleak Moor facing Lileah's army of darkness.

'I needed a change.' she said, at last choosing to answer Thandor's question properly. 'And how did your discussion go with Lothnar – was the duel fixed?'

'Apparently not. Rayna genuinely defeated him, albeit in an unorthodox manner – which he chose not to elaborate upon.'

'Hmm...'

'But your instincts had already confirmed as such – am I right?'

'Thandor, you are rarely ever wrong – it is one of your annoying traits.' she said, offering the Paladin some good-natured backhanded praise. 'Perhaps you should trust my instincts in future?'

'Perhaps I should...' replied Thandor. 'In any event, are you going to elaborate on your brief answer?'

'Rayna represents possibility, and her determination to succeed is infectious. She inspires those around her – take Kirika and her sister, Darlia, for example. These are traits which I admire, and besides, I was caught up in the moment, especially when this one raised his bloody hand.'

'Speaking of which, Nathanar, are you willing to disclose your own thoughts on the matter?' enquired Thandor, who was obviously keen to understand the reason for their decision to enlist with Rayna.

'At a purely local level, it is common knowledge that Ragnar does not desire captaincy over our Order.' replied Nathanar, who was still clearly listening to their conversation. 'Rayna would make a fine Captain, if granted the opportunity to grow into the role.'

'What makes you so certain – if I may ask?' queried Thandor, who seemed genuinely interested in Nathanar's private thoughts.

'I saw her raw abilities first-hand at Scrier's Post – she possesses the qualities required for the role: leadership, informed logical decision making, creative thinking…plus she fights well – she should not have beaten Lothnar, and yet she did.'

'Solid reasoning.'

'And what about you, Thandor? Now that you have heard our reasons, is it not time that you got off of that fence of yours and voiced your own?'

'First I want to see how this latest challenge plays out.'

'Thandor, sometimes you just need to go with your gut on these things. Perhaps you should take a leaf out of Nathanar's new playbook. Besides, it is not as though there is any love lost between you and Ragnar – would you not welcome a change in captaincy?'

Thandor decided not to answer immediately, choosing instead to revert to his habitual nonchalant posture; it was often difficult to read the sometimes-aloof Paladin, although that characteristic – for her at least – was part of his captivating charm. She enjoyed the air of mystery that surrounded him.

'I believe I have troubled you both enough for one cycle.' Thandor eventually replied, clearly ducking her question.

'I am sure there will be trouble enough once we arrive at Bleak Moor – if not sooner.'

'Are your *keen* instincts telling you such?' replied Thandor with a wry smile.

'OK, you can leave now – enjoy your run back to Marcus, at the back of the queue.'

'Take care – both of you.' Thandor replied. 'I would very much like to resume this conversation, *after* we return to the vale.'

'Such positivity – where has this suddenly come from?' asked Nathanar, with a subtle smile.

'Who can say – perhaps this new inspiration of yours is responsible for my altered disposition.'

The Paladin promptly broke step, and began doubling back to Marcus' detachment, which trailed behind them in the distance.

'How do you think he will land on this one?' asked Nathanar, who now marched alongside her.

'Thandor is not one for taking chances. He will investigate all the angles before confirming his position.'

'And what if that position differs from your own?'

'Then I shall find new ways to torment him.'

With the aid of the house guards, they managed to get Cora and Hanarah away from the crowd and into the relative safety of Larissa's warehouse, only a short distance away. Larissa hurriedly shut the door behind them, which helped to muffle the growing din outside. After her arrival, at the original scene of the unrest, the crowd had continued to swell as more and more Freylarkai piled onto the streets, drawn from their homes by the increasing noise outside. The Freylarkai were extremely efficient gossipers, and nothing spread faster than bad news. It was little wonder then that Krashnar's follow up crime had generated so much attention.

'We should be safe here, for a while. How much time do you need?' asked Larissa.

'As much as you can give me. I must concentrate – ergo, I need that mob kept at bay.'

'That *mob* is scared and frightened – they have never seen a Freylarkin of your ability do something like this before.'

'This is not *my* ability; it is the work of a twisted and disturbed mind.' she replied defensively.

Krashnar's works were abhorrent ghastly spectacles – they were not the result of a sane mind. His illicit acts cast a long shadow over those with her ability, despite the achievements wrought by Freylar's shapers, and the necessary role they played in Freylarkin society. For this reason, she had been compelled to exile the nonconformist, banishing him from the vale. It saddened her that a single rogue shaper could cause such unrest.

'We do not have time to debate this.' Larissa replied matter-of-factly. 'Do you need anything?'

'Some of your fabrics to line the floor would be good, as well as two short lengths to gag them.'

'What?! Are you serious?'

'I told you already that this is not my area of expertise. The procedure will be painful, and we can ill afford to incite that crowd any further. If they hear screams, they are likely to force their way in here and cause mayhem. They need to be gagged.'

She could see the conflict in Larissa's eyes, but the dressmaker did as instructed and began lining the floor with an assortment of fabrics; the soft underlay would serve two purposes: to help prevent further harm to both Cora and Hanarah during the procedure, and to soak up the blood. After preparing the space for the separation attempt, Larissa knelt beside the conjoined Freylarkai with two strips of fabric in hand.

'I am sorry, but I must do this.'

Cora was in floods of tears, and shaking badly.

'We understand.' replied Hanarah in a cracked voice. 'Larissa, will you make me a promise?'

'Of course.' replied Larissa, who leaned in closer.

'Our queen lacks conviction – see that she finishes this for me, come what may. I meant what I said about saving my daughter.'

'I understand.' Larissa replied with a grim expression. 'She *will* save your daughter – I promise to make sure of it.'

'Thank you. You are a good friend.'

Larissa gagged the two Freylarkai and then guided them awkwardly towards the makeshift operating theatre. After positioning Cora and Hanarah, ready for the procedure, Larissa wandered towards her with a stony expression.

'That is a promise you cannot keep.' she whispered quietly, ensuring that the others did not overhear her words.

'You are wrong.' replied Larissa sternly, who drew a small blade from the folds of her thick dress. 'You caused this – now you fix it!'

'Vorian, with respect, surely the defense of the vale is no longer our concern – are we not leaving this place?' questioned Dumar.

'It *is* your concern, because The Guardian requested this of us. I made a promise to uphold her request, and as a Knight of the Order, I intend to do so. If you wish to become Knights yourselves, you must learn to work together and support one another. I am requesting your aid, and in cycles to come, you will request my own, and when that time comes, I *will* be there.' he said ardently. 'If you will not do this for your old Order, then please, do this for me – if not for her.'

Dumar turned to the rest of The Vengeful Tears, eager to canvas their thoughts. Fortunately, his brief motivational sermon appeared to have the desired outcome, with none of the former Blades choosing to object.

'Very well.' replied Dumar, turning to face him once more. 'What would you have us do?'

'Thank you.' he replied, followed by a brief nod of respect. 'The house guards are struggling to deal with growing civil unrest, as word of the Narlakai invasion spreads. Their task is to calm the people and coordinate the local militia.'

'Then we are not evacuating?'

'Not on this occasion – this will be a last stand. Our task is to secure and defend the perimeter surrounding the Tri-Spires, giving the house guards time to focus on their own tasks. If there is to be a battle in the vale, we will hold the high ground.'

'And what of this militia?'

'Primarily those with abilities – we cannot have untrained combatants engaged in melee. The rest will help erect defences, before fleeing south to the Ardent Gate.'

'Is The Blade Lord aware of our intentions?'

'No – the plan was his, but he is not aware of our involvement. The Guardian felt it unwise to leave the Tri-Spires unguarded, and both the house guards and the militia will require our leadership.'

'Leadership?'

'Are you not the defenders of Scrier's Post, shield of the vale, of whom I have heard much talk?'

Dumar and the others stiffened their posture in response to his words. Although their appetite for Marcus' battle doctrine had waned since their encounter with the Narlakai, apparently their pride had not. It appeared that he had found the correct threads to tug upon, in order to motivate The Vengeful Tears in Rayna's absence.

'Good – then we have a job to do!'

Cora's muffled screams were too much to bear; tears streamed from her own eyes, making the difficult task requested of her even more so. She tried desperately to convince herself that the pain she inflicted upon them was unavoidable in order to carry out the procedure. In truth – as she had feared – her ability to separate the conjoined flesh was left wanting; she had precious little experience to draw upon, thus Cora and Hanarah both suffered due to her lack of understanding.

'I am sorry – this is new to me.'

She tried again to separate the flesh that bonded Hanarah's torso to her daughter's back, but her efforts only worsened the situation. Part of Hanarah's skin – where her cleavage once existed – tore, causing blood to trickle from the wound, along Cora's back and onto the fabric beneath them. Hanarah bit down hard on her gag, trying hard not to whimper in pain, but the excruciating agony got the better of her, defying her intentions. Despite her mother's hair almost suffocating her, Cora heard the muffled screams and began to shake uncontrollably.

'Larissa, I cannot do this.' she said miserably.

'Yes, you can – and you *will*.'

'I do not know what I am doing; this is not like rock, or some other inanimate object.'

'You changed your eyes.'

'That is different – the two procedures are not alike.'

'Then try harder!'

She tried again to separate the thick line of flesh joining both victims together, but she was unable to do so cleanly, resulting in further blood loss from the mother. She was unable to distribute the conjoined flesh evenly, and with no tolerances to work with, her efforts proved inadequate. Once more Hanarah tried hard to bite down on the pain, but the torment she suffered would not pass silently. Redoubling her efforts, she tried again, this time attempting to direct her ability away from Hanarah, as best she could. Cora cried out in response, almost overcoming the effects of her gag. Hanarah responded immediately, shaking her head violently left and right.

'This is hopeless – I cannot separate them without releasing one of them.'

'Then that is what you must do.' Larissa said coldly.

'I *will not* do it.'

'You cannot walk away from this. You are our queen; it is your job to lead and make difficult decisions, so that we do not have to.'

'Larissa, you *cannot* make me do this!'

Hanarah suddenly began shaking her head in a wild frenzy, trying to shake lose the gag around her mouth. The dressmaker quickly moved to her aid and pulled the fabric down, around Hanarah's neck.

'Release me! Save my daughter and release *me*!'

'No – I will not!' she replied, offering Hanarah a hard stare.

'Larissa, you promised me! Please – save my daughter!'

Larissa remained perfectly still, as she knelt beside Hanarah, carefully considering the mother's desperate plea for help.

'You promised me, no matter the cost – do it for my daughter!'

Without warning, the dressmaker pulled back Hanarah's head then drove her small blade deep into the front of the mother's neck.

She gasped in horror, 'What have you done?!'

'What you should have!' Larissa replied tersely, before withdrawing her blood-soaked weapon.

'Thank…you!' croaked Hanarah, who then began coughing violently as blood rapidly filled her throat.

Blood gushed from the wound, some of which caught her garment, staining it. She froze in horror as Hanarah struggled to breathe, before quickly passing out. Unable to turn, due to her awkward position, Cora tried to look over her shoulder to ascertain what had transpired. Hanarah's head slumped over, causing her daughter's vision to become further obscured by the mass of long hair now blocking

Cora's sight. Though unable to acquire the angle necessary to witness her mother's untimely release, nonetheless, Cora knew instinctively what had happened; Cora's sense of dread was quickly confirmed when blood from her own mother spilled mercilessly down over her. Cora began flailing wildly, desperate to escape the live horror show, of which she had now become the lead star.

'You murderer!' she screamed, unable to turn away from the ghastly sight.

'You have no excuses left to hide behind. Now get on with it – separate her now!'

Enraged by Larissa's action, she unleashed her ability on Krashnar's mutant, no longer concerned by the damage she wrought upon the released mother's body. She ripped Cora's flesh away from Hanarah, causing massive damage in the process. Though Cora remained physically unharmed – relatively speaking – the violent separation made a mess of Hanarah's torso, exposing layers of torn ruddy dermis, sinew and bone. Driven by anger, she pressed on, despite the ghastly sight unfolding before her. Hanarah's ruined body flopped to one side like a rag doll, before falling away entirely, eventually separating itself from Cora's own, as the last robes of stretched skin tore from their moorings. Cora's back was a bloody mess, covered in flaps and loose threads of excess skin. Fortunately, there appeared to be no visible tears in the daughter's own skin. With a decent amount of tidying up, Cora could return to some sense of normality, albeit with a great deal of scarring, both physically and mentally. Numbed by her own actions, she took a few steps backwards and tried to wrap her mind around the horror she had just witnessed. For the last few passes, she had used her ability to construct wonderful trinkets, of both simple and intricate beauty, subject to her mood. Never once had she the desire or inclination to meddle with the flesh – certainly not since tinkering with her own vision, and subsequently learning of their silent overseer. Her actions now left her feeling nauseous and unwell, as though she had committed an unspeakable crime – which she had. Since Larissa was now busying herself with comforting Cora, she moved towards the back of the warehouse, eager to put some distance between herself and the site of the ghastly act. There she sat, alone, replaying the abhorrent images in her mind, whilst struggling to accept what she had done. Twice now, in a single cycle, others had manipulated her, forcing her to perform acts against her better judgement. It dawned on her then that Kirika had a close relationship with the renowned dressmaker, both of whom had actively chosen to undermine her. Clearly, they thought her weak and incapable of ruling over Freylar. She looked towards Larissa at the other end of the warehouse, offering her newest exploiter a cold stare; the dressmaker was tending to Cora's back, cutting away the excess skin using her murderous weapon. Part of her wanted to aid Hanarah's daughter – an innocent victim of the grizzly affair – by tidying up the mess of the enforced separation, but anger stayed her hand.

'You *used* me – perhaps I should offer you the same courtesy.' she muttered, quietly to herself.

He took one last look at the hab's main living space, before exiting and closing the door. Though he had spent only a little under a day in Mr L. Cameron's place of residence, he was glad to see the back of the ugly site. The unfortunate events that had transpired there had changed him irrevocably; like a dark stain, deep in his psyche, the grim experience would stay with him – possibly forever. Time was a great healer, but it would be many years before the memory of the incident faded, losing sufficient clarity to afford him a decent nights' sleep. He exhaled heavily then set off down the starkly lit corridor, towards the gloomy emergency stairwell that took him back down to the ground floor. After quietly descending from level zero-two-nine, he reached the emergency door where he had first accessed the structure. Hearing the door's locks engage, as it closed behind him, was not unlike turning the last page of a poorly written chapter – he did not intend to return to D-zero-zero-three.

'Trix, am I clear?'

There was no response. He wondered if the socially inept software engineer was simply ignoring him – he knew from experience that Trix was more than comfortable with such behaviour.

'Trix, now is not the time to have one of your mood swings – is the way ahead clear?'

'*Yes.*'

He wished dearly that he had access to Trix's NGDF ghost data, but instead Trix was pulling the strings, again. Upon returning to the Wild, he intended to have a stern chat with the hacker, to redefine the terms of their business relationship – although, it seemed unlikely that they would work again alongside one another again. Whilst ultimately they had been successful, their operation had not been without its flaws. Lack of trust between them had been their primary failing. In addition, Trix's inability to cope with changing circumstances, and his controlling disposition in general, had compromised them. Events rarely went according to plan when in the field; it was impractical for

Trix to have control over his every action, especially when he needed to think fast on his feet.

'Thank you.'

It took several hours to return safely to the Wild, and longer still before he made it back to the bolt-hole where he had left Trix the previous night. The software engineer had said very little during his return trip, choosing to speak only when spoken to – specifically during the occasions when he had requested information on Peacekeeper movements. There was clearly something bothering Trix, but he decided it best to tackle the matter in person, after his return; they had quarrelled enough during the operation already, the rest could wait until they were face-to-face.

It was still dark when finally he returned to the hide's location. He brushed aside the local flora noisily, searching for the roof of the subterranean bolt-hole, specifically the sliding access panel which would allow him access. It was strange that Trix had not heard his deliberately noisy approach and slid back the panel to greet him. He reminded himself that Trix was not overly perceptive – at least, not in the physical sense. Eventually, after locating the entrance, he slid back the small mobile section of the hide's roof and peered into the subterranean gloom.

'Trix, it's me.'

There was no response.

'Come on, stop mucking around and light a glow-tube.'

Once again, there was no response.

'Trix! Wake up!'

In all likelihood, Trix had fallen asleep. It would be just like the software engineer to turn in for the night, at the eleventh hour, as opposed to acknowledging his safe return. Trix was selfish by nature, and had no issue using others to achieve his goals. Despite his attempts to alert the hacker, there were no discernible signs of movement below him. On impulse, he dropped to the floor of the hide – half expecting to land on top of Trix – and began fumbling around in the dark, blindly searching for either a glow tube or his deaf bunkmate. Finding neither, he reached for the light which he had taken from the stolen Peacekeeper pack, back at the hab. He placed his fingers over the end of the light before activating it, hoping to dull its luminance. In addition to Trix's notable absence, the bolt-hole itself was curiously tidy; Trix was a slob, and had made his messy presence abundantly felt. The hard compacted earth was devoid of any clutter, except for Trix's data-strap, which lay ominously alone on the floor. He grabbed the strap and pressed his right thumb against it, activating its holographic access panel. Before he could do anything more with the device, a recorded message began playing – it was Trix.

'By the time you view this message, I will be long gone. For what it's worth, I am sorry for parting ways with you so suddenly, and like this. I realise that you do not entirely trust me, but I never lied to you, at least not about the *reason* for our infiltration. However, my perception of the world has since been altered; that reason – for me at least – is no longer acceptable. I thought that I could hide amongst those people in plain sight, but seeing what they did to the Shadow class has changed me. Those *people* deserve to die for their atrocities, and I intend to execute every single one of them.'

There was a long pause before Trix resumed.

'You have skills – extremely useful ones – which I could well use, however, you have a strong moral compass, and you lack conviction; for those reasons you cannot join me in what lies ahead. I am truly sorry that I have cheated you. I have a new raison d'être now, and you must find your own. Do not attempt to search for me – you will fail – and stay out of the heart of the Metropolis. The day will come when the hammer falls, and when it does, it will fall hardest there. The Wild will be spared; I owe you that much. Take care of yourself Fox, and survive – someone needs to retell the events which transpired here.'

The recording ended, then promptly erased itself with ruthless efficiency. He allowed his body to fall gently backwards, carelessly banging his head on the solid earth – his numb state blocked any pain. Lying on his back, staring upwards, he watched the stars above through the hide's open hatch. They shone brightly in the cloudless night sky – a sobering reminder of how insignificant his world truly was. Subconsciously, his mind had tried to bury the revelation Trix had uncovered, but the software engineer's abrupt departure had been the exclamation necessary to wake his reluctant mind from its stupor. He no longer possessed the luxury of denial, and promptly began to succumb to depression. Whilst he lay motionless on the floor of the hide, the damning chorus of Trix's words echoed in his mind:

'You have a strong moral compass, and you lack conviction… I have cheated you…'

SIXTEEN
Secrets

'Rayna, wake up – nap time is over!'

She opened her eyes and saw Natalya standing over her. 'What time is it?'

'It is both dark and late – and the Narlakai are here; is there anything else you would like me to report?' Natalya replied, deliberately mocking her. 'But at least you are fully rested – I suppose that is a good thing.'

'OK, I get the hint. How far out are they?'

'Our scouts report that the front line will see them soon enough; we need to be ready.'

'Help me up.'

She extended her hand and allowed Natalya to pull her to her feet.

'Natalya, do you think I lack conviction?'

The Valkyrie laughed before responding, 'Not at all. You chose to have a moment's sleep, prior to what will likely be a defining battle in the history of our domain, and that is exactly what you did.'

'Very funny.'

She smiled at the Valkyrie's amusing quip. Natalya reminded her of Heldran's lot – she missed the knights' camaraderie.

'I thought so. However, in all seriousness, the Freylarkin I saw in that arena the other cycle, in no way lacked conviction. Furthermore, I would suggest that now is not the time to doubt yourself. A large number of us have chosen to follow you, personally, due to the feats we have seen you accomplish in your short time here in Freylar, in addition to the impossible stories that lie in your wake. For some of us, Rayna, you are an inspiration. Previously bleary-eyed Freylarkin are seeing more clearly now; a result of their staid perception being challenged – by you.'

She was taken aback by Natalya's words. Although Marcus, Kirika and Nathaniel had each touched on her growing popularity, regardless, she had repeatedly dodged the matter, despite the loyalty of The Vengeful Tears, and her strong relationship with the Knights Thranis. However, she had since garnered the respect of The Blades, enough to earn sole commanded of a detachment, including a Paladin and a Valkyrie. There could no longer be room for doubt in her mind. Since being granted a second chance to lead a life of purpose, she had seized the opportunity and run with it; the result of her actions was evidenced on the face of the Valkyrie standing expectantly before her.

In contrast, she thought back to her final days as Callum, in her former life. His time spent in the Wild, after Trix's abrupt departure, had been largely wasted. Aside from his time spent with Kaitlin, he had achieved very little. He had spent the time simply surviving, using Trix's toolbox to harvest additional bio-keys, thereby aiding his resource runs into the metropolis. The morally grey hacker had provided him with an opportunity to strike back at their opressors. However, instead of uniting with Trix, he had allowed his scruples to divide them. Perhaps Trix was right, despite his questionable methods and grey ethics. It dawned on her then that neither world was black and white, as she had originally supposed. Had Trix ultimately been successful or had their separation hindered his plans, she wondered. Despite their opposing ethics, they had achieved the impossible together, hacking into high-level government infrastructure, by exploiting a human weakness. Had they continued to work together, perhaps Callum could have been instrumental in aiding Trix to achieve his final ambition, she mused. But that was another world now, another lifetime, and there was nothing she could do to change that. It was time to move forward, accepting the lessons of both lives.

'You're wrong Trix – I am no longer that person.' she whispered quietly to herself.

'Um…are you feeling OK?' asked Natalya, who appeared confused. 'For a Freylarkin who allegedly does not sleep, I am not convinced that your rest has served you well.'

'On the contrary, I believe I have finally exorcised the demons from my past – it's time now, for me to move forwards. I failed my kin in my former life, but that *will not* happen a second time.'

'Rayna, I am not sure that I understand you.'

'That doesn't matter; all you need do is follow me. I do not care how many horrors Lileah commands forth from the shadows, mark my words, come the break of dawn, we will have sent them back into the abyss.'

A mischievous grin spread across Natalya's face; staring at the Valkyrie was like looking into a mirror. She gave Natalya a playful wink and then they both turned and made their way towards Nathanar and the others, who stood defiantly on the front line, alongside Captain Ragnar's own detachment. Marcus had committed all of The Blades to the war effort, in addition to a cast of supporting Freylarkai under Kirika's watch. The combined force gathered along the southern reach of Bleak Moor, securing the high ground. Kirika's militia consisted largely of personal aides and civilian Freylarkai, the latter of which had been selected for their abilities. They busied themselves preparing the battlefield, working furiously under Marcus' direction to prepare a network of shallow gullies which criss-crossed the ground before them. Shapers worked Firestones into liquid form, before pouring the viscous material into the gullies, created by the telekinetics. What little spare tinder and wadding they had available was also added; the bulk of their resources had been used to fashion torches, dispersed amongst The Blades. Seeing the assembled host set to purpose, moreover its size, strengthened her resolve. The battle ahead promised to be her largest engagement yet, the thought of which set her heart racing.

'Nathanar!' she cried.

The Paladin quickly turned, offering her his full attention, along with those making up her detachment. Some of the neighbouring Blades under Ragnar's command also turned, curious as to what she would say.

'Can I assume that our lot are ready for a fight?'

'Yes commander. They await your order – as do I.'

'Good. I want The Blades to surround me, facing outwards with their weapons drawn.'

She could see the confusion in Nathanar's piercing blue eyes, which appeared to glow in the dark, nonetheless, the Paladin did not question her orders, and commanded The Blades as instructed. The Blades quickly rallied around her as requested, whilst those from other detachments looked on with clear bemusement.

'I want to show you all a little trick, which someone close to me imparted. During the battle, we will have need for what I am about to teach you all. When I give the order to "close", you will all steadily withdraw from your positions and adopt this formation. You will draw the Narlakai in, so that they surround us fully.'

Unsurprisingly, a number of Blades seemed troubled by the formation; they muttered amongst themselves, trying to discern the merit of the seemingly reckless stance.

'Quiet!' said Nathanar sternly, in a tone she was unaccustomed to. The Paladin had clearly been working on projecting his authority, since last they had fought together.

'When I give the order to "turn", you will all do so immediately with your weapons drawn, after which, each of you will promptly close your eyes!'

Sensing the growing tension, she decided it best not to keep The Blades waiting. Casting her mind back to the Ravnarkai ambush, with Heldran and his knights, she clenched her right fist once again, inside of which she began manifesting her inner light. The barely contained light, trapped within the ball of her fist, rapidly approached its crescendo, prompting her to cry out her aforementioned command.

'Turn!'

The disciplined Blades immediately turned around in unison, promptly closing their eyes as instructed. Light exploded violently from her hand, sending out an expansive wave of pure white light. Using Alarielle's experience – now her own – she desperately fought to rein in the expanding light. The light hummed and jittered around them as she held it in place, whilst seeking to guide it towards its new destination – The Blades' weapons – in accordance with her will. The tenuously suspended light abruptly snapped towards her, as if tethered by elastic, ceasing immediately upon contact with the drawn weapons. The retracted light fused with the erect weapons, temporarily disappearing from sight entirely, before reaffirming its presence within its constricted form. The Blades' imbued weapons glowed vibrantly with the redirected light energy, signalling her successful attempt to imbue their arms by merging them with her inner light. Sensing the moment had passed, The Blades slowly began to open their eyes, witnessing first-hand the consequences of her decision to allow Allarielle to impress upon her mind once again. Gasps broke out amongst the gathered Blades. Although most had seen light bringers of greater ability imbue weapons prior to countless other battles, it was apparent that none had previously witnessed such mass-imbuing. The technique was clearly new to them, and one that would permit repurposing of arms during the battle. She turned to Natalya; the Valkyrie held her impressive recurve bow outstretched before her. Light from the bow gently radiated outwards, lighting up the left side of the Valkyrie's face, revealing a playful grin.

'How is this possible?'

'I have never seen such--'

'She is a Sky-Walker; such feats must be commonplace amongst her kin.'

'Quiet!' commanded Nathanar, once more asserting his authority over the detachment. 'We have the means by which to defeat our foes – that it all that matters.'

A sense of renewed purpose descended upon those gathered. There had been no illusion that the horrors they faced were surmountable, given the likely numbers Lileah commanded. However, her unexpected action, and Nathnar's blunt assessment, gave them something to hold onto. The Blade Lord was an accomplished military tactician, but nothing lifted spirits and emboldened morale more than present action. Each now grasped within their hands, possibility, which in turn gave them hope. Despite the future actions of their superiors, the success or failure of The

Blade's campaign was now within their own grasp. By enchanting their weapons, and – more importantly – demonstrating the speed by which such action was possible, she had given them something better than promise, she had offered them something tangible, and they had accepted it.

'Where did you learn such a trick?' boomed a voice to her left.

The Captain of The Blades broke through her contingent's cordon with ease and strode purposefully towards her. Ragnar carried his immense axe in his left hand, and bore a stern expression on his weathered face.

'I never taught you this.'

'No, you did not. Would you like me to teach you?'

Ragnar's expression became grim, leading her to wonder if perhaps she had overstepped the accepted boundaries of her relationship with the giant Freylarkin. There was a lull in their conversation, whilst the Captain considered his response. Ragnar was not known for his patience, however, contrary to his habitual disposition, Ragnar seemed unperturbed by her potentially goading remark – which she had not intended as such. After a moment of reflection, Ragnar's expression appeared to mellow slightly, though it was difficult to be certain amidst the ephemeral shadows which obscured his hard visage.

'That would be useful; a moment of your time now would be appreciated, before the hoard is upon us.'

'Sure.'

The Captain turned and cut a path directly towards his own detachment, pushing past the gathered Blades with ease, like trampling through a field of wheat. The parted Blades maintained their new positions, implying that they felt it unwise on her part to keep Ragnar waiting. Heeding their silent counsel, she followed the Captain towards his intended destination.

'Gather round.' boomed Ragnar, as he approached his detachment. 'The Guardian is about to teach this old wolf a new trick, and you lot have the unenviable assignment of being my test subjects.'

The Captain's unexpected jovial words elicited audible humour amongst The Blades, his habitually gruff disposition tamed by the opportunity she had presented to him. She had not expected Ragnar to react in such a positive manner – quite the opposite in fact. Their relationship had once again matured thanks to her actions during times of conflict. The Captain of The Blades too required something tangible, so it seemed. Having earned a measure of his respect, due to her actions at Scrier's Post, now she had elicited something of greater import; Ragnar had taken his first steps towards treating her as an equal.

'Right you ugly lot, draw your weapons and close your eyes – tightly!'

It felt good to rid herself of the caverns and their confined spaces. Although the Bleak Moor was entirely uninviting – living up to its name – nonetheless, she welcomed the open space and the fresh air. At the time, shortly after abandoning Krashnar's hide, she had chided herself repeatedly for neglecting to clothe herself properly against the cold. She had paid the price for her lack of foresight ever since, although the pain wracking her body helped to distract her from the cruel caress of the approaching winter. The Meldbeast's enthusiastic advance had been unrelenting in its torment, such that she no longer registered the constant agony elicited by its frenetic movements. Her body was now oblivious to the rise and fall of the Meldbeast's torso, her posture adjusting itself automatically to accommodate the beast's constant motion. However, the conclusion of the creature's beleaguered teachings ensured that the cold returned to torment her once more. She could hear her teeth chattering, due to prolonged exposure to the drop in temperature, which had worsened since entering the Bleak Moor; the landscape's low-level scrubland afforded them little to no shelter against the increasing wind – not that the Narlakai seemed to care. She wondered if the soul stealers felt anything, other than the searing touch of the light, or the ecstasy of devouring one's soul. Craning back her neck, to better observe the Night's Lights, the gentle patter of rain touched her face, further mocking her ongoing discomfort.

'Terrific!' she said aloud, sarcastically, giving voice to her increased displeasure.

The Meldbeast snorted in response; perhaps it too mocked her, she mused. The chimera had provided strange company since temporarily parting ways with Krashnar, who had left to infiltrate the vale with the intention of releasing The Guardian menace. She could see the foul moisture from its three mouths as the beast exhaled heavily, breathing hard whilst it thundered back and forth across the landscape, shepherding its dark flock steadily towards the vale. The Meldbeast's stamina was unfathomable, defying the physical exertion it seemingly spent bounding across the moor. The Narlakai, by contrast, drifted effortlessly over the sparse terrain, engaging in erratic bouts of physical movement solely when choosing to taste the air with their foreboding whip-like tendrils. They were near-vacuous entities, containing only fragments of what one might refer to as a soul. This emptiness fuelled their need to fill their hollow cores with the imprisoned souls of others. The Narlakai were thieves, seeking to take that which did not belong to them, in stark contrast to her mount, and herself, who knew only loss – she had lost her home, her femininity, the ability to bear children and now her lover. Despite the worsening conditions – both the weather and her grim state of mind – they had made good progress. The onset of rain would not hinder them. The end game was almost within sight; beyond the Bleak Moor lay the vale, and her quarry. Yet the Freylarkai were not her sole enemy; she needed to be mindful of the sun, despite its weak autumnal presence. After crossing the moor, dawn would rapidly be upon them. She intended to rest the host on the outskirts of the vale, under the relative safety of the trees, thus providing shelter for the Narlakai. It was a risky strategy, given the increased threat of scouts detecting their presence, however, even the Meldbeast required some rest – as did she. Regardless, she was committed now, and would press forwards with their attack, at dusk. If detected, she accepted the need to move ahead of schedule – an inconvenience, though one that would not thwart her plans. Although Darlia had timed their failed invasion better, her lover lacked conviction and had failed to foresee the intervention of The Guardian – neither were concerns she harboured. Krashnar would manage The Guardian, and her own conviction was resolute. She would ensure that the attack was quick, brutal and decisive. Come the following cycle, Mirielle's reign would be in ruin, and The Blades released or scattered to the wind. Any Freylarkai remaining in the vale would bend the knee to her, else be crushed under her heel.

Without any warning, the Meldbeast came to a jarring halt, and would have discarded her from its back if not for Krashnar's grizzly flesh straps, which continued to hold. The chimera sniffed at the air repeatedly with its three lupine heads, using its keen sense of smell to confirm the suspicion already forming in her mind. She quickly invaded the Meldbeast's mind, attempting to discern the cause of its distraction. Something lay ahead of them, upwind, beyond the black horizon, drawing the Meldbeast's attention. The beast's mind articulated the smell, quickly identifying the threat – Freylarkai, a great many of them.

'Damn it, they know we are coming.' she said, spitting the words as though a curse.

Thoughts began to churn in her mind, chief amongst them how the Freylarkai had become aware of her intent. Had Krashnar failed, she mused; assuming the shaper had indeed failed in his assignment, had the Freylarkai used telepaths or scriers to pry knowledge of her assault from him forcibly?

'Stop it! You are over-analysing this – as *she* would have done.' she said aloud, purposefully, trying to block out the wayward thoughts distracting her.

Attempting to out-think The Blade Lord had been Darlia's ploy, and had ultimately led to their defeat. She chided herself for allowing her conviction to wane, if only for a moment. She needed to stay true to herself, and pursue the only path she knew. The Meldbeast's keen senses had given her a distinct advantage, although negated in part by the poor timing of their approach. She considered doubling back her force, but the host had already broken the back of Bleak Moor. Besides, time was against them; they could ill afford to be caught out in the open, subject to the mercy of the sun, along with its fickle cloud cover. Her decision, then, was clear; they would press forwards their attack, with no quarter given. However, knowing that The Blades lay in wait was not without its benefits. She smiled as an amusing thought suddenly occurred to her.

'Since you were the one to bring word of The Blades position to my attention.' she said, directing her gaze towards her mount, 'It seems fitting, therefore, that you should be the one who will gain most from this insight.'

Scrier's Post had felt significantly emptier since Krasus' return to the Tri-Spires. Though she was happy to see the back of the arrogant shaper, his absence had left a noticeable hole in their fledgling community. Even Keshar had made a passing comment on the subject, claiming that the echoes within the sanctuary had gained prominence since the artisan's departure. With the site restored, and once again fit for purpose, she had decided to bolster their community by making contact with others possessing the same ability. To that end, she had maintained contact with the vale, using Sky-Skitters to relay commands to some of Mirielle's most trusted aides, though she was careful not to involve Kayla, who, in all likelihood, would inform Kirika of their secret enterprise. The moment would eventually come when fate would force them to include the Fate Weaver – courtesy of Nathaniel, in all likelihood. In the meantime, anonymity was their closest ally, of which she intended to take full advantage.

She studied the tiny message scroll again, which she held firmly in her hands. Once more, she decoded the scroll's message using a known cipher, ensuring that there was no ambiguity, or misinterpretation on her part. The message contained mixed news. Two potential students had been identified; both were currently journeying north, on a pilgrimage to the sanctuary, and would likely reach Scrier's Post by dawn. Although that news was most welcome, the remainder of the message scroll's contents made for grim reading. The exile Krashnar had returned to the vale – the shocking news had left a pit in her stomach, upon reading the text for the first time. The rogue shaper's motives were largely unknown, but it was known that the exile had released a local Freylarkin, named Riknar, whose mutilated body had been found entangled amongst the bridge piers. A sense of dread gnawed at her after decoding the message, and continued to do so now, whilst she confirmed the disheartening news. During their time spent together, she had learnt a great deal about Keshar, including her family. Riknar was an accomplished fisherman – he was also Keshar's brother. Keshar was hard working, and a most promising student, but the news would probably break her protégé. There were two likely outcomes. Grief-stricken, Keshar, in all likelihood, would succumb to despair, or even a state of depression; either would cause the young scrier to lose focus, severely disrupting her studies, perhaps even undoing the progress they had made thus far. Alternatively, Keshar would journey back to the vale, to be with her family. Either scenario was a setback she could not afford. She would not allow the loss of any momentum at such a critical stage in the site's redevelopment, despite the promise of fresh students. Although they had come to respect one another a great deal, due to their master-apprentice relationship, nonetheless, the dreadful news cradled in her hands would divide them.

'May I come in?' came a voice from behind the door, following a loud knock.

'Come in.'

Keshar quickly entered her private quarters.

'Aleska, I have finished the assignments you set me.'

'Very good – I shall be with you shortly, to further instruct you.'

There was a brief pause; the eager scrier clung to the door, clearly wanting to ask more of her.

'Is there something you wish to ask?'

'Sorry…I was just curious.'

'You need not apologise for your curiosity.' she said, rising from her chair. 'Curious about what?'

'I saw the Sky-Skitter arrive.'

'I see.' she said, making a mental note of Keshar's keen observational skills.

'Is there any news from the vale?'

'As a matter of fact, there is. I was planning to inform you in the morning, but…since you ask, I see no need to wait.'

'Have you been successful?'

'Indeed I have; the next cycle will see our numbers double – two more *young* students will be arriving imminently, to join us.'

'That is wonderful news!' replied Keshar, who was clearly overjoyed.

Whilst they enjoyed each other's company, the obvious generation gap between them meant that certain topics of conversation would always be strained, if not entirely inappropriate. She dearly missed her long talks with Mirielle, and longed for their swift return. Likewise, the prospect of having company her own age seemed to invigorate her apprentice; Keshar appeared quietly thrilled after learning the news that new students would be attending the sanctuary.

'When they arrive, I will need your help to settle them in.'

'I would be delighted to help – I will start making preparations.'

'Very good, but they can wait until the morning.' she said, offering the eager scrier a warm smile. 'Keshar, they will look to you as their senior, therefore, I expect you to impress upon them the boundaries which we have established here. Can I count on you to do this for me?'

'Of course, Aleska. You have taught me well, and I shall pass on what I can, as you have instructed me.'

'Excellent, now please, get some rest.'

Again Keshar loitered by the door, refusing to release her grasp on its frame.

'Am I to assume that there is more that you wish to ask?' she said, raising a scrutinising eyebrow.

'Has there been any word from my family?'

As fate would have it, there it was – the moment she hoped to avoid, entirely, if not for the relentless curiosity of youth. The young Freylarkai of the vale had an inherent need to move forwards, constantly testing the boundaries of their relationships and abilities. This base need reminded her that what they were doing at Scrier's Post was indeed necessary; if left unchecked, Freylarkai of Keshar's ability carried within them the seed of Darlia's successorship. Scrying was an inevitability. The act itself could not be denied to the Freylarkai, though it could be altered, its course redirected to follow a new path. The restoration of Scrier's Post, and Keshar's tutelage, were the first steps upon this new path, which would ultimately shape the Freylarkai for generations to come, by altering their perception of scrying. She would not allow her ambition to be derailed, not least by the incessant questions of one so inexperienced.

'None. Is there anything else?'

'Thank you. I have no further questions.'

'Then I shall see you in the morning – please get some rest.'

Keshar gave her a respectful nod, before seeing herself out, closing the door gently behind her. She waited for a long moment, ensuring that her eager student had in fact withdrawn, having sated her thirst for answers. Convinced that Keshar had indeed turned in for the night, she wandered towards the small hearth in her chamber. Sat upon a metal grill were two Firestones, which crackled softly as they burned vigorously, generating a most welcome light and warmth. With winter fast approaching, she praised herself for having had Krasus shape hearths in the sleeping quarters. The temperature would continue to drop throughout the night, and she could no longer tolerate the cold as she once did – age, it seemed, had a wicked sense of humour. She stared into the hypnotic flames, searching for another way, though none presented itself. Keshar would eventually learn of her brother's release, but if managed carefully, by the time that knowledge reached the scrier's ears, it would matter little to their cause. Others would ultimately fill Keshar's place, and her absence would go largely unnoticed. For now, however, she required the young scrier's presence, thus there was nothing further to consider – the matter was resolved. With a heavy heart, she pulled out the message, which she had concealed within the right sleeve of her thick dress. After decoding the text one last time – to be certain – she offered the tiny scroll to the hungry flames, allowing them to consume yet another secret. Over the passes, she had lost count of the number of times she had watched the greedy flames devour her secrets, but the result was always the same – for every truth consumed, the weight upon her soul increased.

SEVENTEEN
Reprisal

'They are here – on the horizon!' cried a distant telepath, from beyond the gloom.

She cursed her poor sight, envying those born during the winter season; those Freylarkai born later in the pass were habitually blessed with nocturnal vision, a trait that she did not possess. Ragnar – a fellow light bringer – also suffered the same curse; the Captain of The Blades was quite vocal on the matter, choosing to voice his frustrations aloud, for all around to hear.

'How far out are the soul stealers? Where are the wretched things?' boomed the Captain. 'Someone give me a straight answer now, or my axe will be doing the talking!'

She gathered that such public displays of annoyance were perennial, and that Ragnar's unnecessary rants had become a dependable source of pre-battle entertainment for The Blades. She wondered if the Captain was aware of the public's perception of him during such moments, and if in fact the red-haired giant chose to peddle such theatrics deliberately, to ease tension amongst The Blades. Either way, the spectacle was amusing to watch, and was certainly a welcome distraction.

'If he carries on like that, he will struggle to hang onto his voice during the battle, forcing us to listen to the awful moans of the Narlakai instead.'

Natalya's words struck a chord; she remembered well the Narlakai's horrid chorus, the sound of which had managed to lodge itself in her mind, refusing to allow her to let go of it.

'That sound is truly awful.'

'Yes, he can become irksome after a while.'

She laughed at the Valkyrie's obvious humour, entirely at the Captain's expense.

'I think he does it on purpose.' she said, eager to keep their conversation going, as opposed to waiting quietly during the Narlakai's dread march.

'That is Thandor's belief. I am of a similar mind.'

'How well do you know Thandor? I see you both together, frequently.'

'Ha, I am sorry to disappoint you, but it is nothing like that, you understand.' replied Natalya, openly. 'We are good friends, and I value his counsel; he has an annoying habit of being right.'

'Interesting. Does he have any views on the body thief standing next to you?'

'He believes that you are a catalyst for change, with which I am in agreement. You do not possess the combat prowess of a Paladin or Valkyrie, nor Kirika's political awareness. Also, you lack the breadth of Marcus' strategic mindset.'

'Is there an upside to all this?' she interjected, prompting a sort chuckle from Natalya.

'However…you have heart, as well as your tricks, and you are challenging our perceptions, as I mentioned to you earlier. These traits serve you well, and provide a fresh approach to the norm, which is intoxicating.'

'So you're saying I'm toxic?'

'In a good way.'

Both smiled at one another, enjoying the candid nature of their conversation.

'Distance?!' cried Marcus, who stood towards the back of The Blades, surveying his force.

'Two hundred paces, closing steadily.' came the familiar voice from the gloom.

Faint light was starting to creep over the horizon. Before long, dawn would be upon them, though it was unlikely The Blades could weather the Narlakai assault long enough for the rising sun to assist their defence. In any case, cloud cover and the morning haze would likely thwart any such aid by diluting the sun's oppression of the Narlakai. Nevertheless, if they failed to repel Lileah's invasion, both the sun and Vorian's rearguard would be the Freylarkai's only remaining chance of salvation.

'In my experience, those who believe it necessary to publicly affirm their friendship with others are typically masking a deeper connection.'

Natalya looked at her with a puzzled expression, which, after some time, morphed into a wry grin.

'What experience?'

'Fine – you've called my bluff. But it was worth a go.'

'Ha, nice try. Perhaps if those words had not been spoken by a demi-god, they would have carried more weight.'

'I am no demi-god.'

'And the more you deny it, the greater the truth of it. Tell someone you are a queen – it is likely that they will resist the notion. However, act like one, and people will believe that you are such.'

'Are you lecturing me?'

'The point is, you have been acting like a demi-god since you arrived in Freylar, though you never proclaimed to be such. You allowed the Freylarkai to fabricate their own interpretation of you, based on your actions, all of which have cast you in a favourable light.'

'I do not seek a position of authority; I only wish to serve this world better – to make a difference – having made such a hash of my previous life.'

'Yet your attempts to shirk that authority, in the wake of the growing tales of your exploits, are accelerating the very thing that you wish to avoid. You want to fight for the Freylarkai and make our domain a safer place – I see that – but you cannot fulfil such ambition without acquiring the admiration of others. Mirielle built us a home, and her selfless actions garnered our respect and obedience. Now both her former humility and judgement are waning, and her connection to the Freylarkai is growing weaker with each cycle. We do not serve those in power; those in power should serve us, to the best of their ability.'

'Do you oppose Mirielle's rule?'

'Look around you – where is our queen?'

'You realise that my sight is crappy, at best.'

Natalya laughed at her response.

'Whilst I do not understand your bizarre choice of profanity, nonetheless, I get the connotation.'

'I agree that our queen *should* be here.'

'But she is not.' replied Natalya, with a touch of disdain. 'This is a dark time in Freylar's history. Even if we survive this renewed invasion, the Freylarkai will be left in ruin – we will need strong leadership to help us rebuild our society. Let us review Kirika. She sits on the ruling council, but she is no fighter – not in the physical sense that is. Yet she is here, bow in hand, laying the groundwork to aid our defence, in our queen's absence. She stands alongside her sister, the one who brought us word of this attack – one who owes us nothing. Such individuals earn respect and acquire authority through their actions, which ultimately define them, as they do you.'

'I appreciate your insight – are you always this talkative?'

'Well, it is either that, or listen to the Captain.'

They turned their heads in unison, back towards Ragnar; the Captain of The Blades was still hollering, at no one in particular. It was unclear now whether Ragnar continued to play to his audience, or if in fact he was genuinely growing impatient with the enemy's lethargic advance.

'Someone get me a witch – perhaps one of them can tell me where to swing my axe!'

It became clear to her that Ragnar was wasted fighting the ponderous Narlakai; the Captain would likely find a more suitable opponent in the southern lands, engaged in The Hunt. Whilst the Captain continued to indulge in his raucous outbursts, she spied Nathanar wandering over to join them.

'Rayna, I grow tired of listening to that Freylarkin barking at the void. Perhaps now would be a good time to discuss The Blade Lord's strategy? I presume that Marcus has disseminated at least part of his stratagem to you?'

'Your presumption is correct. Whilst I am not privy to the entirety of the plan, I am aware of certain facts. Marcus intends to recreate the battlefield at Scrier's Post.'

'Minor problem: we lack several high walls.' said Natalya sarcastically.

'I doubt even the shapers could fashion anything useful out of this place as a meaningful proxy.' added Nathanar.

'Quite. Which is why he intends to funnel them using fire. The gullies, which Kirika's militia have been diligently preparing, will be ignited, at Marcus' discretion. The archers will also play their part, as they look to hold the flanks – hence all the wadding.'

'Their arrows will be heavy; they won't travel far. And then there is this wretched rain.' Natalya explained.

'Yes, which is why we will have to endure the Captain's rants for a while longer. Marcus' intends to allow the Narlakai to close on us, before we press our attack. He plans to redirect the enemy's flanks with the gullies, before driving them back with our archers, forcing the Narlakai to cluster – the high ground should aid the archers in this.'

'That will send them *all* towards us.' replied Nathanar.

'Yes.' she replied, labouring the word. 'Thus Marcus felt it wise to withhold the plan's specifics.'

'Wonderful – is there anything else you would like to add?' asked Natalya, who was clearly unimpressed with their assignment.

'You won't like it.'

'I do not suppose that I will.'

'Go on, let us hear it.' said Nathanar, maintaining his unfazed expression.

'When we charge the front line, we shall be taking Darlia with--'

Before she could finish her sentence, a foreboding howl echoed across the moor. The dread sound came from the horizon. It reverberated across the landscape, akin to a rumble of thunder, immediately silencing all chatter amongst The Blades, including the Captain's ongoing tirade. The awful sound drew their attention, ushering in with it an unsettled atmosphere that quickly spread throughout their ranks, reminding them of the horrors they were about to face.

'Distance?!'

She felt a strange emptiness after giving up her mount. Though her time with Krashnar's Meldbeast had been short, nonetheless, she had grown attached to the creature in an odd sort of way. Perhaps she just missed the company, she mused. The beast's howl – as she cut through its flesh straps – still rung in her ears; the unforgettable sound was difficult to endure. She could well imagine the pain caused by her blade, as she severed the Meldbeast's skin. Regrettably, the act was necessary in order to improve their chances of success. Thanks to her mental link with the creature, the Meldbeast understood the reason for her actions, although the knowledge did not make the procedure any less painful. The torment she had caused the beast was swiftly returned in kind when descending from her mount; the Meldbeast had assisted – as far as it was able – but the pain that speared through her body when her feet finally contacted with the ground was excruciating. It took her a long moment to recover from the manoeuver. However, once free of her mount, the Meldbeast was able to act upon her new instructions. She ordered the creature to break off from the host; its task was to circle wide, around the enemy's left flank, and attack Marcus' force from the rear. The night was leaving them, but it was still dark enough to provide the Meldbeast adequate cover. In addition, her former mount was capable of breakneck speeds, and its agility was unprecedented – bordering on preternatural – ensuring that it would have no trouble outflanking The Blades unseen.

Without her mount, traversing the moor became a challenge. She chided herself again, this time for her lack of foresight in following Krashnar's advice, leaving the hollow stone crutches he had fashioned for her back at the hide. Although she was able to move freely now, the act of walking was nonetheless still painful; each stride pulled at the metal-infused flesh around her lower abdomen. The cold and the pain caused tears to fall from her eyes, although it would not be long before the art of war distracted her from such irrelevant thoughts. Despite her handicap, she was just about able to keep up with the ponderous Narlakai. The writhing throng of nightmare horrors drifted eerily around her, as she continued to shepherd the dark host south, across the drab landscape. After what felt like an eternity of making very little progress, she caught her first glimpse of the assembled Freylarian host, through whatever means it was that the Narlakai used to see. The elation of nearing her journey's end lifted her soul, relieving the weight of sorrow that had burdened her since parting ways with Darlia. With renewed vigour, she drove the Narlakai forwards, widening their frontage as they advanced purposefully. Krashnar's assumption was correct; her numbers were favourable – significantly so – and she continued to hold sway over the shaper's monstrous pet. If she cared a damn about their fates, she would pity The Blade's pathetic show of force. She wished dearly that Darlia was present, to witness her ascension. There was nothing to stop her now – no high walls, no cover, no Guardian. All that remained was for her to shepherd her black horde across the final stretch of the Bleak Moor, and in doing so sweep away the pitiful resistance standing in her way. The Meldbeast would disrupt Marcus' carefully choreographed formations, unleashing chaos upon The Blades, whilst the Narlakai had their fill of souls. In her mind, she had already won, though determined to thwart her efforts, the weak autumnal sun started to break across the horizon, prompting the darkness to commence its slow retreat.

'You are too late!' she screamed, defiantly. 'The time of the Freylarkai has come to an end.'

It had been a long cycle. After Cora's grizzly operation, followed by the release of her mother, she had overseen the unenviable task of breaking up the Freylarkai mob surrounding Larissa's warehouse. Under her direction, the house guards had eventually managed to subdue the scared spectators, escorting them back to their homes. The process of breaking up the crowd had not been easy, particularly given her refusal to divulge the specifics of what had transpired inside the warehouse. She needed time to marshal her thoughts, to discern the best way of disseminating the ugly news to her people. To that end, she managed to convince Larissa to accompany her to the Tri-Spires, where Cora would receive the best care available. It was a cheap ploy, preying on the dressmaker's emotions, but a necessary one nonetheless. Under the cover of darkness, they escorted Cora quietly to the Tri-Spires, along with the remains of Hanarah's released body. Cora wore a thick fabric over her slender shoulders, to cover the scarring across her back. The body of her mother was wrapped in a blanket, ensuring that even the house guards in attendance were not privy to the truth. Three guards unwittingly carried Hanarah's body back to the Tri-Spires, whilst both she and Larissa aided Cora, who remained weak from her traumatic experience. The young Freylarkin said nothing as they quietly made their way back to the Tri-Spires – even Larissa was surprisingly quiet. The emotional strain she had endured left her feeling stretched and thin. The cycle was one she would sooner forget, but it was not yet over; loose ends needed tidying up, and there was the issue of Larissa, and her own forced exploits – each was accountable, especially Larissa's abhorrent manipulation of her own actions. When finally they arrived at the Tri-Spires, she quickly sought to home her guests.

'Please, use this chamber for the night. You will both be comfortable here. In the meantime, I will have the guards store the other item securely. We will reconvene in the morning, and decide then how best to proceed, *after* I receive word from The Blade Lord, you understand?'

'Understood.' replied Larissa, before escorting Cora into the chamber and closing the door.

She turned and walked towards the guards, who still carried the conspicuous blanket.

'One of you will remain here. Lock the door to the chamber from the outside, and ensure that *no one* leaves or enters the room without my approval. The remainder of you will carry *that* to the chamber at the far end of the corridor. It too will be secured and guarded – no one is to have access.'

'But, with respect, my queen, we are needed to help coordinate and bolster the local militia. Kirika asked that we- -'

'I do not care. Those are her orders – not mine. You will do as I have instructed, is that understood?'

'Yes my queen.' replied the guards, in perfect unison.

Requiring no additional motivation, two of the house guards began carrying Hanarah's body down the corridor, whilst the third quietly secured access to Cora's chamber. She knew that Larissa would be furious, once the dressmaker learned of her true intentions, though none of that mattered right now. Provided Marcus was successful in putting down the resurgence of Darlia's failed invasion, she would deal with Larissa accordingly. However, in the unlikely event that

The Blade Lord failed, she intended for the chamber's door to remain shut.

The Narlakai continued to shorten the gap between them. They were close enough now to allow her to make out their whip-like tendrils, which thrashed and writhed as the soul stealers advanced. The wide silhouette approaching spanned twice the width of their own force; the grim outline suggested that they were significantly outnumbered.

'Close!' cried Rayna.

Immediately, they gathered around The Guardian, with their backs to Rayna and weapons drawn, as per their training. The enchantment previously bestowed upon their arms had since faded. Physical weapons had no effect on the Narlakai's amorphous gaseous bodies; realistically, they could only hope to slow the horrors down, by severing their gangrenous tendrils. However, The Guardian's light gave them a fighting chance; the soul stealers abhorred the light, which was pure anathema to them. With it, they could at least offer some semblance of a fight, despite the overwhelming odds bearing down on them.

'Turn.'

At Rayna's command, she turned around with her eyes tightly shut and raised her quiver, pulled from her back. Light saturated her eyelids, which failed to shield her fully from Rayna's brilliance – the excess light danced wildly across her retinas, with ferocious intensity. After the fleeting moment had passed, she gingerly opened her eyes. Both her stock of arrows, and the quiver securing them, glowed against the approaching dawn, however, this time the result of Rayna's enchantment appeared more intense. The barely contained light within her arrows hummed and jittered, as it fought against its prison, desperately seeking escape. She admired the spirit of her rebellious captive, and welcomed the opportunity to unleash its fury upon the legion of soul stealers advancing towards them.

'To your positions!' cried Nathanar, who held his double-handed sword in his right hand, high above his head.

The Paladin's long weapon glowed fiercely with its imbued light, which ran the length of the blade. Nathanar was tall for a Freylarkin, which – coupled with the height of his sword – helped him to project his authority and embolden those around him. She smiled at the Paladin, who acknowledged her approval; Nathanar nodded politely in return, before moving to the centre-front of their formation, which started rapidly taking shape. She recalled the Paladin's selfless report, which included how he had struggled to make his presence felt during the conflict at Scrier's Post. Now, however, the Paladin's insecurities, which had previously held him back, were receding. Be it his experience of actual command in the field, or his proximity to The Guardian's own actions, she did not care; watching the newly promoted Paladin find his confidence was uplifting. She moved to join Nathanar, leaving space between them for Rayna to fill, who promptly joined the gathering ranks. Post assembly, their detachment formed one half of a concave semi-circle, with the Captain's detachment completing the other half on their left flank. Combined, both detachments formed a curved frontage, along the base of the high ground to their backs, like two cupped hands ready to receive a thrown ball – in this case, the Narlakai. Behind them was Darlia, who stood alone, like an abandoned waif, playing the role of the social pariah. Understandably, The Blades appeared perplexed by their odd formation, but they trusted The Blade Lord. Furthermore, seeing both the Captain and The Guardian readily adopt the strange formation reassured them. Her rank of Valkyrie afforded her some advanced knowledge of Marcus' renowned field tactics, though she was typically apprised of The Blade Lord's designs, only moments prior to their implementation – more of a courtesy than actual involvement. On this occasion, however, The Guardian had seen fit to include her and Nathanar immediately upon learning of Marcus' chosen plan of attack. Rayna – it seemed – valued their input, and welcomed the chance to discuss the merits of the unconventional formation prior to its adoption. After deliberating the strategy, they had unanimously agreed to endorse The Blade Lord's bold tactics, warranted, given the nature of their foe, and their concerning lack of numbers. Two large blocks of archers were deployed on the flanks, behind the ranks of their crescent-shaped formation. Amongst these, the bulk of the force's light bringers had been stationed, their sole objective to imbue arrows, which would rain down on the Narlakai. Marcus' plan involved exposing their archers, offering the Narlakai targets of value. Given the devastation their imbued arrows would inflict upon the black host, it was likely, that Lileah would seek to prioritise their release. The Blade Lord stood impressively between the blocks of archers, surveying the battlefield from his vantage point, maximising the elevated position upon which he and the archers stood. Marcus' intent had been to build a fortification, secured by their unusual concave formation, but to achieve such he required more than The Blades alone could offer, considering their numerical disadvantage. The unenviable task of building the missing pieces of the fortification had been assigned to Kirika, whose militia had since finished preparing the gullies criss-crossing the battlefield. Kirika had taken up position ahead of the main force, some twenty paces before them, along with several of her aides. Fate Weaver had split her unlikely vanguard into two small groups: Kayla and two others held the left flank, whilst Kirika and another took the right. Both groups carried lit torches and crouched, waiting, in anticipation of The Blade Lord's inevitable command.

'What happens if they break?' she whispered.

'Then it's been a pleasure knowing you.' replied Rayna, dryly, who fixed her gaze on Kayla's lot.

The Narlakai were close now, barely forty paces ahead of Kirika's position. Following Rayna's gaze, she could see the nerves starting to manifest in Kayla's camp; Kayla herself was fidgeting noticeably, whilst the others shuffled around nervously, allowing fear to prey upon them.

'Thirty paces!' cried a voice from behind them.

'Hold!' commanded The Blade Lord.

One of the aides, crouched alongside Kayla, suddenly broke, their fear finally getting the better of them. Seeing the Freylarkin hurriedly scrambling away prompted the other nervous torchbearer to follow suit, leaving Kayla alone. She watched as Fate Weaver quickly grabbed the arm of the remaining aide, on the opposing flank, in a vice-like grip, whilst offering Kayla a hard stare across the way.

'Hold your position!' yelled Kirika, sternly.

'Twenty-five paces!'

'Hold!' commanded Marcus' resolutely, once again.

The Blade Lord's dogged disposition when in the field, would not allow Kirika's vanguard a single pace until their task was complete, exactly as he had instructed them. Using civilians to implement such a dangerous ploy was a risky endeavour, but with their numbers stretched, Marcus needed all of The Blades in position, ready for the ensuing battle. Since volunteering for the unenviable assignment, she possessed a deeper level of respect for the renowned scrier. Kirika was proficient with a bow, and could have taken a more passive role at the rear of the army, alongside its archers. Instead, the scrying politician had agreed to be fully exposed, at the front of their host, as bait for the enemy.

'Twenty paces!'

Kayla was beginning to show signs of panic, as the writhing silhouette before them rapidly acquired definition. Sinister vertical maws began opening within the gaseous bodies of the approaching Narlakai; the nightmare horrors sensed the presence of fresh souls, and were readying themselves to feed. In all likelihood, Kayla had never before laid eyes on a soul stealer, let alone an army of them, and at such close proximity. Now, as she reconsidered the facts, The Blade Lord's strategy seemed – to her at least – to border on folly.

'She is going to break. If I get some wadding now, there is still a chance I can hit the mark with my ability.'

'You said it yourself – the arrows will be heavy, and will not travel far.' replied Rayna, 'Besides, accuracy is critical, and the light is poor.'

'Her nerve will not hold.' she said, convinced that their plan was fast unravelling.

'You trust me, right?'

'That is why I am here!'

'Then believe in the fact that I trust Kirika, and the influence she holds over her closest aide.'

'Fifteen paces!'

'Kayla, I believe in you – hold your position!' cried Kirika once more.

Hearing her mentor's voice seemed to tether the young Freylarkin to her post, but Kayla was trembling badly now, and was barely able to hold onto the torch shaking violently in her hand.

'Ten paces!'

'Light the gullies!' cried Marcus mercifully.

The vanguard immediately did as commanded, setting alight the gullies diagonally flanking their formation, reminiscent of a spear with a broken tip. Flames burst into life at the end of the shallow fuel-lined trenches, working their way along the gullies, back towards the flanking archers as they chased Fate Weaver's fast retreating vanguard. The aide alongside Kirika slipped in her haste, planting herself face down on the moor's hard scrubland. It would have been all too easy for Kirika to abandon her charge, thus guaranteeing her own safety, but instead the scrier doubled back to help the Freylarkin scramble back to her feet.

'Ready your weapons!' cried Rayna, who grasped her exotic twin falchions, one in either hand.

To her left she could hear Ragnar, hollering words of damnation at the Narlakai, as the Captain sought to embolden troop morale, moments prior to contact.

Now fully ablaze, the gullies completed their elaborate fortification, engineered by The Blade Lord. Although the flames failed to harm the Narlakai, light from the low-level fiery walls split the enemy's advance, redirecting the soul stealers against Lileah's will. Approximately two thirds of the dark host broke away from the central mass, tracing a diagonal route towards the flanking archers. Marcus' divide and conquer strategy meant that – in the short-term at least –

they only need to concern themselves with the central mass, which continued its forward advance through the breach, artificially created by the exposed gap between the blazing gullies. Their abnormal concave formation now revealed its true potential, allowing them to outflank the Narlakai pouring through the gap in front of them.

'You were right.' she said, nocking an imbued arrow to her bow.

'I guess so – time to put that ability and recurve bow of yours to good use.'

EIGHTEEN
War

'Send them back to the abyss!' boomed Ragnar, as he charged headlong towards the Narlakai, who were now almost entirely upon them.

The Captain swung his enormous axe in a wide arc, its imbued smile reducing everything it touched to an ash-like substance. The particle remnants of the released soul stealers lingered, dancing wildly in the turbulent air. Scores of writhing tendrils flopped to the ground, where they squirmed autonomously, no longer tethered to their former hosts. Logic dictated that his friend be better served using a weapon fashioned exclusively from light, but the Captain was stubborn, and favoured the weight of his monstrous axe. A small part of him wondered if Ragnar enjoyed the showboating, though he quickly reminded himself that the red-haired giant was simply slow to change. In the Captain's haste to engage the enemy, Ragnar had carelessly left himself exposed to the horrors' closely packed ranks, which threatened to engulf the impetuous Captain. With preternatural speed, he drew a throwing knife from the sheath attached to his left arm, before casting it into the heart of a vertical maw forming on the Captain's right flank. The knife's victim gave out a brief sonorous moan, cut short by the Narlakin's release as it disintegrated into dust, before being spirited away by the motion of battle.

'Ragnar, get back in line!' he yelled, trying to pull the Captain back into the fold.

Narlakai were now pouring through the breach, filling the space before them. The black sea of thrashing tendrils reached out with supreme alacrity, seizing the limbs of those less perceptive Blades. Screams filled the battlefield as Blades were dragged unceremoniously to their doom, pulled into the writhing mass, their souls ripe for consumption. The Blades' telekinetics fought hard against the pressure rapidly building in The Blade Lord's kill box, since the range and volume of the Narlakai's appendages made it difficult to engage the enemy.

'Fire!' he heard Marcus cry, in the distance.

The creeping light of dawn immediately received an unexpected assist; a hail of imbued arrows filled the sky over their heads, before raining down on the condensed ranks of the enemy before them. It was a bold manoeuvre, relying on the accuracy of their archers and the front line's ability to hold back the enemy. The carpet of imbued arrows tore through the dark ranks, releasing scores of the horrors. Countless previously trapped souls, now free of their damnable prisons, reached for the sky, desperate to make their belated journey to the Everlife. Light from both the imbued arrows and the formerly trapped souls, supplemented the encroaching light of dawn, creating a hazy light that spilled across the battlefield. Rain continued to fall from the sky, mixing with the ash-like remains of the Narlakai, causing a sticky film to form on the soft ground. A deafening chorus of sonorous moans filled the air whilst the Narlakai reeled from the devastating attack. Despite their losses, however, the soul stealers continued to press against the telekinetics' invisible barrier, which tenuously held the Narlakai at bay.

'Drive them back!' he cried, hoping to give the Captain some respite.

Ragnar remained in the thick of the fighting, like an ancient stone protruding from a fast-flowing stream, refusing to budge, despite the inevitable gradual erosion. The defiant Captain swung his monstrous axe tirelessly, the reach of his menacing weapon barely able to keep his nightmarish crowd at bay, such was the density of the Narlakai's ranks. The Captain's audacity was like a shining beacon, inspiring all those who bore witness, and yet his insane heroics were a weakness – if the Narlakai snuffed out his light, their resolve would rapidly diminish.

'Support the Captain, now!' he screamed, as he continued to fell those soul stealers closest to Ragnar.

The telekinetics pushed once more, causing the Narlakai to ride up like a black wave that threatened to crash down on them. Renewed screams filled the air as more and more Blades were dragged to the ground, to be subsequently pulled into the thrashing black mass. The soulless, desiccated, withered husks of the freshly released were spat back at them,

[missing section emailed to me by Liam, May 2019]

…mercilessly cast into their own ranks, in an attempt to break their fighting spirit. The abhorrent act was difficult to stomach, yet regardless, the dogged Blades valiantly fought on, fuelled by their anger and disgust. Digging deep into their mental reservoirs, those Freylarkai with telekinetic ability drove the Narlakai back again, some of which rode up and over the height of the invisible barrier. The dark stragglers thrashed wildly, amidst their own ranks, desperate to feed in the presence of so many ripe souls, their need to reap insatiable. Despite the horrors now raining down on them, The Blades continued to fight valiantly against the suppressed ranks of the Narlakai, but the enchantment of their weapons was fading fast. The few light bringers they had ran hurriedly between The Blades, imbuing arms as fast as their ability would allow, but without the technique imparted…

imparted to their Captain, coupled with Ragnar's mastery of the light, they were fighting a losing battle.

'Ragnar, get back now, damn it – we need you here!' he screamed at the Captain, who was still belligerently carving out his own personal space in the midst of the enemy's ranks. It was clear that Ragnar had no intention of backing down, his professional pride forbidding such action.

'Nathaniel, assist me!' he cried out, desperately seeking The Teacher's aid.

Realising that no amount of yelling would pull the Captain to his senses, he drew his custom dirks from their slumber and passed through the barrier, wading into the black maelstrom beyond. Nathaniel followed him in – without hesitation – and together they cut a path towards the enraged Captain. Mindful of Ragnar's devastating attacks, they timed their kidnapping to avoid the lethal swing of his axe. Working in unison, they grabbed the Captain around his waist, using all their strength to wrestle him back.

'Get off me!' boomed the Captain.

'Do not test me brother – The Blades need you.' he yelled, fighting against the light bringer's bulk.

'The enchantment is waning.' said Nathaniel.

'We have other light bringers – let them deal with it.'

'They cannot cope. Stop acting like an impetuous child, and do your job.' he said abruptly, deliberately scolding the red-haired giant.

Ragnar growled thunderously in protest, before a sense of understanding eventually took hold; seeing him working together with Nathaniel had been enough to convey the gravity of their words. Realising the truth of the matter, The Captain's resistance quickly receded as Ragnar came to his senses, and together they passed back through the defensive barrier to support their brothers and sisters.

'Damn you Marcus!' she said, venting her frustration aloud, whilst her flanking forces were made to double back. The initial gullies lit by The Blades had not concerned her, however, those trenches subsequently ignited, had. A secondary network of irksome flame barriers had been unexpectedly erected, prior to their contact with the enemy's archers, which had been positioned precariously on the flanks of the hill opposite. She understood now the nature of Marcus' ploy, and the role of bait played magnificently by The Blades' archers. She watched angrily, through the minds of the doleful Narlakai, as her forces ponderously retraced their path, with the intention of reconnecting with the central block. The situation became worse when the archers opened fire, harrying the retreating Narlakai with repeated volleys. The vicious light-imbued arrows rained devastation upon the hapless soul stealers, thinning their ranks as they painstakingly regrouped. Darlia had lamented repeatedly about The Blade Lord's tactical prowess, which she was now witnessing first-hand. Having failed to take her lover's warning seriously, her forces were now paying the price. She toyed with the notion of outflanking the menacing flames, but the inordinate length of The Blade Lord's infernal trenches, coupled with the lethargic pace of the Narlakai – now under fire – meant the option was simply not viable. By the time the Narlakai laboriously navigated their way around the flaming obstacles, The Blades would have eroded the centre of her force, leaving her vulnerable. In any event, The Blade Lord had probably built in contingency for such a manoeuver. The Narlakai were forced to fight on *his* terms, but the weight of numbers remained in her favour; she could absorb the countless losses, however, The Blades could not. Besides, the Freylarkai would eventually break, as opposed to her dark host, which would continue to soldier on in accordance with her will, regardless of casualties suffered. Her mindless troupe of nightmare puppets would weather Marcus' futile resistance, down to the very last.

'Fire your pathetic arrows!' she cried, 'You cannot defeat them all.'

There was also the not-so-small matter of Krashnar's mutilated pet. She opened her mind – made difficult by the turmoil of battle – and searched for the abhorrent creature, seeking to reconnect with her loyal companion. The Meldbeast had swung out wide around The Blades' left flank, to avoid detection, and was now heading towards the enemy's rear. The monstrous beast bounded across the landscape at breakneck speed, bent on making contact with its target. She considered directing the creature towards the enemy's flanks, with the intent of wreaking havoc amongst its archers, but the Meldbeast's keen senses had detected another interesting opportunity – The Blade Lord himself. There was merit in both strategies. Take down the archers and protect the Narlakai's ranks, or destroy The Blades' lynchpin and watch her enemy break and run. She wrestled with the decision, trying to weigh up the pros and cons of both outcomes. Presumably, Marcus' would have no difficulties making the decision, but she had precious little experience with tactical decision making in the field. She cast her mind back to the Narlakai, in particular their ponderous movements; given their lacklustre pace, in all likelihood The Blade's archers would have their way with them before the Meldbeast could alleviate the pressure.

Considering this glaring fact, she convinced herself that Marcus presented the more valuable target, though perhaps she could do better, she mused. Charging The Blade Lord would ultimately be futile; his keen senses would likely detect the Meldbeast's approach, in addition, the auspicious eyes of scriers would be keenly observing his fate. With this in mind, she opened a fresh conduit to the Meldbeast's dominant central head, and proclaimed her will.

'Charge the archers on the left. Do not stop. Run through them. Once you are done, attack The Blade Lord!'

With renewed purpose, the Meldbeast adjusted its course slightly, in accordance with her will, locking its keen senses on the distant target. At thirty paces out, the muscular beast dipped its three heads, before accelerating towards The Blade's left flank, at all speed. She could sense the creature's growing excitement as it rapidly neared its prey, with preternatural speed. Predictably, the Freylarkai spotted the Meldbeast's approach, though it mattered little, since Marcus' forces were unable to react quickly enough to deal with the oncoming juggernaut. The Meldbeast's heads growled ferociously in unison, spreading terror amongst the defenders. The hulking behemoth prepared itself for the inevitable impact by angling its heads down, ready to bludgeon the Freylarkai standing in its path. Disorder quickly spread throughout the archers' ranks – the unprepared Blades began panicking at the sight of the beast's murderous charge. Desperate to avoid the beast's wide trajectory, they collided with one another in their haste, promptly falling to the ground. The Meldbeast thundered through the ranks of the hapless archers with devastating brutality. Those not immediately crushed under the weight of the beast's tread were brutally bludgeoned by its charge.

Their limp broken bodies were launched into the air, before landing horribly, in impossible positions, like discarded rag dolls. A horrid cacophony of battered armour, shattered bones and screams filled the air, as the Meldbeast trampled all those in its path, savagely raking the unit. One of The Blades was brutally laid low by the creature's prehensile tail, its sharp tip raking across the victim's face, tracing a line of acid that ate into their skin. Some of the archers managed to redirect their fire towards the beast, but few of the hastily launched projectiles hit their mark – such was the creature's pace – and those that did seemingly had no effect. Krashnar's pet had endured unimaginable suffering in its genesis, it was therefore folly to think that a few well-placed arrows would bring the hybrid down, optimistically ending its devastating rampage. The defiant Meldbeast paid no attention to The Blades' pathetic projectiles; the beast completed its dreadful charge, as per her command, before adjusting its heading towards The Blade Lord. Marcus had already drawn his bastard sword – the familiar weapon used to cleave Darlia's left hand. The end game was now tantalisingly in sight; The Blade Lord was highly skilled in close combat, but alone, he would offer little resistance for Krashnar's mutilated offspring – of that she was convinced.

It was almost morning by the time she, eventually, retreated to her personal chamber. The cycle had been eventful and long. The events surrounding Kirika and Darlia's fledgling insurrection, Lileah's renewed invasion, and the ugly business with Hanarah, had each consumed a piece of her soul. She felt mentally drained and physically exhausted, wanting nothing more than to collapse onto her bed, and to forget about the troubles that haunted her.

Regrettably, such simple pleasure eluded her grasp. The yoke of leadership refused to relent in its torture, following her all the way to the door of her chamber.

'My queen, we have received a report from the front line.' reported an aide, who had deliberately ambushed her outside of her chamber.

'What news did the Sky-Skitter bring?'

'The message scroll was delivered by dire wolf.'

'Dire wolf?'

'Yes, my queen. Krisis.'

The name was familiar, yet she could not place it; she was tired, and had not the strength of mind remaining to fathom its origin. Instead, she glared at the aide with her vacant eyes, knowing that her presence alone would wrestle the pertinent detail from the nervous Freylarkin's tongue.

'Lothnar's entourage, my Queen.'

'Yes, but what of the message itself?' she snapped, deliberately masking her ignorance.

'The Blade Lord reports that battlefield preparations were carried out successfully, in accordance with the strategy – the terrain is favourable.'

'And the Narlakai?'

'There is no mention of contact with the enemy, at least at the time of the report.'

'I see. When further news arrives, you are to relay word of it to me immediately. Is that clear?'

'Yes, my queen.'

'Please see that I am otherwise not disturbed. You are dismissed.'

'If I may – there is one other matter.'

'What is it?' she replied, wearily.

'The dire wolf – we are unsure what to do with it.'

'It is a wolf; I do not care. Send it back, feed it – do what you like.'

'Yes, my queen.'

The aide quickly scurried away, like a tiny animal running from a predator. She loathed garnering such hollow obedience through fear, yet she found intimidation to be a useful tool when directing her subjects. She seldom enjoyed the idle chatter necessary to soften her command, preferring instead to leave such nuances to both Marcus and Kirika. Given the choice, she would choose to spend her time alone, fashioning her elaborate trinkets in quiet solace, buried in private contemplation. The thought of such peaceful happiness called to her; perhaps she would shape the wooden door before her into a lethal barricade, adorned with sharp wooden barbs and vine-line snares. Yet her reality screamed otherwise, completely at odds with such fanciful musings – the Freylarkai would never allow her isolation. Her mind was losing its focus; she was tired, her vision was waning and she desperately required sleep. Despite her blissful musings, the only thing she immediately required was a bed. She pushed open the heavy doors to her chamber, stepping through into the large circular stone room beyond. The creeping first light of dawn seeped into her chamber, courtesy of its large arched window. The fledgling light refracted through the sea of tiny crystals hanging from the polished stone tree to her right. The gnarled construct toyed with the light, casting ephemeral shapes across the chamber's curved walls. The fleeting designs played tricks on her mind, suggesting the presence of an intruder, when in fact there was none. She quickly put her mind at ease, and began taking off her long thick dress, happy to discard its weight, which had grown heavier throughout the course of the cycle. The garment was now marked with Hanarah's blood, spoiling its otherwise pristine finish. Seeing the dark reddish-black stain sent her mind spinning, reminding her again of her guests currently lodging within the Tri-Spires.

'You will atone for your transgression, Larissa.' she said quietly to herself.

'As will you!' rasped a voice in response, originating from the direction of the crystal-stone tree.

She turned abruptly towards the voice. Her heart was racing, and she could hear the sound of her own rapid breathing loudly in her ears. Something jittered in the gloom, behind the tree, her enhanced vision confirming that she was indeed not alone. Recoiling at the sight, she turned her head towards the chamber door as panic gripped her, dictating her actions. Before she could make good her escape, however, something sharp drove itself through the right-lower quadrant of her abdomen with extreme velocity, jolting her entire body. She instinctively looked down and saw a spear, fashioned from granite, protruding from her body. Panic rapidly gave way to shock, and she found herself curiously inspecting the weapon's trajectory. What she had thought to be a spear was in fact more akin to a lance. The long spike angled upwards from the floor behind her, punctured her body and protruded from her front, the thin shaft of rock preventing her from moving. Cruel laughter echoed from behind the tree, after which a familiar shape emerged from its shadow. One by one, the crystals hanging from the stone tree detached from their moorings, as though plucked by invisible hands. Each fell to the floor, shattering upon impact with the hard surface into hundreds of tiny fragments that littered the ground. The ominous shape began to approach her, offering the shattered remains under its tread no regard.

'Hanarah...how is...this possible?!' she stammered, amidst her stuttered breathing.

'Because of you!' rasped Hanarah, in disgust.

'This...cannot be.' she said, wincing in pain, as the natural faux sedative associated with shock began to fade.

'Of course it can – your will alone made it possible.' the Freylarkin accused her contemptuously, with its wicked tongue.

Hanarah moved awkwardly towards her, like a broken marionette, no longer exclusively under the control of its master. As the scornful Freylarkin made her approach, little details began to reveal themselves, courtesy of her unique sight, confirming that Hanarah was not herself. The Freylarkin's skin was blotchy and off-colour, and in addition she appeared anatomically incorrect – beneath the surface of her skin – and disproportionate, as though sculpted by an amateur artist. Then, finally, the obvious truth of it dawned on her.

'You are...not Hanarah!' she stammered once more, still struggling with her breathing, due to her increasing panic.

Hanarah's eyes changed suddenly; her brown pupils rapidly morphed into two obsidian orbs that fixated on her intently.

'Krashnar!'

'Yesss.' the misshapen Freylarkin hissed, disturbingly. 'Your first exile has returned, triumphantly. So...are you going to welcome me home?'

Dawn was breaking. He glanced up, affording the receding night sky a moment's notice. Elongated trails of light continued to stretch upwards, their wake illuminating the bleak sky. The souls once trapped by the Narlakai now finally began their belated journey towards the Everlife. Refocusing his attention on the battle, more and more of the Narlakai flopped over the top of the telekinetic barrier, pushed forwards by their weight of numbers. The Blades' previously coordinated ranks were now starting to crumble, as the intruding horrors wreaked havoc amidst their lines. The sting of the light bringers' enchantments, coupled with the restraints enforced by the telekinetics, had allowed them to manage their foes. However, the barrier was now beginning to fail, under the relentless press of the dark host, now supported by its redeployed flanks. Arrows imbued with light continued to rain down on the soul stealers' seemingly endless numbers, with little hope of breaking their ranks. Under Lileah's command, the Narlakai were steadfast until the end, refusing to abandon their mistresses' fight, despite their ongoing casualties. Marcus had played a good hand, but numbers were not in The Blades' favour. As was habitually the case, Freylar's enemies continued to outnumber its forces – he failed to recall a time when the reverse was true. Perhaps the Freylarkai were doomed to extinction, their actions only delaying their inevitable fate. He chided himself for such pessimistic thoughts, and promptly redoubled his efforts. The restored enchantment in his falchion – courtesy of the Captain's renewed focus – blazed with anger, desperate to escape its metallic prison and unleash its fury on his enemies. He moved with supreme agility, ducking and diving beneath the thrashing gangrenous tentacles of the Narlakai, turning those he struck to ash. Despite the ruin he visited upon his foes, more Narlakai filled the gaps wrought by his devastating sword arm. The sustained assault of Lileah's dark host slowly eroded their numbers, and as time marched on, The Blades began to tire, hastening further losses. His heart felt heavy once again, as the true gravity of their situation crystallised in his mind. Without a means to break the enemy, there was little hope of The Blades bucking the worsening odds.

Daring to challenge his darkening mood – in the only way she knew how – Rayna doggedly blew apart a fresh column of Narlakai, threatening to divide their conjoined detachments. In her characteristically garish style, Rayna unleashed her raw, unrefined, inner light, which savagely annihilated the soul stealers to his right. The Guardian did not attempt to rein in her ability, and instead allowed her light to run rampant, obliterating those nightmare horrors in its path. Regrettably, Blades also numbered amongst the casualties, their eyes temporarily blinded by Rayna's brilliance. Yet the ends justified the means; once again, The Guardian had called it right, throwing convention in the bin, in favour of a more direct approach. He ran to the aid of several blinded Freylarkai, and – one by one – dragged them away from the front line, away from any immediate danger, whilst they struggled to regain their sight. As he pulled his brothers and sisters to relative safety, he watched as Rayna continued to sunder the Narlakai with her unique fighting style. With keen interest, he watched intently as The Guardian unleased the full power of her exotic Dawnstone twin blades. One he knew intimately – having gifted it to Rayna himself – however, the other aroused shameful memories, ones which were best left forgotten.

'The Ardent Blade.' he whispered to himself.

Adverse to his will, his mind stretched back to a darker time, one that necessitated questionable acts on his part, made possible by the weapon in Rayna's left hand. Seeing the temptress weapon again reminded him of the deeds it compelled, realised by the freedom it granted its bearer. Only one pure of heart could wield the blade without succumbing to the allure it offered. Rayna, however, put the wicked blade to work; The Guardian used the weapon to teleport across the battlefield at speed, bypassing the guard of her opponents entirely, allowing her to strike cleanly, unopposed, at the heart of the enemy. She flitted between the Narlakai, leaving a trail of ash in her wake, which lingered for a moment in the damp air. Despite the soul stealers' relentless writhing and thrashing, it was impossible for the enemy to grapple with The Guardian, who evaded their every attempt. His silver eyes widened, as his mind assembled the pieces of the puzzle, which explained the blade's unlikely presence.

'Nathaniel! Our flank is broken!' cried Lothnar suddenly, approaching rapidly from his left.

'What?!'

'Some kind of abhorrent creature has broken the archers. Marcus fights the beast, but he cannot prevail alone.'

'I will go.' he replied, grimly. 'The Narlakai do not leave casualties for me to heal. Besides, we need you, should we make contact with Lileah.'

'Remain here Teacher!' boomed the Captain, who joined their impromptu council of war.

'You are needed here.' Lothnar proclaimed.

'If we lose Marcus, we lose this fight! No amount of light bringers will save us then!'

He could see the conflict in Lothnar's eyes. They needed Ragnar's light, yet the red-haired giant, with his enormous axe, was the obvious beast-slayer amongst them. In any event, the Captain would not be dissuaded from aiding Marcus, ergo they had no say in the matter, which was resolved before ever being discussed.

'So be it.' replied Lothnar, reluctantly. 'Deal with the menace, then get back here!'

The Captain slapped the nomadic Paladin hard across the back, whilst baring his teeth in a wicked smile.

'Save some for me, brother.'

Ragnar turned, and bounded off up the hill, towards the broken archers, which he could see clearly now, fleeing directly towards them.

'Lothnar, take command of the detachment. I will get the archers back in line.'

'Should I not be the one to rally them?'

'No. I instructed most of them – they *will* heed my command. Your presence will be more impactful here, on the front line, inspiring The Blades. This is a time of heroes, and you are a Paladin – they look up to you.'

'Very well – get them back in line, brother.'

'I shall. Oh, and Lothnar, if they overrun the breach, we *will not* survive this.'

'I understand!'

NINETEEN
Hurt

Like an ever-present shadow, part of her mind lodged itself in the beast's own, observing its fight with The Blade Lord, content to be an eager spectator as the creature spilled Marcus' blood across the moor. Marcus gripped his bastard sword in his right hand, holding his shield with his left. The Blade Lord stood alone, resolutely, in the Meldbeast's line of charge, his stance unyielding and with his unflinching gaze fixed firmly on his attacker. Marcus' staunch disposition came as no surprise to her – she expected nothing less – but failed to even register with her former mount. Krashnar's pet was charged, ready for battle, caring not for the stubbornness of its prey. Delaying the inevitable – in an act of futility – Marcus would remain dogged until the end. The Meldbeast dipped its heads and ran through The Blade Lord, who attempted to side step the creature just moments prior to contact. The tip of Marcus' long blade caught the tail end of the beast's flank, tracing a short red line along its skin that immediately bled into the creature's matted fur. Despite the wound, the Meldbeast's prehensile tail flicked down and left, knocking The Blade Lord's feet out from underneath him. Marcus fell awkwardly to the ground, but recovered quickly whilst the beast circled round, maintaining its momentum, ready for a fresh charge. She laughed wickedly as the Meldbeast ran down The Blade Lord once again, this time leaping towards its target. Marcus dived to his left and attempted to rake the creature's soft underbelly with his blade. Using its supreme agility, the Meldbeast transformed its leap into a forward dive; the chimera tucked in its heads, save for the one on its right, which bit down savagely across

The Blade Lord's weapon, locking the fuller securely between its teeth. The Meldbeast rolled away, propelled by its own momentum, taking the blade with it, violently wrenching the weapon from Marcus' grasp. The force yanked Marcus' right arm brutally, pulling him back down to the ground in a crumpled mess. She laughed again as The Blade Lord stood upright once more, now with his sword arm hanging limply by his side – in all likelihood dislocated by the force of the Meldbeast's attack.

'*Finish him now!*' she conveyed vehemently to the beast. '*Tear him apart!*'

The Meldbeast paced around The Blade Lord in a wide circle; it snorted at the air, savouring its dominance over its prey. Refusing to relinquish its stolen weapon, the Meldbeast's right head continued to grasp Marcus' sword in its jaws. Perhaps, after the battle was over, she would offer the bastard sword to Darlia as a gift – the blade that took her former lover's hand. After a single intimidating lap, the beast ceased parading and began pacing slowly towards The Blades' defeated leader. Marcus held his shield side-on, intent on using it as a weapon, given the absence of his sword. No doubt his shield would make an excellent tool for bludgeoning a Freylarkin, but against the Meldbeast she questioned its effectiveness; the beast's mass alone would be sufficient to mitigate its effects. Krashnar's pet chimera disregarded the improvised weapon, clearly not perceiving it to be a threat. The beast crouched menacingly, flicking its pointed chitin tail left and right, ready to pounce, carefully choosing its moment to strike whilst the battle raged around them.

'*Strike now!*' she commanded impatiently. '*Release him!*'

The creature was about to pounce, when suddenly it released a hideous yelp. Turning abruptly to face a new threat, the Meldbeast saw its own prehensile tail cleanly separated and writhing on the ground. Acidic fluid pooled around the severed end, causing faint smoke to rise from the ground whilst the scrubland beneath was slowly eaten away. Standing behind its severed limb was a massive Freylarkin carrying an enormous axe. The Freylarkin's weapon emitted a soft glow, like the arrows that had rained down on her dark host. She recalled the stories of the Paladins and Valkyries, told to her as a child – in particular, one about the red-haired giant with his massive axe; the Freylarkin standing defiantly before the Meldbeast was Ragnar, Captain of The Blades.

'Pathetic, you are no match for us. Destroy him!'

Krashnar's pet gathered itself, ready to pounce once more, but the Captain had already drawn a backup hand axe, which he threw towards the Meldbeast's central head. The creature turned to evade the incoming projectile, but was unsuccessful; the axe's smile buried itself in the beast's left neck as it turned away, trying to avoid the attack. The remaining two heads gave out an ear-splitting yelp, causing Marcus' bastard sword to fall to the ground with a dull thud. Ragnar's axe remained buried where it had struck; cut off from fresh supplies of blood, the wounded chimera's left head hung limp, causing the creature to list ever so slightly. Blood from the ghastly wound splattered across the moor, and the chimera began shuffling awkwardly, confused, struggling to understand the situation.

'Release him!' she commanded in a scolding manner, seeking to reaffirm her command over the creature's dominant mind. *'Cease cowering and release him now!'*

Following her swift rebuke, the Meldbeast regained its composure, quickly coming about ready for a renewed attack against the irksome Blade Captain. Ragnar now held his monstrous double handed axe with both hands, and had drawn the weapon back, ready to receive the Meldbeast's inevitable charge.

'*Now!*' she commanded, impatiently, allowing her impetuous rage to get the better of her.

The Meldbeast quickly built up speed as it charged again, headlong towards the Captain, with no regard for its own welfare. The defiant Paladin bent slightly at the knees, baring his gritted teeth; the fearless Captain remained steadfast, offering his attacker no quarter. Ragnar's stance was foolish to the extreme – the gallant Freylarkin would be broken irrevocably by the beast's thunderous charge.

'*Goodbye Ragnar!*'

The black tide of writhing tentacles crashing against them was relentless. Destroyed Narlakai were quickly replaced by more, their numbers seemingly without end, yet their own losses were hard felt. Dawn – their only salvation – was now breaking, but its dreary pale sky brought with it little solace. Although the fledgling sun's weak rays came to their aid, the feeble light merely slowed the Narlakai down, an advantage quickly mitigated by their failing telekinetics. The invisible barrier suppressing Lileah's black host was now patchy at best, and Narlakai were now breaking through the unseen breaches, making a mess of The Blades' carefully coordinated ranks. Skirmishes broke out across their formation, with heroes attempting to snuff out the pockets of resistance in an attempt to hold the line with their dwindling numbers. Screams continued to fill the air as more of The

Blades were dragged beneath the dark mass to their inevitable doom. Others were hoisted off the ground, plucked from where they once stood, and tossed into the black abyss. One Narlakin in particular appeared bent on such action; having sated its own appetite, it now felt obligated to feed the souls of the Freylarkai to its dark kin. The soul stealer had thicker tentacles than the rest, and its gaseous mass appeared almost double that of the norm.

'Sister, we must release that threat!'

'Nathanar, take command here – I need to deal with that horror, before its actions break our resolve.' she cried, hoping that he would hear her words over the din.

'Go!' he cried in return. 'We will hold.'

She gave the blue-eyed Paladin a quick nod, before cutting a path directly towards the nightmare, which continued to make short work of her brothers and sisters. Though she had tried her best to decimate the enemy's ranks using her inner light, the continued use of her ability had taken its toll on her body. Both she and the remaining light bringers were tiring fast, plus the Narlakai were inexorably drawn to them; the soul stealers could sense their presence, and thus prioritised the light bringers' release, increasing the risk to those with her ability. Her arms now felt like lead weights, yet she continued to fight on, using Shadow Caster for crowd control and The Ardent Blade to vanquish her foes and accelerate her movements – she dared only imbue the latter, given the nature of the essence imprisoned within its Dawnstone twin. Using her unique blades, she swiftly engaged the standout Narlakin. The soul stealer had wrestled yet another Blade from their ranks, who it now dangled high in the air, with one of its thick tendrils. She fully expected the unfortunate Freylarkin to succumb to the same ill fate as the others molested by the oversized horror, but instead the Narlakin flexed its powerful tendril, hurling the limp armoured body directly towards her. She dived forwards, hitting the ground hard. The abhorrent projectile, flung by her nightmare attacker, narrowly missed her, passing over her head. The body of the unfortunate Freylarkin thumped and clattered across the moor, the violent impact shattering bones and bludgeoning flesh. Before she could get to her feet, the wretched horror wrapped a tentacle around her left arm, squeezing it tight. She lost her grip on The Ardent Blade, and was pulled upright, towards the Narlakin, which began to open its terrifying maw. A long vertical rift formed in the centre of the soul stealer's semi-gaseous body, which pulled the falling rain towards it. Thoughts of Kryshar paralysed her as panic quickly took hold; the disturbing images of the released light bringer's demise continued to haunt her.

'Rayna! You must act!'

Alarielle's words cried out in her mind, quickly bringing her to her senses and giving her the mental kick she desperately needed to function. With supreme effort, struggling against the pull of gravity, she brought Shadow Caster round in a high arc. The blade cut the thick tentacle tethering her to her attacker, and the Narlakin gave out a deep moan as both she and its severed limb fell to the ground. The back of her head pounded against the damp moor, temporarily stunning her, giving the soul stealer time to recover from its wound. More tentacles extended from the Narlakin's gaseous body, quickly wrapping themselves around her arms and legs. The soul stealer wrenched her from the ground yet again, this time squeezing her right arm unbearably tight. She though that perhaps her arm would snap under the immense pressure, but her attacker quickly relented its grip after Shadow Caster fell from her grasp, embedding itself in the cold wet ground. She tried to attack, but the soul stealer violently yanked her limbs in opposite directions, tearing at her muscles. The agony of her stretched limbs disrupted her concentration, causing her to cry out in pain and making it impossible for her to manifest her inner light. The soul stealer continued to widen its abhorrent maw as it drew her in, ripe for devouring. She could feel her soul being pulled from its moorings, as the horror commenced its ugly feeding ritual.

'Rayna, fight it!'

'I can't!' she cried, her muscles feeling as though they were on fire.

'You must try!'

'I am – Alarielle, help me!'

The pain was now immense. Reality began slipping away as her mind began to let go, be it due to the hurt inflicted upon her, or the leeching of her soul. Regardless of the cause, she could sense her body beginning to shut down, no longer able to cope.

'I am sorry sister, but there is no other way. Please forgive me, and accept this as my parting gift.'

The press of Narlakai was now unbearable; her mind felt as though it would explode due to the strain placed upon it. Those with her ability were virtually spent; they could no longer hold back the writhing black abyss which threatened to engulf them all. Pockets of fighting had broken out against soul stealers that had managed to break through their invisible barrier. The Blades were no longer the cohesive fighting force they had been, since the beast engaging The Blade Lord had outflanked their formation, wreaking havoc on their lines. Their formation was now crumbling, and along with it, any chances of success against the overwhelming numbers they continued to face. She wanted nothing more than to unleash her arrows upon their enemy, but they needed the barrier, without which there would be little hope for The Blades' survival.

'I feel useless – tell me what I can do.'

'The Guardian gave you your orders, Darlia – you *will* be needed.'

'Not if that barrier fails. Please, Natalya, allow me to use your weapon.'

Never before had she allowed another to use her bow – such was its personal nature – yet she sympathised with Darlia's feeling of uselessness, knowing that she herself would abhor being in such a position. Despite their brief acquaintance, she felt compelled to aid the wanting scrier; Kirika's elder sibling was willing to help, and The Blades desperately required aid – the time for scruples had passed.

'Very well – take it.'

Darlia quickly took her weapon and gripped the recurve bow tightly in her mechanical claw. The scrier quickly nocked one of her imbued arrows, drew back with her good hand and released. The projectile struck the core of a Narlakin pressed tightly against the collapsing barrier; the soul stealer immediately disintegrated, leaving in its wake a cloud of ash, rapidly absorbed by the maelstrom of battle.

'You are proficient with a bow.'

'I had to be, living for so long in the borderlands.'

Darlia continued to release the Narlakai immediately before them. She could feel the pressure in her mind easing, ever so slightly. Though in the grand scheme of things

Darlia's efforts meant very little, nonetheless, she welcomed any respite the scrier could offer.

'Aim just above the core, the arrows will pass through more cleanly. Too high, however, and they will not release their target.'

Darlia was about to draw again, when the sky above them suddenly lit up once more. A fresh hail of arrows rained down on the black host, immediately easing the pressure on her mind as the imbued projectiles levelled entire ranks of the horrors. She turned her attention towards the hill and saw Nathaniel commanding the left flank; the previously scattered archers were now back in formation, and were already nocking fresh arrows to their bows ready for a second volley. As she directed her attention back towards the front line, she saw The Guardian hoisted high above the battlefield, suspended by numerous thick tentacles which had wrapped themselves tightly around the light bringer's limbs. She watched in dismay as the nightmare pulled Rayna towards its stretched maw, ready to feed.

'Darlia, redirect your fire, now.' she barked, nodding in the direction of The Guardian's attacker.

The scrier quickly redirected her aim, maintaining an iron grip on her bow.

'I cannot hit accurately at that range.'

'Shoot anyway.'

'I might hit her.'

'Do it!

Darlia did as instructed, releasing her grip on the bowstring. The arrow flew high, with Darlia attempting to predict its parabolic curve. Using her ability, she locked onto the fast-moving projectile, barely able to catch it due to her divided attention. Guiding the arrow's trajectory, she used her ability to steer the projectile more accurately. Darlia's arrow punctured the soul stealer, causing part of the Narlakin's immense semi-gaseous body to burn away. Yet despite the devastating wound, the horror continued to function, its will bent on The Guardian's imminent release. Ash and rain were drawn towards the Narlakin, deep into its hideous maw, as it began consuming Rayna's soul, wrenching it from her entangled body.

'Again!' she cried, desperately calling upon Darlia's skill with her bow.

Darlia quickly nocked another arrow to her powerful recurve bow. The competent archer began to draw and aim, though it was painfully obvious to both that they were too late to save the revered light bringer. They watched in disbelief as the remorseless Narlakin ripped Rayna's soul from its host. Torn beyond its point of elasticity, the horror consumed the light bringer's soul, pulling it wholly into its abyss-like rift. After devouring The Guardian's essence, the soul stealer allowed Rayna's empty vessel to fall to the ground, unceremoniously discarded like an unwanted wrapper. Tears of anger rolled down her cheeks as she watched the merciless ruin of Freylar's herald of change. She desperately wanted to cry out for their loss, but the words that could have been, quickly died in her throat, along with her hopes. The invisible barrier holding back the black tide finally gave way, its inevitable collapse ushering forth their inescapable doom.

'We are undone.'

'No, we are not – look!' replied Darlia, whilst redirecting her aim towards the encroaching Narlakai.

The Guardian's hunched body glowed brightly against the morning gloom, like some kind of otherworldly beacon, sent to light their path, before being lost to them entirely. Hope – only moments ago thought lost to her – unexpectedly rekindled itself, as Rayna's body curiously pushed itself to its feet. The light bringer was doubled over, seemingly struggling to contain a raging brilliance manifesting rapidly inside her. Without the strength necessary to hold back the wanton retribution of her ability, a devastating nova exploded outwards from The Guardian. Light shot across the battlefield, blinding all those looking upon it. She tried to turn away from the fierce outburst, but the vicious intensity of the light savagely robbed her of her sight. Around her The Blades screamed in agony, the pain of losing their sight too much to bear. She too cried out, as the world around her abruptly disappeared from view. It took several moments before her senses reoriented themselves, allowing her to think clearly once more.

'Darlia, where are you.' she whimpered, still clawing at her sockets.

'Natalya...I am over here.' replied a cracked voice, to her left.

She followed the sound of Darlia's voice, ultimately tripping over the scrier and landing hard on the ground. Darlia's good hand pressed against her face; the scrier blindly fumbled around, trying to discern if she was hurt from the fall.

'I am fine – albeit, I cannot see.'

'Nor I.' replied Darlia, who grabbed her left shoulder, helping her upright.

'What happened...and what of the Narlakai?'

'I do not know; I saw the light, and then came the screams. It was The Guardian – Rayna seemed to explode.'

The pain in his eyes had been immense. Never before had he witnessed such brilliant light, and without the aid of the renewalists, it would be the last thing The Blades ever saw. He quickly surveyed the battlefield after restoring his own sight; the gullies continued to burn vehemently, but the remainder of the landscape had changed significantly. All around him, The Blades lay on the ground, clutching at their faces or staring vacantly into the distance, no longer able to focus on anyone or anything. Some of the renewalists had already recovered from their blinding trauma, and were scrambling around, tending to the nearest wounded. Behind him he saw Marcus, battered after his fight with the chimera that had broken their ranks. The Blade Lord squinted repeatedly, trying in vain to regain his sight. Close by, he saw the broken remains of the Captain, who lay crushed under the weight of the beast that had attacked them; Ragnar's face had been savagely mauled, with blood staining the wet moor underneath the back of his head. Like the Captain, the creature itself remained perfectly still, unsurprising given the massive axe buried in its central head, and the river of blood pouring from its split skull. Cries of pain sounded all around, and moans of discomfort drifted on the ash-strewn air. Lileah's dark host had suffered greatly during the explosion; only a handful of Narlakai remained, the rest annihilated and scattered on the merciless wind. Hundreds, perhaps thousands, of previously trapped souls commenced their journey to the Everlife; their light mixed with the rain-sodden ash, giving the sky an eerie dirty amber hue, unlike the usually blood-soaked fields which had told the unfortunate tales of most battles he had fought in. At the bottom of the hill, where the fighting had been fiercest, was Rayna. Moments prior to the explosion, he had thought his daughter lost to him for a second time. He recalled the harrowing sight of her attacker devouring her soul, but somehow she now stood upright. Her head was tilted back, and she was crying, pleading perhaps – words that he could not discern – towards the sky. The Guardian seemed oblivious to the destruction she had wrought upon the field of battle. In the distance, beyond the confused light bringer, he saw the instrument of their demise. The immensely potent telepath, Lileah, stood close to a handful of surviving Narlakai. The remorseless exile appeared to be rubbing her eyes, no doubt in a futile attempt to regain her sight. Finally, the opportunity Marcus sought had presented itself.

'See to the Captain's wounds!' he barked towards the nearest active renewalist. 'When you are done, tend to The Blade Lord and the archers.'

The pre-emptive healer nodded in acknowledgement then promptly made his way towards the Captain's ruined body.

'And coordinate the other renewalists!'

He cast his gaze across the battlefield, hurriedly searching for Kirika's elder sibling. He quickly located Darlia, not far from the base of the hill; the former exile was huddled close to Natalya, suggesting that both had also lost the use of their eyes. Sprinting down the hill towards the unlikely duo, he slid to a halt just short of their position.

'Who is there?!' enquired Natalya, clearly startled by his abrupt presence.

'At ease – it is me, Nathaniel.'

'Nathaniel, thank goodness. What has happened?'

'You will see for yourselves soon enough.' he replied, pressing his hands to the sides of their faces. 'This may feel a little uncomfortable.'

Being a master renewalist, restoring their lost sight was a simple enough task; their vision quickly returned, replacing the vacant expression previously etched on their faces with one of shock – both were clearly alarmed by the changed landscape now surrounding them.

'Did Rayna do this?!' asked Natalya, struggling to comprehend that which she already knew to be true.

'We can discuss that later. Our opportunity presents itself – we must act now!'

Stirred by the urgency of his words, Darlia surveyed the landscape, quickly locating her former lover, who was already drawing the few remaining Narlakai towards her.

'You *must* go to her, as we discussed.' he said, fixing Kirika's sister with the intense gaze of his silver orbs.

Darlia's already pale face became even more so; the stark realisation of the task assigned to her clearly weighed heavily on her soul.

'In this, you cannot falter.' he pressed, stressing the gravity of their plight.

'She remains protected.' replied Darlia, meekly.

'We will accompany you, as best we can, though she will not permit us to get close – you understand?'

The exiled scrier said nothing; Darlia remained seated on the ground, staring quietly at Lileah in the distance. Sensing the conflict raging inside Kirika's elder sibling, he began to wonder if Marcus' plan was inherently flawed. He knew first-hand the power of love, specifically the capricious nature of the emotion. If the scrier failed to carry out The Blade Lord's plan, there would be no salvation for their kin. The Blades were spent, and what remained of their force was severely incapacitated. Although The Guardian had eliminated the Narlakai threat, they still required one final decisive push if they were to entertain any realistic chance of victory.

'You came to us for this very reason - this was your design. Please, Darlia, I am begging you, on behalf of all those families back in the vale. Please do not allow Lileah's impetuous nature to rob them of their loved ones.'

'And yet I am asked to rob myself of my own.' replied Darlia, sombrely.

'I cannot begin to fathom the depths of your despair, both past and present. I can only plead for your aid on behalf of our people.'

'Your people, Nathaniel – I was cast out.'

'By the will of one alone.'

'But you allowed it!'

'Yes, and I cannot absolve that mistake; it is a sin that we must endure. However, at the very least, I will make a solemn promise to you that we will learn from that mistake, to prevent history from repeating itself.'

'I can still reason with her.'

'You know that is not true. Any attempt to do so will result in the loss of your advantage.'

'You ask that I give up what remains of my soul, Nathaniel, yet I do not have the strength to do so.'

'I am asking much of you – I know this – and it is all I *can* do. I cannot offer you anything in return to make this right. Darlia, you alone must decide if saving *your* kin is worth the sacrifice asked of you.'

TWENTY
Pursuit

'How did...you get in here?' she said, struggling to convey her words due to the throbbing pain caused by her wound.

'Is it not obvious to you?' the shaper facetiously replied. 'Do your eyes not betray my secrets?'

Slowly Krashnar's true visage revealed itself; Hanarah's voluptuous clean skin gave way to dark lines, stretched across a grubby drawn face, and her fingernails were now dirty and broken. Hanarah's lips dried rapidly, and her groomed hair became matted and unkempt. The reformed Freylarkin now stood hunched before her. Krashnar appeared uglier than she remembered, and looked utterly ridiculous dressed in Hanarah's female attire.

'Surely by now you are familiar with our power?'

'You refer to yourself...the plural?'

'Irrelevant!' snapped the shaper, suggesting that she had touched upon a sensitive matter. 'You have no idea how long I have waited for this moment. Now here you are, ready to become our latest play-thing.'

'You disgust me!' she retorted, wincing in pain again as her vehement response agitated the shaft of rock piercing her body. 'I would sooner court release than amuse your perverse sensibilities.'

'A great pity. Perhaps I should tighten your restraints. Though I would prefer to conserve my strength, so that I might violate your flesh more deeply.'

The dishevelled looking Freylarkin shuffled slowly towards her, utterly disrespecting her personal space. Krashnar pressed his ugly face into the side of her left cheek;

she could feel his malformed nose nuzzling her marble-like skin, the sensation filling her with a sense of dread. After indulging in his brief moment of ecstasy, the vile shaper pulled away, ever so slightly, before flicking out his grotesque long tongue. He dragged the wet coarse flesh upwards, across the side of her face, starting just underneath her jaw, steadily working his way towards her left temple. The disgusting sensation made her skin crawl, and she felt physically sick as he defiled her so brazenly. Fear did its best to paralyse her, both mentally and physically, but she would not allow the abhorrent wretch to violate her any further. Deftly, she slid her right arm behind her back, and gripped the shaft piercing her body. Channelling her ability, she delicately separated the granite lance, either side of her hand, leaving enough length to act as a makeshift weapon. Free from her entrapment, she swiftly took a step back from the shaper, bringing her newly formed cudgel round in a wide arc, catching Krashnar flush against his face. The excruciating pain caused by executing the manoeuvre forced her to relinquish her grip on the weapon. The granite cudgel clattered upon the hard floor, whilst she staggered backwards, struggling to maintain her balance. A moderate length of the crudely shaped lance used to puncture her flesh still protruded from her body, causing immense pain. She called out repeatedly for help, hoping in vain that someone would hear her agonised cries. In the wake of her desperate shouts, loud banging sounded against the doors to her chamber – someone was trying to enter the room, but the thick wooden doors remained firmly shut. More cruel laughter spilled from the recovering shaper's evil tongue; the left side of Krashnar's face was bleeding, where his dirty skin was broken following her attack, yet the returned exile appeared entirely unconcerned.

'Ah, such unexpected spunk – do you even realise the heightened pleasure your futile actions bestow upon me?'

'You are sick...and cruel – I should have ordered Marcus...to release you. Exile was a mercy!'

'Exile is to deny one of their senses – there is no greater sentence, which you are guilty of serving upon others. I will claim you as my prize, and your violations will atone for my shallow existence; your ongoing displeasure will be our delectable pleasure.' the shaper replied hoarsely, before licking his cracked lips.

Further bangs came from the direction of the chamber's doors, distracting her from Krashnar's vile words.

'The Freylarkai on the other side of those doors, who seek to aid their self-serving queen, will not come to your aid – look closer, see for yourself.'

Krashnar had reshaped the granite floor along the base of the doors, forcing the rock to ride up, creating a lip that prevented them from opening. Though his masonry was immensely crude, the results were ultimately effective. In all likelihood, the shaper had carried out the work whilst lurking in the shadow of her tree. She cursed herself for her lack of perception – even with her enhanced sight, she had failed miserably to notice his presence, until it was too late.

'Do not think to test me, *my queen*. Make any attempt to open those doors and I will flay your skin where you stand!'

In light of the severity of the situation, she chose to call his bluff, convinced that her attacker could not carry out his hollow threat without direct physical contact. Feigning critical injury from her wound, she lowered herself slowly to the ground, whimpering submissively as she crouched. In truth, her novice acting skills were barely required, as the shaft – still protruding from her torso – jostled again, inciting further hurt. Krashnar squinted his horrid abyss-like eyes, watching her curiously, as she squirmed before him. When at last her fingertips contacted with the floor, she channelled her ability once more, this time across the length of the room, instantly breaking the barrier sealing the chamber doors.

'Bitch!' cried the shaper, who leapt towards her with sudden preternatural speed.

Krashnar violently grabbed her throat with his sole good hand, forcing her back to the floor. She screamed in agony as the granite shaft penetrating her body shifted once more. Cuts immediately began appearing across her body, as though invisible forces haphazardly took a knife to her unblemished skin. The incisions widened, causing blood to spill from the wounds and onto the floor.

'I warned you! Now suffer our wrath, bitch!'

'You can't leave me – not like this.' she cried, shouting fervently at the artificially lit sky. 'Alarielle!'

Tears filled her eyes, causing the hundreds of souls travelling towards the Everlife to blur together as one, akin to a sphere of light.

'Calm now.'

'What?!' she replied, completely taken aback by the unforgettable voice that suddenly pierced her mind.

'Calm now.' replied the familiar voice, once more.

'You! You are the one who brought me to Freylar.' she said, managing to overcome her shock.

'The Guardian has played their part.'

'What do you mean – did you bring me here, just so that I would feed them to you?!'

'The Guardian's task is complete.'

'Return her to me.'

'That soul does not wish to return.'

'You lie – give her back!'

'That soul belongs to me now – it is not yours to keep.'

'You can't, it will break him, and me! I cannot endure the loss of another. The constant torment is too great; I cannot live this way.'

'You wish to return to your original broken vessel?'

'No – I cannot go back.'

'The Guardian has decided.'

'Decided what?!'

'You will remain here, to guard the souls from those who would keep them from me.'

'You mean the Narlakai?' she replied, blinking away the tears from her eyes.

There was no response to her question. The entity that had brought her to Freylar ceased all communication with her as abruptly as it had commenced their unique dialogue.

'Answer me!' she cried, desperate to learn more from the being. 'Damn it!'

She felt hollow inside, no longer whole, as though part of her soul had been stripped away. Her mind was alone once more, now exclusively her own, no longer required to make space for another in light of her lodger's absence. The feeling of emptiness made her shudder, realising now just how close she had become to Alarielle. Learning of his daughter's departure would ruin Nathaniel – how then was she supposed to break word of Alarielle's release? Furthermore, the entity proclaimed that the decision to move on was Alarielle's own.

How could Nathaniel possibly accept such a thing? Before she could begin to fathom the answer to such questions, Kirika's elder sibling ran straight past her, with both Nathaniel and Natalya in close pursuit. Seeing all three rush frantically past woke her from her reverie. For the first time since her attacker devoured Alarielle's soul, she became acutely aware of her surroundings, and the devastation caused by her unfettered rage. She remembered clearly the events at Scrier's Post, when her eventual recollection of Kaitlin's fate compelled her to unleash her anger against the soul stealers. The result had been destructive, giving The Blades the chance they needed to fend off the invasion, albeit temporarily. This, however, was an extreme version of that previous event. Learning the true fate of the Shadow class, abandonment by Trix, followed by the loss of Alarielle, was too much for her psyche to bear. All the rage, anger and hate, pent-up inside her, had finally unleashed itself, given form courtesy of her ability. The result was truly devastating. The surrounding battlefield had been stripped bare by her loss of control. Everywhere Blades lay on the ground, clutching at their eyes and moaning in pain, whilst a handful of surviving renewalists frantically scrambled around healing the wounded. Amongst them was Galadrick, seconded into Kirika's militia. The Adept renewalist worked fervently, doing his best to undo the damage caused by her indiscriminate attack. She felt sick witnessing first-hand the results of her carelessness. The Freylarkai had finally accepted her, despite her controversial arrival, and in return she had hurt them – first Nathaniel, and now The Blades. Atoning for such mass injury would take everything from her, nevertheless, she vowed to make right her actions. Yet despite the rampant destruction she had unleashed upon the

Freylarkai, the enemy had suffered far worse. Few Narlakai had survived the nova, the rest reduced to ash, which slowly descended to the ground, mixing with the rain to create a thin grey film that covered the moor. The surviving horrors that had somehow weathered the apocalypse were slowly retreating towards a small Freylarkin, who stood alone in the distance. It was towards this same individual whom Darlia, Nathaniel and Natalya currently ran.

'Lileah!' she said aloud, quickly discerning the obvious.

She immediately scanned the battlefield, hoping dearly that the one she sought was not amongst those currently making their journey towards the Everlife. Less than ten paces away she found her prize, blindly wandering across the landscape.

'Lothnar!' she cried, 'You are needed!'

Despite the ambient cries of pain from her fallen brothers and sisters, the Paladin's acute hearing heard her cry, prompting him to adjust his course towards her position. Fighting off her exhaustion, she ran towards Lothnar, stopping just short of his seemingly aimless wandering.

'Lothnar, it's me.'

'Rayna?'

'The Narlakai are almost spent. Lileah stands alone, but I cannot approach her without your help.'

'You *must* guide me!' he said, holding out his right arm.

'I understand – hold onto me tightly.'

She permitted the Paladin to grab her arm, and together they began jogging towards the vengeful exile who had wrought so much destruction upon their kin. She steered them via the site of Alarielle's release, stooping en route to retrieve her Dawnstone blades. When bringing her head back up, she saw Nathaniel go down hard, clutching his head and releasing the grip on his falchion. Forcing The Teacher to abandon his weapon was no mean feat, but to seem him taken down so easily was alarming. Deep down she already knew that she would share the same fate as Nathaniel, but none of that actually mattered. They would each play their part, hoping to distract Lileah as best they could. The only thing that mattered now was Darlia, in particular, the scrier's resolve.

Darlia was quick on her feet, despite the weight of her mechanical hand; she ran directly towards Lileah, paying no heed to the Narlakai gathering around the spiteful young telepath. The scrier was either supremely confident in her ability to foresee the future, and thus evade the soul stealers entirely, or she fancied the likelihood of Lileah choosing not to attack, preying on the heartstrings of her former lover. Regardless, she did not share Darlia's seemingly unwavering faith. Aiming her recurve bow with her left hand, she raised her weapon and drew back its bowstring, ready to shoot. She was an excellent shot, even at speed. Hitting the Narlakai would not be the issue; clearing them in time, however, was another matter. Fortunately, the light from Rayna's apocalyptic outburst had rejuvenated the enchantment previously bestowed upon her arrows, giving her the weapons necessary to assault the remainder of Lileah's dark host. However, before she could fire, Nathaniel suddenly went down hard. The master renewalist cried out in pain whilst clutching his head, completely undone by the power of Lileah's malicious mind. She considered breaking off her assault to aid Nathaniel, but there was little point in doing so. In all likelihood, she would be the target of Lileah's next attack; she needed to ensure Darlia's safe passage, before her fate inevitably followed The Teacher's own. She released her bowstring, sending one of her enchanted arrows towards a surviving Narlakin. The arrow speared through the horror's core, instantly disintegrating it. As the arrow left its target, she brought it around in a wide arc using her mind, sending it racing towards another of the soul stealers. Whilst steering her first shot – using her telekinesis – she hastily released a second arrow, which she also dared to guide simultaneously with her mind. The arrows curved through the air, puncturing multiple targets, creating plumes of ash in Darlia's path. The wilful scrier continued her charge, running straight through the clouds of ash that lingered for a short time in the air, before the rain ultimately had its way with them. The enchantment on her projectiles already in flight waned with each target they struck; each obliterated Narlakin sapped a portion of the light imprisoned within them, eventually rendering them ineffective. Nonetheless, their wanton destruction provided her a relatively unobstructed long shot at the powerful telepath. She nocked another of her arrows to her recurve bow, drew back once more and released the vicious projectile towards Lileah. Steering the arrow past Darlia and several intervening Narlakai, she willed the arrow well beyond its normal range, accelerating the projectile with the power of her mind. The arrow raced towards its target, striking the telepath cleanly in the centre of her chest. To her dismay, the arrow smashed upon impact, splintering in to numerous tiny pieces that quickly fell to the ground.

'What the--'

Intense pain stabbed her mind, stealing the use of her legs and causing her vision to black out for a second time. She fell hard upon the ground, bruising and scraping her body against the moor as her body slid to a halt. The agony in her mind was debilitating; she writhed on the wet ground clutching at her head, in a futile attempt to shield herself from the immensely powerful attack. So extreme was the pain that she began to wretch uncontrollably – the horrendous experience was unlike anything she had previously endured. Flashes of random colour assaulted her vision, as Lileah continued to scramble her mind with her vicious ability. She screamed in pain, convinced that she would never see Freylar again.

Abruptly, the pain subsided and her vision returned. She looked up to see Lothnar crouched next to her. The nomadic Paladin bore an intense expression, yet his eyes were eerily vacant, suggesting that he had not yet recovered from The Guardian's attack. She pushed herself off the floor and quickly retrieved her recurve bow. Nathaniel was also now back on his feet and raced to join them.

'Nathaniel, what is happening?!' she cried out.

'He is disrupting her ability, but I must assist him.' replied The Teacher, coming to an abrupt stop beside them.

Nathaniel placed his hands against Lothnar's head and began to shore up the Paladin's crumbling mind, hoping that together they could stalemate their attacker long enough to make a difference.

'Natalya, you must help Darlia and Rayna – go!'

She scrambled to her feet and ran towards Lileah once more. Her body ached from her fall and her head throbbed, but she pushed through the pain, bent on ridding Freylar of its spiteful attacker. Darlia was close now, hotly pursued by Rayna, some twenty paces back; The Guardian had sheathed her falchions and was running full pelt. Releasing more of her arrows, she took down several more of the soul stealers forming Lileah's makeshift entourage with her augmented projectiles. She reached for another of her arrows, only to find that there were no more; amidst the carnage of battle, she had uncharacteristically lost count of the arrows remaining in her quiver.

'Damn it!'

She discarded her bow and channelled her remaining strength through her legs, trying her utmost to catch up with Rayna, who by now had pulled away notably. Her body ached from the punishment it had endured, though she would not falter; a great many of The Blades had sacrificed themselves to create an opportunity to vanquish their foe – it was just the three of them now.

'Again!'

At his command, Dumar and the others pushed against the doors once more. Unexpectedly, this time the doors to the queen's chamber opened wide, catching a number of The Vengeful Tears by surprise and causing them to stumble to their knees. He peered into the queen's room and saw Mirielle, lying on her back, crying in pain. A wretch of a Freylarkin had one hand around her throat, along with a sinister grin stretched across his face. The unsavoury intruder – clearly a male – appeared malformed and unkempt; his left hand was a couple of fingers short, and he had black pupil-less eyes.

'Protect the Queen!'

Dumar was the first of The Vengeful Tears to cross the threshold on his feet. Upon breaching the chamber, a row of granite spikes thrust forth from the stone floor. The spikes drove forwards at an angle, narrowly missing Dumar, who possessed the agility necessary to avoid being impaled by the ad hoc spears. The number of spikes increased, creating a crescent-shaped barbed stone barrier around the chamber doors. He drew his ardent sword and took a heavy swing at one of the spikes, eager to test their resilience. The blade glanced off the surface of the granite spear, at best chipping the unnatural construct. It was abundantly clear, following his unsuccessful attack, that they would not be breaching the mysterious shaper's defences through traditional means. Furthermore, any attempts to fly over or scale the spikes would likely result in more of the stakes being formed. Frustration tormented him; they stood less than eight paces from the queen, yet they were unable to provide assistance.

'Damn it!' said Dumar angrily, clearly agitated by their inability to help.

Beyond the barrier, Mirielle struggled against her attacker. Unnatural things were happening to their bodies; their flesh warped and bones deformed, as each tried to counter and subdue the other, employing the more ghastly aspect of their ability. Freylar's queen was undeniably strong, but her wounds were grievous, thus her attacker held the advantage. Without their aid, there was little chance of Mirielle fending off her attacker. In her wounded state, she was only delaying the inevitable.

'Calm down. Panic leads to confusion.'

'We can fly over.'

'No! He will impale us all.'

'Then why does he not release us now and be done with it!'

'Because he *wants* us to watch! Look at his face – he is enjoying this.'

'The sick bastard! Vorian, we are useless!'

'Breathe…assess the battlefield, it will aid us.'

'But there is *nothing* – only the light.'

Despite his obvious frustration, Dumar's keen perception served him well. Light from the morning sun crept into the chamber through its large arched window, bathing them in the weak light of dawn. He quickly raised his ardent blade and caught the light along the edge of the weapon, using the Knights' battle-code as a means of distracting Mirielle's attacker.

'Get ready!' he said, ensuring The Vengeful Tears were prepared to fight.

Angling his ardent blade, he redirected the morning light towards Mirielle's attacker. The irksome light caught the rogue shaper's left eye flush, causing him to lose focus temporarily. The Queen capitalised on the shaper's momentary lapse in concentration, channelling her ability into the piece of granite still protruding from her body. The granite shaft elongated rapidly, puncturing her adversary's body with its newly formed razor-sharp point. Both cried out in pain, although Mirielle used the agonising respite by slapping her right hand hard to the floor, subsequently destroying the barrier between them, which obliterated into tiny fragments that filled the air.

'Charge!' cried Dumar, leaping towards Mirielle's attacker.

The rogue shaper quickly stood up, revealing his ridiculous attire. He lashed out with his left hand, catching Dumar's shield flush. The unexpected force of the strike sent the ill-prepared Freylarkin across the room, crashing into the wall opposite with a heavy thump. Another of The Vengeful Tears drew back their falchion, ready to strike Mirielle's vicious assailant, but was subsequently caught by a brutal uppercut. The immense force of the impact smashed the Freylarkin's head back, snapping their neck with an awful sounding crack. The savage impact caused the broken body to leave the ground; it hurtled across the room, towards the Queen's stone tree. The broken remains impaled themselves on the artificial construct with a sickening crunch. Blood gushed from the punctured corpse, washing the tree's inflexible branches with a fresh coat of crimson. What was once a beautiful sight was now a gruesome totem for the released, the tree's delicate crystal leaves were smashed, replaced by blood-splattered gore.

'Do not relent!' he cried, seeking to press their advantage.

With the rogue shaper distracted, he hoped that Freylar's queen would aid their cause, but Mirielle continued to lay on the floor, writhing in pain. Another of The Vengeful Tears was propelled across the chamber by further violent attacks, yet their dogged persistence gave him the opportunity he needed to break their untenable stalemate. Realising that piecemeal close combat was not a sustainable option, he pulled a knife from his belt and threw it towards their attacker. Though he had toyed occasionally with throwing weapons, back at the Ardent Gate, he was by no means skilled at ranged combat, evidenced by the blade's poor location of impact. In his haste to deal with the threat, he inadvertently hooked his throw, causing the knife's flight to deviate from its intended course. It buried itself in the shaper's right thigh, causing the leg to give out beneath him, forcing him onto his knees.

'Encircle him – now!' he barked, coordinating The Vengeful Tears.

Those still on their feet hastily formed a loose circle around the assailant, whilst the others sought to recover and join their formation. He quickly slotted into the ring-fence, ensuring that he stood between the rogue shaper and Freylar's queen.

'On my command.' he cried, directing his ardent sword towards their quarry.

The shaper groaned loudly in pain, before spitting several audible curses, realising now that the odds were stacked against him. Mirielle's assailant pulled the knife from his thigh – prompting further groans of discomfort – yet no blood stains surfaced on the fabric of the ridiculous outfit he wore. Instead, a black substance appeared to secrete from the wound, which moved of its own volition down the shaper's leg and across the floor towards them.

'Release it!' he cried to the dumbstruck Freylarkin closest to the tar-like substance.

The Vengeful Tear attempted to squash the black liquid under their heel, but the agile substance moved rapidly, narrowly avoiding the fate he had intended for it. Using the disturbing distraction to his advantage, the wounded shaper grunted and abruptly stood up. Limping with surprising speed, the unnatural Freylarkin moved quickly towards the arched window, breaking through their formation, batting aside those blocking his path. Unexpectedly, the mad shaper hurled himself through the window's wide opening, quickly disappearing from view. Breaking formation, he raced towards the window and looked down, watching in disbelief as their attacker plummeted towards the ground, like a heavy stone cast from a great height. Averting his certain doom, the Freylarkin extended what appeared to be a set of grotesque looking flesh-coloured wings. They tore through the fabric covering the shaper's back and rapidly unfurled, revealing the true extent of their colossal size. The large wings acted like sails; they caught the air magnificently, catapulting the shaper swiftly across the vale. Using his newly formed membranous wings to glide effortlessly, Mirielle's attacker made good his escape, across the river, headed north. Though he tried desperately not to show it, the frustration of allowing the queen's attacker to escape irked him. Freylar had been dealt yet another hammer blow by its enemies, but there was nothing useful to be gained by griping about the past, or flagellating oneself for failed action. Turning his back to the window, he carefully surveyed the destruction littering the chamber. Despite the obvious fractures and bruising, The Vengeful Tears stood doggedly before him, albeit groaning in unison, awaiting further orders. They had gotten off lightly – except for the poor wretch still impaled on Mirielle's tree. The Queen, however, was not so lucky. Her wounds were extensive, and her body looked twisted and deformed. The occasional broken bone he could minister to – he was proficient with a splint – but the damage wrought by the rogue shaper was extensive, and well beyond his skill to heal.

'Someone, get me a renewalist – now!'

TWENTY ONE
Duplicity

Had she properly considered her plan, there would have been a good chance that she would have remained by Natalya's side. Instead, she ran towards Lileah, oblivious of the Narlakai threat that still lingered. Her actions were both careless and ill-conceived, and in no way motivated by logical thinking. Yet her broken soul knew the truth of the matter, in particular, that which she needed to accomplish. Doubt was not a factor – the stakes were too high for any misgivings. Therefore, she allowed what remained of her soul to guide her reckless actions, throwing all sense of caution to the wind as she charged headlong towards her former lover. As she narrowed the gap between herself and Lileah, she called upon the aid of her ability, engaging her second sight. Choosing to scry her own future, she saw several of the Narlakai disintegrate before her; they burst into clouds of ash that lingered in the damp air, viciously cut down by needles of light that steered around her. The light-imbued arrows curved through the air, hunting voraciously for further prey. The arrows had been fired by Natalya – of that she was certain – their deadly signature plain to read. Knowing that the Valkyrie intended to cover her approach, she disengaged her second sight, doing her utmost to increase her speed. Dipping her head, she ran faster than she had previously dared since the loss of her hand. Though her mechanical prosthetic encumbered her movement, regardless, its twisted creator possessed the foresight to ensure its lightweight construction. Despite its awkward design, the weight of her ornate bronze mechanical claw did little to detract from her speed. True to her scrying, the needles of light came to her aid, spearing those Narlakai daring to obstruct her path. She ran through the plumes of ash and those untethered souls, no longer bound by their abhorrent prisons. She squinted her eyes, preventing the ash from interfering with her vision, but she could not evade the harrowing touch of the released, which brushed against her as she continued to run. Regardless of any consent, thoughts from the released assaulted her psyche. They flooded her mind, painting vivid pictures of the lives they had lead, sharing their experiences with her, as if desperate to communicate, having been denied that basic right by their former captors. The world around her appeared to stand still, whilst the images cascaded through her mind. Visual cues, representing the milestones that define oneself, were planted in her mind, forcing her to relive – if only in summary – the lives of others. Images of loved ones, friends, achievements and hardships assailed her, along with the emotions that accompanied them. The joy and sorrow she felt was overwhelming, but she welcomed the heartfelt experiences, allowing them to fill her soul; what had once been a desolate thing, since her exile from Freylar, was now full of life's experiences, albeit those of others. She no longer felt alone; the ethereal touch of the newly freed souls, now embarking on their final journey to the Everlife, somehow emboldened her. Though her love for Lileah had helped her to overcome the hardships of living on the fringes of society, those feelings were but a small measure of the ones now filling her. Having sated their need to communicate, the souls severed their connection and ceased invading her mind. The world around her swiftly resumed, and she was running once more, although there was something different now – her surroundings remained the same, but she had not. The psychic transfer of experiences had altered her disposition, irrevocably. She was no longer the shattered exile who had once lain broken on the grubby floor of Krashnar's hide. Her impromptu encounter had changed her, instilling in her a reason to carry on. Now, she had a duty of care to the loved ones left behind by the departing souls, whose fates had been previously unknown. Armed with their collective knowledge, she would seek out the relations of those now traveling to the Everlife, go to them, and apprise them of the memories of their loved ones. No story deserved to go untold, and she would be the one to tell them. The renewed sense of purpose galvanised her, giving her fresh resolve. There remained only one obstacle in her way; she needed to end one chapter and begin another. Trying hard to block out the pain in her thighs, she pushed on, channelling what physical strength she was still able to draw upon down into her legs. The gap between her and Lileah was now less than thirty paces, close enough perhaps for her to begin her ploy. She pressed forwards with dogged determination, running through more of the ash-like plumes, brushing up against more of the departing souls, all desperate to share their stories with her before their departure. Their unforgivable imprisonment increased her ire, and her loathing towards the Narlakai. She felt deep shame, having once used them as allies of convenience against her kin. The sins she had committed were abhorrent, surely punishable by release, or the relentless devotion of her remaining cycles towards atonement – if that was even possible. Regardless of her fate, ending the current nightmare, and providing closure for those left behind, was the least she could do.

Another arrow flew past her, this time towards the immensely powerful telepath responsible for Freylar's ongoing ruin. The projectile struck Lileah's torso flush, immediately splintering upon impact. Krashnar had fashioned Lileah's body well – given the circumstances – therefore mitigating the effects of such futile attacks. The petite Freylarkin turned her head and stared vacantly towards her. Lileah's grubby face was devoid of emotion. She looked more akin to a mechanical doll now, given her expressionless face, and the work wrought upon her body by their cruel surrogate father. The distant sound of a female voice screamed from behind her – no doubt another victim of Lileah's vicious mind. Regrettably, she could not afford the audible distress her attention; the only thing that mattered now was in fact herself. She needed to confront Lileah. There was no other fit for the task, for which she alone was uniquely suited.

'Lileah – I was wrong! Please, let me beg your forgiveness!' she cried.

His right arm throbbed incessantly as it hung loosely by his side. He tried to raise it, with every intention of blindly retrieving his sword, but it no longer responded to his will. A nearby renewalist, who had been tending to Ragnar, rushed to his side, eager to lend aid.

'Please, hold still my lord.' said the healer, placing his hands against his temples.

Slowly his vision began to return, and with it the all too familiar grim reality of war. Fierce fighting had ravaged the battlefield; few troops on either side remained standing, underlining the macabre brutality of war. The renewalist reached for his arm, distracting him from the surrounding carnage, including the distressing sight of Ragnar's ruined body.

'It is nothing – see to the Captain.'

'My lord, I have done all that I can for him. The Teacher has ordered us to restore sight to the archers.'

'That is now your priority – go!'

The renewalist quickly ran off towards the nearest incapacitated Blade wielding a bow. Others had already done the same, and the first of the ranged attackers were now slowly rising to their feet.

'All of you, to me – now!' he commanded, seeking to reform a detachment of the skilled long-range fighters.

The disorientated archers promptly responded to the familiar sound of his voice, and began to assemble piecemeal around him. The number of Blades remaining was worryingly low. He quickly surveyed the battlefield; his brief assessment suggested that at least half of their force was gone. Irrevocably mauled corpses, well beyond the skill of any renewalist, littered the hill where the enemy's savage chimera had reaped its fill. In addition, countless dried empty husks lay strewn across the wet moor, their souls torn from their moorings and devoured by Lileah's dark host. Furthermore, the surviving Blades were predominantly incapacitated, their sight obliterated by the impromptu explosion of light. Although they now possessed the numerical advantage, following the devastating effects of the indiscriminate light, the fortification he had worked so hard to engineer was in tatters. The Blades were out of position, and their chain of command disrupted. Looking at the hazy ash filled sky, there was now little chance that the breaking dawn would aid their fight. Fresh clouds also gathered, adding further credence to his grim analysis. The feeble new light of dawn struggled to penetrate the murky sky, mitigating its effects on the remaining Narlakai. The battle had failed to play out entirely according to his will; no great surprise, given the unpredictability of war. Even Freylar's scriers found it difficult to foresee the nuances that would affect its overall outcome. Some, more than others, saw more clearly, including Kirika, but ultimately their kind only served as guides. In this instance, she had aided him in preparing the battlefield well, but the time for clever stratagems was over. The only thing that mattered now was the release of Lileah – at any cost.

'Archers, ready your bows.' he commanded, unwilling to wait for their ranks to swell.

The hastily assembled archers formed a rough line, facing towards the gap in the fuel-lined trenches, which continued to blaze near the bottom of the hill.

'See your target.' he said, pointing towards two figures in the distance.

'My lord, at that range we cannot--'

'I will see to it.' he barked in return.

He was confident in his ability to guide some of the arrows to their mark, though less so about not hitting Darlia in the process. Still, he did not require Kirika's sibling to negotiate terms with Lileah, her distraction alone was sufficient for his plan.

'Draw!'

The assembled archers pulled at their bowstrings and aimed their weapons. Without his ability to steer their shots, it was almost certain that the arrows would not find their mark as such range. However, with guidance from his mind, he felt assured that the spiteful telepath would soon meet her doom. Lileah had already evaded The Blades' reach once – he would not permit such mercy a second time.

'On my mark.'

He cleared his mind of all things save for the nocked arrows, resting in wait at the behest of their eagle-eyed masters. He focused intently on the distant target, picturing Lileah in his mind's eye. All other concerns melted into nothingness, such was his determination to put an end to the blight suckling at Freylar's bosom.

'Fi--'

Before he could finish issuing his command, agonising pain splintered his mind. The severity of the torment robbed him of his legs; they immediately buckled at the knees, sending him hard to the ground in a crumpled heap. His vision doubled, making it impossible for him to focus, further adding to the misery of the suffering he endured. Anguished screams cried out around him, suggesting that the archers shared his fate. He tried to fight through the ongoing torment, but the debilitating attack rooted him to the ground, where he writhed in pain, clutching at this head.

She could sense Darlia's presence, although her compromised vision failed to render the pertinent details necessary to identify her former lover. Her ruined vision handicapped her, but she could still sense the pieces on the board with her mind. Losing the use of her sight was an obvious hindrance, but her ability alone was enough to force the Freylarkai's compliance. After ensuring victory, she would coerce a renewalist to aid her, thus restoring her sight. Perhaps, in time, the revered healers would also restore some of her femininity, of which she had been so cruelly robbed. In addition to Darlia, she could sense others rapidly closing in on her, and then there was Lothnar. The tenacious Paladin clearly did not know when to quit; she had already defeated the second-rate telepath at Scrier's Post, though his ego clearly refused to accept his previous good hiding courtesy of her vastly superior mental prowess. She had enjoyed their previous encounter, but Lothnar's interference was now becoming tiresome. She no longer had the luxury of time, given the hazy sun's unwanted presence just over the horizon. Furthermore, the Narlakai had suffered a catastrophic blow, the cause of which she was uncertain. Worse still, she had lost her connection to the Meldbeast, thus she was no longer in the mood for childish games. She felt the feeble presence of Lothnar's mind pressing upon her own; the nomadic Paladin tried desperately to disrupt her psychic connections, but the breadth of his resistance was insignificant against her own power. Lothnar's foolish attempts to thwart her ability would forever prove futile. Focusing the full ferocity of her mind on The Blade's master telepath, she sent a mental hammer blow towards the Paladin. The severity of the psychic attack sent the rival telepath reeling from the impact. Lothnar immediately ceased his pointless attempts to impede her, sinking back into mental obscurity where he belonged.

'I warned you before to stay down – know your place!'

No longer hindered by the irksome telepath, she resumed gathering what remained of the Narlakai towards her, mindful of the others still closing on her position, including her former lover. Darlia's presence was curious – she had expected the formidable scrier to remain at Krashnar's hide, sinking deeper into her self-inflicted state of depression. Instead, her former lover unexpectedly raced towards her. Perhaps Darlia sought a final audience with her, hoping desperately to change her direction, she mused. On the other hand, maybe her former lover had found renewed perspective. Either way, Darlia's presence was puzzling. Hastily, she tried to glean information from the scrier's mind, but without her consent, and amid the distractions of war, such a task was far from simple, despite the power she wielded. Interestingly, Darlia's mind was cluttered with thoughts seemingly not her own. Someone, or something, had left multiple impressions on her mind. The myriad thoughts were fresh and raw, from which Darlia seemed to draw renewed purpose. Unable to unravel the mystery of her former lover's changed disposition, she focused her mind's eye on two Freylarkin in hot pursuit. Both were proceeding directly towards her, their minds full of hate and hostility. She recognised one as the archer who had skilfully shot her before Lothnar interfered with her righteous retribution. The other, however, was alien to her – just another Blade with foolish notions of ending her invasion. Once again, she called upon her ability, unleashing the fury of her mind. By her will alone she invaded the minds of the two approaching Freylarkai, mentally ravaging them and leaving both prone upon the wet moor. She heard their cries in the distance as they crashed to the ground, writhing in agony under the heel of her mind. She considered obliterating their psyches entirely, but was subsequently distracted by the sound of Darlia's voice, calling to her.

'Lileah – I was wrong! Please, let me beg your forgiveness!'

Darlia's unexpected words caught her off guard, breaking her concentration; hearing the scrier's familiar tone proved more disruptive than the feeble opposition offered by The Blade's most formidable telepath. Without any conscious thought on her part, her mind ceased tormenting its quarry, automatically focusing on Darlia's voice instead.

'Please forgive me.' cried Darlia once more.

'Why are you here?!' she cried, uncertain as to the distance between them.

'I am here.' replied Darlia, struggling to catch her breath.

'Why have you come here?' she repeated her question, this time in a softer, quieter, tone.

Darlia moved closer; she saw a myriad of contrasting colours that shifted with her former lover's movements, defining her outline, but nothing in the way of any discernible detail. Resorting to her other senses, she listened to the sound of Darlia's heavy breathing, as the exhausted scrier sought to compose herself.

'You should not be here – it is not safe.'

'I had to.'

'Why are you here – why now?'

'Tell me, what is your name child?'

'I am no child!' replied the gaunt looking female.

'Forgive me; I believed you to be younger than in fact you are.'

'You know nothing of it – including my name.'

'Are you always this hostile?'

'Go away!'

'No.'

The young Freylarkin scowled at her, then turned her back and moved away, towards another gloomy crevasse in the rock face.

'What are you looking for?' she said, closing her distance with the feral-looking Freylarkin.

'None of your business. Now leave me alone – or else!'

'Or else what?'

A sharp pain suddenly stabbed at her mind, causing her to stumble to the dusty ground. The unexpected discomfort was unlike anything she had felt before. It split her mind suddenly, temporarily disrupting her bodily functions.

'Or else that. Now go away!'

'No.' she groaned in response, trying to compose herself.

'Are you stupid?'

'No, I am angry.' she said, raising her left stump.

The grubby Freylarkin stared intently at the space where her left hand used to be. She watched with painful amusement as the petite stray stood on the tips of her toes, trying to better her low-level vantage point.

'You can come closer and look, if you like – see it in all its grizzly splendour.'

'Does it hurt?' asked the Freylarkin, moving closer to examine her stump.

'It used to, but now it mainly itches. Sometimes the itching drives me mad.'

She lowered her ruined arm, thus affording her interested audience a better view of her ruddy coloured stump. She could still recall the agony of the shock amputation, when The Blade Lord savagely took her hand at the behest of Queen Mirielle. Marcus had used his unforgiving bastard sword to cleave her hand from its moorings with a single strike. In that moment – which she had failed to foresee – everything had changed, or rather, *she* had changed. Anger, hate, revulsion, and every dark emotion in between surfaced to the fore, bent on steering her down a path of vengeance; in the wake of her unjust exile, revenge had become her newest bedfellow.

'So what do you think?'

'How did it happen?' replied the scrawny female, inquisitively.

'Would you like to hear my story?'

'Yes.'

'OK – but we will have no more of your nonsense, you understand?'

'Fine.'

She glanced around, looking for somewhere to sit, but was eminently disappointed; with the obvious exception of the rock face, there was little of note in their desolate surroundings. In the end, she decided to sit on the dusty floor, having grown accustomed to the harsh reality of life in the Narlakai borderlands. She looked up towards the female, who continued to stand, watching over her.

'Stand if you like, but this is a long story – if told properly.'

There was no response, however, seeing the wisdom in her words, the rebellious female sat down opposite, with legs crossed, regarding her expectantly. She promptly began her tale, deciding it best not to keep her keen audience waiting, at which time approximately two paces separated them. By the time she had recounted her sad story, the grubby waif had used the time to gingerly edge closer, such that only a single pace now lied between them. She wiped a tear from her cheek, using the back of her good hand, and did her best to offer a warm smile.

'I hate them too.' said the female.

There was a lull in their lacklustre conversation, during which they stared at one another, content in their comfortable silence. Time passed, during which grey clouds started to gather overhead, bringing with them the threat of rain. The Narlakai borderlands were perpetually bleak and desiccated;

when moisture ultimately graced the dry lands, its welcome gift made little difference to their perpetual arid state.

The female suddenly rose to her feet, and without a word resumed her search along the rock face.

'You will not find shelter amongst these rocks – I have already searched them.' she said, pushing herself upright with the aid of her good hand.

She quickly brushed her clothes, temporarily removing the habitual dust that clung to them – it was impossible to maintain any decorum amidst the inhospitable lands.

'Trust me – you will not find anything of note.'

'I have nowhere else to go.'

'Then come with me.'

The dishevelled Freylarkin paused for a moment, before slowly turning to face her.

'Why do you care, when no one else will?'

She approached the young female, who took a step back warily, and offered her hand. Gingerly, her new acquaintance reciprocated, touching the tips of her outstretched fingers with her own.

'I care, because I share your pain of being cast aside, to be shunned by your own kin, and denied everything you know and love. You desperately scrabble along the edge of society, subconsciously searching for a way back in. However, this is no longer your true calling. You are done with Freylar's pretence, and its haughty inhabitants, but you do not know how to live in this new domain of yours – it is alien to you.'

'That is not true.'

'Yes, it is.'

'How would you know?'

'Because I have seen it.'

'What?!'

'I have looked into your past, and have seen you habitually clinging to such places, trying to find shelter and a place where you belong. This is not it – but I can offer you a measure of what you seek.'

'I do not understand. How can you know all this?'

'I told you – I have seen it. Just now, when we touched, you revealed your past to me.'

'You are a scrier!'

'Yes – Freylar's greatest. But they fear my ability, or at least that bitch Mirielle does.'

The female Freylarkin, with her short raven-black hair, glowered at her menacingly. She could feel the telepath attempting to sift through her mind, searching for truth in order to validate her words.

'There is nothing for you here. Come with me, and we can hate them together. We can rule over this barren land and bide our time in the comfort of the shadows, whilst I scry their fates in order to engineer their demise.'

The youth continued to regard her sternly. After what seemed like an eternity, the grubby waif softened her expression, though only slightly.

'My name is Lileah.'

TWENTY TWO
Release

'Why are you here – why now?'

She engaged her second sight, using her ability to scry their future, though only as clearly as her level of skill would permit. The ongoing tumult of war made it extremely difficult to predict their fate – the actions of every Freylarkin present had the potential to influence their destiny. She sifted through the tranche of possible futures lying in wait for them, finally settling on one which revealed itself to her clearer than any other. In her vision, a volley of arrows thumped into the wet ground surrounding them. Two of the projectiles hit Lileah; one pierced her right shoulder and the other struck the flesh-metal of her torso, splintering upon impact. The expression on the scornful telepath's face in the wake of the attack painted a grim tale. After recovering from the shock of the surprise offensive, Lileah's face contorted with anger. At first, she thought her former lover's rage to be a result of the arrow shaft protruding from her shoulder. However, following Lileah's vacant gaze, she quickly discovered the cause to be something far worse. Looking down, she saw that a third arrow had struck herself; its head had evidently pierced her back and was now protruding from her blood-soaked belly. She dropped to the ground, and the visions became darker, the last of which depicted Lileah screaming with wild fury – an image she would struggle to forget. There was little doubt in her mind that the vengeful telepath would unleash the unfettered ferocity of her mind, in all likelihood ending what remained of The Blades.

'They mean to shoot us!' she proclaimed, bringing an abrupt end to her reverie.

'When?'

'Now!'

She watched anxiously as Lileah scoured the battlefield with her mind, searching fervently for renewed threats. The telepath's face twitched, and soon distant screams cried out in agony from behind her.

'You should have come with me – together we can rule this domain.' said Lileah, having apparently dealt with the threat.

'I realise my transgressions at last. But what matters now is that I am here.'

'So you now stand with me?'

'I have always been with you – since the day we first met, and for all of the cycles we shared together in each other's arms. You opened your soul to me, allowed me in, thus I understand your pain – there is no excuse for the horrors visited upon you.' she replied, emphatically.

'She was supposed to protect us – as Freylar's ruler, it was her responsibility! Instead, she allowed those bastards to continue violating me, hoping that their ghastly exploits would go unnoticed and shatter my resolve, rendering me submissive. I was nothing more than an irritant to her, a blot on her *exemplary* reign – I doubt she even knew my name.'

'She knows it now!'

'That bitch is unable to manage conflict! My desperate pleas for help fell on her deaf ears. She tried to sweep me under the carpet, maintaining the pretence of serenity during her rule.' continued Lileah, whose vacant eyes began to water.

'She *will* atone for her inaction – this, I swear to you!' she replied, ardently, whilst taking a step closer.

'*I* will be the one to pass sentence. When I am done here, with The Blades, there will be no one to stand in my way. I will hunt down those who stole my childhood from me, and I shall feed her to them, sating their abhorrent personal amusement! I will make her suffer, as I did; she will endure the same humiliation that was visited upon me.'

'And after...what happens then?'

'Perhaps I will have Freylar's queen build her own prison, out there, amongst the inhospitable rocks, where she can rot in the shadow of the unjust society she created.'

'What of the others – the ones who physically abused you?'

'Once I am done with them...release. They deserve nothing less for their atrocities.'

She was close now, enough to touch her former lover. Slowly, she slid her arms around Lileah's waist, drawing the vengeful Freylarkin in close. Despite Lileah's extraordinary mental capabilities, she was still a lost little child, in desperate need of love from the mother she never had. Lileah had been abandoned during her childhood, and thus no longer recalled her birth parents' countenance; in a sense, she had become a surrogate mother for the unwanted telepath. It was unsurprising then, that Lileah welcomed her embrace – despite their recent differences – desperately clamouring for her love. During her traumatic upbringing, the waif had been passed from pillar to post, forced to scratch out a living on the fringe of society – by contrast, she had only experienced hardship in more recent passes. Regretably, given the depths of hatred ingrained on Lileah's psyche from such a young age, it was impossible to imagine her former lover recovering from the childhood trauma. Indeed, her attempts to scry a different outcome had all lead to naught.

'I am sorry for leaving you – you deserve better.' she said, sliding her prosthetic hand around the back of Lileah's head.

'You did not leave me – it was I who left you.' replied the telepath, with surprise sincerity. 'I realise now that you were not ready for the difficult task ahead. I understand the reason for your hesitation – no doubt, the safety of your sister is a concern. But together, we can end this, and take back that which was denied to us, including your sister.'

Using the claw Krashnar had fashioned for her, she carefully pressed Lileah's head to her bosom, where she held it gently.

'No, *you* misunderstand.'

She pressed her lips slowly to the top of Lileah's head, lingering, struggling to make peace with their shared fate. Her former lover's embrace was no longer warm and inviting. Instead, the flesh-metal used to fashion Lileah's torso was cold to the touch – it felt like a prison, one designed to keep her out. The sudden realisation that she would never again truly embrace her former lover made her weep uncontrollably. Tears filled her eyes, and her newly restored vision started to blur.

'I am sorry for leaving *you*. This needs to end, and there is only one way. Please forgive me…child.'

In a final act of mercy for the irrevocably troubled telepath, she clenched her bladed claw, crushing Lileah's head within its vice-like grip.

Ragnar brought his colossal axe down on to the beast's central head, burying it into the top of the chimera's skull. Ordinarily, she would have expected such a devastating blow to release its victim instantaneously, however, the dark sorceries used to engineer the construct allowed it to continue its onslaught. The chimera's bulk smashed into Ragnar, regardless of the devastating wound dealt to it by the veteran Paladin. Ragnar's body flew through the air some five or six paces, before crashing upon the moor in a broken heap. After completing its devastating charge, the creature came to a gradual halt, then began to pace around in a seemingly confused manner. It was unclear how the beast continued to function, with its left head lame and the smile of Ragnar's axe still buried in the top of the central dome. Despite its injuries, the beast reared its right head and sniffed at the air, before turning towards the body of the fallen light bringer. The chimera haphazardly stumbled towards the Captain's prone body, leaving behind it a trickle of blood. Eventually its colossal shadow eclipsed Ragnar's body, at which point the beast lowered its right head and proceeded to maul the Captain's face. She gasped with shock as Ragnar suddenly raised his arms and began wrestling with the chimera's last surviving head. The Captain's movements appeared to be restricted to his torso and above, implying that he was paralysed from the waist down. Despite the obvious handicap, Ragnar fought on, using the brute strength of his arms to apply a three-quarter chancery around his attacker's neck. The beast tried to lift its right head, repeatedly, in a futile attempt to break Ragnar's facelock, but only succeeded in banging the back of the Captain's head upon the wet ground. Ragnar's right arm fumbled blindly at his side, trying desperately to draw a dirk strapped to his waist whilst maintaining the vicious lock with his left. The exasperated beast repeatedly beat the Captain's broken body against the moor, eventually causing Ragnar to lose his hold. Sensing victory, the chimera's surviving head lunged at the Captain, tearing more of Ragnar's flesh from his face, oblivious to the dirk he now held in his right hand. The dogged Blade Captain grimaced defiantly, then drove the dagger into the side of the chimera's right head. The beast reared up, howling in pain, before listing right and crumpling to the ground. The beast's prone body fell upon the Captain, pinning Ragnar to the ground with its enormous bulk. Deeply saddened by the outcome, she watched intently as the Captain use the last of his strength to turn his head to the side to better observe the ongoing battle. Despite the black tidal wave that threatened to engulf The Blades, the Captain appeared to have a coy smile on his face. Seeing the subtle gesture raised her spirits; the Captain was a proud Freylarkin, and a fierce fighter – the red-haired giant clearly approved of the manner of his release. The Captain had always feared the prospect of fading quietly into obscurity, stuck behind a wooden desk, whilst poorly managing the affairs of The Blades. Ragnar deserved nothing less than an honourable release in battle, versus an adversary worthy of his attention. Fate – it seemed – had granted his wish, and so the Captain welcomed his release. She watched with great sadness as Ragnar passed beyond their reach, but not before whispering his final words, which she expertly read on his dying lips.

'So much for that favour, Thandor...'

She was confident that justifiably tall tales would be told about the Captain's epic final battle, as he fought to his last breath to defend The Blade Lord – indeed, she vowed that such would happen. Although they had shared a turbulent relationship, nonetheless, she respected his commitment to Freylar's defence. His heroic deeds would become verse, and, in time, a statue would no doubt be erected in his likeness to honour his service to The Blades – the latter, she would personally see done, thereby ensuring Ragnar's place in history.

She disengaged her second sight and surveyed the rest of the battlefield. In the distance, she saw Darlia, who stood out against the grim backdrop of broken bodies due to her distinct mechanical claw. Her sister was hunched over and appeared to be weeping. Lying on the ground adjacent to them was the prone body of a small Freylarkin, minus its head. The scrubland around the body was black – likely the result of massive blood loss from the open neck soaking the moor.

'Lileah!' she said aloud, affirming her thoughts.

True to her word, her sister had brought an end to the conflict, though it had already reaped a heavy price from The Blades; hundreds had been released during the fighting with Lileah's defeated host. Yet there was some solace: if not for Rayna, their casualties would have been significantly worse – if indeed they had won at all. Without The Guardian's impromptu intervention, it was almost a given that Lileah would have forged her bloody path to the steps of the Tri-Spires. She counted herself amongst those fortunate enough to have been spared the light's devastating touch; if not for her repeated scrying, she too would have found herself groping around blindly upon the moor.

'So…it is done.' said Marcus, who joined her unexpectedly.

The Blade Lord cradled his lame right forearm, using his left. His fight with the savage chimera had dislocated the limb, if not broken it entirely. It was the first time she recalled seeing Marcus defeated in combat. Typically, The Blade Lord's supreme guile assured him of victory, but the severe lack of numbers had ultimately been his undoing.

Marcus had used The Blades well, but ultimately, there had been too few.

'No – this is not over. What we see here is only the half of it.'

'The politics can wait – the Freylarkai need time to mourn their losses.'

'Agreed. However, there *will* be a reckoning Marcus. This is not something that you or I can evade, either through clever strategy or the careful manipulation of fate.'

'I understand.'

'This – everything you see before you – needs to be accounted for. *This*, needs a purpose.'

'I understand.'

'Do you?' she said, turning to face The Blade Lord. 'The Blades will not survive this – at least, not in their current state. Change is coming Marcus, and whatever that change is, it will offer us no more mercy than the wrath of a shattered exile.'

'Forgive me Kirika – but I cannot do this now.'

'Marcus, I am not without compassion. Go, mourn your loss. Once the dust has settled here, I will see to it that he receives full honours – he will have his pyre.'

'Thank you.' replied Marcus sombrely. 'I will leave details of the clean-up in your capable hands.'

'Marcus.' she said, as The Blade Lord turned to walk away. 'There will come a time when you *need* to pick a side in all this.'

Marcus paused for a moment, considering her words. After a brief moment of reflection, he responded quietly, before walking away.

'I understand.'

The inside of her head pounded incessantly, though she could see clearly once more, for which she was extremely grateful. Someone was shouting behind her, but it took her body a moment to reset itself, after which she recognised the voice calling to her.

'I'm fine.' she replied, eventually responding to the repeated cries.

She stood up from the wet moor and pushed aside her sodden red hair, which clung to her face, doing its best to obscure her vision. Instinctively she turned towards the voice and saw Natalya. The Valkyrie wobbled as she walked slowly towards her, clearly suffering the aftereffects of the psychic trauma that had laid them low during the final moments of the battle. Her gaze drifted towards the scenes unfolding behind Natalya; her eyes flitted across the landscape, taking in the aftermath of battle that was left in the wake of Lileah's invasion. She watched as renewalists continued to scramble between survivors, doing their best to assist The Blades who had inadvertently suffered her wrath following Alarielle's release. Most had now recovered their sight and were wandering around aimlessly in small isolated groups, though many were still handicapped, fumbling around on the wet ground. The battle was clearly over, and what little remained of Lileah's dark host was no longer a concern. The few remaining Narlakai slowly drifted away, back towards the borderlands, in full retreat. The soul stealers had been decimated, but so too had The Blades. At best, they numbered less than a few hundred, and of those still on the ground, not all were moving. The remainder were now withered husks, slowly decomposing in the dreary rain. So many had sacrificed themselves defending Freylar, and in return, their souls had been snatched from their bodies. Now they provided nourishment for *something*, well beyond their understanding. Knowing that she had freed so many, only to send them to their potential doom, sickened her; the fact that the Narlakai had initiated the process was of little comfort. Ultimately, her rebirth in Freylar had come with a heavy price – was she any better than the metropolis' unjust government, she mused. In any event, she felt like she had betrayed the Freylarkai, acting inadvertently as an agent for her onetime benefactor. The entity's cryptic words had rocked her world, again. According to the enigma, the Narlakai were a cancer of sort, preventing it from fulfilling its own purpose. What then, was the purpose of the Freylarkai, and moreover, the Ravnarkai, who excelled at perpetuating death – were they in fact, the preferred species? The outrageous notion only contributed to the pounding in her head. It was in that moment that she truly began to understand the Queen's obsession with the thing in the sky. Mirielle's eyes, and her loose psychic connection to the entity, were little more than maddening tools that afforded them a brief glimpse of a larger picture, of which the Freylarkai were blissfully unaware. It occurred to her then that the entity – or sphere of light, as she knew it – had no designation, or name – at least, none that she knew of. Perhaps, in order to understand a thing, one first needed to give it a name. She decided then that she would henceforth refer to it as The Deceiver.

'Rayna.' cried Natalya once more, 'It is over – look!'

She quickly spun around following the direction of the Valkyrie's outstretched hand. Less than ten paces away she saw Darlia, cradling the body of a young Freylarkin, whose torso appeared to be fashioned from some kind of metal alloy. The body was missing its head, and blood spilled from its neck due to what appeared to be a brutal decapitation. Darlia herself was in floods of tears, and her mechanical claw covered with gore. Part of her had expected this of the disgraced scrier, suspecting that little good would come from trying to dissuade Lileah. Nonetheless, she had hoped for a better outcome – Darlia deserved a measure of happiness, given her unjust exile and the risk she took by returning to Freylar. Yet it was not to be. All those caught up in the conflict had ultimately suffered, loosing respected comrades and loved ones – such was the outcome of any war. The battle for Scrier's Post had rocked The Blades at the grass roots, but this latest incursion had devastated their ranks. It would take tens of passes for their Order to recover its losses – if indeed it survived the coming cycles. Darlia continued to weep for Lileah, understandably so given the closeness they had apparently shared together in exile. As with The Blades, Darlia too would struggle to deal with the repercussions caused by the invasion. She recounted her own experience of taking a life, and wondered if somehow she could find a way to pass on the impression imparted to her by Alarielle. In all likelihood, the talented scrier would need to find her own way of managing the burden of guilt, which she would ultimately shoulder for the remainder of her cycles.

'She's a victim in all this.' she said, airing her thoughts aloud. 'As were The Blades.'

Before Natalya could respond, Nathanar raced towards them with a sense of urgency etched on his face.

'What is it?' she asked, dreading the answer to her question.

'It is the Captain.' replied Nathanar, struggling to regain his breath.

'What of Ragnar?' asked Natalya, whose expression had darkened.

'Some kind of abhorrent monster – with three heads – outflanked us during the battle. It devastated the archers, and almost released The Blade Lord himself.' reported Nathanar, before pausing again to catch his breath. 'The Captain intervened and released the beast, but…'

'But what?' she asked, knowing what would come next.

'He did not survive the encounter – we have lost the Captain.'

'Damn it!'

'Rayna, The Blades will not survive this. When they learn of Ragnar's release, it will break the Order.' said Natalya flatly.

'Agreed – we need to find a way to cauterise the wound, before it gets infected.' said Nathanar.

'I'm sensing that you already have a solution in mind.' she said, focusing her attention on Nathanar's piercing blue eyes.

'You will not like it.'

'No, I don't suppose that I will.' she said, with a weary sigh, quickly discerning the Paladin's intent from his body language alone.

'Can I assume that you are on board with this?' the Paladin enquired with a hard stare.

'On board with what?' asked Natalya, with obvious frustration.

'Do I have a choice?'

'Not really.'

'Ha – you've been spending too much time with me.'

The Paladin smiled, then turned his back on them and ran off towards a group of Blades loitering – probably in shock – on the battlefield. Natalya turned to her with a mixture of confusion and annoyance etched on her face.

'It may not work.'

'What may not work?!' asked Natalya, irritably. 'You have yet to explain this confounding means of communication which you two have obviously developed.'

'If this works, it won't come as a surprise to you.'

'Do not become the part-time aloof, like Thandor – it does not suit you Rayna. We value your plain speak, and your honesty.'

'And I value your candid counsel.' she said, offering Natalya an infectious smile, followed by a characteristically maddening playful wink. 'Look behind you – witness the trouble caused by the one whom we have led astray.'

Nathanar stood before them, in the distance, alongside Kirika, both of whom had raised their left hands high above their heads. Those Blades standing either side of the pair had adopted the exact same stance, and all had cut the open palms of their hands, allowing blood to trickle down their arms onto the moor. Behind the renowned scrier, others had followed suit, and beyond those, a rapidly increasing number of Blades were copying the actions of those already openly declaring their support for her. Part of her had feared the loss of their respect – having robbed them of their sight – but those fears were apparently unwarranted. She knew now that war had a strange way of creating bonds of fellowship between survivors; she had witnessed it once already, at Scrier's Post, and now – albeit with a scrier aiding her – history was repeating itself. Together they stood silently alongside one another, watching with interest as more and more of The Blades followed suit, until eventually, almost all of those with their vision restored had openly declared their support.

'He has become quite the agitator, don't you think?'

'Rayna, I dearly hope that you know what you are getting yourself into. I fear that you have ended one war, only to incite another.' replied Natalya, emphatically.

Despite the grim prophecy, Natalya drew a small blade from the belt around her waist and ran the edge of the blade across the palm of her left hand, before raising it above her head. Natalya then turned to her with a mischievous smile stretched across her face and gave her a playful wink.

'So…what happens next?'

– www.thechroniclesoffreylar.com –

If you enjoyed volume three of The Chronicles of Freylar, I would greatly appreciate an online review from you on the Amazon store. You can also 'Become a Blade Aspirant' on the website and join the ranks of The Blades.

DRAMATIS PERSONAE

Ruling Council of Freylar
Kirika 'Fate Weaver', Valkyrie
Marcus 'The Blade Lord', Paladin –
Commander of The Blades
Mirielle, Queen

The Blades
Dumar, Blade Novice –
The Vengeful Tears
Lothnar, Paladin
Natalya, Valkyrie
Nathanar, Paladin
Nathaniel 'The Teacher', Blade Master
Ragnar, Paladin –
Captain of The Blades
Rayna 'The Guardian', Blade Adept
Thandor, Paladin

Knights Thranis
Anika, Knight
Falkai, Knight
Gedrick, Knight Captain
Heldran, Knight Lord
Loredan, Knight Restorant
Vorian, Knight
Xenia, Knight
Zephir, Knight

House Guard
Ralnor, Guard

Deceased Freylarkai
Alarielle, Blade Adept
Caleth, Blade Lord
Katrin, Knight
Kryshar, Blade Aspirant
Morin, Knight

Civilian Freylarkai
Aleska, Retired Valkyrie
Cora, Store Proprietor
Galadrick,
Hanarah, Store Proprietor
Kayla, Administrative Aide
Keshar,
Krasus,
Larissa, Dressmaker
Riknar, Fisherman

Exiled Freylarkai
Darlia
Krashnar
Lileah

Dire Wolves
Krisis

Orders
Knights Thranis
The Blades

Races
Freylarkai
Narlakai
Ravnarkai

Humans
Austin 'Trix'
Callum 'Fox'
Kaitlin Delarouse

Printed in Great Britain
by Amazon